☞ **W9-CUB-281**

OTHER BOOKS BY *Albert Camus*

Awarded the Nobel Prize for Literature in 1957

NOTEBOOKS 1942–1951   1965
(*Carnets*, janvier 1942–mars 1951)

NOTEBOOKS 1935–1942   1963
(*Carnets*, mai 1935–fevrier 1942)

RESISTANCE, REBELLION, AND DEATH   1961
(*Actuelles*—A Selection)

THE POSSESSED (*Les Possédés*)   1960

CALIGULA AND THREE OTHER PLAYS   1958
(*Caligula, Le Malentendu, L'Etat de siège, Les Justes*)

EXILE AND THE KINGDOM (*L'Exil et le Royaume*)   1958

THE FALL (*La Chute*)   1957

THE MYTH OF SISYPHUS AND OTHER ESSAYS   1955
(*Le Mythe de Sisyphe*)

THE REBEL (*L'Homme révolté*)   1954

THE PLAGUE (*La Peste*)   1948

THE STRANGER (*L'Etranger*)   1946

These are BORZOI BOOKS,
published in New York by Alfred A. Knopf

LYRICAL
AND
CRITICAL ESSAYS

LYRICAL
AND
CRITICAL ESSAYS

BY *Albert Camus*

❦❦ ❦❦❦ ❦❦

EDITED AND WITH NOTES BY PHILIP THODY
TRANSLATED FROM THE FRENCH
BY ELLEN CONROY KENNEDY

ALFRED : A · KNOPF · *NEW YORK*

1968

THIS IS A BORZOI BOOK
PUBLISHED BY ALFRED A. KNOPF, INC.

Introduction

ALTHOUGH Camus's greatest achievements as a creative writer are undoubtedly to be found in his novels and his plays, his literary career nevertheless both began and ended with the publication of a volume of essays. Between the appearance of *L'Envers et l'Endroit* in 1937 and the publication of his Nobel Prize speeches in 1958, he developed and extended his use of the essay form to express both his personal attitude toward life and certain artistic values. He also wrote articles on political topics, and a selection of these, under the title *Actuelles*, takes up three volumes of his complete works. But these articles, however perfect their style, did not really fall under Camus's definition of the essay. For him, it was first and foremost what its etymology suggests: an attempt to express something, a trying out of ideas and forms, an experiment. It was not a polemical tool, although it could put forward very specific ideas. It was an attempt to record impressions and ideas that could later be used in other, more imaginative works. This is why the first two collections of essays included in this translation, *L'Envers et l'Endroit* (*The Wrong Side and the Right Side*) and *Noces* (*Nuptials*), provide so natural a commentary on Camus's first novel, *L'Etranger* (*The Stranger*), and his first major philosophical work, *Le Mythe de Sisyphe* (*The Myth of Sisyphus*). He is exploring, within the context of his own immediate experience, the ideas of the absurdity of the world, the inevitability of death, and the importance of the physical life, which will later be cast into a more

v

intellectual mold in the philosophical work and into a more perfectly controlled artistic form in the novel. The Camus that emerges from these pages is, on an intellectual level, the young pagan rejecting Christianity, and the Mediterranean sensualist already preparing that criticism of Northern metaphysics which informs *L'Homme révolté* (*The Rebel*). He is also, on the more human level, the son seeking to communicate with his mother, the young man trying to come to terms with old age, and the lover of nature endeavoring to express this love in words.

The third volume of essays, *L'Eté* (*Summer*), has less unity of tone and subject matter than the first two. It brings together texts ranging over a wider period and already bears signs of that intense disillusionment with French political life that formed the starting point for *La Chute* (*The Fall*) in 1956. It also shows Camus as an ironically detached observer of his native Algeria, concerned less with the intensity of its physical joys than with the occasionally charming naïveté of its provincial culture. The first essays in *Summer* date from before the Second World War, and are again the working out of an experience that was to find its way into one of Camus's major works, though this time in a less central position. The evocation of Oran at the beginning of *La Peste* (*The Plague*) clearly stems from essays such as *The Minotaur, or Stopping in Oran,* and offers in itself an example of the transition which Camus was making in that book from a provincial to a world-wide frame of reference. Camus is not, of course, suggesting that the lyrical or the humorous account which he gives of Algerian life is the whole story. The Algerian reports translated in *Resistance, Rebellion, and Death* have to be read side by side with the essays in *Nuptials* or in *Summer* if an accurate picture is to emerge of the relationship between Camus and his native land. His love for Algeria was essentially lucid. But it was in that land, as all these essays show, that he found his truest and most lasting inspiration.

Camus began his career as a literary critic when he was twenty-five and was working as a journalist on the left-wing newspaper *Alger-Républicain*. Of the twenty or so short articles he published on literary topics before this newspaper was virtually forced to close down by the French authorities in North Africa, only three are translated here. The reviews of Sartre's first novel, *La Nausée*, and of his short stories, *Le Mur*, present an obvious interest for the enthusiasm that Camus showed for Sartre's work at a time when the two had never met, and for the very considerable difference of attitude that already separated the two men. By the time he wrote the other literary essays included in the second part of this collection, Camus had already passed beyond the stage when he was required to provide a review of a particular length to match the requirements of a newspaper. He could now write more fully, exploring the different philosophical and aesthetic problems that he had already encountered in his own work: the problems of language, the nature of tragedy, the conflict within Europe between Mediterranean and Northern values, the scope and nature of the novel. Except for his enthusiasm for Faulkner, his literary preferences were classical and traditional: Madame de Lafayette, Stendhal, Tolstoy, Melville, and Martin du Gard attracted him most as novelists, the Greeks, Shakespeare, and the Spanish playwrights of the Golden Age as dramatists. It is as a record of the ideals which inspired him rather than of the influences which he underwent that his later literary criticism is so valuable.

Like the essays in *The Wrong Side and the Right Side* or in *Nuptials*, the texts in the third part of this volume are particularly valuable for the light which they throw on Camus as a creative writer. Both *The Stranger* and *The Plague* have been widely interpreted and criticized. This is how Camus thought they should be approached and how he felt they could be defended against the criticisms sometimes made of them. His three interviews also clarify his attitude toward his work as a whole, and particularly toward *The Myth of Sisyphus* and *The Rebel.* These too were essays, but of a more perfect and finished kind: the expression within an intellectual and historical context of an attitude toward life already worked out in lyrical terms.

PHILIP THODY

For her generous counsel during the preparation of this volume, the editor and translator are much indebted to Germaine Brée.

Contents

PART II

CRITICAL ESSAYS

PART III

CAMUS ON HIMSELF

I

LYRICAL ESSAYS

I
THE WRONG SIDE
AND
THE RIGHT SIDE

(L'Envers et L'Endroit)

---

to Jean Grenier

Preface, 1958

THE ESSAYS collected in this volume were written in
1935 and 1936 (I was then twenty-two) and published a
year later in Algeria in a very limited edition. This edition
has been unobtainable for a long time and I have always
refused to have *The Wrong Side and the Right Side*
reprinted.

There are no mysterious reasons for my stubbornness. I reject nothing of what these writings express, but
their form has always seemed clumsy to me. The prejudices on art I cherish in spite of myself (I shall explain
them further on) kept me for a long time from consider-
ing their republication. A great vanity, it would seem,
leading one to suppose that my other writings satisfy
every standard. Need I say this isn't so? I am only more
aware of the inadequacies in *The Wrong Side and the
Right Side* than of those in my other work. How can I
explain this except by admitting that these inadequacies
concern and reveal the subject closest to my heart. The
question of its literary value settled, then, I can confess
that for me this little book has considerable value as

5

testimony. I say for me, since it is to me that it reveals and from me that it demands a fidelity whose depth and difficulties I alone can know. I should like to try to explain why.

Brice Parain often maintains that this little book contains my best work. He is wrong. I do not say this, knowing how honest he is, because of the impatience every artist feels when people are impertinent enough to prefer what he has been to what he is. No, he is wrong because at twenty-two, unless one is a genius, one scarcely knows how to write. But I understand what Parain, learned enemy of art and philosopher of compassion, is trying to say. He means, and he is right, that there is more love in these awkward pages than in all those that have followed.

Every artist thus keeps within himself a single source which nourishes during his lifetime what he is and what he says. When that spring runs dry, little by little one sees his work shrivel and crack. These are art's wastelands, no longer watered by the invisible current. His hair grown thin and dry, covered with thatch, the artist is ripe for silence or the salons, which comes to the same thing. As for myself, I know that my source is in *The Wrong Side and the Right Side,* in the world of poverty and sunlight I lived in for so long, whose memory still saves me from two opposing dangers that threaten every artist, resentment and self-satisfaction.

Poverty, first of all, was never a misfortune for me: it was radiant with light. Even my revolts were brilliant with sunshine. They were almost always, I think I can say this without hypocrisy, revolts for everyone, so that every life might be lifted into that light. There is no certainty my heart was naturally disposed to this kind of love. But circumstances helped me. To correct a natural indifference, I was placed halfway between poverty and the sun. Poverty kept me from thinking all was well under the sun and in history; the sun taught me that history was not everything. I wanted to change lives, yes, but not the world which I worshipped as divine. I suppose this is how I got started on my present difficult career, innocently stepping onto the tightrope upon which I move painfully forward, unsure of reaching the end. In other words, I became an artist, if it is true that there is no art without refusal or consent.

In any case, the lovely warmth that reigned over my childhood freed me from all resentment. I lived on almost nothing, but also in a kind of rapture. I felt infinite strengths within me: all I had to do was find a way to use them. It was not poverty that got in my way: in Africa, the sun and the sea cost nothing. The obstacle lay rather in prejudices or stupidity. These gave me every opportunity to develop a "Castilian pride" that has done me much harm, that my friend and teacher Jean Grenier is right to make fun of, and that I tried in vain to correct, until I realized that there is a fatality in human natures. It seemed better to accept my pride and try to make use of it, rather than give myself, as Chamfort would put it, principles stronger than my character. After some soul-searching, however, I can testify that among my many weaknesses I have never discovered that most widespread failing, envy, the true cancer of societies and doctrines.

I take no credit for so fortunate an immunity. I owe it to my family, first of all, who lacked almost everything and envied practically nothing. Merely by their silence, their reserve, their natural sober pride, my people, who did not even know how to read, taught me the most valuable and enduring lessons. Anyhow, I was too

7

absorbed in feeling to dream of things. Even now, when I
see the life of the very rich in Paris, there is compassion
in the detachment it inspires in me. One finds many
injustices in the world, but there is one that is never
mentioned, climate. For a long time, without realizing it,
I thrived on that particular injustice. I can imagine the
accusations of our grim philanthropists, if they should
happen to read these lines. I want to pass the workers off
as rich and the bourgeois as poor, to prolong the happy
servitude of the former and the power of the latter. No,
that is not it. For the final and most revolting injustice is
consummated when poverty is wed to the life without
hope or the sky that I found on reaching manhood in the
appalling slums of our cities: everything must be done so
that men can escape from the double humiliation of
poverty and ugliness. Though born poor in a working-
class neighborhood, I never knew what real misfortune
was until I saw our chilling suburbs. Even extreme Arab
poverty cannot be compared to it, because of the difference in climate. But anyone who has known these indus-
trial slums feels forever soiled, it seems to me, and responsible for their existence.

What I have said is nonetheless true. From time
to time I meet people who live among riches I cannot even
imagine. I still have to make an effort to realize that
others can feel envious of such wealth. A long time ago, I
once lived a whole week luxuriating in all the goods of
this world: we slept without a roof, on a beach, I lived on
fruit, and spent half my days alone in the water. I
learned something then that has always made me react to
the signs of comfort or of a well-appointed house with
irony, impatience, and sometimes anger. Although I live
without worrying about tomorrow now, and therefore
count myself among the privileged, I don't know how to

own things. What I do have, which always comes to me
without my asking for it, I can't seem to keep. Less from
extravagance, I think, than from another kind of parsi-
mony: I cling like a miser to the freedom that disappears
as soon as there is an excess of things. For me, the
greatest luxury has always coincided with a certain bare-
ness. I love the bare interiors of Spanish or North African
houses. Where I prefer to live and work (and what is
more unusual, where I would not mind dying) is in a
hotel room. I have never been able to succumb to what
is called home life (so often the very opposite of an
inner life); "bourgeois" happiness bores and terrifies me.
This incapacity is nothing to brag about: it has made no
small contribution to my worst faults. I don't envy anyone
anything, which is my right, but I am not always mindful
of the wants of others and this robs me of imagination,
that is to say, kindness. I've invented a maxim for my own
personal use: "We must put our principles into great
things, mercy is enough for the small ones." Alas! We
invent maxims to fill the holes in our own natures. With
me, a better word for the aforementioned mercy would be
indifference. The results, as one can imagine, are less
than miraculous.

But all I want to emphasize is that poverty does
not necessarily involve envy. Even later, when a serious
illness temporarily deprived me of the natural vigor that
always transfigured everything for me, in spite of the
invisible infirmities and new weaknesses this illness
brought, I may have known fear and discouragement, but
never bitterness. The illness surely added new limitations, the hardest ones, to those I had already. In the end
it encouraged that freedom of the heart, that slight detachment from human concerns, which has always saved
me from resentment. Since living in Paris I have learned

9

this is a royal privilege. I've enjoyed it without restrictions or remorse, and until now at any rate, it has illuminated my whole life. As an artist, for example, I began by admiring others, which in a way is heaven on earth. (The present custom in France, as everyone knows, is to launch and even to conclude one's literary career by choosing an artist to make fun of.) My human passions, like my literary ones, have never been directed *against* others. The people I have loved have always been better and greater than I. Poverty as I knew it taught me not resentment but a certain fidelity and silent tenacity. If I have ever forgotten them, either I or my faults are to blame, not the world I was born into.

The memory of those years has also kept me from ever feeling satisfied in the exercise of my craft. Here, as simply as I can, I'd like to bring up something writers normally never mention. I won't even allude to the satisfaction one supposedly feels at a perfectly written book or page. I don't know whether many writers experience it. As far as I'm concerned, I don't think I've ever found delight in re-reading a finished page. I will even admit, ready to be taken at my word, that the success of some of my books has always surprised me. Of course, rather shabbily, one gets used to it. Even today, though, I feel like an apprentice compared to certain living writers I rank at their true worth. One of the foremost is the man to whom these essays were dedicated as long as twenty years ago.[1] Naturally, a writer has some joys he lives for and that do satisfy him fully. But for me, these come at the moment of conception, at the instant when the subject reveals itself, when the articulation of the work

[1] *Jean Grenier was Camus's philosophy teacher at the Lycée d'Alger and later at the University of Algiers. It was under his direction that Camus undertook research for his Diplôme*

Preface

sketches itself out before the suddenly heightened awareness, at those delicious moments when imagination and
intelligence are fused. These moments disappear as they
are born. What is left is the execution, that is to say, a
long period of hard work.

On another level, an artist also has the delights of
vanity. The writer's profession, particularly in French
society, is largely one of vanity. I say this without scorn,
and with only slight regret. In this respect I am like
everyone else; who is impervious to this ridiculous dis-
ease? Yet, in a society where envy and derision are the
rule, the day comes when, covered with scorn, writers pay
dearly for these poor joys. Actually, in twenty years of
literary life, my work has brought very few such joys,
fewer and fewer as time has passed.

Isn't it the memory of the truths glimpsed in *The
Wrong Side and the Right Side* that has always kept me
from feeling at ease in the public exercise of my craft
and has prompted the many refusals that have not always won me friends? By ignoring compliments and hom-
ages we lead the person paying those compliments to
think we look down on him, when in fact we are only
doubting ourselves. By the same token, if I had shown
the mixture of harshness and indulgence sometimes
found in literary careers, if like so many others I had
exaggerated a bit, I might have been looked upon more
favorably, for I would have been playing the game. But
what's to be done, the game does not amuse me! The ambitions of a Lucien de Rubempré or a Julien Sorel often
disconcert me in their naïveté and their modesty. Nietzsche's, Tolstoy's, or Melville's overwhelm me, precisely

*d'études supérieures, which he successfully completed in 1936,
on* Métaphysique chrétienne et néoplatonisme. —P.T.

11

because of their failure. I feel humility, in my heart of hearts, only in the presence of the poorest lives or the greatest adventures of the mind. Between the two is a society I find ludicrous.

Sometimes on those opening nights at the theater, which are the only times I ever meet what is insolently referred to as "all Paris," it seems to me that the audience is about to vanish, that this fashionable world does not exist. It is the others who seem real to me, the tall figures sounding forth upon the stage. Resisting the impulse to flee, I make myself remember that every one in the audience also has a rendezvous with himself: that he knows it and will doubtless be keeping it soon. Immediately he seems like a brother once more; solitudes unite those society separates. Knowing this, how can one flatter this world, seek its petty privileges, agree to congratulate every author of every book, and openly thank the favorable critic. Why try to seduce the enemy, and above all how is one to receive the compliments and admiration that the French (in the author's presence anyway, for once he leaves the room! . . .) dispense as generously as Pernod or the fan magazines. I can't do it and that's a fact. Perhaps there is a lot of that churlish pride of mine here, whose strength and extent I know only too well. But if this were all, if only my vanity were involved, it seems to me that I ought to enjoy compliments, superficially at least, instead of repeatedly being embarrassed by them. No, the vanity I share with others comes mostly when I react to criticisms that have some measure of truth. It's not conceit that makes me greet compliments with that stupid, ungrateful look I know so well, but (along with the profound indifference that haunts me like a natural infirmity) a strange feeling that comes over me: "You're missing the point . . ." Yes, they are missing the point, and that is why a reputation, as it's called, is sometimes so hard to bear that one takes a kind of malicious pleasure in doing everything one can to lose it. On the other hand, re-reading *The Wrong Side and the Right Side* for this edition after so many years, I know instinctively that certain pages, despite their inadequacies, *are* the point. I mean that old woman, a silent mother, poverty, light on the Italian olive trees, the populated loneliness of love— all that in my opinion reveals the truth.

Since these pages were written I have grown older and lived through many things. I have learned to recognize my limits and nearly all my weaknesses. I've learned less about people, since their destiny interests me more than their reactions, and destinies tend to repeat each other. I've learned at least that other people do exist, and that selfishness, although it cannot be denied, must try to be clear-sighted. To enjoy only oneself is impossible, I know, although I have great gifts in this direction. If solitude exists, and I don't know if it does, one should certainly have the right to dream of it occasionally as paradise. I do from time to time, like everyone else. Yet two tranquil angels have always kept me from that paradise: one has a friend's face, the other an enemy's. Yes, I know all this and I've also learned or nearly learned the price of love. But about life itself I know no more than what is said so clumsily in *The Wrong Side and the Right Side*.

"There is no love of life without despair of life," I wrote, rather pompously, in these pages. I didn't know at the time how right I was; I had not yet been through years of real despair. They came, and managed to destroy everything in me except an uncontrolled appetite for life. I still suffer from this both fruitful and destructive passion that bursts through even the gloomiest pages of *The*

Wrong Side and the Right Side. It's been said we really *live* for only a few hours of our life. This is true in one sense, false in another. For the hungry ardor one can sense in these essays has never left me; in the last analysis, this appetite is life at its best and at its worst. I've certainly tried to correct its worst effects. Like everyone, I've done my best to improve my nature by means of ethics. Alas, the price has been high. With energy, something I've a good deal of, one sometimes manages to behave morally, but never to *be* moral. To long for morality when one is a man of passion is to yield to *in*justice at the very moment one speaks of justice. Man sometimes seems to me a walking injustice: I am thinking of myself. If I now have the impression I was wrong, or that I lied sometimes in what I wrote, it is because I do not know how to treat my iniquity honestly. Surely I've never claimed to be a just man. I've only said that we should try to be just, and also that such an ambition involves suffering and unhappiness. But is this distinction so important? And can the man who does not even manage to make justice prevail in his own life preach its virtues to other people? If only we could live according to honor— that virtue of the unjust! But our society finds the word obscene; "aristocratic" is a literary and philosophical insult. I am not an aristocrat, my reply is in this book: here are my people, my teachers, my ancestry; here is what, through them, links me with everyone. And yet I do need honor, because I am not big enough to do without it!

What does it matter? I merely wanted to show that if I have come a long way since this book, I have not made much progress. Often, when I thought I was moving forward, I was losing ground. But, in the end, my needs, my errors, and my fidelities have always brought me back to the ancient path I began to explore in *The*

Wrong Side and the Right Side, whose traces are visible in everything I've done since, and along which on certain mornings in Algiers, for example, I still walk with the same slight intoxication.

If this is so, why have I so long refused to produce this feeble testimony? First of all because, I must repeat, I have artistic scruples just as other men have moral and religious ones. If I am stuck with the notion "such things are not done," with taboos in general rather alien to my free nature, it's because I am the slave, and an admiring one, of a severe artistic tradition. Since this uneasiness may be at war with my profound anarchy, it strikes me as useful. I know my disorder, the violence of certain instincts, the graceless abandon into which I can throw myself. In order to be created, a work of art must first of all make use of the dark forces of the soul. But not without channeling them, surrounding them with dikes, so that the water in them rises. Perhaps my dikes are still too high today. From this, the occasional stiffness . . . Someday, when a balance is established between what I am and what I say, perhaps then, and I scarcely dare write it, I shall be able to construct the work I dream of. What I have tried to say here is that in one way or another it will be like *The Wrong Side and the Right Side* and that it will speak of a certain form of love. The second reason I've kept these early essays to myself will then be clear: clumsiness and disorder reveal too much of the secrets closest to our hearts; we also betray them through too careful a disguise. It is better to wait until we are skillful enough to give them a form that does not stifle their voice, until we know how to mingle nature and art in fairly equal doses; in short, to be. For being consists of being able to do everything at the same time. In art, everything comes at once or not at all; there is no light without flame. Stendhal once cried: "But my soul is a fire which suffers if it does not blaze." Those who are like him in this should create only when afire. At the height of the flame, the cry leaps straight upward and creates words which in their turn reverberate. I am talking here about what all of us, artists unsure of being artists, but certain that we are nothing else, wait for day after day, so that in the end we may agree to live.

Why then, since I am concerned with what is probably a vain expectation, should I now agree to republish these essays? First of all because a number of readers have been able to find a convincing argument.[2] And then, a time always comes in an artist's life when he must take his bearings, draw closer to his own center, and then try to stay there. Such is my position today, and I need say no more about it. If, in spite of so many efforts to create a language and bring myths to life, I never manage to rewrite *The Wrong Side and the Right Side*, I shall have achieved nothing. I feel this in my bones. But nothing prevents me from dreaming that I shall succeed, from imagining that I shall still place at the center of this work the admirable silence of a mother and one man's effort to rediscover a justice or a love to match this silence. In the dream that life is, here is man, who finds his truths and loses them on this mortal earth, in order to return through wars, cries, the folly of justice and love, in short through pain, toward that tranquil land where death itself is a happy silence. Here still . . . Yes, nothing prevents one from dreaming, in the very hour of exile, since at least I know this, with sure and certain

[2] A simple one. "This book already exists, but in a small number of copies sold by booksellers at a very high price. Why should wealthy readers be the only ones with the right to read it?" Why indeed?

knowledge: a man's work is nothing but this slow trek to rediscover, through the detours of art, those two or three great and simple images in whose presence his heart first opened. This is why, perhaps, after working and producing for twenty years, I still live with the idea that my work has not even begun. From the moment that the republication of these essays made me go back to the first pages I wrote, it was mainly this I wanted to say.

Irony

❦❦ ❦❦❦ ❦❦

Two years ago, I knew an old woman. She was suffering from an illness that had almost killed her. The whole of her right side had been paralyzed. Only half of her was in this world while the other was already foreign to her. This bustling, chattering old lady had been reduced to silence and immobility. Alone day after day, illiterate, not very sensitive, her whole life was reduced to God. She believed in him. The proof is that she had a rosary, a lead statue of Christ, and a stucco statue of Saint Joseph carrying the infant Jesus. She doubted her illness was incurable, but said it was so that people would pay attention to her. For everything else, she relied on the God she loved so poorly.

One day someone did pay attention to her. A young man. (He thought there was a truth and also knew that this woman was going to die, but did not worry about solving this contradiction.) He had become genuinely interested in the old woman's boredom. She felt it. And his interest was a godsend for the invalid. She was eager to talk about her troubles: she was at the end of her tether, and you have to make way for the rising generation. Did she get bored? Of course she did. No one spoke to her. She had been put in her corner, like a dog. Better to be done with it once and for all. She would sooner die than be a burden to anyone.

Her voice had taken on a quarrelsome note, like someone haggling over a bargain. Still, the young man understood. Nonetheless, he thought being a burden on others was better than dying. Which proved only one thing: that he had surely never been a burden to any one. And of course he told the old lady—since he had seen the rosary: "You still have God." It was true. But even here she had her troubles. If she happened to spend rather a long time in prayer, if her eyes strayed and followed a pattern in the wallpaper, her daughter would say: "There she is, praying again!" "What business is that of yours?" the invalid would say. "It's none of my business, but eventually it gets on my nerves." And the old woman would fall silent, casting a long, reproachful look at her daughter.

The young man listened to all this with an immense, unfamiliar pain that hurt his chest. And the old woman went on: "She'll see when she's old. She'll need it too."

You felt that this old woman had been freed of everything except God, wholly abandoned to this final evil, virtuous through necessity, too easily convinced that what still remained for her was the only thing worth loving, finally and irrevocably plunged into the wretchedness of man in God. But if hope in life is reborn, God is powerless against human interests.

They had sat down at table. The young man had been invited to dinner. The old lady wasn't eating, because it is difficult to digest in the evening. She had stayed in her corner, sitting behind the young man who had been listening to her. And because he felt he was being watched he couldn't eat very much. Nevertheless, the dinner progressed. They decided to extend the party by going to the cinema. As it happened, there was a funny film on that week. The young man had blithely accepted, without thinking about the person who continued to exist behind his back.

The guests had risen from table to go and wash their hands before leaving. There was obviously no question of the old lady's going too. Even if she hadn't been half-paralyzed, she was too ignorant to be able to understand the film. She said she didn't like the movies. The truth was she couldn't understand them. In any case, she was in her corner, vacantly absorbed in the beads of her rosary. This was where she put all her trust. The three objects she kept near her represented the material point where God began. Beyond and behind the rosary, the statue of Christ, or of Saint Joseph, opened a vast, deep blackness in which she placed all her hope.

Everyone was ready. They went up to the old lady to kiss her and wish her a good night. She had already realized what was happening and was clutching her rosary tightly in her hand. But it was plain this showed as much despair as zeal. Everyone else had kissed her. Only the young man was left. He had given her an affectionate handshake and was already turning away. But she saw that the one person who had taken an interest in her was leaving. She didn't want to be alone. She could already feel the horror of loneliness, the long, sleepless hours, the frustrating intimacy with God. She was afraid, could now rely only on man, and, clinging to the one person who had shown any interest in her, held on to his hand, squeezing it, clumsily thanking him in order to justify this insistence. The young man was embarrassed. The others were already turning round to tell him to hurry up. The movie began at nine and it was better to arrive early so as not to have to wait in line.

He felt confronted by the most atrocious suffering he had ever known: that of a sick old woman left behind by people going to the movies. He wanted to leave and escape, didn't want to know, tried to draw back his hand. For a moment, he felt an intense hatred for the old woman, and almost slapped her hard across the face.

Finally he managed to get away, while the invalid, half rising from her armchair, watched with horror as the last certainty in which she could have found rest faded away. Now there was nothing to protect her. And, defenseless before the idea of death, she did not know exactly what terrified her, but felt that she did not want to be alone. God was of no use to her. All He did was cut her off from people and make her lonely. She did not want to be without people. So she began to cry.

The others were already outside in the street. The young man was gripped with remorse. He looked up at the lighted window, a great dead eye in the silent house. The eye closed. The old woman's daughter told the young man: "She always turns the light off when she's by herself. She likes to sit in the dark." [1]

[1] *Roger Quillot, in his notes to the second volume of Camus's works published in the* Bibliothèque de la Pléiade *in 1965, traces the ideas Camus expresses in these essays to the very first literary sketches written in 1932, when he was only nineteen. A manuscript belonging to Camus's first wife, Simone Hié, presents the themes of loneliness and old age, and specifically mentions the old woman left behind by the young people who go to the cinema. In 1935 Camus sketched a plan for these essays that indicates he intended to center them around the son's relationship with his mother. He first had the idea of writing a preface*

The old man brought his eyebrows triumphantly together, waggling a sententious forefinger. "When I was a young man," he said, "my father used to give me five francs a week out of my wages as pocket money to last me till the following Saturday. Well, I still managed to save. First of all, when I went to see my fiancée, I walked four miles through the open country to get there and four miles to get back. Just you listen to me now, young men just don't know how to amuse themselves nowadays." There were three young men sitting at a round table with this one old man. He was describing his petty adventures —childish actions overblown, incidents of laziness celebrated as victories. He never paused in his story, and, in a hurry to tell everything before his audience left, mentioned only those portions of his past he thought likely to impress them. Making people listen was his only vice: he refused to notice the irony of the glances and the sudden mockery that greeted him. The young man saw in him the usual old bird for whom everything was marvelous in his day, while he thought himself the respected elder whose experience carries weight. The young don't know that experience is a defeat and that we must lose everything in order to win a little knowledge. He had suffered. He never mentioned it. It's better to seem happy. And if he were wrong about this, he would have been even more

---

to a new edition of these essays in 1949, and read part of this one to Quillot in 1954. The essays were originally published in 1937, by the small firm of Charlot, in Algiers. The account of Camus's home life in the last section of Irony *and in the essay* The Wrong Side and the Right Side *include the most openly autobiographical passages in all of his work. His father was killed at the first battle of the Marne in 1914 (cf. page 38), and he lived with his mother, his grandmother, and his elder brother Lucien in the working-class suburb of Belcourt in Algiers. —*P.T.

mistaken to try to make people sympathize with him. What do an old man's sufferings matter when life absorbs you completely? He talked on and on, wandering blissfully through the grayness of his mutterings. But it couldn't last. He needed an ending, and the attention of his listeners was waning. He wasn't even funny any longer; he was old. And young men like billiards and cards, which take their minds off the imbecility of everyday work.

Soon he was alone, despite his efforts and the lies he told to enliven his story. With no attempt to spare his feelings, the young men had left. Once again he was alone. No longer to be listened to: that's the terrible thing about being old. He was condemned to silence and loneliness. He was being told that he would soon be dead. And an old man who is going to die is useless, he is even an insidious embarrassment. Let him go. He ought to go. Or, if not, to shut up is the least he can do. He suffers, because as soon as he stops talking he realizes that he is old. Yet he did get up and go, smiling to everyone around him. But the faces he saw were either indifferent, or convulsed by a gaiety that he had no right to share. A man was laughing: "She's old, I don't deny it, but sometimes the best stews are made in old pots." Another, already more seriously: "Well, we're not rich but we eat well. Look at my grandson now, he eats more than his father. His father needs a pound of bread, he needs two! And you can pile on the sausage and Camembert. And sometimes when he's finished he says: 'Han, han!' and keeps on eating." The old man moved away. And with his slow step, the short step of the donkey turning the wheel, he walked through the crowds of men on the long pavements. He felt ill and did not want to go home. Usually he was quite happy to get home to his table and the oil lamp,

24

the plates where his fingers mechanically found their places. He still liked to eat his supper in silence, the old woman on the other side of the table, chewing over each mouthful, with an empty head, eyes fixed and dead. This evening, he would arrive home later. Supper would have been served and gone cold, his wife would be in bed, not worrying about him since she knew that he often came home unexpectedly late. She would say: "He's in the moon again," and that would be that.

death

Now he was walking along with his gently insistent step. He was old and alone. When a life is reaching its end, old age wells up in waves of nausea. Everything comes down to not being listened to any more. He walks along, turns at the corner of the street, stumbles, and almost falls. I've seen him. It's ridiculous, but what can you do about it? After all, he prefers being in the street, being there rather than at home, where for hours on end fever veils the old woman from him and isolates him in his room. Then, sometimes, the door slowly opens and gapes ajar for a moment. A man comes in. He is wearing a light-colored suit. He sits down facing the old man and the minutes pass while he says nothing. He is motionless, just like the door that stood ajar a moment ago. From time to time he strokes his hair and sighs gently. When he has watched the old man for a long time with the same heavy sadness in his eyes, he leaves, silently. The latch clicks behind him and the old man remains, horrified, with an acid and painful fear in his stomach. Out in the street, however few people he may meet, he is never alone. His fever sings. He walks a little faster: tomorrow everything will be different, tomorrow. Suddenly he realizes that tomorrow will be the same, and, after tomorrow, all the other days. And he is crushed by this irreparable discovery. It's ideas like this that kill one. Men

routine

25

kill themselves because they cannot stand them—or, if they are young, they turn them into epigrams.

Old, mad, drunk, nobody knows. His will be a worthy end, tear-stained and admirable. He will die looking his best, that is to say, he will suffer. That will be a consolation for him. And besides, where can he go? He will always be old now. Men build on their future old age. They try to give this old age, besieged by hopelessness, an idleness that leaves them with no defense. They want to become foremen so they can retire to a little house in the country. But once they are well on in years, they know very well this is a mistake. They need other men for protection. And as far as he was concerned, he needed to be listened to in order to believe in his life. The streets were darker and emptier now. There were still voices going by. In the strange calm of evening they were becoming more solemn. Behind the hills encircling the town there were still glimmers of daylight. From somewhere out of sight, smoke rose, imposingly, behind the wooded hilltops. It rose slowly in the sky, in tiers, like the branches of a pine tree. The old man closed his eyes. As life carried away the rumblings of the town, and the heavens smiled their foolish, indifferent smile, he was alone, forsaken, naked, already dead.

Need I describe the other side of this fine coin? Doubtless, in a dark and dirty room, the old woman was laying the table. When dinner was ready she sat down, looked at the clock, waited a little longer, and then began to eat a hearty meal. She thought to herself: "He is in the moon." That would be that.

There were five of them living together: the grandmother, her younger son, her elder daughter, and the daughter's two children. The son was almost dumb;

the daughter, an invalid, could think only with difficulty; and of the two children, one was already working for an insurance company while the other was continuing his studies. At seventy, the grandmother still dominated all these people. Above her bed you could see a portrait taken of her five years before, upright in a black dress that was held together at the neck by a medallion, not a wrinkle on her face. With enormous clear, cold eyes, she had a regal posture she relinquished only with increasing age, but which she still sometimes tried to recover when she went out.

It was these clear eyes that held a memory for her grandson which still made him blush. The old woman would wait until there were visitors and would ask then, looking at him severely, "Whom do you like best? Your mother or your grandmother?" The game was even better when the daughter was present. For the child would always reply: "My grandmother," with, in his heart, a great surge of love for his ever silent mother. Then, when the visitors were surprised at this preference, the mother would say: "It's because she's the one who brought him up."

It was also because the old woman thought that love is something you can demand. The knowledge that she herself had been a good mother gave her a kind of rigidity and intolerance. She had never deceived her husband, and had borne him nine children. After his death, she had brought up her family energetically. Leaving their little farm on the outskirts, they had ended up in the old, poor part of the town where they had been living for a long time.

And certainly this woman was not lacking in qualities. But to her grandsons, who were at the age of absolute judgments, she was nothing but a fraud. One of their uncles had told them a significant story: he had gone to pay a visit to his mother-in-law, and from the outside had seen her sitting idly at the window. But she had come to the door with a duster in her hand and had apologized for carrying on working by saying that she had so little free time left after doing her housework. And it must be confessed that this was typical. She fainted very easily after family discussions. She also suffered from painful vomiting caused by a liver complaint. But she showed not the slightest discretion in the practice of her illness. Far from shutting herself away, she would vomit noisily into the kitchen garbage can. And when she came back into the room, pale, her eyes running with tears from the effort, she would remind anyone who begged her to go to bed that she had to get the next meal ready and carry on in running the house: "I do everything here." Or again: "I don't know what would become of you without me."

The children learned to ignore her vomitings, her "attacks" as she called them, as well as her complaints. One day she went to bed and demanded the doctor. They sent for him to humor her. On the first day he diagnosed a slight stomach upset, on the second a cancer of the liver, on the third a serious attack of jaundice. But the younger of the two children insisted on seeing all this as yet another performance, a more sophisticated act, and felt no concern. This woman had bullied him too much for his initial reaction to be pessimistic. And there is a kind of desperate courage in being lucid and refusing to love. But people who play at being ill can succeed: the grandmother carried simulation to the point of death. On her last day, her children around her, she began freeing herself of the fermentations in her intestines. She turned and spoke with simplicity to her grandson: "You see," she said, "I'm farting like a little pig." She died an hour later.

As for her grandson, he now realized that he had not understood a thing that was happening. He could not free himself of the idea that he had just witnessed the last and most monstrous of this woman's performances. And if he asked himself whether he felt any sorrow, he could find none at all. Only on the day of the funeral, because of the general outburst of tears, did he weep, but he was afraid of being insincere and telling lies in the presence of death. It was on a fine winter's day, shot through with sunlight. In the pale blue sky, you could sense the cold all spangled with yellow. The cemetery overlooked the town, and you could see the fine transparent sun setting in the bay quivering with light, like a moist lip.

None of this fits together? How very true! A woman you leave behind to go to the movies, an old man to whom you have stopped listening, a death that redeems nothing, and then, on the other hand, the whole radiance of the world. What difference does it make if you accept everything? Here are three destinies, different and yet alike. Death for us all, but his own death to each. After all, the sun still warms our bones for us.

Between Yes and No

 ❦❦ ❦❦❦ ❦❦

IF IT IS true that the only paradises are those we have
lost, I know what name to give the tender and inhuman
something that dwells in me today. An emigrant returns
to his country. And I remember. The irony and tension
fade away, and I am home once more. I don't want to
ruminate on happiness. It is much simpler and much
easier than that. For what has remained untouched in
these hours I retrieve from the depths of forgetfulness is
the memory of a pure emotion, a moment suspended in
eternity. Only this memory is true in me, and I always
discover it too late. We love the gentleness of certain
gestures, the way a tree fits into a landscape. And we
have only one detail with which to recreate all this love,
but it will do: the smell of a room too long shut up, the
special sound of a footstep on the road. This is the way it
is for me. And if I loved then in giving myself, I finally
became myself, since only love restores us.

Slow, peaceful, and grave, these hours return,
just as strong, just as moving—there is a kind of vague
desire in the dull sky. Each rediscovered gesture reveals

me to myself. Someone once said to me: "It's so difficult
to live." And I remember the tone of voice. On another
occasion, someone murmured: "The worst blunder is still
to make people suffer." When everything is over, the
thirst for life is gone. Is this what's called happiness? As
we skirt along these memories, we clothe everything in
the same quiet garb, and death looks like a backdrop
whose colors have faded. We turn back into ourselves.
We feel our distress and like ourselves the better for it.
Yes, perhaps that's what happiness is, the self-pitying
awareness of our unhappiness.

It is certainly like that this evening. In this Moorish café, at the far end of the Arab town, I recall not a
moment of past happiness but a feeling of strangeness. It
is already night. On the walls, canary-yellow lions pursue
green-clad sheiks among five-branched palm trees. In a
corner of the café, an acetylene lamp gives a flickering
light. The real light comes from the fire, at the bottom of
a small stove adorned with yellow and green enamel. The
flames light up the middle of the room, and I can feel
them reflected on my face. I sit facing the doorway and
the bay. Crouched in a corner, the café owner seems to be
looking at my glass, which stands there empty with a
mint leaf at the bottom. There is no one in the main
room, noises rise from the town opposite, while further
off in the bay lights shine. I hear the Arab breathe heavily, and his eyes glow in the dusk. Is that the sound of the
sea far off? The world sighs toward me in a long rhythm,
and brings me the peace and indifference of immortal
things. Tall red shadows make the lions on the walls
sway with a wavelike motion. The air grows cool. A fog-
horn sounds at sea. The beams from the lighthouse begin
to turn: one green, one red, and one white. And still the
world sighs its long sigh. A kind of secret song is born of

this indifference. And I am home again. I think of a child living in a poor district. That neighborhood, that house! There were only two floors, and the stairs were unlit. Even now, long years later, he could go back there on the darkest night. He knows that he could climb the stairs without stumbling once. His very body is impregnated with this house. His legs retain the exact height of the steps; his hand, the instinctive, never-conquered horror of the bannister. Because of the cockroaches.

On summer evenings, the workingmen sit on their balconies. In his apartment, there was only one tiny window. So they would bring the chairs down, put them in front of the house, and enjoy the evening air. There was the street, the ice-cream vendor next door, the cafés across the way, and the noise of children running from door to door. But above all, through the wide fig trees there was the sky. There is a solitude in poverty, but a solitude that gives everything back its value. At a certain level of wealth, the heavens themselves and the star-filled night are nature's riches. But seen from the very bottom of the ladder, the sky recovers its full meaning: a priceless grace. Summer nights mysterious with crackling stars! Behind the child was a stinking corridor, and his little chair, splitting across the bottom, sank a little beneath his weight. But, eyes raised, he drank in the pure night. Sometimes a large tram would rattle swiftly past. A drunk would stand singing at a street corner, without disturbing the silence.

The child's mother sat as silently. Sometimes, people would ask her: "What are you thinking about?" And she would answer: "Nothing." And it was quite true. Everything was there, so she thought about nothing. Her life, her interests, her children were simply there, with a presence too natural to be felt. She was frail, had diffi-

32

culty in thinking. She had a harsh and domineering mother who sacrificed everything to a touchy animal pride and had long held sway over her weak-minded daughter. Emancipated by her marriage, the daughter came home obediently when her husband died. He died a soldier's death, as they say. One could see his gold-framed military medal and *croix de guerre* in a place of honor. The hospital sent the widow the small shell splinter found in his body. She kept it. Her grief has long since disappeared. She has forgotten her husband, but still speaks of her children's father. To support these children, she goes out to work and gives her wages to her mother, who brings them up with a whip. When she hits them too hard, the daughter tells her: "Don't hit them on the head." Because they are her children she is very fond of them. She loves them with a hidden and impartial love. Sometimes, on those evenings he's remembering, she would come back from her exhausting work (as a cleaning woman) to find the house empty, the old woman out shopping, the children still at school. She would huddle in a chair, gazing in front of her, wandering off in the dizzy pursuit of a crack along the floor. As the night thickened around her, her muteness would seem irredeemably desolate. If the child came in, he would see her thin shape and bony shoulders, and stop, afraid. He is beginning to feel a lot of things. He is scarcely aware of his own existence, but this animal silence makes him want to cry with pain. He feels sorry for his mother; is this the same as loving her? She has never hugged or kissed him, for she wouldn't know how. He stands a long time watching her. Feeling separate from her, he becomes conscious of her suffering. She does not hear him, for she is deaf. In a few moments, the old woman will come back, life will start up again: the round light cast by the kerosene lamp, the oilcloth on the table, the shouting, the swearing. Meanwhile, the silence marks a pause, an immensely long moment. Vaguely aware of this, the child thinks the surge of feeling in him is love for his mother. And it must be, because after all she is his mother.

She is thinking of nothing. Outside, the light, the noises; here, silence in the night. The child will grow, will learn. They are bringing him up and will ask him to be grateful, as if they were sparing him pain. His mother will always have these silences. He will suffer as he grows. To be a man is what counts. His grandmother will die, then his mother, then he.

His mother has given a sudden start. Something has frightened her. He looks stupid standing there gazing at her. He ought to go and do his homework. The child has done his homework. Today he is in a sordid café. Now he is a man. Isn't that what counts? Surely not, since doing homework and accepting manhood leads to nothing but old age.

Still crouching in his corner, the Arab sits with his hands clasped round his feet. The scent of roasting coffee rises from the terraces and mingles with the excited chatter of young voices. The hooting of a tugboat adds its grave and tender note. The world is ending here as it does each day, and all its measureless torments now give rise to nothing but this promise of peace. The indifference of this strange mother! Only the immense solitude of the world can be the measure of it. One evening, they had called her son—he was already quite grown up —to his mother's side. A fright had brought on a serious mental shock. She was in the habit of going out on the balcony at the end of the day. She would take a chair and lean her mouth against the cold and salty iron of the rail-

34

ing. Then she would watch the people going past. Behind her, the night would gradually thicken. In front of her, the shops would suddenly light up. The street would fill with people and lights. She would gaze emptily out until she forgot where she was. On this particular evening, a man had loomed up behind her, dragged her backward, knocked her about, and run away when he heard a noise. She had seen nothing, and fainted. She was in bed when her son arrived. He decided, on the doctor's advice, to spend the night with her. He stretched out on the bed, by her side, lying on the top of the blankets. It was summer. The fear left by the recent drama hung in the air of the overheated room. Footsteps were rustling and doors creaked. The smell of the vinegar used to cool his mother's brow floated in the heavy air. She moved restlessly about, whimpering, sometimes giving a sudden start, which would shake him from his brief snatches of sleep. He would wake drenched in sweat, ready to act—only to fall back heavily after glancing at his watch on which the night light threw dancing shadows. It was only later that he realized how much they had been alone that night. Alone against the others. The "others" were asleep, while they both breathed the same fever. Everything in the old house seemed empty. With the last midnight trams all human hope seemed drained away, all the certainties of city noises gone. The house was still humming with their passage; then little by little everything died away. All that remained was a great garden of silence interrupted now and then by the sick woman's frightened moans. He had never felt so lost. The world had melted away, taking with it the illusion that life begins again each morning. Nothing was left, his studies, ambitions, things he might choose in a restaurant, favorite colors. Nothing but the sickness and death he felt surrounded by . . . And yet, at the very moment that the world was crumbling, he was alive. Finally he fell asleep, but not without taking with him the tender and despairing image of two people's loneliness together. Later, much later, he would remember this mingled scent of sweat and vinegar, this moment when he had felt the ties attaching him to his mother. As if she were the immense pity he felt spread out around him, made flesh, diligently, without pretense, playing the part of a poor old woman whose fate moves men to tears.

Now the ashes in the grate are beginning to choke the fire. And still the same sigh from the earth. The perfect song of a *derbouka* is heard in the air, a woman's laughter above it. In the bay, the lights come closer— fishing vessels no doubt, returning to harbor. The triangle of sky I see from where I am sitting is stripped of its daylight clouds. Choked with stars, it quivers on a pure breeze and the padded wings of night beat slowly around me. How far will it go, this night in which I cease to belong to myself? There is a dangerous virtue in the word simplicity. And tonight I can understand a man wanting to die because nothing matters anymore when one sees through life completely. A man suffers and endures misfortune after misfortune. He bears them, settles into his destiny. People think well of him. And then, one evening, he meets a friend he has been very fond of, who speaks to him absent-mindedly. Returning home, the man kills himself. Afterwards, there is talk of private sorrows and secret dramas. No, if a reason really must be found, he killed himself because a friend spoke to him carelessly. In the same way, every time it seems to me that I've grasped the deep meaning of the world, it is its simplicity that always overwhelms me. My mother, that evening, and its strange indifference. On another occasion, I was living in a villa in the suburbs, alone with a dog, a couple

36

of cats and their kittens, all black. The mother cat could
not feed them. One by one, all the kittens died. They filled
the room with their filth. Every evening, when I arrived
home, I would find one lying stiff, its gums laid bare. One
evening, I found the last one, half eaten by the mother. It
stank already. The stench of death mingled with the
stench of urine. Then, with my hands in the filth and the
stench of rotting flesh reeking in my nostrils, I sat down
in the midst of all this misery and gazed for hour after
hour at the demented glow in the cat's green eyes as it
crouched motionless in the corner. Yes. And it is just like
that this evening. When we are stripped down to a certain point, nothing leads anywhere any more, hope and
despair are equally groundless, and the whole of life can
be summed up in an image. But why stop there? Simple,
everything is simple, the lights alternating in the lighthouse, one green, one red, one white; the cool of the
night; and the smell of the town and the poverty that
reach me from below. If, this evening, the image of a
certain childhood comes back to me, how can I keep from
welcoming the lesson of love and poverty it offers? Since
this hour is like a pause between yes and no, I leave hope
or disgust with life for another time. Yes, only to capture
the transparency and simplicity of paradises lost—in an
image. And so it was not long ago, in a house in an old
part of town, when a son went to see his mother. They sat
down facing each other, in silence. But their eyes met:

"Well, mother."

"Well, here we are."

"Are you bored? I don't talk much."

"Oh, you've never talked much."

And though her lips do not move her face lights
up in a beautiful smile. It's true, he never talked much to
her. But did he ever need to? When one keeps quiet, the

37

situation becomes clear. He is her son, she is his mother. She can say to him: "You know."

She is sitting at the foot of the divan, her feet together, her hands together in her lap. He, on his chair, scarcely looks at her and smokes ceaselessly. A silence.

"You shouldn't smoke so much."

"I know."

The whole feeling of the neighborhood rises through the window: the accordion from the café next door, the traffic hurrying in the evening, the smell of the skewers of grilled meat eaten between small, springy rolls of bread, a child crying in the road. The mother rises and picks up her knitting. Her fingers are clumsy, twisted with arthritis. She works slowly, taking up the same stitch three or four times or undoing a whole row with a dull ripping sound.

"It's a little cardigan. I'll wear it with a white collar. With this and my black coat, I'll be dressed for the season."

She has risen to turn on the light.

"It gets dark early these days."

It was true. Summer was over and autumn had not yet begun. Swifts were still calling in the gentle sky.

"Will you come back soon?"

"But I haven't left yet. Why do you mention that?"

"Oh, it was just to say something."

A trolley goes by. A car.

"Is it true I look like my father?"

"The spitting image. Of course, you didn't know him. You were six months old when he died. But if you had a little moustache!"

He mentioned his father without conviction. No memory, no emotion. Probably he was very ordinary. Besides, he had been very keen to go to war. His head was split open in the battle of the Marne. Blinded, it took him a week to die; his name is listed on the local war memorial.

"When you think about it," she says, "it was better that way. He would have come back blind or crazy. So, the poor man . . ."

"That's right."

What is it then that keeps him in this room, except the certainty that it's still the best thing to do, the feeling that the whole *absurd* simplicity of the world has sought refuge here.

"Will you be back again?" she says. "I know you have work to do. Just from time to time . . ."

But where am I now? And how can I separate this deserted café from that room in my past? I don't know any longer whether I'm living or remembering. The beams from the lighthouse are here. And the Arab stands in front of me telling me that he is going to close. I have to leave. I no longer want to make such dangerous descents. It is true, as I take a last look at the bay and its light, that what wells up in me is not the hope of better days but a serene and primitive indifference to everything and to myself. But I must break this too limp and easy curve. I need my lucidity. Yes, everything is simple. It's men who complicate things. Don't let them tell us any stories. Don't let them say about the man condemned to death: "He is going to pay his debt to society," but: "They're going to chop his head off." It may seem like nothing. But it does make a little difference. There are some people who prefer to look their destiny straight in the eye.

Death in the Soul [1]

❦❦ ❦❦❦ ❦❦

I ARRIVED in Prague at six in the evening. Right away, I took my bags to the checkroom. I still had two hours to look for a hotel. And I was full of a strange feeling of liberty because I no longer had two suitcases hanging on my arms. I came out of the station, walked by some gardens, and suddenly found myself in the middle of the Avenue Wenceslas, swarming with people at that time of evening. Around me were a million human beings who had been alive all this time whose existence had never concerned me. They were alive. I was thousands of kilometers from home. I could not understand their language. They walked quickly, all of them. And as they

[1] *This essay was inspired by Camus's 1936 visit to Prague. According to his own working notebooks, the* Carnets, *he finished it in 1937 after the last essay in* The Wrong Side and the Right Side, *"Love of Life." His decision to place it before "Love of Life" in the finished volume suggests that an upsurge of happiness can follow closely after the experience of man's solitude. The "two sides of the cloth," evoked by the French title of the essays,* L'Envers et l'Endroit, *are thus closely linked together.* —P.T.

overtook and passed me, they cut themselves off from me. I felt lost.

I had little money. Enough to live on for six days. After that, friends would be joining me. Just the same, I began to feel anxious. So I started looking for a cheap hotel. I was in the new part of the town, and all the places I came upon were glittering with lights, laughter, and women. I walked faster. Something in my rapid pace already seemed like flight. Toward eight in the evening, exhausted, I reached the old town. Drawn by a modest-looking hotel with a small doorway, I enter. I fill in the form, take my key. I have room number 34, on the third floor. I open the door to find myself in a most luxurious room. I look to see how much it costs: twice as expensive as I'd thought. The money question is suddenly acute. Now I can live only scrimpingly in this great city. My distress, still rather vague a few moments ago, fixes itself on this one point. I feel uneasy, hollow and empty. Nevertheless, a moment of lucidity: I have always been credited, rightly or wrongly, with the greatest indifference to money. Why should I be worried? But already my mind is working. I must get something to eat, I start walking again and look for a cheap restaurant. I should spend no more than ten crowns on each meal. Of all the restaurants I see, the least expensive is also the least attractive. I walk up and down in front of it. The people inside begin to notice my antics: I have to go in. It is a rather murky cellar, painted with pretentious frescoes. The clientele is fairly mixed. A few prostitutes, in one corner, are smoking and talking seriously to one another. A number of men, for the most part colorless and of indeterminate age, sit eating at the tables. The waiter, a colossus in a greasy dinner jacket, leans his enormous, expressionless head in my direction. I quickly make a random choice of a dish from what, for me, is an incomprehensible menu. But it seems there is need for explanations. The waiter asks a question in Czech. I reply with what little German I know. He does not know German. I'm at a loss. He summons one of the girls, who comes forward in the classic pose, left hand on hip, cigarette in the right, smiling moistly. She sits down at my table and asks questions in a German I judge as bad as my own. Everything becomes clear. The waiter was pushing the *plat du jour*. Game for anything, I order it. The girl talks to me but I can't understand her anymore. Naturally, I say yes in my most sincere tone of voice. But I am not with it. Everything annoys me, I hesitate, I don't feel hungry. I feel a twinge of pain and a tightness in my stomach. I buy the girl a glass of beer because I know my manners. The *plat du jour* having arrived, I start to eat: a mixture of porridge and meat, ruined by an unbelievable amount of cumin. But I think about something else, or rather of nothing at all, staring at the fat, laughing mouth of the woman in front of me. Does she think I am inviting her favors? She is already close to me, starts to make advances. An automatic gesture from me holds her back. (She was ugly. I have often thought that if she had been pretty I would have avoided everything that happened later.) I was afraid of being sick, then and there, in the midst of all those people ready to laugh; still more afraid of being alone in my hotel room, without money or enthusiasm, reduced to myself and my miserable thoughts. Even today, I still wonder with embarrassment how the weary, cowardly creature I then became could have emerged from me. I left. I walked about in the old town, but unable to stomach my own company any longer, I ran all the way to my hotel, went to bed, and waited for sleep, which came almost at once.

Any country where I am not bored is a country that teaches me nothing. That was the kind of remark I tried out to cheer myself up. Need I describe the days that followed? I went back to my restaurant. Morning and evening, I endured that atrocious, sickening cumin-flavored food. As a result, I walked around all day with a constant desire to vomit. I resisted the impulse, knowing one must be fed. Besides, what did this matter compared to what I would have had to endure if I had tried a new restaurant? Here, at least, I was "recognized." People gave me a smile even if they didn't speak to me. On the other hand, anguish was gaining ground. I paid too much attention to that sharp twinge of pain in my head. I decided to organize my days, to cover them with points of reference. I stayed in bed as late as possible and the days were consequently shorter. I washed, shaved, and methodically explored the town. I lost myself in the sumptuous baroque churches, looking for a homeland in them, emerging emptier and more depressed after a disappointing confrontation with myself. I wandered along the Vltava and saw the water swirling and foaming at its dams. I spent endless hours in the immense, silent, and empty Hradchin district. At sunset, in the shadow of its cathedral and palaces, my lonely footsteps echoed in the streets. Hearing them, the panic seized me again. I had dinner early and went to bed at half past eight. The sun pulled me out of myself. I visited churches, palaces and museums, tried to soften my distress in every work of art. A classic dodge: I wanted my rebellion to melt into melancholy. But in vain. As soon as I came out, I was a stranger again. Once, however, in a baroque cloister at the far end of the town, the softness of the hour, the bells tinkling slowly, the clusters of pigeons flying from the old tower, and something like a scent of herbs and nothingness gave rise within me to a tear-filled silence that almost delivered me. Back at the hotel that evening, I wrote the following passage in one sitting: I reproduce it here unchanged, since its very pomposity reminds me of how complex my feelings were: "What other profit can one seek to draw from travel? Here I am, stripped bare, in a town where the signs are strange, unfamiliar hieroglyphics, with no friends to talk to, in short, without any distraction. I know very well that nothing will deliver me from this room filled with the noises of a foreign town, to lead me to the more tender glow of a fireside or a place I'm fond of. Should I shout for help? Unfamiliar faces would appear. Churches, gold, incense, everything flings me back into this daily life where everything takes its color from my anguish. The curtain of habits, the comfortable loom of words and gestures in which the heart drowses, slowly rises, finally to reveal anxiety's pallid visage. Man is face to face with himself: I defy him to be happy . . . And yet this is how travel enlightens him. A great discord occurs between him and the things he sees. The music of the world finds its way more easily into this heart grown less secure. Finally stripped bare, the slightest solitary tree becomes the most tender and fragile of images. Works of art and women's smiles, races of men at home in their land and monuments that summarize the centuries, this is the moving and palpable landscape that travel consists of. Then, at twilight, this hotel room where once again the hollow feeling eats at me, as if my soul were hungry." Need I confess that all this was just a means of getting to sleep? I can admit it now. What I remember of Prague is the smell of cucumbers soaked in vinegar that you buy at any street corner to eat between your fingers. Their bitter, piquant scent would awaken my anguish and quicken it as soon as I crossed the threshold of my hotel. That, and perhaps a certain tune played on an accordion as well. Beneath my windows, a blind, one-armed man would sit on his instrument, holding it in place with one buttock while opening and shutting it with his good hand. It was always the same childish, tender tune that woke me every morning, abruptly returning me to the unadorned reality in which I was floundering.

I remember too that on the banks of the Vltava I would suddenly stop, and seized by the scent or the melody, carried almost beyond myself, would murmur: "What does it mean? What does it mean?" But I had doubtless not yet gone over the edge. On the fourth day, at about ten in the morning, I was getting ready to go out. I wanted to see a certain Jewish cemetery I'd not been able to find the day before. Someone knocked at the door of the next room. After a moment's silence, they knocked again. A long knock this time, but apparently there was no answer. A heavy step went down the stairs. Without paying attention to what I was doing, my mind empty, I wasted a few moments reading the instructions for a shaving cream that I had already been using for a month. The day was heavy. A coppery light fell from the grey sky on the spires and domes of old Prague. As they did every morning, the newsboys were calling the name of a newspaper, *Narodni Politika*. I tore myself with difficulty from the torpor that was overcoming me. But just as I was going out, I passed the bellman who looked after my particular floor, armed with a bunch of keys. I stopped. He knocked again, for a long time. He tried to open the door. No success. It must have been bolted on the inside. More knocks. The room sounded so ominously empty that, depressed as I was, I left without asking any questions. But out in the Prague streets a painful foreboding pursued

me. How shall I ever forget the bellman's silly face, the
funny way his polished shoes curled upward, the button
missing from his jacket? I had lunch finally, but with a
growing feeling of disgust. At about two in the afternoon,
I went back to my hotel.

The staff was whispering in the lobby. I climbed
the stairs rapidly, the quicker to face what I was expecting. It was just as I'd thought. The door of the room was
half open, so that all that could be seen was a high,
blue-painted wall. But the dull light I mentioned earlier
threw two shadows on this screen: that of the dead man
lying on the bed and a policeman guarding the body. The
two shadows were at right angles to each other. The light
overwhelmed me. It was authentic, a real light, an afternoon light, signifying life, the sort of light that makes
one aware of living. He was dead. Alone in his room. I
knew it was not suicide. I dashed back into my room and
threw myself on the bed. A man like so many others,
short and fat as far as I could tell from his shadow. He
had probably been dead for quite a while. And life had
gone on in the hotel, until the bellman had thought of
calling him. He had come without suspecting anything
and died, alone. Meanwhile, I had been reading the advertisement for my shaving cream. I spent the afternoon in
a state that would be hard to describe. I lay on my bed,
thinking of nothing, with a strange heaviness in my
heart. I cut my nails. I counted the cracks in the floor-
boards. "If I can count up to a thousand . . ." At fifty or
sixty, I gave up. I couldn't go on. I could understand
nothing of the noises outside. Once, though, in the corridor, a stifled voice, a woman's voice, said in German: "He
was so good." Then I thought desperately of home, of my
own town on the shores of the Mediterranean, of its
gentle summer evenings that I love so much, suffused in

46

green light and filled with young and beautiful women. It was days since I had uttered a single word and my heart was bursting with the cries and protests I had stifled. If anyone had opened his arms to me, I would have wept like a child. Toward the end of the afternoon, broken with weariness, I stared madly at the door handle, endlessly repeating a popular accordion tune in my empty head. At that moment I had gone as far as I could. I had no more country, city, hotel room, or name. Madness or victory, humiliation or inspiration—was I about to *know*, or to be destroyed? There was a knock at the door and my friends came in. I was saved, if disappointed. I believe I even said: "I'm glad to see you again." But I'm sure I stopped there, and that in their eyes I still looked like the man they had left.

I left Prague not long after. And I certainly took an interest in what I saw later. I could note down such and such an hour in the little Gothic cemetery of Bautzen, the brilliant red of its geraniums and the blue morning sky. I could talk about the long, relentless, barren plains of Silesia. I crossed them at daybreak. A heavy flight of birds was passing in the thick, misty morning, above the sticky earth. I also liked Moravia, tender and grave, with its distant, pure horizons, its roads bordered with sour plum trees. But inside I still felt the dizziness of those who have gazed too long into a bottomless pit. I arrived in Vienna, left a week later. Still the numbness held me captive.

Yet in the train taking me from Vienna to Venice, I was waiting for something. I was like a convalescent fed on bouillon wondering how his first crust of bread will taste. Light was about to break through. I know now what it was: I was ready to be happy. I'll mention only the six days I lived on a hill near Vicenza. I am still there,

47

or rather, I still find myself there again occasionally, when the scent of rosemary brings it flooding back.

I enter Italy. A land that fits my soul, whose signs I recognize one by one as I approach. The first houses with their scaly tiles, the first vines flat against a wall made blue by sulphur dressings, the first clothes hung out in the courtyards, the disorder of the men's untidy, casual dress. And the first cypress (so slight and yet so straight), the first olive tree, the dusty fig tree. The soul exhausts its revolts in the shady piazzas of small Italian towns, in noontimes when pigeons look for shelter, in slowness and sloth—passion melts by degrees into tears, and then, Vicenza. Here the days revolve from the day-break, swollen with roosters' crowing to the unequalled evenings, sweetish and tender, silky behind the cypress trees, their long hours measured by the crickets' chirping. The inner silence that accompanies me rises from the slow pace that leads from each of these days to the next. What more can I long for than this room opening on the plain below, with its antique furniture and its hand-made lace. I have the whole sky on my face and I feel as if I could follow these slow, revolving days forever, spinning motionlessly with them. I breathe in the only happiness I can attain—an attentive and friendly awareness. I spend the whole day walking about: from the hill, I go down to Vicenza or else further into the country. Every person I meet, every scent on this street is a pretext for my measureless love. Young women looking after a children's summer camp, the ice-cream vendor's horn (his cart is a gondola on wheels, pushed by two handles), the displays of fruit, red melons with black pips, translucent, sticky grapes—all are props for the person who can no longer be alone.[2] But the cicadas'

[2] That is to say, everybody.

48

tender and bitter chirping, the perfume of water and stars one meets on September nights, the scented paths among the lentisks and the rosebushes, all these are signs of love for the person forced to be alone.[3] Thus pass the days. After the dazzling glare of hours filled with sun, the evenings come, in the splendid golden backdrop of the sun setting behind the darkness of the cypress trees. I walk along the road toward the crickets one hears from far away. As I advance, one by one they begin to sing more cautiously, and then fall silent. I move forward slowly, oppressed by so much ardent beauty. Behind me, one by one, the crickets' voices swell once more: a mystery hangs in this sky from which beauty and indifference descend. In a last gleam of light, I read on the front of a villa: *"In magnificentia naturae, resurgit spiritus."* This is where I should stop. Already the first star shines, three lights gleam on the hill opposite, night has fallen suddenly, unannounced. A breeze murmurs in the bushes behind me, the day has fled, leaving its sweetness behind.

I had not changed, of course. It was simply that I was no longer alone. In Prague, I was suffocating, surrounded by walls. Here, I was face to face with the world, and liberated from myself. I people the universe with forms in my own likeness. For I have not yet spoken of the sun. Just as it took me a long time to realize my attachment and love for the world of poverty in which I spent my childhood, only now can I see the lesson of the sun and the land I was born in. A little before noon I went out and walked toward a spot I knew that looked out over the immense plain of Vicenza. The sun had almost reached its zenith, the sky was an intense, airy blue. The light it shed poured down the hillsides, clothing cypresses

---

[3] That is to say, everybody.

49

and olive trees, white houses and red roofs in the warm-
est of robes, then losing itself in the plain that was steam-
ing in the sun. Each time I had the same feeling of being
laid bare. The horizontal shadow of that little fat man
was still inside me. And what I could touch with my
finger in these plains whirling with sunlight and dust, in
these close-cropped hills all crusty with burnt grass, was
one form, stripped to its essentials, of that taste for nothingness that I carried within me. This country restored
my very heart, and put me face to face with my secret
anguish. It was and yet was not the anguish I had felt in
Prague. How can I explain it? Certainly, looking at this
Italian plain, peopled with trees, sunshine, I grasped better than I had before this smell of death and inhumanity
that had now been pursuing me for a month. Yes, this
fullness without tears, this peace without joy that filled
me was simply a very clear awareness of what I did not
like—renunciation and disinterest. In the same way, the
man who is about to die, and knows it, takes no interest
in what will happen to his wife, except in novels. He
realizes man's vocation, which is to be selfish—that is
to say, someone who despairs. For me, this country held
no promise of immortality. What would be the point of
feeling alive once more in the soul, if I had no eyes to see
Vicenza, no hands to touch the grapes of Vicenza, no skin
to feel the night's caress on the road from Monte Berico to
the Villa Valmarana?

Yes, all this was true. But the sun filled me also
with something else that I cannot really express. At this
extreme point of acute awareness everything came together, and my life seemed a solid block to be accepted or
rejected. I needed a grandeur. I found it in the confrontation between my deep despair and the secret indifference
of one of the most beautiful landscapes in the world. I

drew from it the strength to be at one and the same time both courageous and aware. So difficult and paradoxical a thing was enough for me. But perhaps I have exaggerated a bit what I felt then so sincerely. I often think of Prague and the mortal days I spent there. I'm back in my own town again. Occasionally, though, the sour smell of cucumbers and vinegar reawakens my distress. Then I need to think of Vicenza. Both are dear to me, and I find it hard to separate my love of light and life from my secret attachment to the experience of despair that I have tried to describe. It will be clear already that I don't want to bring myself to choose between them. In the suburbs of Algiers, there is a little cemetery with black iron gates. If you go the far end, you look out over the valley with the sea in the distance. You can spend a long time dreaming before this offering that sighs with the sea. But when you retrace your steps, you find a slab that says "Eternal regrets" on an abandoned grave. Fortunately, there are idealists to tidy things up.

Love of Life

AT NIGHT in Palma, life recedes slowly toward the tune-filled café district behind the market: the streets are dark and silent until one comes upon latticed doorways where light and music filter through. I spent almost a whole night in one of these cafés. It was a small, very low room, rectangular, painted green and hung with pink garlands. The wooden ceiling was covered with tiny red light bulbs. Miraculously fitted into this minute space were an orchestra, a bar with multicolored bottles, and customers squeezed shoulder to shoulder so tight they could hardly breathe. Just men. In the middle, two square yards of free space. Glasses and bottles streamed by as the waiter carried them to all four corners of the room. No one was completely sober. Everyone was shouting. Some sort of naval officer was belching alcohol-laden compliments into my face. An ageless dwarf at my table was telling me his life story. But I was too tense to listen. The orchestra was playing tunes one could only catch the rhythm of, since it was beaten out by every foot in the place. Some-

times the door would open. In the midst of shouts, a new
arrival would be fitted in between two chairs.[1]

Suddenly, ·the cymbals clashed, and a woman
leaped swiftly into the tiny circle in the middle of the
cabaret. "Twenty-one," the officer told me. I was stupe-
fied. The face of a young girl, but carved in a mountain of
flesh. She might have been six feet tall. With all her fat
she must have weighed three hundred pounds. Hands on
her hips, wearing a yellow net through which a checker-
board of white flesh swelled, she was smiling; and each
corner of her mouth sent a series of small ripples of flesh
moving toward her ears. The excitement in the room
knew no bounds. One felt this girl was known, loved,
expected. She was still smiling. She looked around at the
customers, still silent and smiling, and wiggled her belly
forward. The crowd roared, then demanded a song that
everyone seemed to know. It was a nasal Andalusian tune
accompanied by a strong three-beat rhythm from the
drums. She sang, and at each beat mimed the act of
love with her whole body. In this monotonous and passionate movement, real waves of flesh rose from her hips
and moved upward until they died away on her shoulders. The room seemed stunned. But pivoting around
with the refrain, seizing her breasts with both hands and
opening her red, moist mouth, the girl took up the tune in
chorus with the audience, until everyone stood upright in
the tumult.

As she stood in the center, feet apart, sticky with
sweat, hair hanging loose, she lifted her immense torso,
which burst forth from its yellow netting. Like an un-

[1] There is a certain freedom of enjoyment that defines
true civilization. And the Spanish are among the few peoples in
Europe who are civilized.

clean goddess rising from the waves, her eyes hollow, her forehead low and stupid, only a slight quivering at her knees, like a horse's after a race, showed she was still living. In the midst of the foot-stamping joy around her, she was like an ignoble and exalting image of life, with despair in her empty eyes and thick sweat on her belly . . .

Without cafés and newspapers, it would be difficult to travel. A paper printed in our own language, a place to rub shoulders with others in the evenings enable us to imitate the familiar gestures of the man we were at home, who, seen from a distance, seems so much a stranger. For what gives value to travel is fear. It breaks down a kind of inner structure we have. One can no longer cheat—hide behind the hours spent at the office or at the plant (those hours we protest so loudly, which protect us so well from the pain of being alone). I have always wanted to write novels in which my heroes would say: "What would I do without the office?" or again: "My wife has died, but fortunately I have all these orders to fill for tomorrow." Travel robs us of such refuge. Far from our own people, our own language, stripped of all our props, deprived of our masks (one doesn't know the fare on the streetcars, or anything else), we are completely on the surface of ourselves. But also, soul-sick, we restore to every being and every object its miraculous value. A woman dancing without a thought in her head, a bottle on a table, glimpsed behind a curtain: each image becomes a symbol. The whole of life seems reflected in it, insofar as it summarizes our own life at the moment. When we are aware of every gift, the contradictory intoxications we can enjoy (including that of lucidity) are indescribable. Never perhaps has any land but the Mediterranean carried me so far from myself and yet so near.

The emotion I felt at the café in Palma probably came from this. On the other hand, what struck me in the empty district near the cathedral, at noon, among the old palaces with their cool courtyards, in the streets with their scented shadows, was the idea of a certain "slowness." No one in the streets. Motionless old women in the miradors. And, walking along past the houses, stopping in courtyards full of green plants and round, gray pillars, I melted into this smell of silence, losing my limits, becoming nothing more than the sound of my footsteps or the flight of birds whose shadows I could see on the still sunlit portion of the walls. I would also spend long hours in the little Gothic cloister of San Francisco. Its delicate, precious colonnade shone with the fine, golden yellow of old Spanish monuments. In the courtyard there were rose laurels, fake pepper plants, a wrought-iron well from which hung a long, rusty metal spoon. Passers-by drank from it. I still remember sometimes the clear sound it made as it dropped back on the stone of the well. Yet it was not the sweetness of life that this cloister taught me. In the sharp sound of wingbeats as the pigeons flew away, the sudden, snug silence in the middle of the garden, in the lonely squeaking of the chain on its well, I found a new and yet familiar flavor. I was lucid and smiling before this unique play of appearances. A single gesture, I felt, would be enough to shatter this crystal in which the world's face was smiling. Something would come undone—the flight of pigeons would die and each would slowly tumble on its outstretched wings. Only my silence and immobility lent plausibility to what looked so like an illusion. I joined in the game. I accepted the appearances without being taken in. A fine, golden sun gently warmed the yellow stones of the cloister. A woman was drawing water from the well. In an hour, a minute, a second, now perhaps, everything might collapse. And yet this miracle continued. The world lived on, modest, ironic, and discreet (like certain gentle and reserved forms of women's friendship). A balance continued, colored, however, by all the apprehension of its own end.

There lay all my love of life: a silent passion for what would perhaps escape me, a bitterness beneath a flame. Each day I would leave this cloister like a man lifted from himself, inscribed for a brief moment in the continuance of the world. And I know why I thought then of the expressionless eyes of Doric Apollos or the stiff, motionless characters in Giotto's paintings.[2] It was at these moments that I truly understood what countries like this could offer me. I am surprised men can find certainties and rules for life on the shores of the Mediterranean, that they can satisfy their reason there and justify optimism and social responsibility. For what struck me then was not a world made to man's measure, but one that closed in upon him. If the language of these countries harmonized with what echoed deeply within me, it was not because it answered my questions but because it made them superfluous. Instead of prayers of thanksgiving rising to my lips, it was this *Nada* whose birth is possible only at the sight of landscapes crushed by the sun. There is no love of life without despair of life.

In Ibiza, I sat every day in the cafés that dot the harbor. Toward five in the evening, the young people would stroll back and forth along the full length of the jetty; this is where marriages and the whole of life are arranged. One cannot help thinking there is a certain grandeur in beginning one's life this way, with the whole

[2] The decadence of Greek sculpture and the dispersion of Italian art begin with the appearance of smiles and expression in the eyes, as if beauty ended where the mind begins.

world looking on. I would sit down, still dizzy from the day's sun, my head full of white churches and chalky walls, dry fields and shaggy olive trees. I would drink a sweetish syrup, gazing at the curve of the hills in front of me. They sloped gently down to the sea. The evening would grow green. On the largest of the hills, the last breeze turned the sails of a windmill. And, by a natural miracle, everyone lowered his voice. Soon there was nothing but the sky and musical words rising toward it, as if heard from a great distance. There was something fleeting and melancholy in the brief moment of dusk, perceptible not only to one man but also to a whole people. As for me, I longed to love as people long to cry. I felt that every hour I slept now would be an hour stolen from life . . . that is to say from those hours of undefined desire. I was tense and motionless, as I had been during those vibrant hours at the cabaret in Palma and at the cloister in San Francisco, powerless against this immense desire to hold the world between my hands.

I know that I am wrong, that we cannot give ourselves completely. Otherwise, we could not create. But there are no limits to loving, and what does it matter to me if I hold things badly if I can embrace everything? There are women in Genoa whose smile I loved for a whole morning. I shall never see them again and certainly nothing is simpler. But words will never smother the flame of my regret. I watched the pigeons flying past the little well at the cloister in San Francisco, and forgot my thirst. But a moment always came when I was thirsty again.

The Wrong Side and the Right Side

SHE WAS a lonely and peculiar woman. She kept in close touch with the Spirits, took up their causes, and refused to see certain members of her family who had a bad reputation in this world where she found refuge.

One day, she received a small legacy from her sister. These five thousand francs, coming at the end of her life, turned out to be something of an encumbrance. They had to be invested. If almost everyone is capable of using a large fortune, the difficulty begins when the sum is a small one. The woman remained true to herself. Nearing death, she wanted shelter for her old bones. A real opportunity occurred. A lease had just expired in the local cemetery. On this plot the owners had erected a magnificent, soberly designed black marble tomb, a genuine treasure in fact, which they were prepared to let her have for four thousand francs. She purchased the vault. It was a safe investment, immune to political upheavals or fluctuations in the stock market. She had the inner grave prepared, and kept it in readiness to receive her body. And, when everything was finished, she had her name carved on it in gold letters.

The transaction satisfied her so completely that she was seized with a veritable love for her tomb. At first, she went to see how the work was progressing. She ended up by paying herself a visit every Sunday afternoon. It was the only time she went out, and it was her only amusement. Toward two in the afternoon, she made the long trip that brought her to the city gates where the cemetery was. She would go into the little tomb, carefully close the door behind her, and kneel on the *prie-dieu*. It was thus, quite alone with herself, confronting what she was and what she would become, rediscovering the link in a chain still broken, that she effortlessly pierced the secret designs of Providence. A strange symbol even made her realize one day that in the eyes of the world she was dead. On All Saints' Day, arriving later than usual, she found the doorstep of her tomb piously strewn with violets. Some unknown and tenderhearted passers-by, seeing the tomb devoid of flowers, had had the kind thought of sharing their own, and honored her neglected memory.

And now I think about these things again. I can see only the walls of the garden on the other side of my window. And a few branches flowing with light. Higher still, more foliage and, higher still, the sun. But all I can perceive of the air rejoicing outside, of all the joy spread across the world, are the shadows of branches playing on my white curtains. Also five rays of sunlight patiently pouring the scent of dried grass into the room. A breeze, and the shadows on the curtains come to life. If a cloud passes over the sun, the bright yellow of a vase of mimosas leaps from the shadow. This is enough: when a single gleam begins, I'm filled with a confused and whirling joy. It is a January afternoon that puts me this way, face to face with the wrong side of the world. But the cold remains at the bottom of the air. Covering everything a film of sunlight that would crack beneath your finger, but which clothes everything in an eternal smile. Who am I and what can I do but enter into this play of foliage and light? Be this ray of sunlight in which my cigarette burns away, this softness and discreet passion breathing in the air. If I try to reach myself, it is at the bottom of this light. And if I try to understand and savor this delicate taste which reveals the secret of the world, it is myself that I find at the depth of the universe. Myself, that is to say, this extreme emotion which frees me from my surroundings.

In a moment—other things, other men, and the graves they purchase. But let me cut this minute from the cloth of time. Others leave a flower between pages, enclosing in them a walk where love has touched them with its wing. I walk too, but am caressed by a god. Life is short, and it is sinful to waste one's time. They say I'm active. But being active is still wasting one's time, if in doing one loses oneself. Today is a resting time, and my heart goes off in search of itself. If an anguish still clutches me, it's when I feel this impalpable moment slip through my fingers like quicksilver. Let those who wish to turn their backs upon the world. I have nothing to complain of, since I can see myself being born. At the moment, my whole kingdom is of this world. This sun and these shadows, this warmth and this cold rising from the depths of the air: why wonder if something is dying or if men suffer, since everything is written on this window where the sun sheds its plenty as a greeting to my pity? I can say and in a moment I shall say that what counts is to be human and simple. No, what counts is to be true, and then everything fits in, humanity and simplicity. When am I truer than when I am the world? My cup

brims over before I have time to desire. Eternity is there
and I was hoping for it. What I wish for now is no longer
happiness but simply awareness.

One man contemplates and another digs his
grave: how can we separate them? Men and their absurdity? But here is the smile of the heavens. The light swells
and soon it will be summer. But here are the eyes and
voices of those I must love. I hold onto the world with
every gesture, to men with all my gratitude and pity. I do
not want to choose between the right and wrong sides of
the world, and I do not like a choice to be made. People
don't want one to be lucid and ironic. They say: "It shows
you're not nice." I can't see how this follows. Certainly, if
I hear someone called an immoralist, my translation is
that he needs to give himself an ethic; if I hear of another
that he despises intelligence, I realize that he cannot bear
his doubts. But this is because I don't like people to cheat.
The great courage is still to gaze as squarely at the light
as at death. Besides, how can I define the link that leads
from this all-consuming love of life to this secret despair?
If I listen to the voice of irony,[3] crouching underneath
things, slowly it reveals itself. Winking its small, clear
eye, it says: "Live as if . . ." In spite of much searching,
this is all I know.

After all, I am not sure that I am right. But if I
think of that woman whose story I heard, this is not what
is important. She was going to die, and her daughter
dressed her for the tomb while she was alive. Actually, it
seems it's easier to do so before the limbs are stiff. Yet it's
odd all the same to live among people who are in such a
hurry.

[3] That *guarantee of freedom* Barrès speaks of.

II

NUPTIALS

[1938]

(Noces)

---

*The hangman strangled Cardinal Carrafa
with a silken rope that broke: two further
attempts were necessary. The Cardinal looked
at the hangman without deigning to utter a word.*

Stendhal, *La Duchesse de Palliano*

Note to the 1950 edition

THESE ESSAYS *were originally written in 1936 and 1937, and a small number of copies were published in Algiers in 1938. This new edition reproduces them without any changes, in spite of the fact that their author has not ceased to consider them as essays, in the precise and limited meaning of the term.*

Nuptials at Tipasa[1]

IN THE spring, Tipasa is inhabited by gods and the gods speak in the sun and the scent of absinthe leaves, in the silver armor of the sea, in the raw blue sky, the flower-covered ruins, and the great bubbles of light among the heaps of stone. At certain hours of the day the country-side is black with sunlight. The eyes try in vain to perceive anything but drops of light and colors trembling on the lashes. The thick scent of aromatic plants tears at the throat and suffocates in the vast heat. Far away, I can just make out the black bulk of the Chenoua, rooted in the hills around the village, moving with a slow and heavy rhythm until finally it crouches in the sea.

The village we pass through to get there already opens on the bay. We enter a blue and yellow world and

[1] *Tipasa is a village on the Mediterranean coast, about fifty miles from Algiers. Camus went there frequently in 1935 and 1936. A manuscript exists of a first sketch for this essay, written in 1936, but the first typewritten copy dates from July 1937. Certain phrases, however, already occur in the* Carnets *for 1936.* —P.T.

are welcomed by the pungent, odorous sigh of the Algerian summer earth. Everywhere, pinkish bougainvillaea hangs over villa walls; in the gardens the hibiscus are still pale red, and there is a profusion of tea roses thick as cream, with delicate borders of long, blue iris. All the stones are warm. As we step off the buttercup yellow bus, butchers in their little red trucks are making their morning rounds, calling to the villagers with their horns.

To the left of the port, a dry stone stairway leads to the ruins, through the mastic trees and broom. The path goes by a small lighthouse before plunging into the open country. Already, at the foot of this lighthouse, large red, yellow, and violet plants descend toward the first rocks, sucked at by the sea with a kissing sound. As we stand in the slight breeze, with the sun warming one side of our faces, we watch the light coming down from the sky, the smooth sea and the smile of its glittering teeth. We are spectators for the last time before we enter the kingdom of ruins.

After a few steps, the smell of absinthe seizes one by the throat. The wormwood's gray wool covers the ruins as far as the eye can see. Its oil ferments in the heat, and the whole earth gives off a heady alcohol that makes the sky flicker. We walk toward an encounter with love and desire. We are not seeking lessons or the bitter philosophy one requires of greatness. Everything seems futile here except the sun, our kisses, and the wild scents of the earth. I do not seek solitude. I have often been here with those I loved and read on their features the clear smile the face of love assumes. Here, I leave order and moderation to others. The great free love of nature and the sea absorbs me completely. In this marriage of ruins and springtime, the ruins have become stones again, and losing the polish imposed on them by men, they have reverted to nature. To celebrate the return of her prodigal daughters Nature has laid out a profusion of flowers. The heliotrope pushes its red and white head between the flagstones of the forum, red geraniums spill their blood over what were houses, temples, and public squares. Like the men whom much knowledge brings back to God, many years have brought these ruins back to their mother's house. Today, their past has finally left them, and nothing distracts them from the deep force pulling them back to the center of all that falls.

How many hours have I spent crushing absinthe leaves, caressing ruins, trying to match my breathing with the world's tumultuous sighs! Deep among wild scents and concerts of somnolent insects, I open my eyes and heart to the unbearable grandeur of this heat-soaked sky. It is not so easy to become what one is, to rediscover one's deepest measure. But watching the solid backbone of the Chenoua, my heart would grow calm with a strange certainty. I was learning to breathe, I was fitting into things and fulfilling myself. As I climbed one after another of the hills, each brought a reward, like the temple whose columns measure the course of the sun and from which one can see the whole village, its white and pink walls and green verandas. Like the basilica on the East hill too, which still has its walls and is surrounded by a great circle of uncovered ornamented coffins, most of them scarcely out of the earth, whose nature they still share. They used to contain corpses; now sage and wallflowers grow in them. The Sainte-Salsa basilica is Christian, but each time we look out through a gap in the walls we are greeted by the song of the world: hillsides planted with pine and cypress trees, or the sea rolling its white horses twenty yards away. The hill on which Sainte-Salsa is built has a flat top and the wind

67

blows more strongly through the portals. Under the morning sun, a great happiness hovers in space.

Those who need myths are indeed poor. Here the gods serve as beds or resting places as the day races across the sky. I describe and say: "This is red, this blue, this green. This is the sea, the mountain, the flowers." Need I mention Dionysus to say that I love to crush mastic bulbs under my nose? Is the old hymn that will later come to me quite spontaneously even addressed to Demeter: "Happy is he alive who has seen these things on earth"? How can we forget the lesson of sight and seeing on this earth? All men had to do at the mysteries of Eleusis was watch. Yet even here, I know that I shall never come close enough to the world. I must be naked and dive into the sea, still scented with the perfumes of the earth, wash them off in the sea, and consummate with my flesh the embrace for which sun and sea, lips to lips, have so long been sighing. I feel the shock of the water, rise up through a thick, cold glue, then dive back with my ears ringing, my nose streaming, and the taste of salt in my mouth. As I swim, my arms shining with water flash into gold in the sunlight, until I fold them in again with a twist of all my muscles; the water streams along my body as my legs take tumultuous possession of the waves—and the horizon disappears. On the beach, I flop down on the sand, yield to the world, feel the weight of flesh and bones, again dazed with sunlight, occasionally glancing at my arms where the water slides off and patches of salt and soft blond hair appear on my skin.

Here I understand what is meant by glory: the right to love without limits. There is only one love in this world. To clasp a woman's body is also to hold in one's arms this strange joy that descends from sky to sea. In a moment, when I throw myself down among the absinthe plants to bring their scent into my body, I shall know, appearances to the contrary, that I am fulfilling a truth which is the sun's and which will also be my death's. In a sense, it is indeed my life that I am staking here, a life that tastes of warm stone, that is full of the sighs of the sea and the rising song of the crickets. The breeze is cool and the sky blue. I love this life with abandon and wish to speak of it boldly: it makes me proud of my human condition. Yet people have often told me: there's nothing to be proud of. Yes, there is: this sun, this sea, my heart leaping with youth, the salt taste of my body and this vast landscape in which tenderness and glory merge in blue and yellow. It is to conquer this that I need my strength and my resources. Everything here leaves me intact, I surrender nothing of myself, and don no mask: learning patiently and arduously how to live is enough for me, well worth all their arts of living.

Shortly before noon, we would come back through the ruins to a little café by the side of the port. How cool was the welcome of a tall glass of iced green mint in the shady room, to heads ringing with colors and the cymbals of the sun! Outside were the sea and the road burning with dust. Seated at the table, I would try to blink my eyelids so as to catch the multicolored dazzle of the white-hot sky. Our faces damp with sweat, but our bodies cool in light clothing, we would flaunt the happy weariness of a day of nuptials with the world.

The food is bad in this café, but there is plenty of fruit, especially peaches, whose juice drips down your chin as you bite into them. Gazing avidly before me, my teeth closing on a peach, I can hear the blood pounding in my ears. The vast silence of noon hangs over the sea. Every beautiful thing has a natural pride in its own beauty, and today the world is allowing its pride to seep from every pore. Why, in its presence, should I deny the joy of living, as long as I know everything is not included in this joy? There is no shame in being happy. But today the fool is king, and I call those who fear pleasure fools. They've told us so much about pride: you know, Lucifer's sin. Beware, they used to cry, you will lose your soul, and your vital powers. I have in fact learned since that a certain pride . . . But at other times I cannot prevent myself from asserting the pride in living that the whole world conspires to give me. At Tipasa, "I see" equals "I believe," and I am not stubborn enough to deny what my hands can touch and my lips caress. I don't feel the need to make it into a work of art, but to describe it, which is different. Tipasa seems to me like a character one describes in order to give indirect expression to a certain view of the world. Like such characters, Tipasa testifies to something, and does it like a man. Tipasa is the personage I'm describing today, and it seems to me that the very act of caressing and describing my delight will insure that it has no end. There is a time for living and a time for giving expression to life. There is also a time for creating, which is less natural. For me it is enough to live with my whole body and bear witness with my whole heart. Live Tipasa, manifest its lessons, and the work of art will come later. Herein lies a freedom.

I never spent more than a day at Tipasa. A moment always comes when one has looked too long at a landscape, just as it is a long time before one sees enough of it. Mountains, the sky, the sea are like faces whose barrenness or splendor we discover by looking rather than seeing. But in order to be eloquent every face must be seen anew. One complains of growing tired too quickly, when one ought to be surprised that the world seems new only because we have forgotten it.

Toward evening I would return to a more formal section of the park, set out as a garden, just off the main road. Leaving the tumult of scents and sunlight, in the cool evening air, the mind would grow calm and the body relaxed, savoring the inner silence born of satisfied love. I would sit on a bench, watching the countryside expand with light. I was full. Above me drooped a pomegranate tree, its flower buds closed and ribbed like small tight fists containing every hope of spring. There was rosemary behind me, and I could smell only the scent of its alcohol. The hills were framed with trees, and beyond them stretched a band of sea on which the sky, like a sail becalmed, rested in all its tenderness. I felt a strange joy in my heart, the special joy that stems from a clear conscience. There is a feeling actors have when they know they've played their part well, that is to say, when they have made their own gestures coincide with those of the ideal character they embody, having entered somehow into a prearranged design, bringing it to life with their own heartbeats. That was exactly what I felt: I had played my part well. I had performed my task as a man, and the fact that I had known joy for one entire day seemed to me not an exceptional success but the intense fulfillment of a condition which, in certain circumstances, makes it our duty to be happy. Then we are alone again, but satisfied.

Now the trees were filled with birds. The earth would give a long sigh before sliding into darkness. In a moment, with the first star, night would fall on the theater of the world. The dazzling gods of day would return to their daily death. But other gods would come. And, though they would be darker, their ravaged faces too would come from deep within the earth.

For the moment at least, the waves' endless crashing against the shore came toward me through a space dancing with golden pollen. Sea, landscape, silence, scents of this earth, I would drink my fill of a scent-laden life, sinking my teeth into the world's fruit, golden already, overwhelmed by the feeling of its strong, sweet juice flowing on my lips. No, it was neither I nor the world that counted, but solely the harmony and silence that gave birth to the love between us. A love I was not foolish enough to claim for myself alone, proudly aware that I shared it with a whole race born in the sun and sea, alive and spirited, drawing greatness from its simplicity, and upright on the beaches, smiling in complicity at the brilliance of its skies.

The Wind at Djemila[1]

❧❧ ❧❧❧ ❧❧

THERE are places where the mind dies so that a truth
which is its very denial may be born. When I went to
Djemila, there was wind and sun, but that is another
story. What must be said first of all is that a heavy,
unbroken silence reigned there—something like a perfectly balanced pair of scales. The cry of birds, the soft
sound of a three-hole flute, goats trampling, murmurs
from the sky were just so many sounds added to the
silence and desolation. Now and then a sharp clap, a
piercing cry marked the upward flight of a bird huddled
among the rocks. Any trail one followed—the pathways
through the ruined houses, along wide, paved roads
under shining colonnades, across the vast forum between
the triumphal arch and the temple set upon a hill—
would end at the ravines that surround Djemila on every

[1] *Camus went to Djémila in the spring of 1936, in a small
tourist plane chartered by some of his friends. In the* Carnets
*for 1936, there are references to this visit, but the actual essay
does not seem to have been written until the following year.* —P.T.

73

side, like a pack of cards opening beneath a limitless sky. And one would stand there, absorbed, confronted with stones and silence, as the day moved on and the mountains grew purple surging upward. But the wind blows across the plateau of Djemila. In the great confusion of wind and sun that mixes light into the ruins, in the silence and solitude of this dead city, something is forged that gives man the measure of his identity.

It takes a long time to get to Djemila. It is not a town where you stop and then move further on. It leads nowhere and is a gateway to no other country. It is a place from which travelers return. The dead city lies at the end of a long, winding road whose every turning looks like the last, making it seem all the longer. When its skeleton, yellowish as a forest of bones, at last looms up against the faded colors of the plateau, Djemila seems the symbol of that lesson of love and patience which alone can lead us to the world's beating heart. There it lies, among a few trees and some dried grass, protected by all its mountains and stones from vulgar admiration, from being picturesque, and from the delusions of hope.

We had wandered the whole day in this arid splendor. The wind, which we had scarcely felt at the beginning of the afternoon, seemed to increase as the hours went by, little by little filling the whole countryside. It blew from a gap in the mountains, far to the East, rushing from beyond the horizon, leaping and tumbling among the stones and in the sunlight. It whistled loudly across the ruins, whirled through an amphitheater of stones and earth, bathing the heaps of pock-marked stone, circling each column with its breath and spreading out in endless cries on the forum, open to the heavens. I felt myself whipping in the wind like a mast, hollowed at the waist. Eyes burning, lips cracking, my skin became so dry

it no longer seemed mine. Until now, I had been decipher-
ing the world's handwriting on my skin. There, on my
body, the world had inscribed the signs of its tenderness
or anger, warming with its summer breath or biting with
its frosty teeth. But rubbed against for so long by the
wind, shaken for more than an hour, staggering from resistance to it, I lost consciousness of the pattern my body
traced. Like a pebble polished by the tides, I was polished
by the wind, worn through to the very soul. I was a
portion of the great force on which I drifted, then much
of it, then entirely it, confusing the throbbing of my own
heart with the great sonorous beating of this omnipresent
natural heart. The wind was fashioning me in the image
of the burning nakedness around me. And its fugitive
embrace gave me, a stone among stones, the solitude of a
column or an olive tree in the summer sky.

    The violent bath of sun and wind drained me of
all strength. I scarcely felt the quivering of wings inside
me, life's complaint, the weak rebellion of the mind.
Soon, scattered to the four corners of the earth, self-
forgetful and self-forgotten, I am the wind and within it,
the columns and the archway, the flagstones warm
to the touch, the pale mountains around the deserted
city. And never have I felt so deeply and at one and the
same time so detached from myself and so present in the
world.

    Yes, I am present. And what strikes me at this mo-
ment is that I can go no further—like a man sentenced
to life imprisonment, to whom everything is present.
But also like a man who knows that tomorrow will be the
same, and every other day. For when a man becomes
conscious of what he is now, it means he expects nothing
further. If there are landscapes like moods, they are the
most vulgar. All through this country I followed some-

75

thing that belonged not to me but to it, something like a taste for death we both had in common. Between the columns with their now lengthening shadows anxieties dissolved into the air like wounded birds. And in their place came an arid lucidity. Anxiety springs from living hearts. But calm will hide this living heart: this is all I can see clearly. As the day moved forward, as the noises and lights were muffled by the ashes falling from the sky, deserted by myself, I felt defenseless against the slow forces within me that were saying no.

Few people realize that there is a refusal that has nothing to do with renunciation. What meaning do words like future, improvement, good job have here? What is meant by the heart's progress? If I obstinately refuse all the "later on's" of this world, it is because I have no desire to give up my present wealth. I do not want to believe that death is the gateway to another life. For me, it is a closed door. I do not say it is a step we must all take, but that it is a horrible and dirty adventure. Everything I am offered seeks to deliver man from the weight of his own life. But as I watch the great birds flying heavily through the sky at Djemila, it is precisely a certain weight of life that I ask for and obtain. If I am at one with this passive passion, the rest ceases to concern me. I have too much youth in me to be able to speak of death. But it seems to me that if I had to speak of it, I would find the right word here between horror and silence to express the conscious certainty of a death without hope.

We live with a few familiar ideas. Two or three. We polish and transform them according to the societies and the men we happen to meet. It takes ten years to have an idea that is really one's own—that one can talk about. This is a bit discouraging, of course. But we gain from this a certain familiarity with the splendor of the world. Until then, we have seen it face to face. Now we need to step aside to see its profile. A young man looks the world in the face. He has not had time to polish the idea of death or of nothingness, even though he has gazed on their full horror. That is what youth must be like, this harsh confrontation with death, this physical terror of the animal who loves the sun. Whatever people may say, on this score at least, youth has no illusions. It has had neither the time nor the piety to build itself any. And, I don't know why, but faced with this ravined landscape, this solemn and lugubrious cry of stone, Djemila, inhuman at nightfall, faced with this death of colors and hope, I was certain that when they reach the end of their lives, men worthy of the name must rediscover this confrontation, deny the few ideas they had, and recover the innocence and truth that gleamed in the eyes of the Ancients face to face with destiny. They regain their youth, but by embracing death. There is nothing more despicable in this respect than illness. It is a remedy against death. It prepares us for it. It creates an apprenticeship whose first stage is self-pity. It supports man in his great effort to avoid the certainty that he will die completely. But Djemila . . . and then I feel certain that the true, the only, progress of civilization, the one to which a man devotes himself from time to time, lies in creating conscious deaths.

What always amazes me, when we are so swift to elaborate on other subjects, is the poverty of our ideas on death. It is a good thing or a bad thing, I fear it or I summon it (they say). Which also proves that everything simple is beyond us. What is blue, and how do we think "blue"? The same difficulty occurs with death. Death and colors are things we cannot discuss. Nonetheless, the important thing is this man before me, heavy as earth, who prefigures my future. But can I really think about it?

I tell myself: I am going to die, but this means nothing, since I cannot manage to believe it and can only experience other people's death. I have seen people die. Above all, I have seen dogs die. It was touching them that overwhelmed me. Then I think of flowers, smiles, the desire for women, and realize that my whole horror of death lies in my anxiety to live. I am jealous of those who will live and for whom flowers and the desire for women will have their full flesh and blood meaning. I am envious because I love life too much not to be selfish. What does eternity matter to me. You can be lying in bed one day and hear someone say: "You are strong and I owe it to you to be honest: I can tell you that you are going to die"; you're there, with your whole life in your hands, fear in your bowels, looking the fool. What else matters: waves of blood come throbbing to my temples and I feel I could smash everything around me.

But men die in spite of themselves, in spite of their surroundings. They are told: "When you get well . . . ," and they die. I want none of that. For if there are days when nature lies, there are others when she tells the truth. Djemila is telling the truth tonight, and with what sad, insistent beauty! As for me, here in the presence of this world, I have no wish to lie or to be lied to. I want to keep my lucidity to the last, and gaze upon my death with all the fullness of my jealousy and horror. It is to the extent I cut myself off from the world that I fear death most, to the degree I attach myself to the fate of living men instead of contemplating the unchanging sky. Creating conscious deaths is to diminish the distance that separates us from the world and to accept a consummation without joy, alert to rapturous images of a world forever lost. And the melancholy song

78

of the Djemila hills plunges this bitter lesson deeper in my soul.

Toward evening, we were climbing the slopes leading to the village and, retracing our steps, listened to explanations: "Here is the pagan town; this area outside the field is where the Christians lived. Later on . . ." Yes, it is true. Men and societies have succeeded one another in this place; conquerors have marked this country with their noncommissioned officer's civilization. They had a vulgar and ridiculous idea of greatness, measuring the grandeur of their empire by the surface it covered. The miracle is that the ruin of their civilization is the very negation of their ideal. For this skeleton town, seen from high above as evening closes in and white flights of pigeons circle round the triumphal arch, engraved no signs of conquest or ambition on the sky. The world always conquers history in the end. The great shout of stone that Djemila hurls between the mountains, the sky, and the silence—well do I know its poetry: lucidity, indifference, the true signs of beauty or despair. The heart tightens at the grandeur we've already left behind. Djemila remains with its sad watery sky, the song of a bird from the other side of the plateau, the sudden, quick scurrying of goats along the mountainside, and, in the calm, resonant dusk, the living face of a horned god on the pediment of an altar.

Summer in Algiers [1]

to Jacques Heurgon

THEY are often secret, the love affairs we have with cities. Old towns like Paris, Prague, and even Florence are closed in upon themselves in such a way as to delimit their domain. But Algiers and a few other privileged coastal towns open into the sky like a mouth or a wound. What one can fall in love with in Algiers is what everybody lives with: the sea, visible from every corner, a certain heaviness of the sunlight, the beauty of the people. And, as usual, such generosity and lack of shame emit a more secret perfume. In Paris, one can yearn for space and for the beating of wings. Here, at least, man has everything he needs, and his desires thus assured, can take the measure of his riches.

[1] *This essay contains what is perhaps Camus's most highly idealized descriptions of the Algerian working class. Jacques Heurgon was, in 1939, professor at the Faculté des Lettres in Algiers, and editor of the review* Rivages *in which the passage on page 86 about the mint pastilles first appeared in February 1939.*

One probably has to live a long time in Algiers to understand how desiccating an excess of nature's blessings can be. There is nothing here for people seeking knowledge, education, or self-improvement. The land contains no lessons. It neither promises nor reveals anything. It is content to give, but does so profusely. Everything here can be seen with the naked eye, and is known the very moment it is enjoyed. The pleasures have no remedies and their joys remain without hope. What the land needs are clear-sighted souls, that is to say, those without consolation. It asks that we make an act of lucidity as one makes an act of faith. A strange country, which gives the men it nourishes both their splendor and their misery. It is not surprising that the sensual riches this country offers so profusely to the sensitive person should coincide with the most extreme deprivation. There is no truth that does not also carry bitterness. Why then should it be surprising if I never love the face of this country more than in the midst of its poorest inhabitants?

Throughout their youth, men find a life here that matches their beauty. Decline and forgetfulness come later. They have wagered on the flesh, knowing they would lose. In Algiers, to the young and vital everything is a refuge and a pretext for rejoicing: the bay, the sun, games on the red and white terraces overlooking the sea, the flowers and stadiums, the cool-limbed girls. But for the man who has lost his youth there is nothing to hang on to, and no outlet for melancholy. Elsewhere—on Italian terraces, in European cloisters, or in the shape of the hills in Provence—there are places where a man can shed his humanity and gently find salvation from himself. But everything here demands solitude and young blood. On his deathbed, Goethe called for light, and this is a historic remark. In Belcourt and Bab-el-Oued, old men sitting at the back of cafés listen to the young, with brilliantined hair, boasting of their exploits.

It is summer in Algiers that grants us these beginnings and these endings. During the summer months, the town is deserted. But the poor and the sky remain. We go down with them to the harbor and its treasures: the water's gentle warmth and the women's brown bodies. In the evening, swollen with these riches, the people return to oilcloth and kerosene lamp, the meager furniture of their existence.

In Algiers, you don't talk about "going swimming" but about "knocking off a swim." I won't insist. People swim in the harbor and then go rest on the buoys. When you pass a buoy where a pretty girl is sitting, you shout to your friends: "I tell you it's a seagull." These are healthy pleasures. They certainly seem ideal to the young men, since most of them continue this life during the winter, stripping down for a frugal lunch in the sun at noontime every day. Not that they have read the boring sermons of our nudists, those protestants of the body (there is a way of systematizing the body that is as exasperating as systems for the soul). They just "like being in the sun." It would be hard to exaggerate the significance of this custom in our day. For the first time in two thousand years the body has been shown naked on the beaches. For twenty centuries, men have strived to impose decency on the insolence and simplicity of the Greeks, to diminish the flesh and elaborate our dress. Today, reaching back over this history, young men sprinting on the Mediterranean beaches are rediscovering the magnificent motion of the athletes of Delos. Living so close to other bodies, and through one's own body, one finds it has its own nuances, its own life, and, to venture an absurdity, its

82

own psychology.[2] The evolution of the body, like that of the mind, has its history, its reversals, its gains, and its losses. With only this nuance: color. Swimming in the harbor in the summertime, you notice that everybody's skin changes at the same time from white to gold, then to brown, and at last to a tobacco hue, the final stage the body can attain in its quest for transformation. Overlooking the harbor is a pattern of white cubes, the Casbah. From water level, people's bodies form a bronzed frieze against the glaring white background of the Arab town. And, as one moves into August and the sun grows stronger, the white of the houses grows more blinding and the skins take on a darker glow. How then can one keep from feeling a part of this dialogue between stone and flesh, keeping pace with the sun and the seasons? One spends whole mornings diving to peals of laughter in splashing water, on long canoe trips paddling around the red and black freighters (the Norwegian ones smell of all sorts of wood, the German ones reek of oil, the ones going from port to port along the coast smell of wine and old casks). At the hour when the sun spills from every corner of the sky, an orange canoe laden with brown bodies carries us home in one mad sprint. And when, suddenly ceasing the rhythmic stroking of its double fruit-colored

[2] May I be foolish enough to say that I don't like the way Gide exalts the body? He asks it to hold back desire in order to make it more intense. This brings him close to those who, in the slang of brothels, are termed "weirdies" or "oddballs." Christianity also seeks to suspend desire. But, more naturally, sees in this a mortification. My friend Vincent, who is a cooper and junior breast-stroke champion, has an even clearer view of things. He drinks when he is thirsty, if he wants a woman tries to sleep with her, and would marry her if he loved her (this hasn't happened yet). Then he always says: "That feels better!"—an energetic summary of the apology one could write for satiety.

83

wings, we glide into the quiet inner harbor, how can I doubt that what I lead across the silken waters is a cargo of tawny gods, in whom I recognize my brothers?

At the other end of town, summer already offers us the contrast of its other wealth: I mean its silences and boredom. These silences do not always have the same quality, depending on whether they occur in shadow or sunlight. There is a noontime silence on the government square. In the shade of the trees that grow along each side, Arabs sell penny glasses of iced lemonade, perfumed with orange blossom. Their cry of "cool, cool" echoes across the empty square. When it fades away, silence falls again under the sun: ice moves in the merchant's pitcher, and I can hear it tinkling. There is a siesta silence. On the streets around the docks, in front of the squalid barber shops, one can measure it in the melodious buzzing of the flies behind the hollow reed curtains. Elsewhere, in the Moorish cafés of the Casbah, it is bodies that are silent, that cannot drag themselves away, leave the glass of tea, and rediscover time in the beating of their pulse. But, above all, there is the silence of the summer evenings.

These brief moments when day trembles into night must swarm with secret signs and calls to be so closely linked to Algiers in my heart. When I have been away from this country for some time, I think of its twilights as promises of happiness. On the hills looking down over the town, there are paths among the mastic and the olive trees. And it is toward them that my heart turns then. I can see sheaves of black birds rising against the green horizon. In the sky, suddenly emptied of its sun, something releases its hold. A whole flock of tiny red clouds stretches upward until it dissolves into the air. Almost immediately afterward appears the first star, which had been taking shape and growing harder in the thickness of the heavens. And then, sudden and all-enveloping, the night. What is so unique in these fleeting evenings of Algiers that they free so many things in me? They leave a sweetness on my lips that vanishes into the night before I have time to weary of it. Is this the secret of their persistence? The tenderness of this country is overwhelming and furtive. But at least our heart gives way to it completely. The dance hall at Padovani Beach is open every day. And, in this immense rectangular box, open to the sea all along one side, the poor youngsters of the district come to dance until evening. Often, I would wait there for one particular moment. In the daytime, the dance hall is protected by a sloping wooden roof. When the sun has gone down it is removed. The hall fills with a strange green light, born in the double shell of sky and sea. When you sit far from the windows, you can see only the sky, and, like puppets in a shadow theater, the faces of the dancers floating past, one after another. Sometimes they play a waltz, and the dark profiles revolve like cutout figures on a turntable. Night comes quickly and with it the lights. I shall never be able to describe the thrill and the secret enchantment of this subtle moment. I remember a magnificent, tall girl who had danced all one afternoon. She was wearing a necklace of jasmine on her close-fitting blue dress, which was damp with sweat right down the back. She was laughing and throwing back her head as she danced. Passing in front of the tables, she left behind a mingled scent of flowers and flesh. When evening came, I could no longer see her body pressed against her partner, but the white of her jasmine and the black of her hair swirled one after the other against the sky, and when she threw back her breasts I could hear her laugh and see her partner's silhouette lean suddenly forward. I owe my idea of innocence to evenings like these. And I am learning not to separate these beings charged with violence from the sky in which their desires revolve.

At the neighborhood movie houses in Algiers, they sometimes sell pastilles with engraved red mottoes that express everything needed for the birth of love: (A) questions: "When will you marry me?"; "Do you love me?"; (B) replies: "Madly"; "Next spring." After having prepared the ground, you pass them to the girl next to you, who answers in kind or simply plays dumb. At Belcourt, there have been marriages arranged like this, whole lives decided in an exchange of mint candies. And this gives a good picture of the childlike people of this country.

The hallmark of youth, perhaps, is a magnificent vocation for easy pleasures. But, above all, the haste to live borders on extravagance. In Belcourt, as in Bab-el-Oued, people marry young. They start work very early, and exhaust the range of human experience in ten short years. A workingman of thirty has already played all his cards. He waits for the end with his wife and children around him. His delights have been swift and merciless. So has his life. And you understand then that he is born in a land where everything is given to be taken away. In such abundance and profusion, life follows the curve of the great passions, sudden, demanding, generous. It is not meant to be built, but to be burned up. So reflection or self-improvement are quite irrelevant. The notion of hell, for example, is nothing more than an amusing joke here. Only the very virtuous are allowed such fancies. And I even think that virtue is a meaningless word in Algeria. Not that these men lack principles. They have their code of morality, which is very well defined. You "don't let your mother down." You see to it that your wife is respected in the street. You show consideration to pregnant women. You don't attack an enemy two to one, because "that's dirty." If anyone fails to observe these elementary rules "He's not a man," and that's all there is to it. This seems to me just and strong. There are still many of us who observe the highway code, the only disinterested one I know. But at the same time, shopkeeper morality is unknown. I have always seen the faces around me take on an expression of pity at the sight of a man between two policemen. And, before finding out whether the man was a thief, a parricide, or simply an eccentric, people said: "Poor fellow," or again, with a touch of admiration: "He's a real pirate, that one!"

There are peoples born for pride and for life. It is they who nourish the most singular vocation for boredom, they too who find death the most repulsive. Apart from sensual delights, Algerian amusements are idiotic. A bowling club, fraternal society dinners, cheap movies, and communal celebrations have for years now been enough to keep the over-thirty age group entertained. Sundays in Algiers are among the dreariest anywhere. How would these mindless people know how to disguise the deep horror of their lives with myths? In Algiers, everything associated with death is either ridiculous or detestable. The people have neither religion nor idols and die alone after having lived in a crowd. I know no place more hideous than the cemetery on the boulevard Bru, which is opposite one of the most beautiful landscapes in the world. A fearful sadness rises from the accumulated bad taste of its black monuments, revealing death's true face. "Everything passes," the heart-shaped ex-votos read, "but memory." And they all insist on the ridiculous eternity provided at so small a price by the hearts of those who loved us. The same phrases serve all forms of despair. They are addressed to the deceased and speak in the second person singular: "Our memory will never abandon thee"—a gloomy pretense by means of which one lends a body and desires to what is, at best, a black liquid. In another spot, in the midst of a stupefying display of flowers and marble birds, is this reckless vow: "Never shall thy grave lack flowers." But one is quickly reassured: the words are carved around a gilded stucco bouquet, a great timesaver for the living (like those flowers called "everlasting," which owe their pompous name to the gratitude of those who still jump on moving buses). Since one must move with the times, the classical warbler is sometimes replaced by a breath-taking pearly airplane, piloted by a silly-looking angel who, disregarding all logic, has been provided with a magnificent pair of wings.

Still, how can I explain it, these images of death never quite separate themselves from life? The values are closely linked. The favorite joke of Algerian undertakers, driving by in an empty hearse, is to shout "Like a ride, honey?" to the pretty girls they meet along the way. There is nothing to keep one from finding this symbolic, if in somewhat bad taste. It may also seem blasphemous to greet the news of someone's death with a wink of the left eye and the comment "Poor guy, he won't sing any more." Or, like the woman from Oran who had never loved her husband: "The Lord gave him to me, the Lord hath taken him away." But when all is said and done, I don't see what is sacred about death, and I am, on the contrary, very aware of the difference between fear and respect. Everything breathes the horror of death in this country that is an invitation to life. And yet it is beneath the walls of this very cemetery that the young men of Belcourt arrange their meetings and the girls let themselves be kissed and fondled.

I fully realize that such people cannot be accepted by everyone. Intelligence does not occupy the place here that it does in Italy. This race is indifferent to the mind. It worships and admires the body. From this comes its strength, its naïve cynicism, and a puerile vanity that leads it to be severely criticized. People commonly reproach its "mentality," that is to say, its particular mode of life and set of values. And it is true that a certain intensity of living involves some injustice. Yet here are a people with no past, with no traditions, though not without poetry. Their poetry has a hard, sensual quality I know very well; it is far from tender, even from the tenderness of the Algerian sky; it is the only poetry, in fact, that moves me and restores me. The opposite of a civilized people is a creative one. These barbarians lounging on the beaches give me the foolish hope that, perhaps without knowing it, they are modeling the face of a culture where man's greatness will finally discover its true visage. These people, wholly engaged in the present, live with neither myths nor consolation. Investing all their assets on this earth, they are left defenseless against death. The gifts of physical beauty have been heaped upon them. And, also the strange greediness that always goes along with wealth that has no future. Everything people do in Algiers reveals a distaste for stability and a lack of regard for the future. People are in a hurry to live, and if an art were to be born here it would conform to the hatred of permanence that led the Dorians to carve their first column out of wood. And still, yes, one can find a certain moderation as well as a constant excess in the strained and violent faces of these people, in this summer sky emptied of tenderness, beneath which all truths can be told and on which no deceitful divinity has traced the signs of hope or of redemption. Between this sky and the faces turned toward it there is nothing on which to hang a mythology, a literature, an ethic, or a religion—only stones, flesh, stars, and those truths the hand can touch.

To feel one's ties to a land, one's love for certain men, to know there is always a place where the heart can find rest—these are already many certainties for one man's life. Doubtless they are not enough. But at certain moments everything yearns for this homeland of the soul. "Yes, it is to this we must return." What is strange about finding on earth the unity Plotinus longed for? Unity expresses itself here in terms of sea and sky. The heart senses it through a certain taste of the flesh that constitutes its bitterness and greatness. I am learning that there is no superhuman happiness, no eternity outside the curve of the days. These ridiculous and essential assets, these relative truths are the only ones that move me. I have not enough soul to understand the other, "ideal" ones. Not that we should behave as beasts, but I can see no point in the happiness of angels. All I know is that this sky will last longer than I shall. And what can I call eternity except what will continue after my death? What I am expressing here is not the creature's complacency about his condition. It is something quite different. It is not always easy to be a man, even less to be a man who is pure. But to be pure means to rediscover that country of the soul where one's kinship with the world can be felt, where the throbbing of one's blood mingles with the violent pulsations of the afternoon sun. It is a well-known fact that we always recognize our homeland at the moment we are about to lose it. Men whose self-torments are too great are those whom their native land rejects. I have no desire to be crude or to seem to exaggerate. But after all what denies me in this life is first of all what kills me. Everything that exalts life at the same time increases its absurdity. In the Algerian summer I learn that only one thing is more tragic than suffering, and that is the life of a happy man. But this can also be the path to a greater life, since it can teach us not to cheat.

Many people, in fact, affect a love of life in order to avoid love itself. They try to enjoy themselves and "to experiment." But this is an intellectual attitude. It takes a rare vocation to become a sensualist. A man lives out his life without the help of his mind, with its triumphs and defeats, its simultaneous loneliness and companionship. Seeing those men from Belcourt who work, take care of their wives and children, often without a word of complaint, I think that one can feel a certain shame. I certainly have no illusions. There is not much love in the lives I am describing. I should say rather that there is no longer very much. But at least they have eluded nothing. There are some words that I have never really understood, such as sin. Yet I think I know that these men have never sinned against life. For if there is a sin against life, it lies perhaps less in despairing of it than in hoping for another life and evading the implacable grandeur of the one we have. These men have not cheated. They were gods of the summer at twenty in their thirst for life, and they are still gods today, stripped of all hope. I have seen two of them die. They were full of horror, but silent. It is better that way. From the mass of human evils swarming in Pandora's box, the Greeks brought out hope at the very last, as the most terrible of all. I don't know any symbol more moving. For hope, contrary to popular belief, is tantamount to resignation. And to live is not to be resigned.

Such at least is the bitter lesson of summers in Algiers. But already the season trembles and the summer passes. After so much violence and tension, the first September rains are like the first tears of a liberated land, as if for a few days this country were bathed in tenderness. Yet at the same time the carob trees emit the scent of love across Algeria. In the evening or after the rain, the whole earth lies, its belly moistened with a bitter almond-scented seed, at rest from having yielded all summer long to the sun. And once again this fragrance consecrates the nuptials of man and earth, and gives rise in us to the only truly virile love in this world: one that is generous and will die.

The Desert[1]

❧❧ ❧❧❧ ❧❧

to Jean Grenier

LIVING, of course, is rather the opposite of expressing. If I am to believe the great Tuscan masters, it means bearing triple witness, in silence, fire, and immobility. It takes a long time to realize that one can encounter the faces in these Tuscan paintings any day of the week in the streets of Florence or Pisa. But of course we no longer know how to see the real faces of those around us. We no longer look at our contemporaries, eager only for those points of reference in them that determine our behavior. We prefer its most vulgar poetry to the face itself. As for Giotto and Piero della Francesca, they are perfectly aware that a man's feelings are nothing. Surely everyone has a heart. But the great simple, eternal emotions around which the love of living revolves—hatred, love, tears, and joys—

[1] *This essay is based largely on the visit that Camus made to Italy in September 1937. This was his second visit to Italy, and he had been there for the first time in 1936, immediately after the disastrous stay in Prague described on pages 40–7. Many of the ideas expressed in this essay were first elaborated in the* Carnets *for September 1937.* —P.T.

93

these grow deep inside a man and mold the visage of his destiny, like the grief that makes Mary clench her teeth in Giottino's "Entombment." In the immense friezes of Tuscan churches I make out crowds of angels, their features scarcely traced, but in each mute and passionate face I recognize a solitude.[2]

What matters are not picturesque qualities, episodes, shades of color, or emotional effects. What counts is not poetry. What counts is truth. And I call truth anything that continues. There is a subtle lesson in thinking that, in this respect, only painters can satisfy our hunger. This is because they have the privilege of making themselves novelists of the body. Because they work in that magnificent and trivial matter called the present. And the present always shows itself in a gesture. They do not paint a smile, a fleeting moment of modesty, of regret, or of expectation, but a face with the shape of its bones and the warmth of its blood. What they have expelled from these faces molded for eternity is the curse of the mind: at the price of hope. For the body knows nothing of hope. All it knows is the beating of its own heart. Its eternity consists of indifference. As in the "Scourging of Christ" by Piero della Francesca, where, in a freshly washed courtyard, both the tortured Christ and the thick-set executioner reveal the same detachment in their attitudes. This is because the torment has no sequel. Its lesson ends with the frame around the canvas. Why should a man who expects no tomorrow feel emotion? The impassiveness and the greatness that man shows when he has no hope, the eternal present, is precisely

[2] *In his notes to this essay in* Pléiade II, *p. 1361, Louis Faucon points out that Malraux expressed similar ideas on Piero della Francesca in a review entitled* Verve *in 1937–8, before developing them in* Les Voix du Silence. —P.T.

what perceptive theologians have called hell. And hell, as everyone knows, also consists of bodily suffering. The Tuscan painters stop at the body and not at its destiny. There are no prophetic paintings. And it is not in museums that we must seek reasons to hope.

The immortality of the soul, it is true, engrosses many noble minds. But this is because they reject the body, the only truth that is given them, before using up its strength. For the body presents no problems, or, at least, they know the only solution it proposes: a truth which must perish and which thus acquires a bitterness and nobility they dare not contemplate directly. Noble minds would rather have poetry than the body, for poetry concerns the soul. Clearly, I am playing on words. But it is also clear that all I wish to do by calling it truth is consecrate a higher poetry: the dark flame that Italian painters from Cimabue to Francesca have raised from the Tuscan landscape as the lucid protestation of men thrown upon an earth whose splendor and light speak ceaselessly to them of a nonexistent God.

Sometimes indifference and insensitivity permit a face to merge with the mineral grandeur of a landscape. Just as certain Spanish peasants come to resemble their own olive trees, so the faces in Giotto's pictures, shorn of the insignificant shadows that reveal the soul, finally merge with Tuscany itself in the only lesson it freely offers: the exercise of passion at the expense of feeling, a mixture of asceticism and pleasure, a resonance common to both man and the earth and by which man, like the earth, defines himself as halfway between wretchedness and love. There are not many truths the heart can be sure of. I realized this one evening as the shadows were beginning to drown the vines and olive trees of the Florentine countryside in a vast and silent sadness. But sadness in this country is never anything but a commentary on beauty. And as the train traveled on through the evening I felt a tension in me slowly relaxing. Can I doubt today that even with the face of sadness, one could call it happiness?

Yes, Italy also lavishes on every landscape the lesson illustrated by its men. But it is easy to miss our chance of happiness, for it is always undeserved. The same is true of Italy. And if its grace is sudden, it is not always immediate. More than any other country, Italy invites us to deepen an experience that paradoxically seems to be complete on first acquaintance. This is because it begins by pouring out its poetry the better to disguise its truth. Italy's first enchantments are rites of forgetfulness: the laurel roses of Monaco, flower-filled Genoa with its smell of fish, and blue evenings on the Ligurian coast. Then finally Pisa, and with it an Italy which has lost the rather tawdry charm of the Riviera. But it is still a land of easy virtue, so why not lend ourselves for a time to its sensual grace? There is nothing urging me on while I am here (I am deprived of the joys of the harried tourist,[3] since a cheap ticket compels me to spend a certain time in the town "of my choice"). My patience for love and understanding seems endless on this first evening when, dead tired and starved, I enter Pisa, greeted on the station platform by ten loudspeakers bellowing out a flood of sentimental songs to an almost entirely youthful crowd. I already know what I expect. After the life here has surged around me, the strange moment will come, when, with the cafés closed and the silence suddenly restored, I'll walk through the short,

[3] *The reference here is to Henry de Montherlant's series of novels entitled* Les Voyageurs traqués, *published in the 1930's.* —P.T.

96

dark streets toward the center of the town. The black and gold Arno, the green and yellow monuments, the empty town—how can I describe the neat and sudden subterfuge that transforms Pisa at ten each evening into a strange stage-set of silence, water, and stone. "In such a night as this, Jessica!" Here, on this unique stage, gods appear with the voices of Shakespeare's lovers . . . We must learn how to lend ourselves to dreaming when dreams lend themselves to us. Already I can hear in the depth of this Italian night the strains of the more private song that people come to look for here. Tomorrow, and only tomorrow, the countryside will round out in the morning light. Tonight I am a god among gods, and as Jessica flies off "on the swift steps of love," I mingle my voice with Lorenzo's. But Jessica is only a pretext; this surge of love goes beyond her. Yes, I think Lorenzo is not so much in love with her as grateful to her for allowing him to love. Why should I dream this evening of the lovers of Venice and forget Verona's? Because there is nothing here that invites us to cherish unhappy lovers. Nothing is more vain than to die for love. What we ought to do is live. A living Lorenzo is better than a Romeo in his grave, despite his rosebush. Then why not dance in these celebrations of living love—and sleep in the afternoons on the lawn of the Piazza del Duomo, surrounded by monuments there will always be time enough to visit, drink from the city's fountains where the water is lukewarm but so fluid, and look once more for the face of that laughing woman with the long nose and proud mouth. All we need understand is that this initiation prepares us for higher illuminations. These are the dazzling processions that lead to the Dionysian mysteries at Eleusis. It is in joy that man prepares his lessons and when his ecstasy is at its highest pitch that the flesh becomes conscious and consecrates its communion with a sacred mystery whose symbol is black blood. It is now that the self-forgetfulness drawn from the ardor of that first Italy prepares us for the lesson that frees us from hope and from our history. These twin truths of the body and of the moment, at the spectacle of beauty—how can we not cling to them as to the only happiness we can expect, one that will enchant us but at the same time perish?

The most loathsome materialism is not the kind people usually think of, but the sort that attempts to let dead ideas pass for living realities, diverting into sterile myths the stubborn and lucid attention we give to what we have within us that must forever die. I remember that in Florence, in the cloister of the dead at the Santissima Annunziata, I was carried away by something I mistook for distress, which was only anger. It was raining. I was reading the inscriptions on the tombstones and ex-votos. One man had been a tender father and a faithful husband; another, at the same time the best of husbands and a skillful merchant. A young woman, a model of all the virtues, had spoken French *"si come il nativo."* There was a young girl, who had been the hope of her whole family, *"ma la gioia è pellegrina sulla terra."* None of this affected me. Nearly all of them, according to the inscriptions, had resigned themselves to dying, doubtless because they accepted their other duties. Children had invaded the cloister and were playing leapfrog over the tombstones that strove to perpetuate their virtues. Night was falling, and I had sat down on the ground, my back against a column. A priest smiled at me as he went by. In the church, an organ was playing softly, and the warm color of its pattern sometimes emerged behind the children's shouts. Alone against the column, I was like someone seized by the throat, who shouts out his faith as if it were his last word. Everything in me protested against such a resignation. "You must," said the inscriptions. But no, and my revolt was right. This joy that was moving forward, indifferent and absorbed like a pilgrim treading on the earth, was something that I had to follow step by step. And, as to the rest, I said no. I said no with all my strength. The tombstones were teaching me that it was pointless, that life is *"col sol levante, col sol cadente."* But even today I cannot see what my revolt loses by being pointless, and I am well aware of what it gains.

Besides, that is not what I set out to say. I would like to define a little more clearly a truth I felt then at the very heart of my revolt and of which this revolt was only an extension, a truth that stretched from the tiny last roses in the cloister of Santa Maria Novella to the women on that Sunday morning in Florence, their breasts free beneath their light dresses, and their moist lips. On every church corner, that Sunday morning, there were displays of flowers, their petals thick and shining, bejeweled with spots of water. I found in them then a kind of "simplicity" as well as a reward. There was a generous opulence in the flowers and in the women, and I could not see that desiring the latter was much different from longing for the former. The same pure heart sufficed for both. It's not often a man feels his heart is pure. But when he does, it is his duty to call what has so singularly purified him truth, even if this truth may seem a blasphemy to others, as is the case with what I thought that day. I had spent the morning in a Franciscan convent, at Fiesole, full of the scent of laurel. I had stood for a long time in a little courtyard overflowing with red flowers, sunlight, and black and yellow bees. In one corner there was a green watering can. Earlier, I had visited the monks' cells, and seen their little tables, each adorned with a skull. Now, the garden testified to their inspiration. I had turned back toward Florence, down the hill that led toward the town lying open with all its cypress trees. I felt this splendor of the world, the women and the flowers, was a kind of justification for these men. I was not sure that they were not also the justification for all men who know that an extreme level of poverty always meets the wealth and luxury of the world. Between the life of these Franciscans enclosed among columns and flowers and the life of the young men of the Padovani beach in Algiers who spend the whole year in the sun, I felt there was a common resonance. If they strip themselves bare, it is for a greater life (and not for another life). At least, that is the only valid meaning of such expressions as "deprivation" and "stripping oneself bare." Being naked always carries a sense of physical liberty and of the harmony between hand and flowers—the loving understanding between the earth and a man delivered from the human— ah! I would be a convert if this were not already my religion. No, what I have just said cannot be a blasphemy —any more than if I say that the inner smile of Giotto's portraits of Saint Francis justifies those who have a taste for happiness. For myths are to religion what poetry is to truth: ridiculous masks laid upon the passion to live.

Shall I go further? The same men at Fiesole who live among red flowers keep in their cells the skull that nourishes their meditations. Florence at their windows and death on their tables. A certain continuity in despair can give birth to joy. And when life reaches a certain temperature, our soul and our blood mingle and live at ease in contradiction, as indifferent to duty as to faith. I am no longer surprised that a cheerful hand should thus have summarized its strange notion of honor on a wall in

Pisa: *"Alberto fa l'amore con la mia sorella."* I am no longer surprised that Italy should be the land of incests, or at least, what is more significant, of admitted incests. For the path that leads from beauty to immorality is tortuous but certain. Plunged deep in beauty, the mind feeds off nothingness. When a man faces landscapes whose grandeur clutches him by the throat, each movement of his mind is a scratch on his perfection. And soon, crossed out, scarred and rescarred by so many overwhelming certainties, man ceases to be anything at all in face of the world but a formless stain knowing only passive truths, the world's color or its sun. Landscapes as pure as this dry up the soul and their beauty is unbearable. The message of these gospels of stone, sky, and water is that there are no resurrections. Henceforth, from the depths of the deserts that the heart sees as magnificent, men of these countries begin to feel temptation. Why is it surprising if minds brought up before the spectacle of nobility, in the rarefied air of beauty, remain unconvinced that greatness and goodness can live in harmony. An intelligence with no god to crown its glory seeks for a god in what denies it. Borgia, on his arrival in the Vatican, exclaims: "Now that God has given us the papacy, let us hasten to enjoy it." And he behaves accordingly. "Hasten" is indeed the word. There is already a hint of the despair so characteristic of people who have everything.

Perhaps I am mistaken. For I was in fact happy in Florence, like many others before me. But what is happiness except the simple harmony between a man and the life he leads? And what more legitimate harmony can unite a man with life than the dual consciousness of his longing to endure and his awareness of death? At least he learns to count on nothing and to see the present as the only truth given to us "as a bonus." I realize that people talk about Italy, the Mediterranean, as classical countries where everything is on a human scale. But where is this, and where is the road that leads the way? Let me open my eyes to seek my measure and my satisfaction! What I see is Fiesole, Djemila, and ports in the sunlight. The human scale? Silence and dead stones. All the rest belongs to history.

And yet this is not the end. For no one has said that happiness should be forever inseparable from optimism. It is linked to love—which is not the same thing. And I know of times and places where happiness can seem so bitter that we prefer the promise of it. But this is because at such times or places I had not heart enough to love—that is, to persevere in love. What we must talk of here is man's entry into the celebration of beauty and the earth. For now, like the neophyte shedding his last veils, he surrenders to his god the small change of his personality. Yes, there is a higher happiness, where happiness seems trivial. In Florence, I climbed right to the top of the Boboli gardens, to a terrace from which I could see Mount Oliveto and the upper part of the town as far as the horizon. On each of the hills, the olive trees were pale as little wisps of smoke, and the stronger shoots of the cypresses stood out against their light mist, the nearer ones green and the further ones black. Heavy clouds spotted the deep blue of the sky. As the afternoon drew to a close, a silvery light bathed everything in silence. At first the hilltops had been hidden in clouds. But a breeze had risen whose breath I could feel on my cheek. As it blew, the clouds behind the mountains drew apart like two sides of a curtain. At the same time, the cypress trees on the summit seemed to shoot up in a single jet against the sudden blue of the sky. With them, the whole hillside and landscape of stones and olive trees rose slowly back into sight. Other clouds appeared. The curtain closed. And the hill with its cypress trees and houses vanished once more. Then the same breeze, which was closing the thick folds of the curtain over other hills, scarcely visible in the distance, came and pulled them open here anew. As the world thus filled and emptied its lungs, the same breath ended a few seconds away and then, a little further off, took up again the theme of a fugue that stone and air were playing on a world-scale. Each time, the theme was repeated in a slightly lower key. As I followed it into the distance, I became a little calmer. Reaching the end of so stirring a vision, with one final glance I took in the whole range of hills breathing in unison as they slipped away, as if in some song of the entire earth.

Millions of eyes, I knew, had gazed at this landscape, and for me it was like the first smile of the sky. It took me out of myself in the deepest sense of the word. It assured me that but for my love and the wondrous cry of these stones, there was no meaning in anything. The world is beautiful, and outside it there is no salvation. The great truth that it patiently taught me is that the mind is nothing, nor even the heart. And that the stone warmed by the sun or the cypress tree shooting up against the suddenly clear sky mark the limits of the only universe in which "being right" is meaningful: nature without men. And this world annihilates me. It carries me to the end. It denies me without anger. As that evening fell over Florence, I was moving toward a wisdom where everything had already been overcome, except that tears came into my eyes and a great sob of poetry welling up within me made me forget the world's truth.

· · ·

It is on this moment of balance I must end: the strange moment when spirituality rejects ethics, when happiness springs from the absence of hope, when the mind finds its justification in the body. If it is true that every truth carries its bitterness within, it is also true that every denial contains a flourish of affirmations. And this song of hopeless love born in contemplation may also seem the most effective guide for action. As he emerges from the tomb, the risen Christ of Piero della Francesca has no human expression on his face—only a fierce and soulless grandeur that I cannot help taking for a resolve to live. For the wise man, like the idiot, expresses little. The reversion delights me.

But do I owe this lesson to Italy, or have I drawn it from my own heart? It was surely in Italy that I became aware of it. But this is because Italy, like other privileged places, offers me the spectacle of a beauty in which, nonetheless, men die. Here again truth must decay, and what is more exalting? Even if I long for it, what have I in common with a truth that is not destined to decay? It is not on my scale. And to love it would be pretense. People rarely understand that it is never through despair that a man gives up what constituted his life. Impulses and moments of despair lead toward other lives and merely indicate a quivering attachment to the lessons of the earth. But it can happen that when he reaches a certain degree of lucidity a man feels his heart is closed, and without protest or rebellion turns his back on what up to then he had taken for his life, that is to say, his restlessness. If Rimbaud dies in Abyssinia without having written a single line, it is not because he prefers adventure or has renounced literature. It is because "that's how things are," and because when we reach a certain stage of awareness we finally acknowledge something which each of us, according to our particular vocation, seeks not to understand. This clearly involves undertaking the survey of a certain desert. But this strange desert is accessible only to those who can live there in the full anguish of their thirst. Then, and only then, is it peopled with the living waters of happiness.

Within reach of my hand, in the Boboli gardens, hung enormous golden Chinese persimmons whose bursting skin oozed a thick syrup. Between this light hill and these juicy fruits, between the secret brotherhood linking me to the world and the hunger urging me to seize the orange-colored flesh above my hand, I could feel the tension that leads certain men from asceticism to sensual delights and from self-denial to the fullness of desire. I used to wonder, I still wonder at this bond that unites man with the world, this double image in which my heart can intervene and dictate its happiness up to the precise limit where the world can either fulfill or destroy it. Florence! One of the few places in Europe where I have understood that at the heart of my revolt consent is dormant. In its sky mingled with tears and sunlight, I learned to consent to the earth and be consumed in the dark flame of its celebrations. I felt . . . but what word can I use? What excess? How can one consecrate the harmony of love and revolt? The earth! In this great temple deserted by the gods, all my idols have feet of clay.

III
SUMMER

(L' Eté)

But you, you were born for a limpid day.
Hölderlin

WHILE *the essays in* The Wrong Side and the Right Side *and* Nuptials *were all written and published within a relatively short time, and express attitudes closely connected with a particular period in Camus's life, those included in* L'Été *in 1954 cover a much wider period. As his own note to page 109 indicates, he began writing* Le Minotaur ou la Halte d'Oran *as early as 1939, although the essay was not finally published until February 1946, when it appeared in the thirteenth number of the review* L'Arche. *It was subsequently published by Charlot, in Algiers, and was made available to the general reading public in France only in 1954. In contrast, the first brief notes for* The Sea Close By *were written in October 1949 (see* Carnets II, Gallimard; *1964, p. 290; Alfred A. Knopf edition, p. 228), and the essay itself was published in a review in 1954.*

    Oran was a town that Camus knew very well. In the first volume of his Carnets, *he refers to two visits that he made there in 1939, and it was the birthplace of his second wife, Francine Faure, whom he married in 1940.* La Peste *is set in Oran, and the insistence upon the ordinary, down-to-earth, and commercial atmosphere of the city is an important theme in the novel.* —P.T.

The Minotaur, or Stopping in Oran

❦❦ ❦❦❦ ❦❦

to Pierre Galindo

THIS *essay dates from 1939—something the reader should bear in mind in judging what Oran might be like today. Violent protests emanating from this beautiful town have in fact assured me that all the imperfections have been (or will be) remedied. The beauties celebrated in this essay, have, on the other hand, been jealously protected. Oran, a happy and realistic city, no longer needs writers. It is waiting for tourists.*

(1953)

THERE are no more deserts. There are no more islands. Yet one still feels the need of them. To understand this world, one must sometimes turn away from it; to serve men better, one must briefly hold them at a distance. But where can the necessary solitude be found, the long breathing space in which the mind gathers its strength and takes stock of its courage? There are still the great cities. But they must meet certain conditions.

The cities Europe offers are too full of murmurs from the past. A practiced ear can still detect the rustling of wings, the quivering of souls. We feel the dizziness of the centuries, of glory and revolutions. We are reminded of the clamor in which Europe was forged. There is not enough silence.

109

Paris is often a desert for the heart, but sometimes, from the height of Père-Lachaise, a wind of revolution suddenly fills this desert with flags and vanquished grandeurs. The same is true of certain Spanish towns, of Florence or Prague. Salzburg would be peaceful without Mozart. But now and then the great cry of Don Juan plunging into hell runs across the Salzach. Vienna seems more silent, a maiden among cities. Its stones are no more than three centuries old, and their youth has known no sadness. But Vienna stands at a crossroads of history. The clash of empires echoes around her. On certain evenings when the sky clothes itself in blood, the stone horses on the monuments of the Ring seem about to take flight. In this fleeting instant, when everything speaks of power and history, you can distinctly hear the Ottoman empire crashing under the charge of the Polish cavalry. Here, too, there is not enough silence.

It is certainly this well-populated solitude that men look for in the cities of Europe. At least, men who know what they want. Here, they can choose their company, take it and leave it. How many minds have been tempered in the walk between a hotel room and the old stones of the Ile Saint-Louis! It is true that others died of loneliness. But it was here, in any case, that those who survived found reasons to grow and for self-affirmation. They were alone and yet not alone. Centuries of history and beauty, the burning evidence of a thousand past lives, accompanied them along the Seine and spoke to them both of traditions and of conquests. But their youth urged them to call forth this company. There comes a time, there come times in history, when such company is a nuisance. "It's between the two of us now," cries Rastignac as he confronts the vast mustiness of Paris. Yes, but two can also be too many!

Deserts themselves have taken on a meaning; poetry has handicapped them. They have become the sacred places for all the world's suffering. What the heart requires at certain moments is just the opposite, a place without poetry. Descartes, for his meditations, chose as his desert the busiest commercial city of his time. There he found his solitude, and the chance to write what is perhaps the greatest of our virile poems: "The first (precept) was never to accept anything as true unless I knew without the slightest doubt that it was so." One can have less ambition and yet the same longing. But for the last three centuries Amsterdam has been covered with museums. To escape from poetry and rediscover the peacefulness of stones we need other deserts, and other places without soul or resources. Oran is one of these.

THE STREET

I have often heard people from Oran complain about their town: "There are no interesting people here." But you wouldn't want them if there were! A number of high-minded people have tried to acclimate this desert to the customs of another world, faithful to the principle that no one can genuinely serve art or ideas without cooperation from others.[1] The result is that the only edifying circles are those of poker players, boxing and bowling fans, and local clubs. At least their atmosphere is natural. After all, there is a kind of greatness that doesn't lend itself to elevation. It is sterile by nature. And anyone who wants to find it leaves the clubs behind to descend into the street.

[1] In Oran, you meet Gogol's Klestakoff. He yawns and then says: "I feel we ought to concern ourselves with higher things."

The streets of Oran are reserved for dust, pebbles, and heat. If it rains there is a flood and a sea of mud. But rain or shine, the shops have the same absurd, extravagant look. All the bad taste of Europe and the Orient meets in Oran. There, pell-mell, are marble greyhounds, Swan Lake ballet dancers, Diana the Huntress in green galalith, discus throwers and harvesters, everything that serves as wedding or birthday presents, the whole depressing crew that some joker of a businessman endlessly conjures up to fill our mantelpieces. But the relentless bad taste reaches a point of baroque extravagance where all can be forgiven. Behold, embellished with dust, the contents of one shop window: ghastly plaster-cast models of tortured feet, a batch of Rembrandt sketches "given away at 150 francs each," a quantity of "practical jokes and tricks," tricolor wallets, an eighteenth-century pastel drawing, a mechanical plush donkey, bottles of *eau de Provence* for preserving green olives, and a wretched wooden Virgin with an indecent smile. (So that no one will be left in ignorance, the management has placed a label at its feet: "Wooden virgin.")

You can find in Oran: [2]

1. Cafés whose grease-covered countertops are strewn with the feet and wings of flies, where the proprietor never stops smiling although the place is always empty. A "small black coffee" used to cost twelve sous and a "large" eighteen;

2. Photographers' shops where techniques have not progressed since the invention of sensitized paper. They display a singular fauna, never encountered in the

---

[2] *These features of life in Oran were first noted down by Camus when he visited Oran in 1939. (See* Carnets I, *pp. 188–90, 221–6; Alfred A. Knopf edition, pp. 158–60, 186–92).* —P.T.

street, ranging from a pseudo sailor leaning with one elbow on a console table to a marriageable maiden in a dowdy dress, simpering with dangling arms against a sylvan background. It can be assumed that these are not copies from nature but original creations;

3. An edifying abundance of undertakers. This is not because more people die in Oran than elsewhere, but simply, I suppose, because they make more fuss about it.

The endearing simplicity of this nation of shopkeepers even extends to their advertising. The program of a local movie theater describes a third-rate coming attraction. I note the adjectives "magnificent," "splendid," "extraordinary," "marvelous," "overwhelming," and "stupendous." In conclusion, the management informs the public of the considerable sacrifices it has had to make in order to be able to present this astonishing production. The price of seats, however, will remain the same.

It would be wrong to assume that this merely shows the taste for exaggeration peculiar to Mediterranean countries. What the authors of this remarkable advertisement are really doing is giving proof of their psychological perspicacity. They need to overcome the indifference and profound apathy people have in this country when faced with a choice between two entertainments, two jobs, and often, even between two women. One decides only when compelled to do so. And the advertisers are perfectly aware of this. They will go to American extremes, since the same exasperating conditions exist in both places.

Finally, the streets of Oran reveal the two main pleasures of the local young people: having their shoes shined, and promenading in these same shoes along the boulevard. To understand fully the first of these two sensual delights, you must entrust your shoes at ten o'clock on a Sunday morning to the shoe shiners on the boulevard Gallieni. There, perched on a high armchair, one can enjoy the peculiar satisfaction that even the layman derives from the spectacle of men as deeply and visibly in love with their work as are the shoe cleaners of Oran. Everything is worked out to the last detail. Several brushes, three kinds of polishing rags, shoe polish mixed with gasoline: one would think the operation concluded as a perfect shine rises beneath the application of the soft brush. But the same eager hand puts a second coat of polish on the gleaming surface, rubs it, dulls it, drives the cream into the very heart of the leather and then creates, with the same brush, a double and truly definitive shine that flashes forth from the depths.

The marvels thus obtained are then exhibited to the connoisseurs. To really appreciate the pleasures offered by the boulevard, you must attend the costume balls organized by the young people of Oran every evening in the town's main thoroughfares. "Fashionable" Oranians between the ages of sixteen and twenty model their elegance on American movie stars, disguising themselves every night before dinner. With curly, brilliantined hair flowing from under a felt hat pulled down over the left ear while its brim obliterates the right eye, the neck encircled in a collar generous enough to receive the continuation of the hair, the microscopic knot of the tie held in place by the strictest of pins, a jacket hanging half way down the thighs and nipped in at the hips, light-colored trousers hanging short, and shoes gleaming above triple soles, these youths click along the sidewalks, sounding their unshakable self-confidence with their steel-tipped shoes. In every detail they attempt to imitate the style, the brashness, the superiority of Mr. Clark Gable. This is why, thanks to their rather careless pronunciation, the town's more critical citizens have nicknamed these young men "The Clarques."

In any case, the main boulevards of Oran are invaded late every afternoon by an army of amiable adolescents who take the greatest pains to look like gangsters. Since the young girls know they have been destined since birth to marry these tender-hearted ruffians, they too flaunt the make-up and elegance of the great American actresses. The same cynics consequently christen them "Marlenes." Thus, when on the evening boulevards the chirping of birds rises from the palm trees to the sky, scores of Clarques and Marlenes meet, and size each other up appreciatively, happy to be alive and to make believe, indulging for an hour in the bliss of perfect existences. What we are witnessing here, to quote the envious, are meetings of the American delegation. The words reveal the bitterness of those over thirty who have no part in such games. They fail to see these daily congresses of youth and romantic love for what they are— the parliaments of birds one finds in Hindu literature. But no one, on the boulevards of Oran, discusses the problem of Being, or worries about the way to perfection. There is only the fluttering of wings, the flaunting of outspread tails, flirtations between victorious graces, all the rapture of a careless song that fades with the coming of night.

Already I hear Klestakoff: "We must concern ourselves with higher things." Alas, he is quite capable of doing so. A little encouragement, and in a few years time he will populate this desert. But, for the time being, a slightly secretive soul can find deliverance in this facile town, with its parade of made-up maidens so incapable of ready-made emotion that the ruse of their borrowed coquetry is immediately uncovered. Concern ourselves with higher things! We would do better to use our eyes: Santa Cruz carved out of the rock, the mountains, the flat sea, the violent wind and the sun, the tall cranes in the docks, the sheds, the quays, and the gigantic flights of stairs that scale the rock on which the town is set, and in the town itself the games and the boredom, the tumult and the solitude. Perhaps none of this is elevated enough. But the great value of such overpopulated islands is that in them the heart can strip itself bare. Silence is possible now only in noisy towns. From Amsterdam, Descartes writes the aging Guez de Balzac, "I go walking every day in the confusion of a great people, with as much freedom and quiet as you must find in your country lanes."

THE DESERT IN ORAN

Compelled to live facing a glorious landscape, the people of Oran have overcome this formidable handicap by surrounding themselves with extremely ugly buildings. You expect a town opening on the sea, washed and refreshed by the evening breezes. But except for the Spanish district,[3] you find a city with its back to the sea, built turning in upon itself, like a snail. Oran is a long circular yellow wall, topped by a hard sky. At first, one wanders around the labyrinth, looking for the sea as for Ariadne's sign. But one turns around and around in the stifling yellow streets. In the end, the Oranians are devoured by the Minotaur of boredom. The Oranians have long since stopped wandering. They have let the monster eat them.

No one can know what stone is all about until he has been to Oran. In this dustiest of cities, the pebble is

---

[3] And the new boulevard Front-de-Mer.

king. It is so much revered that merchants display it in their windows, either as a paperweight or simply for its appearance. People pile them up along the streets, doubtless for pure visual pleasure, since a year later the pile is still there. Things which elsewhere derive their poetry from being green here take on a face of stone. The hundred or so trees that can be found in the business section of the town have been carefully covered with dust. They are a petrified forest, their branches exuding an acrid, dusty smell. In Algiers, the Arab cemeteries have the gentleness they are known for. In Oran, above the Ras-el-Aïn ravine, facing the sea for once, laid out against the blue sky are fields of chalky, crumbly pebbles set blindingly on fire by the sun. In the midst of these dead bones of the earth, here and there a crimson geranium lends its life and fresh blood to the landscape. The whole town is held fast in a stone vise. Seen from the Planters, the cliffs that hold it in their grip are so thick that the landscape loses its reality in so much mineral. Man is an outlaw. So much heavy beauty seems to come from another world.

If one can define the desert as a place with no soul where the sky alone is king, then Oran awaits its prophets. All around and above the town Africa's brutal nature is resplendent in its burning glory. It shatters the ill-chosen décor men have laid upon it, thrusting its violent cries between each house and down on all the rooftops. As one climbs one of the roads along the side of Santa Cruz mountain, what appears at first are the scattered, brightly colored cubes of Oran. A bit higher, and already the jagged cliffs surrounding the plateau crouch into the sea like red beasts. A little higher still and great whirlpools of sun and wind blanket the untidy town, blowing and battering through its scattered confusion in all four corners of the rocky landscape. Confronted here are man's magnificent anarchy and the permanence of an unchanging sea. Enough to raise along the mountain road a mounting, overwhelming scent of life.

There is something implacable about deserts. The mineral sky of Oran, its trees and streets coated with dust unite to create this thick, impassive world in which the mind and heart are never diverted from themselves or their single subject, which is man. I am speaking here of difficult retreats. People write books about Florence and Athens. These towns have formed so many European minds that they must have a meaning. They maintain the power to sadden or excite. They calm a certain hunger of the soul whose proper food is memory. But how can one feel tender in a town where nothing appeals to the mind, where even ugliness is anonymous, where the past is reduced to nothing? Emptiness, boredom, an indifferent sky: what enticements do these places offer? Solitude, doubt, and perhaps human beings. For a certain race of men, human beings, wherever they are beautiful, are a bitter homeland. Oran is one of the thousand capitals such men possess.

SPORTS

The Central Sporting Club, in the rue du Fondouk, in Oran, is presenting an evening of boxing, which it claims will be appreciated by those who really love the sport. What this actually means is that the boxers whose names are on the posters are far from being champions, that some of them will be stepping into the ring for the first time, and that you can therefore count on the courage, if not the skill, of the contestants. Electrified by an Oranian's promise that "blood will flow," I find myself this evening among the real lovers of the sport.

It would appear that the fans never demand comfort. A ring has been erected at the far end of a kind of whitewashed, garishly lit garage, with a corrugated iron roof. Folding chairs have been set up on all four sides of the ropes. These are the "ringside seats." Other seats have been set up the length of the hall, and at the far end there is a wide open space known as the "promenade," so named because not one of the five hundred people standing there can take out his pocket handkerchief without causing a serious accident. A thousand men and two or three women—of the type who, according to my neighbor, "always want to show off"—are breathing in this rectangular box. Everyone is sweating ferociously. While we wait for the young hopefuls to step into the ring, an immense loudspeaker grinds out Tino Rossi. Ballads before butchery.

The true fan has limitless patience. The match scheduled for nine o'clock has not yet started at half past, and yet no one complains. It is a warm spring evening, and the smell of men in shirt sleeves is intoxicating. Vigorous discussions are punctuated with the periodic popping of lemonade corks and the tireless lamentations of the Corsican singer. A few late arrivals squeeze into the audience as a spotlight rains blinding light on the ring. The amateur fights begin.

These "white hopes," or beginners, who fight for pleasure, are always anxious to prove it by massacring each other at the first opportunity, with a fine disregard for technique. None of them has ever lasted more than three rounds. Tonight's hero is a certain "Kid Avion," who ordinarily sells lottery tickets on café terraces. At the beginning of the second round, his opponent took an unfortunate dive out of the ring under the impact of a propellerlike fist.

The crowd has grown a little more excited, though still polite. Gravely, it inhales the sacred scent of liniment. It contemplates this series of slow rites and confused sacrifices, rendered even more authentic by the expiatory patterns thrown against the whiteness of the wall by the struggling shadows. These are the formal prologue of a savage and calculated religion. Only later comes the trance.

And, at this very moment, the loudspeaker introduces Amar, "the hometown tough who has never surrendered," against Pérez, "the Algerian puncher." An outsider might well misinterpret the howls that greet the presentation of the boxers in the ring. He would imagine this was some sensational fight in which the two rivals were going to settle a personal quarrel well known to the public. It is, indeed, a quarrel that they are going to settle, but one that, for the last hundred years, has mortally divided Algiers and Oran. A few hundred years ago, these two North African towns would already have bled each other white, as Florence and Pisa did in happier times. Their rivalry is all the stronger for being based on absolutely nothing. Having every reason to love each other, they hate all the more intensely. The Oranians accuse the Algerians of being "stuck-up." The Algerians insinuate that Oranians have no manners. Such insults are more scathing than one might think, since they are metaphysical. And, because they cannot besiege each other, Oran and Algiers meet, struggle, and exchange insults in the field of sport and in competition over statistics and public works.

A page of history is therefore unfolding in the ring. And the hometown tough guy, supported by a thousand howling voices, is defending a way of life and the pride of a province against Pérez. Truth compels me to say that Amar is making his points badly. His arguments are out of order: he lacks reach. The Algerian puncher, on the other hand, is long enough in the arm and makes his points persuasively against his opponent's eyebrow. The Oranian flaunts his colors triumphantly, amid the howls of the frenzied spectators. In spite of repeated encouragement from the gallery and from my neighbor, in spite of the fearless "Slug him," "Give him hell," the insidious cries of "foul," "Oh, the referee didn't see it," the optimistic "He's pooped," "He's had it," the Algerian is declared winner on points to the accompaniment of interminable booing. My neighbor, who likes to talk about the sporting spirit, applauds ostentatiously, whispering to me in a voice hoarse from shouting: "They won't be able to say *there* that Oranians are rude."

But in the hall itself a number of unscheduled fights have already broken out. Chairs are brandished in the air, the police force their way through, the excitement is at its height. To calm these good people and contribute to the restoration of silence, the "management" instantly entrusts the loudspeaker with the thunderous march *Sambre-et-Meuse*. For a few moments the hall takes on a wondrous aspect. Confused bunches of fighters and benevolent referees wave to and fro beneath the policemen's grasp, the gallery is delighted and urges them to further efforts with wild cries, cock-a-doodle-doos, or ironic catcalls soon drowned in the irresistible flood of military music.

But the announcement that the main fight is about to start is enough to restore calm. This happens quickly, with no flourishes, the way actors leave the stage as soon as the play is over. In the most natural way in the world, hats are dusted, chairs put back in their place, and every face immediately assumes the benign expression of the respectable spectator who has paid for his seat at a family concert.

In the last fight of the evening a French naval champion confronts an Oranian boxer. This time it is the latter who has the advantage of reach. But in the first few rounds his superiority does not appeal much to the crowd, which is sleeping off its excitement, convalescing. Everyone is still out of breath. The applause seems unfelt; the whistling half-hearted. The spectators split into two camps, as they must do if order is to prevail. But each man's choice yields to the indifference of great weariness. If the Frenchman holds in the clinches, if the Oranian forgets that one does not punch with the head, ·the boxer is bowled over by a broadside of hisses but immediately put back on his feet with a salvo of applause. It is not until the seventh round that Sport reappears as the fans begin to rouse from their fatigue. The Frenchman has actually hit the canvas and anxious to regain points has charged at his opponent. "Here we go," says my neighbor. "Now comes the bullfight." And that is just what it is. Bathed in sweat under the implacable lights, the two boxers open their guard, close their eyes, and swing. They push with their knees and shoulders, exchange blood, and snort with fury. At the same moment, the spectators rise and punctuate each hero's effort. They take the blows, return them, echoing them in a thousand harsh and panting voices. Those who arbitrarily picked their favorite stick stubbornly to their choices, and get passionate about it. Every ten seconds my right ear is pierced by my neighbor's shouting: "Come on, blue-jacket! Get him, sailor," while a spectator in front of us shouts *Anda, hombre!* to the Oranian. The hombre and the blue-jacket go to it, egged on in this white-washed temple of cement and corrugated tin by a crowd completely given over to these low-brow gods. Every dull thud on the gleaming chests echoes in enormous vibrations through the very body of the crowd, who, along with the boxers themselves, give the fight their all.

In this atmosphere, the announcement of a draw is badly received. It runs contrary to what, in the crowd, is an utterly Manichaean vision: there is good and evil, the winner and the loser. One must be right if one isn't wrong. The result of this impeccable logic is immediately expressed by two thousand energetic lungs accusing the judges of being either bought or sold. But the blue-jacket has embraced his opponent in the ring and drinks in his fraternal sweat. This is enough to make the crowd effect an immediate about-face and burst into applause. My neighbor is right: they are not uncivilized.

The crowd spilling out now into a night filled with silence and stars has just fought the most exhausting kind of battle. The people say nothing, they slip furtively away, too exhausted for post-mortems. There is good and evil; this religion is merciless. The cohort of the faithful is now nothing more than a bunch of black and white shadows disappearing into the night. Strength and violence are lonely gods; they do not serve memory. They simply scatter their miraculous fistfuls in the present. They correspond to these people without a past who celebrate their communions around the boxing ring. Their rites are a bit trying, but they simplify everything. Good and evil, the winner and the loser: At Corinth, two temples stood side by side—the Temple of Violence, the Temple of Necessity.

MONUMENTS

For many reasons that have as much to do with economy as with metaphysics, one can say that Oranian style, if such a thing exists, finds clear and forceful expression in that singular edifice known as the *Maison du Colon*. Oran is scarcely lacking in monuments. The city has its quota of Imperial Marshals, ministers, and local benefactors. You come across them in little, dusty squares, as resigned to rain as to sun, converted like everything else to stone and boredom. Yet they represent something imported. In this happy barbarity they are unfortunate traces of civilization.

On the other hand, Oran has raised altars and rostrums in its own honor. Needing a building to house the innumerable agricultural organizations that provide the country a livelihood, they decided to erect it in the most solid materials, placing it at the center of the business district, a convincing representation of their virtues: *La Maison du Colon*. Judging from this building, these virtues are three in number: boldness of taste, love of violence, and a sense of historical synthesis. Egypt, Babylon, and Munich have collaborated in this delicate construction—a large cake resembling an immense inverted cup. Multicolored stones are set along each side of the roof, to the most startling effect. The brightness of the mosaic is so persuasive that all one can discern at first is a shapeless dazzle. But closer inspection reveals a meaning to the fully alerted attention: a gracious settler, in bow tie and sun helmet, is receiving the homage of a procession of slaves clad as nature intended.[4] Finally, the edifice with all these illuminations has been erected at the center of an intersection, amid the bustle of the tiny gondola-shaped tramways whose squalor is one of the town's charms.

Oran is, moreover, very attached to the two lions that stand in its main square. Since 1888 they have sat

[4] As one can see, another quality of the Algerian race is candor.

majestically on either side of the staircase leading up to the town hall. Their creator was named Cain. They look imperious and are short in the body. It's said that at night they descend one after the other from their pedestals and pad silently around the darkened square, occasionally stopping to urinate thoughtfully beneath the tall, dusty fig trees. These are rumors, of course, to which Oranians lend an indulgent ear. But the whole thing's unlikely.

Despite some research, I have not been able to develop any great enthusiasm for Cain. All I have discovered is that he enjoyed a reputation as a skillful depicter of animals. Nonetheless, I often think of him—a tendency the mind acquires in Oran. An artist whose name has a certain echo, who gave this town a work of no importance. Several hundred thousand men have grown familiar with the jovial beasts he placed in front of a pretentious town hall. This is one kind of artistic success. These two lions doubtless bear witness, like thousands of works on the same order, to something quite different from talent. Other men were able to create "The Night Watch," "Saint Francis Receiving the Stigmata," "David," or "The Exaltation of the Flower." Cain stuck two grinning cats in the town square of a trading province overseas. But David one day will crumble along with Florence, while these lions perhaps will be saved from disaster. Once again, they hint at something further.

Can I clarify this idea? These statues are both insignificant and solid. The mind has made no contribution to them, matter a very large one. Mediocrity seeks to endure by any means, including bronze. We refuse its claims to eternity, but it makes them every day. Isn't mediocrity itself eternity? In any case, there is something touching about this perseverance; it has its lesson, the lesson offered by all Oran's monuments and by the city

itself. For an hour a day, once in a while, you are compelled to take an interest in something that is not important. The mind can profit from such moments of calm.
This is how it takes the cure, and because these moments
of humility are absolutely necessary to the mind, it seems
to me this opportunity for mental relaxation is better
than many others. Everything perishable seeks to endure.
Let's admit that everything wishes to endure. Man's
works have no other meaning, and in this respect Cain's
lions have the same chance of success as the ruins at
Angkor. This inclines us to be modest.

There are other monuments in Oran, or, at least,
that is what we must call them since they too are repre-
sentative of their town, in perhaps a more significant
way. They are the excavations now being made along the
coast line for a distance of ten kilometers. The ostensible
reason is to transform the brightest of bays into an enormous port. Actually, it is still another opportunity for
man to pit himself against stone.

In the canvases of certain Flemish masters, you
see the insistent recurrence of an admirably spacious
theme: building the Tower of Babel. There are immense
landscapes, rocks reaching up into the sky, escarpments
teeming with workmen, animals, ladders, strange machines, ropes, and beams. Man is in the picture only to
bring out the inhuman vastness of the construction. This
is what comes to mind along the coast west of Oran.

Clinging to immense slopes are rails, pick-up
trucks, cranes, and miniature railways . . . Through
whistles, dust, and smoke, toylike locomotives twist
around vast blocks of stone under a devouring sun. Night
and day a nation of ants swarms over the smoking car-
cass of the mountain. Scores of men, hanging from the
same rope against the cliff face, their bellies pressed to

the handles of pneumatic drills, quiver day after day in mid-air, unloosing whole patches of stone that crash down in a roar of dust. Further along, trucks dump their loads from the top of the slopes, and the rocks, suddenly launched toward the sea, roll and dive into the water, each heavy block followed by a shower of lighter stones. At regular intervals, in the dead of night or in the middle of the day, explosions shake the whole mountain and raise the very sea itself.

What man is doing with these excavations is launching a head-on attack against stone. And if we could for a moment forget the harsh slavery that makes this work possible, we would be filled with admiration. These stones, wrenched from the mountain, help man in his designs. They pile up beneath the first waves, gradually emerge, and finally take shape as a jetty that will soon be covered with men and machines daily moving further out to sea. Vast steel jaws gnaw unceasingly at the cliff's belly, swivel round, and disgorge their excess rubble into the sea. As the face of the cliff sinks lower, the whole coast pushes the sea relentlessly backward.

Stone, of course, cannot be destroyed. All one can do is move it around. In any case, it will always outlast the men who use it. For the moment, it supports their determination to act. Even that determination is doubtless quite gratuitous. But to move things around is man's work: he must choose between doing that or doing nothing at all.[5] Clearly, the Oranians have chosen. For years to come they will keep piling rocks along the coast and into its indifferent bay. In a hundred years, that is to say, tomorrow, they will have to start again. But today these

[5] This essay deals with one particular temptation. One must have known it. Then one can act or not act, but knowing what the terms are.

heaps of rock express the men who move in and out among them, their faces masked in dust and sweat. The true monuments of Oran are still its stones.

ARIADNE'S STONE

The people of Oran, it would seem, are like that friend of Flaubert's who, from his deathbed, cast a last look on this irreplaceable earth and cried out: "Close the window, it's too beautiful." They have closed the window, they have walled themselves in, they have exorcised the landscape. But Le Poitevin died, and the days continued to follow one another just the same. Just as the sea and land beyond the yellow walls of Oran continue their indifferent dialogue. This permanence in the world has always had a charm for man. It excites him and drives him to despair. The world never has more than one thing to say; it is interesting, then boring. But, in the long run, it triumphs through obstinacy. It is always right.

At the very gates of Oran, nature speaks more insistently. Immense stretches of wasteland, covered with fragrant brush, lie in the direction of Canastel. There, the wind and sun speak only of solitude. Rising over Oran is Santa Cruz Mountain, with its plateau and the thousand ravines leading to it. Roads once traveled by coaches cling against the hillsides overlooking the sea. In January, some are covered with flowers. Buttercups and daisies transform them into sumptuous paths, embroidered in white and yellow. Enough has been said about Santa Cruz. But if I had to describe it, I would forget the sacred processions climbing its harsh slopes on great feast days to evoke other pilgrims who find their way in solitude through the red stones, mounting above the motionless

bay, to consecrate one perfect, luminous hour to its bare-
ness.

Oran also has deserts of sand: its beaches. The
ones near the city gates are empty only in winter and in
spring. They are plateaus then, covered with asphodels,
and dotted with small, bare villas among the flowers.
Below them growls the sea. Yet the sun, the slight wind,
the whiteness of the asphodels, the harsh blue of the sky
already foreshadow the summer and the golden youth
swarming over the beach, long hours on the sand, and
the sudden gentleness of evening. Each year there is a
new harvest of flower maidens on these shores. Apparently, they only last the season. The next year other
warm blossoms, still little girls with bodies hard as buds
the summer before, take their place. Descending from
the plateau at eleven in the morning, all this young flesh,
scarcely covered by its motley garments, flows across the
sand like a multicolored wave.

One must go farther (yet strangely near the place
where two hundred thousand men turn in circles) to
find a landscape still virgin: long, empty dunes on which
the passage of men has left no other trace than a worm-
eaten hut. From time to time, an Arab shepherd leads
the black and beige spots of his herd of goats across
the top of the dunes. On these beaches in the province of
Oran each summer morning feels like the world's first.
Each dusk feels like the last, a solemn death proclaimed
at sunset by a final light that darkens every shade. The
sea is aquamarine, the road the color of dried blood, the
beach yellow. Everything vanishes with the green sun; an
hour later, the dunes are streaming with moonlight.
These are boundless nights beneath a shower of stars.
Storms occasionally drift across them, and flashes of

lightning shoot along the dunes, turn the sky pale, casting an orange-glow upon the sand or in our eyes.

But this cannot be shared in words. It must be lived. So much solitude and grandeur make these places unforgettable. In the mild early dawn, beyond the small, still black and bitter waves, a new being cleaves the scarcely endurable waters of the night. The memory of these joys holds no regret, and that is how I know that they were good. After so many years, they are still there, somewhere in this heart that finds fidelity so difficult. And I know that today, if I want to go back, the same sky will still pour its cargo of stars and breezes upon the deserted dunes. These are the lands of innocence.

But innocence needs sand and stone. And man has forgotten how to live with them. At least, this appears to be the case, since he has enclosed himself in this strange town where boredom slumbers. Yet it is this confrontation which gives Oran its value. The capital of boredom, besieged by innocence and beauty, is hemmed in by an army of as many soldiers as stones. At certain times, though, how tempted one feels in this town to defect to the enemy! How tempting to merge oneself with these stones, to mingle with this burning, impassive universe that challenges history and its agitations! A vain temptation, no doubt. But every man has a deep instinct that is neither for destruction nor creation. Simply the longing to resemble nothing. In the shade of the warm buildings of Oran, on its dusty asphalt, one sometimes hears this invitation. For a while, it seems, minds which yield to it are never disappointed. They have the shades of Eurydice and the sleep of Isis. These are the deserts where thought recovers its strength, the cool hand of evening on a troubled heart. No vigil can be kept upon this Mount of Olives; the mind joins and sanctions the sleeping Apostles. Were they really wrong? They did have their revelation after all.

Think of Sakia-Mouni in the desert. He spent long years there, crouching motionless and looking up to heaven. The gods themselves envied him this wisdom and this fate of stone. Swallows had nested in his stiff and outstretched hands. But, one day, off they flew, following the call of distant lands. And the man who had killed in himself desire and will, glory and sadness, began to weep. And so it is that flowers spring from rock. Yes, let us consent to stone when we must. It too can give us the secret and the rapture that we seek in faces. Of course, it cannot last. But what is there that can? Faces lose their secrets and there we are, reduced once more to the bondage of desire. And if stone can do no more for us than can the human heart, it can at least do just as much.

"To be nothing!" For thousands of years this cry has inspired millions of men to revolt against desire and suffering. Its echoes have traveled over centuries and oceans, coming to rest on the oldest sea in the world. They still reverberate softly against the solid cliffs of Oran. Without knowing it, everyone in this country follows this precept. Of course, it's almost in vain. Nothingness lies within our grasp no more than does the absolute. But since we welcome as evidence of grace the eternal signs revealed in roses or in the suffering of men, let us not reject the rare invitations to sleep the earth offers. These have as much truth as the others.

Here, perhaps, is the Ariadne's thread of this frenzied and somnambulistic city. We acquire the virtues, the wholly provisional virtues, of a certain boredom. To be spared, we must say "yes" to the Minotaur. It is an ancient, fertile wisdom. Above the sea, lying silent at the foot of the red cliffs, we need only to balance ourselves precisely between the two massive headlands, to the right and to the left, that are washed in the clear water. In the chugging of a coastguard vessel crawling out to sea bathed in radiant light, you can distinctly hear the muffled call of glittering, inhuman forces: the Minotaur's farewell.

It is noon, the day itself stands at a point of balance. His rite accomplished, the traveler receives the price of his deliverance: the little stone, dry and soft as an asphodel, that he picks up on the cliff. For the initiate, the world is no heavier to carry than that stone. The burden of Atlas is easy; all one need do is choose his moment. One realizes then that for an hour, a month, a year, these shores can lend themselves to freedom. They offer the same uncritical welcome to the monk, the civil servant, or the conqueror. There were days when I expected to run into Descartes or Cesare Borgia in the streets of Oran. It didn't happen. But perhaps someone else will be more fortunate than I. A great action, a great undertaking, virile meditation used to call for the solitude of a desert or a convent. It was there that men kept vigil over the weapons of their minds. What better place to keep these vigils now than in the emptiness of a large town built to last a long time in the midst of mindless beauty?

Here is the small stone, soft as an asphodel. It lies at the beginning of everything. Flowers, tears (if you insist), departures and struggles are for tomorrow. In the middle of the journey, when the heavens open their fountains of light into vast, resounding space, the headlands all along the coast look like a fleet of ships impatient to weigh anchor. These heavy galleons of rock and light tremble on their keels as if in preparation for a voyage to the island of the sun. Oh, the mornings in Oran! From high on the plateaus, the swallows swoop down into the immense cauldrons of simmering air. The whole coast is ready for departure, a thrill of adventure runs along it. Tomorrow, perhaps, we shall set sail together.

1939

The Almond Trees

✿✿ ✿✿✿ ✿✿

"Do you know," Napoleon once said to Fontanes, "what astounds me most about the world? The impotence of force to establish anything. There are only two powers in the world: the sword and the mind. In the end, the sword is always conquered by the mind." [1]

Conquerors, you see, are sometimes melancholy. They have to pay some price for so much vainglory. But what a hundred years ago was true of the sword is no longer true today of the tank. Conquerors have made progress, and the dismal silence of places without intelligence has been established for years at a time in a lacerated Europe. At the time of the hideous wars of Flanders, Dutch painters could still perhaps paint the cockerels in their farmyards. The Hundred Years War has likewise been forgotten, and yet the prayers of Silesian mystics still linger in some hearts. But today, things have

[1] *Camus first noted down the remark by Napoleon in his* Carnets *in 1939, and sketched out a description of the almond trees later the same year. (See* Carnets I, *pp. 186, 196; Alfred A. Knopf edition, pp. 156, 165–6.)*

134

changed; the painter and the monk have been drafted—
we are one with the world. The mind has lost that regal
certainty which a conqueror could acknowledge; it exhausts itself now in cursing force, for want of knowing
how to master it.

Some noble souls keep on deploring this, saying it
is evil. We do not know if it is evil, but we know it is a
fact. The conclusion is that we must come to terms with
it. All we need know, then, is what we want. And what we
want precisely is never again to bow beneath the sword,
never again to count force as being in the right unless it
is serving the mind.

The task is endless, it's true. But we are here to
pursue it. I do not have enough faith in reason to sub-
scribe to a belief in progress or to any philosophy of
history. I do believe at least that man's awareness of his
destiny has never ceased to advance. We have not overcome our condition, and yet we know it better. We know
that we live in contradiction, but we also know that we
must refuse this contradiction and do what is needed to
reduce it. Our task as men is to find the few principles
that will calm the infinite anguish of free souls. We must
mend what has been torn apart, make justice imaginable
again in a world so obviously unjust, give happiness a
meaning once more to peoples poisoned by the misery of
the century. Naturally, it is a superhuman task. But superhuman is the term for tasks men take a long time to
accomplish, that's all.

Let us know our aims then, holding fast to the
mind, even if force puts on a thoughtful or a comfortable
face in order to seduce us. The first thing is not to despair. Let us not listen too much to those who proclaim
that the world is at an end. Civilizations do not die so
easily, and even if our world were to collapse, it would

not have been the first. It is indeed true that we live in tragic times. But too many people confuse tragedy with despair. "Tragedy," Lawrence said, "ought to be a great kick at misery." [2] This is a healthy and immediately applicable thought. There are many things today deserving such a kick.

When I lived in Algiers, I would wait patiently all winter because I knew that in the course of one night, one cold, pure February night, the almond trees of the Vallée des Consuls would be covered with white flowers. I would marvel then at the sight of this fragile snow resisting the rains and the wind from the sea. Yet every year it lasted just long enough to prepare the fruit.

There is no symbol here. We will not win our happiness with symbols. We'll need something more solid. I mean only that sometimes, when life weighs too heavily today in a Europe still full of misery, I turn toward those shining lands where so much strength is still intact. I know them too well not to realize that they are the chosen land where courage and contemplation can live in harmony. Thinking of them teaches me that if we are to save the mind we must ignore its gloomy virtues and celebrate its strength and wonder. Our world is poisoned by its misery, and seems to wallow in it. It has utterly surrendered to that evil which Nietzsche called the spirit of heaviness. Let us not add to this. It is futile to weep over the mind, it is enough to labor for it.

[2] *The quotation from D. H. Lawrence is taken from a letter written to A. W. McLeod on October 6, 1912: "I hate Bennett's resignation. Tragedy ought to be like a great kick at misfortune." Camus first noted it down in* Carnets I, *p. 183, in 1939; Alfred A. Knopf edition, p. 153.*

A first version of this text appeared in La Tunisie Française *on January 25, 1941.* —P.T.

But where are the conquering virtues of the mind? The same Nietzsche listed them as mortal enemies to heaviness of the spirit. For him, they are strength of character, taste, the "world," classical happiness, severe pride, the cold frugality of the wise. More than ever, these virtues are necessary today, and each of us can choose the one that suits him best. Before the vastness of the undertaking, let no one forget strength of character. I don't mean the theatrical kind on political platforms, complete with frowns and threatening gestures. But the kind that through the virtue of its purity and its sap, stands up to all the winds that blow in from the sea. Such is the strength of character that in the winter of the world will prepare the fruit.

1940

Prometheus in the Underworld[1]

I felt the Gods were lacking
as long as there was nothing to oppose them.

Lucian, *Prometheus in the Caucasus*

WHAT DOES Prometheus mean to man today? One could doubtless claim this God-defying rebel as the model of contemporary man and his protest thousands of years ago in the deserts of Scythia as culminating in the unparalleled historical convulsion of our day. But, at the same time, something suggests that this victim of persecution is still among us and that we are still deaf to the great cry of human revolt of which he gives the solitary signal.

Modern man indeed endures a multitude of suffering on the narrow surface of this earth; for the man deprived of food and warmth, liberty is merely a luxury that can wait; all he can do is suffer a little more, as if it were only a question of letting liberty and its last witnesses vanish a bit more. Prometheus was the hero who loved men enough to give them fire and liberty, technol-

---

[1] *This essay was first published in 1947 by Palimugre, in Paris.*

ogy and art. Today, mankind needs and cares only for technology. We rebel through our machines, holding art and what art implies as an obstacle and a symbol of slavery. But what characterizes Prometheus is that he cannot separate machines from art. He believes that both souls and bodies can be freed at the same time. Man today believes that we must first of all free the body, even if the mind must suffer temporary death. But can the mind die temporarily? Indeed, if Prometheus were to reappear, modern man would treat him as the gods did long ago: they would nail him to a rock, in the name of the very humanism he was the first to symbolize. The hostile voices to insult the defeated victim would be the very ones that echo on the threshold of Aeschylean tragedy: those of Force and Violence.

Am I yielding to the meanness of our times, to naked trees and the winter of the world? But this very nostalgia for light is my justification: it speaks to me of another world, of my true homeland. Does this nostalgia still mean something to some men? The year the war began, I was to board a ship and follow the voyage of Ulysses. At that time, even a young man without money could entertain the extravagant notion of crossing the sea in quest of sunlight. But I did what everyone else did at the time. I did not get on that ship. I took my place in the queue shuffling toward the open mouth of hell. Little by little, we entered. At the first cry of murdered innocence, the door slammed shut behind us. We were in hell, and we have not left it since. For six long years we have been trying to come to terms with it. Now we glimpse the warm ghosts of fortunate islands only at the end of long, cold, sunless years that lie ahead.

How then, in this damp, dark Europe, can we avoid hearing with a quiver of regret and difficult complicity the cry the aged Chateaubriand uttered to Ampère departing for Greece: "You won't find a leaf from the olive trees or a single grape left of the ones I saw in Attica. I even miss the grass that grew there in my day. I haven't had the strength to make a patch of heather grow." [2] And we too, for all our youthful blood, sunk as we are in the terrible old age of this last century, sometimes miss the grass that has always grown, the olive leaf that we'll no longer go to look at just to see it, and the grapes of liberty. Man is everywhere, and everywhere we find his cries, his suffering, and his threats. With so many men gathered together, there is no room for grasshoppers. History is a sterile earth where heather does not grow. Yet men today have chosen history, and they neither could nor should turn away from it. But instead of mastering it, they agree a little more each day to be its slave. Thus they betray Prometheus, this son "both bold in thought and light of heart." This is how they revert to the wretchedness of the men Prometheus tried to save. "They saw without seeing, heard without listening, like figures in a dream."

Yes, one evening in Provence, one perfect hill, one whiff of salt are enough to show us that everything still lies before us. We need to invent fire once more, to settle down once again to the job of appeasing the body's hunger. Attica, liberty, and its grape-gathering, the bread of the soul, must come later. What can we do about this but cry to ourselves: "They will never exist any more, or they will exist for others," and do what must be done so that others at least do not go begging? We who feel this so painfully, and yet who try to accept it without bitter-

[2]*Camus first noted down this quotation from Chateaubriand in July 1945. See* Carnets II, *p. 136; Alfred A. Knopf edition, p. 104.* —P.T.

ness, are we lagging behind, or are we forging ahead, and will we have the strength to make the heather grow again?

We can imagine how Prometheus would have replied to this question that rises from our century. Indeed, he has already given his answer: "I promise you, O mortals, both improvement and repair, if you are skillful, virtuous and strong enough to achieve them with your own hands." If, then, it is true that salvation lies in our own hands, I will answer Yes to the question of the century, because of the thoughtful strength and the intelligent courage I still feel in some of the people I know. "O Justice, O my mother," cries Prometheus, "you see what I am made to suffer." And Hermes mocks the hero: "I am amazed that, being a God, you did not foresee the torment you are suffering." "I did see it," replies the rebel. The men I've mentioned are also the sons of justice. They, too, suffer from the misery of all men, knowing what they do. They know all too well that blind justice does not exist, that history has no eyes, and that we must therefore reject its justice in order to replace it as much as possible with the justice conceived by the mind. This is how Prometheus returns in our century.

Myths have no life of their own. They wait for us to give them flesh. If one man in the world answers their call, they give us their strength in all its fullness. We must preserve this myth, and ensure that its slumber is not mortal so that its resurrection is possible. I sometimes doubt whether men can be saved today. But it is still possible to save their children, both body and mind. It is possible to offer them at the same time the chance for happiness and beauty. If we must resign ourselves to living without beauty, and the freedom that is a part of beauty, the myth of Prometheus is one of those that will remind us that any mutilation of man can only be temporary, and that one serves nothing in man if one does not serve the whole man. If he is hungry for bread and heather, and if it is true that bread is the more necessary, let us learn how to keep the memory of heather alive. At the darkest heart of history, Promethean men, without flinching from their difficult calling, will keep watch over the earth and the tireless grass. In the thunder and lightning of the gods, the chained hero keeps his quiet faith in man. This is how he is harder than his rock and more patient than his vulture. His long stubbornness has more meaning for us than his revolt against the gods. Along with his admirable determination to separate and exclude nothing, which always has and always will reconcile mankind's suffering with the springtimes of the world.

1946

A Short Guide to Towns Without a Past

✸✸ ✸✸✸ ✸✸

THE SOFTNESS of Algiers is rather Italian. The cruel glare of Oran has something Spanish about it. Constantine, perched high on a rock above the Rummel Gorges, is reminiscent of Toledo. But Spain and Italy overflow with memories, with works of art and exemplary ruins. Toledo has had its El Greco and its Barrès. The cities I speak of, on the other hand, are towns without a past. Thus they are without tenderness or abandon. During the boredom of the siesta hours, their sadness is implacable and has no melancholy. In the morning light, or in the natural luxury of the evenings, their delights are equally ungentle. These towns give nothing to the mind and everything to the passions. They are suited neither to wisdom nor to the delicacies of taste. A Barrès or anyone like him would be completely pulverized.

Travelers with a passion for other people's passions, oversensitive souls, aesthetes, and newlyweds have nothing to gain from going to Algiers. And, unless he had a divine call, a man would be ill-advised to retire and live there forever. Sometimes, in Paris, when people I respect ask me about Algeria, I feel like crying out: "Don't go there." Such joking has some truth in it. For I can see what they are expecting and know they will not find it. And, at the same time, I know the attractions and the subtle power of this country, its insinuating hold on those who linger, how it immobilizes them first by ridding them of questions and finally by lulling them to sleep with its everyday life. At first the revelation of the light, so glaring that everything turns black and white, is almost suffocating. One gives way to it, settles down in it, and then realizes that this protracted splendor gives nothing to the soul and is merely an excessive delight. Then one would like to return to the mind. But the men of this country— and this is their strength—seem to have more heart than mind. They can be your friends (and what friends!), but you can never tell them your secrets. This might be considered dangerous here in Paris, where souls are poured out so extravagantly and where the water of secrets flows softly and endlessly along among the fountains, the statues, and the gardens.

This land most resembles Spain. With no traditions Spain would be merely a beautiful desert. And unless one happens to have been born there, there is only one race of men who can dream of withdrawing forever to the desert. Having been born in this desert, I can hardly think of describing it as a visitor. Can one catalogue the charms of a woman one loves dearly? No, one loves her all of a piece, if I may use the expression, with one or two precise reasons for tenderness, like a favorite pout or a particular way of shaking the head. Such is my long-standing liaison with Algeria, one that will doubtless never end and that keeps me from being completely lucid. All anyone can do in such a case is to persevere and make a kind of abstract list of what he loves in the thing he loves. This is the kind of academic exercise I can attempt here on the subject of Algeria.

First there is the beauty of the young people. The Arabs, of course, and then the others. The French of Algeria are a bastard race, made up of unexpected mixtures. Spaniards and Alsatians, Italians, Maltese, Jews, and Greeks have met here. As in America, such raw intermingling has had happy results. As you walk through Algiers, look at the wrists of the women and the young men, and then think of the ones you see in the Paris *métro*.

The traveler who is still young will also notice that the women are beautiful. The best place in Algiers to appreciate this is the terrace of the Café des Facultés, in the rue Michelet, on a Sunday morning in April. Groups of young women in sandals and light, brightly colored dresses walk up and down the street. You can admire them without inhibitions: that is what they come for. The Cintra bar, on the boulevard Galliéni in Oran, is also a good observatory. In Constantine, you can always stroll around the bandstand. But since the sea is several hundred kilometers away, there is something missing in the people you meet there. In general, and because of this geographical location, Constantine offers fewer attractions, although the quality of its ennui is rather more delicate.

If the traveler arrives in summer, the first thing to do, obviously, is to go down to the beaches surrounding the towns. He will see the same young people, more dazzling because less clothed. The sun gives them the somnolent eyes of great beasts. In this respect, the beaches of Oran are the finest, for both nature and women are wilder there.

As for the picturesque, Algiers offers an Arab

town, Oran a Negro village and a Spanish district, and Constantine a Jewish quarter. Algiers has a long necklace of boulevards along the sea; you must walk there at night. Oran has few trees, but the most beautiful stone in the world. Constantine has a suspension bridge where the thing to do is have your photograph taken. On very windy days, the bridge sways to and fro above the deep gorges of the Rummel, and you have the feeling of danger.

I recommend that the sensitive traveler, if he goes to Algiers, drink *anisette* under the archways around the harbor, go to La Pêcherie in the morning and eat freshly caught fish grilled on charcoal stoves; listen to Arab music in a little café on the rue de la Lyre whose name I've forgotten; sit on the ground, at six in the evening, at the foot of the statue of the duc d'Orléans, in Government Square (not for the sake of the duke, but because there are people walking by, and it's pleasant there); have lunch at Padovani's, which is a kind of dance hall on stilts along the seashore, where the life is always easy; visit the Arab cemeteries, first to find calm and beauty there, then to appreciate at their true value the ignoble cities where we stack our dead; go and smoke a cigarette in the Casbah on the rue de Bouchers, in the midst of spleens, livers, lungs, and intestines that drip blood on everything (the cigarette is necessary, these medieval practices have a strong smell).

As to the rest, you must be able to speak ill of Algiers when in Oran (insist on the commercial superiority of Oran's harbor), make fun of Oran when in Algiers (don't hesitate to accept the notion that Oranians "don't know how to live"), and, at every opportunity, humbly acknowledge the surpassing merit of Algiers in comparison to metropolitan France. Once these concessions have

146

been made, you will be able to appreciate the real superiority of the Algerian over the Frenchman—that is to say, his limitless generosity and his natural hospitality.

And now perhaps I can stop being ironic. After all, the best way to speak of what one loves is to speak of it lightly. When Algeria is concerned, I am always afraid to pluck the inner cord it touches in me, whose blind and serious song I know so well. But at least I can say that it is my true country, and that anywhere in the world I recognize its sons and my brothers by the friendly laughter that fills me at the sight of them. Yes, what I love about the cities of Algeria is not separate from their inhabitants. That is why I like it best there in the evening when the shops and offices pour into the still, dim streets a chattering crowd that runs right up to the boulevards facing the sea and starts to grow silent there, as night falls and the lights from the sky, from the lighthouses in the bay, and from the streetlamps merge together little by little into a single flickering glow. A whole people stands meditating on the seashore then, a thousand solitudes springing up from the crowd. Then the vast African nights begin, the royal exile, and the celebration of despair that awaits the solitary traveler.

No, you must certainly not go there if you have a lukewarm heart or if your soul is weak and weary! But for those who know what it is to be torn between yes and no, between noon and midnight, between revolt and love, and for those who love funeral pyres along the shore, a flame lies waiting in Algeria.

1947

Helen's Exile[1]

✴✴ ✴✴✴ ✴✴

THE MEDITERRANEAN has a solar tragedy that has nothing to do with mists. There are evenings, at the foot of
mountains by the sea, when night falls on the perfect
curve of a little bay and an anguished fullness rises from
the silent waters. Such moments make one realize that if
the Greeks knew despair, they experienced it always
through beauty and its oppressive quality. In this golden
sadness, tragedy reaches its highest point. But the despair of our world—quite the opposite—has fed on ugliness and upheavals. That is why Europe would be ignoble
if suffering ever could be.

We have exiled beauty; the Greeks took arms for
it. A basic difference—but one that goes far back. Greek
thought was always based on the idea of limits. Nothing

[1] *This text, written in August 1948 and originally dedicated to the poet René Char, one of Camus's close personal
friends, first appeared in the* Cahiers du Sud *in 1948. The ideas
that it expresses form the basis for many of the political and
philosophical arguments developed in* L'Homme révolté (The
Rebel) *in 1951.* —P.T.

148

was carried to extremes, neither religion nor reason, because Greek thought denied nothing, neither reason nor religion. It gave everything its share, balancing light with shade. But the Europe we know, eager for the conquest of totality, is the daughter of excess. We deny beauty, as we deny everything that we do not extol. And, even though we do it in diverse ways, we extol one thing and one alone: a future world in which reason will reign supreme. In our madness, we push back the eternal limits, and at once dark Furies swoop down upon us to destroy. Nemesis, goddess of moderation, not of vengeance, is watching. She chastises, ruthlessly, all those who go beyond the limit.

The Greeks, who spent centuries asking themselves what was just, would understand nothing of our idea of justice. Equity, for them, supposed a limit, while our whole continent is convulsed by the quest for a justice we see as absolute. At the dawn of Greek thought, Heraclitus already conceived justice as setting limits even upon the physical universe itself: "The sun will not go beyond its bounds, for otherwise the Furies who watch over justice will find it out." We, who have thrown both universe and mind out of orbit, find such threats amusing. In a drunken sky we ignite the suns that suit us. But limits nonetheless exist and we know it. In our wildest madness we dream of an equilibrium we have lost, and which in our simplicity we think we shall discover once again when our errors cease—an infantile presumption, which justifies the fact that childish peoples, inheriting our madness, are managing our history today.

A fragment attributed to the same Heraclitus states simply: "Presumption, regression of progress." And centuries after the Ephesian, Socrates, threatened by the death penalty, granted himself no superiority other than this: he did not presume to know what he did not know. The most exemplary life and thought of these centuries ends with a proud acknowledgment of ignorance. In forgetting this we have forgotten our virility. We have preferred the power that apes greatness—Alexander first of all, and then the Roman conquerors, whom our school history books, in an incomparable vulgarity of soul, teach us to admire. We have conquered in our turn, have set aside the bounds, mastered heaven and earth. Our reason has swept everything away. Alone at last, we build our empire upon a desert. How then could we conceive that higher balance in which nature balanced history, beauty, and goodness, and which brought the music of numbers even into the tragedy of blood? We turn our back on nature, we are ashamed of beauty. Our miserable tragedies have the smell of an office, and their blood is the color of dirty ink.

That is why it is indecent to proclaim today that we are the sons of Greece. Or, if we are, we are sons turned renegade. Putting history on the throne of God, we are marching toward theocracy, like those the Greeks called barbarians, whom they fought to the death in the waters of Salamis. If we really want to grasp the difference, we must look to the one man among our philosophers who is the true rival of Plato. "Only the modern city" Hegel dares to write, "offers the mind the grounds on which it can achieve awareness of itself." We live in the time of great cities. The world has been deliberately cut off from what gives it permanence: nature, the sea, hills, evening meditations. There is no consciousness any more except in the streets because there is history only in the streets, so runs the decree. And, consequently, our most significant works demonstrate the same prejudice. One looks in vain for landscapes in the major European writers since Dostoevski. History explains neither the natural universe which came before it, nor beauty which stands above it. Consequently it has chosen to ignore them. Whereas Plato incorporated everything—nonsense, reason, and myths—our philosophers admit nothing but nonsense or reason, because they have closed their eyes to the rest. The mole is meditating.

It was Christianity that began to replace the contemplation of the world with the tragedy of the soul. But Christianity at least referred to a spiritual nature, and therefore maintained a certain fixity. Now that God is dead, all that remains are history and power. For a long time now, the whole effort of our philosophers has been solely to replace the idea of human nature with the idea of situation and ancient harmony with the disorderly outbursts of chance or the pitiless movement of reason. While the Greeks used reason to restrain the will, we have ended by placing the impulse of the will at the heart of reason, and reason has therefore become murderous. For the Greeks, values existed a priori and marked out the exact limits of every action. Modern philosophy places its values at the completion of action. They are not, but they become, and we shall know them completely only at the end of history. When they disappear, limits vanish as well, and since ideas differ as to what these values will be, since there is no struggle which, unhindered by these same values, does not extend indefinitely, we are now witnessing the Messianic forces confronting one another, their clamors merging in the shock of empires. Excess is a fire, according to Heraclitus. The fire is gaining ground; Nietzsche has been overtaken. It is no longer with hammer blows but with cannon shots that Europe philosophizes.

Nature is still there, nevertheless. Her calm skies

and her reason oppose the folly of men. Until the atom too bursts into flame, and history ends in the triumph of reason and the death agony of the species. But the Greeks never said that the limit could not be crossed. They said it existed and that the man who dared ignore it was mercilessly struck down. Nothing in today's history can contradict them.

Both the historical mind and the artist seek to remake the world. But the artist, through an obligation of his very nature, recognizes limits the historical mind ignores. This is why the latter aims at tyranny while the passion of the artist is liberty. All those who struggle today for liberty are in the final analysis fighting for beauty. Of course, no one thinks of defending beauty solely for its own sake. Beauty cannot do without man, and we shall give our time its greatness and serenity only by sharing in its misery. We shall never again stand alone. But it is equally true that man cannot do without beauty, and this is what our time seems to want to forget. We tense ourselves to achieve empires and the absolute, seek to transfigure the world before having exhausted it, to set it to rights before having understood it. Whatever we may say, we are turning our backs on this world. Ulysses, on Calypso's island, is given the choice between immortality and the land of his fathers. He chooses this earth, and death with it. Such simple greatness is foreign to our minds today. Others will say that we lack humility, but the word, all things considered, is ambiguous. Like Dostoevski's buffoons who boast of everything, rise up to the stars and end by flaunting their shame in the first public place, we simply lack the pride of the man who is faithful to his limitations—that is, the clairvoyant love of his human condition.

"I hate my time," wrote Saint-Exupéry before his

death, for reasons that are not far removed from those I have mentioned. But, however overwhelming his cry may be, coming from someone who loved men for their admirable qualities, we shall not take it as our own. Yet what a temptation, at certain times, to turn our backs on this gaunt and gloomy world. But this is our time and we cannot live hating ourselves. It has fallen so low as much from the excess of its virtues as from the greatness of its faults. We shall fight for the one among its virtues that has ancient roots. Which virtue? Patroclus's horses weep for their master, dead in battle. All is lost. But Achilles takes up the battle and victory comes at the end because friendship has been murdered: friendship is a virtue.

It is by acknowledging our ignorance, refusing to be fanatics, recognizing the world's limits and man's, through the faces of those we love, in short, by means of beauty—this is how we may rejoin the Greeks. In a way, the meaning of tomorrow's history is not what people think. It is in the struggle between creation and the inquisition. Whatever the price artists will have to pay for their empty hands, we can hope for their victory. Once again, the philosophy of darkness will dissolve above the dazzling sea. Oh, noonday thought, the Trojan war is fought far from the battleground! Once again, the terrible walls of the modern city will fall, to deliver Helen's beauty, "its soul serene as the untroubled waves."

1948

The Enigma[1]

✿✿ ✿✿✿ ✿✿

WAVES of sunlight, pouring from the topmost sky, bounce
fiercely on the countryside around us. Everythings grows
quiet beneath its force, and Mount Luberon, over there, is

[1] *This essay, composed in 1950, was also dedicated to
René Char. As it shows, Camus suffered a great deal from the
failure of French critics and journalists to realize that his attitude was constantly evolving, and that* L'Etranger (The
Stranger) *and* Le Mythe de Sisyphe (The Myth of Sisyphus) *did
not necessarily contain all his ideas. Later on, even before the
publication of* L'Homme révolté (The Rebel) *had led to violent
public quarrels with André Breton in 1951 and Jean-Paul Sartre
in 1952, Camus's pessimism about his relationship with his public
and his literary colleagues became even more marked. Thus, on
page 321 of* Carnets II *(Alfred A. Knopf edition, p. 252) he
noted that "Paris begins by serving a work of art and pushes it.
But once it is established, then the fun begins. It is essential to
destroy it. Thus there are, in Paris, as in certain streams in Bra-
zil, thousands of little fish whose job this is. They are tiny, but
innumerable. Their whole head, if I may say so, is in their teeth.
And they completely remove the flesh from a man in five minutes,
leaving nothing but the bare bones. They then go away, sleep a
little, and begin again." —*P.T.

154

merely a vast block of silence that I listen to unceasingly. I listen carefully, someone is running toward me in the distance, invisible friends call to me, my joy grows, just as years ago. Once again, a happy enigma helps me to understand everything.

Where is the absurdity of the world? Is it this resplendent glow or the memory of its absence? With so much sun in my memory, how could I have wagered on nonsense? People around me are amazed; so am I, at times. I could tell them, as I tell myself, that it was in fact the sun that helped me, and that the very thickness of its light coagulates the universe and its forms into a dazzling darkness. But there are other ways of saying this, and I should like, faced with the white and black clarity that, for me, has always been the sign of truth, to explain in simple terms what I feel about this absurdity which I know too well to allow anyone to hold forth on it without making certain nuances. The very fact of talking about it, after all, will lead us back to the sun.

No man can say what he is. But sometimes he can say what he is not. Everyone wants the man who is still searching to have already reached his conclusions. A thousand voices are already telling him what he has found, and yet he knows that he hasn't found anything. Should he search on and let them talk? Of course. But, from time to time, one must defend himself. I do not know what I am looking for, cautiously I give it a name, I withdraw what I said, I repeat myself, I go backward and forward. Yet people insist I identify my term or terms, once and for all. Then I object; when things have a label aren't they lost already? Here, at least, is what I can try to say.

If I am to believe one of my friends, a man always has two characters: his own, and the one his wife thinks he has. Substitute society for wife and we shall understand how a particular expression, used by a writer to describe a whole context of emotions, can be isolated by the way people comment on it and laid before its author every time he tries to talk about something else. Words are like actions: "Are you the father of this child?" "Yes." "Then he is your son." "It is not as simple as that, not at all!" Thus Gerard de Nerval, one filthy night, hanged himself twice, once for himself because he was unhappy, and a second time for his legend, which now helps some people to live. No one can write about real unhappiness, or about certain moments of happiness, and I shall not try to do so here. But, as far as legends are concerned, we can describe them, and, for a moment at least, believe that we have dispelled them.

A writer writes to a great extent to be read (let's admire those who say they don't, but not believe them). Yet more and more, in France, he writes in order to obtain that final consecration which consists of not being read. In fact, from the moment he can provide the material for a feature article in the popular press, there is every possibility that he will be known to a fairly large number of people who will never read his works because they will be content to know his name and to read what other people write about him. From that point on he will be known (and forgotten) not for what he is, but according to the image a hurried journalist has given of him. To make a name in literature, therefore, it is no longer indispensable to write books. It is enough to be thought of as having written one which the evening papers will have mentioned and which one can fall back on for the rest of one's life.

There is no doubt that such a reputation, great or small, will be undeserved. But what can be done about it?

Let us rather admit that the inconvenience may also be beneficial. Doctors know that certain illnesses are desirable: they compensate, in some way, for a functional disorder which, without them, might express itself in some more serious disturbance. Thus there are fortunate constipations and providential attacks of arthritis. The flood of words and hasty judgments, which nowadays drowns all public activity in an ocean of frivolity, at least endows the French writer with a modesty he constantly needs in a nation that, furthermore, gives a disproportionate importance to his calling. To see one's name in two or three newspapers I could mention is so harsh a trial that it must inevitably involve some spiritual benefit. Praise be, then, to a society that teaches us so cheaply, every day, by its very homage, that the greatness it honors is worthless. The louder its noise, the quicker it dies. It evokes the flaxen fires Alexander VI often had burned before him to remind him that the glory of this world vanishes like smoke.

But let's leave irony aside. It is enough to say that an artist must resign himself good humoredly and allow what he knows is an undeserved image of himself to lie about in dentists' waiting rooms and at the hairdresser's. I know a fashionable writer who, according to such sources, supposedly spent every night presiding over Bacchanalian orgies, where nymphs were clothed in nothing but their hair and fauns had gloomy fingernails. One might have wondered how he found the time to write a series of books that fill several library shelves. Like most of his colleagues, this writer actually spends his nights sleeping in order to spend long hours every day at his desk, and drinks Vichy water so as not to strain his liver. This does not prevent the average Frenchman, whose Saharan sobriety and mania for cleanliness are well known, from growing indignant at the idea of our writers teaching people to drink and not to wash. There is no dearth of examples. I personally can furnish an excellent cheap recipe for securing a reputation for austerity. I actually have so weighty a reputation, a source of great amusement to my friends (as far as I'm concerned, it rather makes me blush, since I know how little I deserve it). It's enough, for instance, to decline the honor of dining with a newspaper editor of whom you do not have a high opinion. Even simple decency cannot be imagined except by reference to some twisted sickness of the soul. No one will ever imagine that if you refuse this editor's dinner, it may be not only because you haven't a very high opinion of him, but also because your greatest fear in the world is being bored—and what is more boring than a typical Parisian dinner?

One must therefore submit. But, from time to time, you can try to readjust the sights, and repeat that you can't always be a painter of the absurd and that no one can believe in a literature of despair. Of course, it is always possible to write, or to have written, an essay on the notion of the absurd. But after all, you can also write about incest without necessarily having hurled yourself on your unfortunate sister, and I have nowhere read that Sophocles ever thought of killing his father and dishonoring his mother. The idea that every writer necessarily writes about himself and depicts himself in his books is one of the puerile notions that we have inherited from Romanticism. It is by no means impossible—quite the opposite—that a writer should be interested first and foremost in other people, or in his time, or in well-known myths. Even if he does happen to put himself on stage, it is only very exceptionally that he talks about what he is really like. A man's works often retrace the story of his nostalgias or his temptations, practically never his own history especially when they claim to be autobiographical. No man has ever dared describe himself as he is.

On the other hand, as far as such a thing is possible, I should like to have been an objective writer. What I call an objective author is one who chooses themes without ever taking himself as the subject. But the modern mania of identifying the author with his subject matter will not allow him this relative creative liberty. Thus does one become a prophet of the absurd. Yet what else have I done except reason about an idea I discovered in the streets of my time? That I have nourished this idea (and part of me nourishes it still) along with my whole generation goes without saying. I simply set it far enough away so that I could deal with it and decide on its logic. Everything that I've been able to write since shows this plainly enough. But it is more convenient to exploit a cliché than a nuance. They've chosen the cliché: so I'm as absurd as ever.

What is the point of saying yet again that in the experience which interested me, and which I happened to write about, the absurd can be considered only as a point of departure—even though the memory and feeling of it still accompany the farther advances. In the same manner, with all due sense of proportion, Cartesian doubt, which is systematic, was not enough to make Descartes a skeptic. In any case, how can one limit oneself to saying that nothing has meaning and that we must plunge into absolute despair? Without getting to the bottom of things, one can at least mention that just as there is no absolute materialism, since merely to form this word is already to acknowledge something in the world apart from matter, there is likewise no total nihilism. The moment you say that everything is nonsense you express something meaningful. Refusing the world all meaning amounts to abolishing all value judgments. But living, and eating, for example, are in themselves value judgments. You choose to remain alive the moment you do not allow yourself to die of hunger, and consequently you recognize that life has at least a relative value. What, in fact, does "literature of despair" mean? Despair is silent. Even silence, moreover, is meaningful if your eyes speak. True despair is the agony of death, the grave or the abyss. If he speaks, if he reasons, above all if he writes, immediately the brother reaches out his hand, the tree is justified, love is born. Literature of despair is a contradiction in terms.

Of course, a certain optimism is not my speciality. Like all men of my age, I grew up to the sound of the drums of the First World War, and our history since that time has remained murder, injustice, or violence. But real pessimism, which does exist, lies in outbidding all this cruelty and shame. For my part, I have never ceased fighting against this dishonor, and I hate only the cruel. I have sought only reasons to transcend our darkest nihilism. Not, I would add, through virtue, nor because of some rare elevation of the spirit, but from an instinctive fidelity to a light in which I was born, and in which for thousands of years men have learned to welcome life even in suffering. Aeschylus is often heartbreaking; yet he radiates light and warmth. At the center of his universe, we find not fleshless nonsense but an enigma, that is to say, a meaning which is difficult to decipher because it dazzles us. Likewise, to the unworthy but nonetheless stubborn sons of Greece who still survive in this emaciated century, the scorching heat of our history may seem unendurable, but they endure it in the last analysis because they want to understand it. In the center of our work, dark though it may be, shines an inexhaustible sun, the same sun that shouts today across the hills and plain.

After this, the flaxen fire can burn; who cares what we appear to be and what we usurp? What we are, what we have to be, are enough to fill our lives and occupy our strength. Paris is a wondrous cave, and its inhabitants, seeing their own shadows reflected on the far wall, take them for the only reality there is. The same is true of the strange, fleeting renown this town dispenses. But we have learned, far from Paris, that there is a light behind us, that we must turn around and cast off our chains in order to face it directly, and that our task before we die is to seek through any words to identify it. Every artist is undoubtedly pursuing his truth. If he is a great artist, each work brings him nearer to it, or, at least, swings still closer toward this center, this buried sun where everything must one day burn. If he is mediocre, each work takes him further from it, the center is then everywhere, the light disintegrates. But the only people who can help the artist in his obstinate quest are those who love him, and those who, themselves lovers or creators, find in their own passion the measure of all passion, and hence know how to criticize.

Yes, all this noise . . . when peace would be to love and create in silence! But we must learn to be patient. One moment more, the sun seals our mouths.

1950

Return to Tipasa

❦❦ ❦❦❦ ❦❦

You sailed away from your father's dwelling
With your heart on fire, Medea! And you passed
Between the rocky gates of the seas;
And now you sleep on a foreign shore.

Medea

FOR FIVE DAYS the rain had been falling unceasingly on
Algiers, finally drenching the sea itself. From the heights
of an apparently inexhaustible sky, unending sheets of
rain, so thick they were viscous, crashed into the gulf.
Soft and gray like a great sponge, the sea heaved in the
shapeless bay. But the surface of the water seemed almost motionless beneath the steady rain. At long intervals, however, a broad and imperceptible movement
raised a murky cloud of steam from the sea and rolled it
into the harbor, below a circle of soaking boulevards. The
town itself, its white walls running with damp, gave off
another cloud of steam that billowed out to meet the first.
Whichever way you turned you seemed to be breathing
water, you could drink the very air.

Looking at this drowned sea, seeing in December

an Algiers that was still for me the city of summers, I walked about and waited. I had fled from the night of Europe, from a winter of faces. But even the town of summers was emptied of its laughter, offering me only hunched and streaming backs. In the evening, in the fiercely lit cafés where I sought refuge, I read my age on faces I recognized without knowing their names. All I knew was that these men had been young when I was, and that now they were young no longer.

I stayed on, though, without any clear idea of what I was waiting for, except, perhaps, the moment when I could go back to Tipasa. It is certainly a great folly, and one that is almost always punished, to go back to the places of one's youth, to want to relive at forty the things one loved or greatly enjoyed at twenty. But I was aware of this folly. I had already been back to Tipasa once, not long after those war years that marked for me the end of my youth. I hoped, I think, to rediscover there a liberty I was unable to forget. Here, more than twenty years ago, I had spent whole mornings wandering among the ruins, breathing the scent of absinthe, warming myself against the stones, discovering the tiny, short-lived roses that survive in springtime. Only at noon, when even the crickets are silenced by the heat, would I flee from the avid blaze of an all-consuming light. Sometimes, at night, I would sleep open-eyed beneath a sky flowing with stars. I was alive at those moments. Fifteen years later, I found my ruins again. A few steps from the first waves, I followed the streets of the forgotten city across the fields covered with bitter trees; and, on the hills overlooking the bay, could still caress their pillars, which were the color of bread. But now the ruins were surrounded by barbed wire, and could be reached only through official entrances. It was also forbidden, for reasons sanctioned, it would seem, by morality, to walk there after dark; by day, one would meet an official guard. That morning, doubtless by chance, it was raining across the whole sweep of the ruins.

Bewildered, walking through the lonely, rain-soaked countryside, I tried at least to recover the strength that has so far never failed me, that helps me to accept what is, once I have realized I cannot change it. I could not, of course, travel backward through time and restore to this world the face I had loved, which had disappeared in a single day a long time before. On the second of September, 1939, I did not go to Greece, as I had planned. Instead, the war enveloped us, then Greece itself. This distance, these years separating the warm ruins from the barbed wire, were also within me, as I stood that day staring at tombs filled with black water or beneath the dripping tamarisk trees. Raised above all in the spectacle of a beauty that was my only wealth, I had begun in plenty. The barbed wire came later—I mean tyrannies, war, policings, the time of revolt. We had had to come to terms with night: the beauty of daytime was only a memory. And in this muddy Tipasa, even the memory was growing dim. No room now for beauty, fullness, or youth! In the light cast by the flames, the world had suddenly shown its wrinkles and its afflictions, old and new. It had suddenly grown old, and we had too. I knew the ardor I had come in search of could only be roused in someone not expecting it. There is no love without a little innocence. Where was innocence? Empires were crumbling, men and nations were tearing at one another's throats; our mouths were dirtied. Innocent at first without knowing it, now we were unintentionally guilty: the more we knew, the greater the mystery. This is why we busied ourselves, oh mockery, with morality. Frail in spirit, I dreamed of virtue! In the days of innocence, I did not know morality existed. Now I knew it did, and could not live up to it. On the promontory I had loved in former days, between the drenched pillars of the ruined temple, I seemed to be walking behind someone whose footsteps I could still hear on the tombstones and mosaics, but whom I would never catch up with again. I went back to Paris, and stayed for some years before returning home again.

During all these years, however, I had a vague feeling of missing something. Once you have had the chance to love intensely, your life is spent in search of the same light and the same ardor. To give up beauty and the sensual happiness that comes with it and devote one's self exclusively to unhappiness requires a nobility I lack. But, after all, nothing is true that compels us to make it exclusive. Isolated beauty ends in grimaces, solitary justice in oppression. Anyone who seeks to serve the one to the exclusion of the other serves no one, not even himself, and in the end is doubly the servant of injustice. A day comes when, because we have been inflexible, nothing amazes us anymore, everything is known, and our life is spent in starting again. It is a time of exile, dry lives, dead souls. To come back to life, we need grace, a homeland, or to forget ourselves. On certain mornings, as we turn a corner, an exquisite dew falls on our heart and then vanishes. But the freshness lingers, and this, always, is what the heart needs. I had to come back once again.

And, in Algiers a second time, still walking under the same downpour that I felt had not stopped since what I thought was my final departure, in the midst of this immense melancholy smelling of rain and sea, in spite of the misty sky, the sight of people's backs fleeing beneath the deluge, the cafés whose sulphurous light decomposed everyone's face, I persisted in my hopes. Anyway, didn't I know that rain in Algiers, although it looks as if it would go on forever, nonetheless does stop suddenly, like the rivers in my country that swell to a flood in two hours, devastate acres of land, and dry up again in an instant? One evening, in fact, the rain stopped. I waited still one more night. A liquid morning rose, dazzling, over the pure sea. From the sky, fresh as a rose, washed and rewashed by the waters, reduced by each successive laundering to its most delicate and clearest texture, a quivering light fell, endowing each house, each tree, with a palpable shape and a magic newness. The earth must have risen in just such a light the morning the world was born. Once again I set out for Tipasa.

There is not a single one of these sixty-nine kilometers of highway that is not filled for me with memories and sensations. A violent childhood, adolescent daydreams to the hum of the bus's engines, mornings, the freshness of young girls, beaches, young muscles always tensed, the slight anguish that the evening brings to a sixteen-year-old heart, the desire to live, glory, and always the same sky, for months on end, with its inexhaustible strength and light, as companion to the years, a sky insatiable, one by one devouring victims lying crucified upon the beach at the funereal hour of noon. Always the same sea as well, almost impalpable in the morning air, glimpsed again on the horizon as soon as the road, leaving the Sahel and its hills with their bronze-colored vineyards, dipped down toward the coast. But I did not stop to look at it. I wanted to see the Chenoua again—that heavy, solid mountain, carved all in one piece and running along the west side of Tipasa Bay before descending into the sea. You see it from far away, long before you get

there, as a light blue haze still mingling with the sea. But
gradually it condenses as you come nearer, until it takes
on the color of the waters surrounding it, like an immense and motionless wave brutally caught in the very
act of breaking over a suddenly calm sea. Nearer still,
almost at the gates of Tipasa, you see its frowning mass,
brown and green, the old, unshakable, moss-covered god,
port and haven for its sons, of whom I am one. I was
gazing at it as I finally crossed the barbed wire and stood
among the ruins. And, in the glorious December light, as
happens only once or twice in lives that may later be
described as heaped with every blessing, I found exactly
what I had come in search of, something which in spite
of time and in spite of the world was offered to me and
truly to me alone, in this deserted nature. From the olive-
strewn forum, one could see the village down below. Not
a sound came from it; wisps of smoke rose in the limpid
air. The sea also lay silent, as if breathless beneath the
unending shower of cold, glittering light. From the Chenoua, a distant cock crow alone sang the fragile glory of
the day. Across the ruins, as far as one could see, there
were nothing but pitted stones and absinthe plants, trees
and perfect columns in the transparence of the crystal
air. It was as if the morning stood still, as if the sun had
stopped for an immeasurable moment. In this light and
silence, years of night and fury melted slowly away. I
listened to an almost forgotten sound within myself, as if
my heart had long been stopped and was now gently
beginning to beat again. And, now awake, I recognized
one by one the imperceptible sounds that made up the
silence: the *basso continuo* of the birds, the short, light
sighing of the sea at the foot of the rocks, the vibration of
the trees, the blind song of the columns, the whispering
of the absinthe plants, the furtive lizards. I heard all this,

and also felt the waves of happiness rising up within me. I felt that I had at last come back to harbor, for a moment at least, and that from now on this moment would never end. But soon afterward the sun rose visibly a degree higher in the sky. A blackbird chirped its brief prelude and immediately, from all around, bird voices exploded with a strength, a jubilation, a joyful discord, an infinite delight. The day moved on. It was to carry me through till evening.

At noon, on the half-sandy slopes, strewn with heliotropes like a foam that the furious waves of the last few days had left behind in their retreat, I gazed at the sea, gently rising and falling as if exhausted, and quenched two thirsts that cannot be long neglected if all one's being is not to dry up, the thirst to love and the thirst to admire. For there is only misfortune in not being loved; there is misery in not loving. All of us, today, are dying of this misery. This is because blood and hatred lay bare the heart itself; the long demand for justice exhausts even the love that gave it birth. In the clamor we live in, love is impossible and justice not enough. That is why Europe hates the daylight and can do nothing but confront one injustice with another. In order to prevent justice from shriveling up, from becoming nothing but a magnificent orange with a dry, bitter pulp, I discovered one must keep a freshness and a source of joy intact within, loving the daylight that injustice leaves unscathed, and returning to the fray with this light as a trophy. Here, once more, I found an ancient beauty, a young sky, and measured my good fortune as I realized at last that in the worst years of our madness the memory of this sky had never left me. It was this that in the end had saved me from despair. I had always known that the ruins of Tipasa were younger than our drydocks or our debris. In Tipasa, the world is born again each day in a light always new. Oh light! The cry of all the characters in classical tragedy who come face to face with their destinies. I knew now that their final refuge was also ours. In the depths of winter, I finally learned that within me there lay an invincible summer.

Once more I left Tipasa, returning to Europe and its struggles. But the memory of that day sustains me still and helps me meet both joy and sorrow with equanimity. In the difficult times we face, what more can I hope for than the power to exclude nothing and to learn to weave from strands of black and white one rope tautened to the breaking point? In everything I've done or said so far, I seem to recognize these two forces, even when they contradict each other. I have not been able to deny the light into which I was born and yet I have not wished to reject the responsibilities of our time. It would be too easy to set against the gentle name Tipasa other names more sonorous and more cruel: there is, for man today, an inner path that I know well from having traveled both ways upon it, which leads from the summits of the mind to the capitals of crime. And, doubtless, one can always rest, sleep on the hillside or settle into crime. But if we give up a part of what exists, we must ourselves give up being; we must then give up living or loving except by proxy. Thus there is a will to live without refusing anything life offers: the virtue I honor most in this world. From time to time, at least, it's true that I would like to have practiced it. Since few times require to the extent ours does that one be as equal to the best as to the worst, to avoid nothing and keep a double memory alive is precisely what I would like to do. Yes, there is beauty and there are the humiliated. Whatever difficulties the enterprise may present, I would like never to be unfaithful either to the one or the other.

But this still sounds like ethics, and we live for something that transcends ethics. If we could name it, what silence would follow! East of Tipasa, the hill of Sainte-Salsa, evening has come to life. It is still light, of course, but an invisible waning of the light announces the sunset. A wind rises, gentle as the night, and suddenly the untroubled sea chooses its way and flows like a great barren river across the horizon. The sky darkens. Then begins the mystery, the gods of night, and what lies beyond pleasure. But how can this be expressed? The little coin I carry back from here has one clear side, the face of a beautiful woman that reminds me of what I've learned in the course of this day, while the other side, which I feel beneath my fingers homeward bound, has been eaten away. What does this lipless mouth express if not what another, mysterious voice within me says, that daily teaches me my ignorance and my happiness:

> The secret I am looking for is buried in a valley of olive trees, beneath the grass and cold violets, around an old house that smells of vines. For more than twenty years I have wandered over this valley, and over others like it, questioning dumb goatherds, knocking at the door of empty ruins. Sometimes, when the first star shines in a still, clear sky, beneath a rain of delicate light, I have thought that I knew. I did know, in fact. Perhaps I still know. But no one is interested in this secret, doubtless I myself do not desire it, and I cannot cut myself off from my own people. I live with my family, who believe they reign over rich and hideous cities, built of stones and mists. Day and

night it raises its voice, and everything yields beneath it while it bows down to nothing: it is deaf to all secrets. Its power sustains me and yet bores me, and I come to be weary of its cries. But its unhappiness is my own, we are of the same blood. I too am sick, and am I not a noisy accomplice who has cried out among the stones? Thus I try to forget, I march through our cities of iron and fire, I smile bravely at the night, I welcome the storms, I will be faithful. In fact, I have forgotten: henceforth, I shall be deaf and active. But perhaps one day, when we are ready to die of ignorance and exhaustion, I shall be able to renounce our shrieking tombs, to go and lie down in the valley, under the unchanging light, and learn for one last time what I know.

1953

The Sea Close By[1]

❦❦ ❦❦❦ ❦❦

Logbook

I GREW UP *with the sea and poverty for me was sumptuous; then I lost the sea and found all luxuries gray and poverty unbearable. Since then, I have been waiting. I wait for the homebound ships, the house of the waters, the limpidity of day. I wait patiently, am polite with all my strength. I am seen walking by on fine, sophisticated streets, I admire landscapes, I applaud like everyone, shake hands, but it is not I who speak. Men praise me, I dream a little, they insult me, I scarcely show surprise. Then I forget, and smile at the man who insulted me, or am too courteous in greeting the person I love. Can I help it if all I remember is one image? Finally they summon me to tell them who I am. "Nothing yet, nothing yet . . ."*

[1] *This essay first appeared in the* Nouvelle Nouvelle Revue Française *in 1954. Camus first noted down his intention of writing an essay on the sea in* Carnets II, *p. 290, (Alfred A. Knopf edition, p. 228) when he remarked that "the desperate man has no native land. I knew that the sea existed, and that is why I lived in the midst of this mortal time." —*P.T.

I surpass myself at funerals. Truly, I excel. I walk slowly through the iron-strewn suburbs, taking the wide lanes planted with cement trees that lead to holes in the cold ground. There, beneath the slightly reddened bandage of the sky, I watch bold workmen inter my friends beneath six feet of earth. If I toss the flower a clay-covered hand holds out to me, it never misses the grave. My piety is exact, my feelings as they should be, my head suitably inclined. I am admired for finding just the right word. But I take no credit: I am waiting.

I have been waiting for a long time. Sometimes, I stumble, I lose my touch, success evades me. What does it matter, I am alone then. I wake up at night, and, still half asleep, think I hear the sound of waves, the breathing of waters. Fully awake, I recognize the wind in the trees and the sad murmur of the empty town. Afterward, all my art is not too much to hide my anguish or clothe it in the prevailing fashion.

At other times, it's the opposite, and I am helped. On certain days in New York, lost at the bottom of those stone and steel shafts where millions of men wander, I would run from one shaft to the next, without seeing where they ended, until, exhausted, I was sustained only by the human mass seeking its way out. But, each time, there was the distant honking of a tugboat to remind me that this empty well of a city was an island, and that off the tip of the Battery the water of my baptism lay in wait for me, black and rotting, covered with hollow corks.

Thus, I who own nothing, who have given away my fortune, who camp in all my houses, am still heaped, when I choose, with every blessing; I can set sail at any hour, a stranger to despair. There is no country for those who despair, but I know that the sea precedes and follows me, and I hold my madness ready. Those who love and are separated can live in grief, but this is not despair: they know that love exists. This is why I suffer, dry-eyed, in exile. I am still waiting. A day comes, at last . . .

The sailors' bare feet beat softly on the deck. We are setting sail at daybreak. The moment we leave the harbor a short, gusty wind vigorously brushes the sea, which curls backward in small, foamless waves. A little later, the wind freshens and strews the sea with swiftly vanishing camellias. Thus, throughout the morning, we hear our sails slapping above a cheerful pond. The waters are heavy, scaly, covered with cool froth. From time to time the waves lap against the bow; a bitter, unctuous foam, the gods' saliva, flows along the wood and loses itself in the water, where it scatters into shapes that die and are reborn, the hide of some white and blue cow, an exhausted beast that floats for a long time in our wake.

Ever since our departure, the seagulls have been following our ship, apparently without effort, almost without moving their wings. Their fine, straight navigation scarcely leans upon the breeze. Suddenly, a loud plop at the level of the kitchens stirs up a greedy alarm among the birds, throwing their fine flight into confusion and sending up a fire of white wings. The seagulls whirl madly in every direction and then with no loss of speed drop from the fight one by one and dive toward the sea. A few seconds later they are together again on the water, a quarrelsome farmyard that we leave behind, nesting in the hollow of the wave, slowly picking through the manna of the scraps.

At noon, under a deafening sun, the sea is so exhausted it scarcely finds the strength to rise. When it falls back on itself it makes the silence whistle. After an hour's cooking, the pale water, a vast white-hot iron sheet, sizzles. In a minute it will turn and offer its damp side, now hidden in waves and darkness, to the sun.

We pass the gates of Hercules, the headland where Antaeus died. Beyond, there is ocean everywhere; on one side we pass the Horn and the Cape of Good Hope, the meridians wed the latitudes, the Pacific drinks the Atlantic. At once, setting course for Vancouver, we sail slowly toward the South Seas. A few cable lengths away, Easter Island, Desolation, and the New Hebrides file past us in convoy. Suddenly, one morning, the seagulls disappear. We are far from any land, and alone, with our sails and our engines.

Alone also with the horizon. The waves come from the invisible East, patiently, one by one; they reach us, and then, patiently, set off again for the unknown West, one by one. A long voyage, with no beginning and no end . . . Rivers and streams pass by, the sea passes and remains. This is how one ought to love, faithful and fleeting. I wed the sea.

The high seas. The sun sinks and is swallowed by the fog long before it reaches the horizon. For a brief moment, the sea is pink on one side and blue on the other. Then the waters grow darker. The schooner slides, minute, over the surface of a perfect circle of thick, tarnished metal. And, at the most peaceful hour, as evening comes, hundreds of porpoises emerge from the water, frolic around us for a moment, then flee to the horizon where there are no men. With them gone, silence and the anguish of primitive waters are what remain.

. . .

A little later still, we meet an iceberg on the Tropic. Invisible, to be sure, after its long voyage in these warm waters, but still effective: it passes to starboard, where the rigging is briefly covered with a frosty dew, while to port the day dies without moisture.

Night does not fall at sea. It rises, rather, toward the still pale sky, from the depths of waters an already drowned sun gradually darkens with its thick ashes. For a brief moment, Venus shines alone above the black waves. In the twinkling of an eye, stars swarm in the liquid night.

The moon has risen. First it lights the water's surface gently, then climbs higher and inscribes itself in the supple water. At last, at its zenith, it lights a whole corridor of sea, a rich river of milk which, with the motion of the ship, streams down inexhaustibly toward us across the dark ocean. Here is the faithful night, the cool night I called for in the rollicking lights, the alcohol, the tumult of desire.

We sail across spaces so vast they seem unending. Sun and moon rise and fall in turn, on the same thread of light and night. Days at sea, as similar each to the other as happiness . . .

This life rebellious to forgetfulness, rebellious to memory, that Stevenson speaks of.

Dawn. We sail perpendicularly across the Tropic of Cancer, the waters groan and are convulsed. Day breaks over a surging sea, full of steel spangles. The sky is white with mist and heat, with a dead but unbearable glare, as if the sun had turned liquid in the thickness of the clouds, over the whole expanse of the celestial vault. A sick sky over a decomposing sea. As the day draws on, the heat grows in the white air. All day long, our bow noses out clouds of flying fish, tiny iron birds, forcing them from their hiding places in the waves.

In the afternoon, we meet a steamer bound for home. The salute our foghorns exchange with three great prehistoric hoots, the signals of passengers lost at sea warning there are other humans present, the gradually increasing distance between the two ships, their separation at last on the malevolent waters, all this fills the heart with pain. These stubborn madmen, clinging to planks tossed upon the mane of immense oceans, in pursuit of drifting islands: what man who cherishes solitude and the sea will ever keep himself from loving them?

In the very middle of the Atlantic, we bend beneath the savage winds that blow endlessly from pole to pole. Each cry we utter is lost, flies off into limitless space. But this shout, carried day after day on the winds, will finally reach land at one of the flattened ends of the earth and echo timelessly against the frozen walls until a man, lost somewhere in his shell of snow, hears it and wants to smile with happiness.

I was half asleep in the early afternoon sun when a terrible noise awoke me. I saw the sun in the depths of the sea, the waves reigning in the surging heavens. Suddenly, the sea was afire, the sun flowed in long icy draughts down my throat. The sailors laughed and wept around me. They loved, but could not forgive one another. I recognized the world for what it was that day. I decided to accept the fact that its good might at the same time be evil and its transgressions beneficial. I realized that day that there were two truths, and that one of them ought never to be uttered.

The curious austral moon, looking slightly pared, keeps us company for several nights and then slides rapidly from the sky into the sea, which swallows it. The Southern Cross, the infrequent stars, the porous air remain. At the same instant, the wind ceases. The sky rolls and pitches above our immobile masts. Engine dead, sails hove to, we are whistling in the warm night as the water beats amicably against our sides. No commands, the machines are silent. Why indeed should we continue and why return? Our cup runneth over, a mute rapture lulls us invincibly to sleep. There are days like this when all is accomplished; we must let ourselves flow with them, like swimmers who keep on until exhausted. What can we accomplish? I have always concealed it from myself. Oh bitter bed, princely couch, the crown lies at the bottom of the seas.

In the morning, the lukewarm water foams gently under our propeller. We put on speed. Toward noon, traveling from distant continents, a herd of walruses cross our path, overtake us, and swim rhythmically to the north, followed by multicolored birds which from time to time alight upon their tusks. This rustling forest slowly vanishes on the horizon. A little later the sea is covered with strange yellow flowers. Toward evening, for hour after hour, we are preceded by an invisible song. Comfortably, I fall asleep.

All sails stretched to the keen breeze, we skim across a clear and rippling sea. At top speed, our helm goes hard to port. And toward nightfall, correcting our course again, listing so far to starboard that our sails skim the water, we sail rapidly along the side of a southern continent I recognize from having once flown blindly over it in the barbarous coffin of an airplane. I was an idle king and my chariot dawdled; I waited for the sea but it never came. The monster roared, took off from the guano fields of Peru, hurled itself above the beaches of the Pacific, flew over the fractured white vertebrae of the Andes and then above the herds of flies that cover the immense Argentinian plain, linking in one swoop the milk-drowned Uruguayan meadows to Venezuela's black rivers, landing, roaring again, quivering with greed at the sight of new empty spaces to devour, and yet never failing to move forward or at least doing so only with a convulsed, obstinate slowness, a fixed, weary, and intoxicated energy. I felt I was dying in this metallic cell and dreamed of bloodshed and orgies. Without space, there is neither innocence nor liberty! When a man cannot breathe, prison means death or madness; what can he do there but kill and possess? But today I have all the air I need, all our sails slap in the blue air, I am going to shout at the speed, we'll toss our sextants and compasses into the sea.

Our sails are like iron under the imperious wind. The coast drifts at full speed before our eyes, forests of royal coconut trees whose feet are bathed by emerald lagoons, a quiet bay, full of red sails, moonlit beaches. Great buildings loom up, already cracking under the pressure of the virgin forest that begins in the back yards; here and there a yellow ipecac or a tree with violet branches bursts through a window; Rio finally crumbles away behind us and the monkeys of the Tijuca will laugh and gibber in the vegetation that will cover its new ruins. Faster still, along wide beaches where the waves spread out in sheaves of sand, faster still, where the Uruguayan sheep wade into the sea and instantly turn it yellow. Then, on the Argentinian coast, great crude piles of faggots, set up at regular intervals, raise slowly grilling halves of oxen to the sky. At night, the ice from Tierra del Fuego comes and beats for hours against our hull, the ship hardly loses speed and tacks about. In the morning, the single wave of the Pacific, whose cold foam boils green and white for thousands of kilometers along the Chilean coast, slowly lifts us up and threatens to wreck us. The helm avoids it, overtakes the Kerguelen Islands. In the sweetish evening the first Malayan boats come out to meet us.

"To sea! To sea!" shouted the marvelous boys in one of the books from my childhood. I have forgotten everything about that book except this cry. "To sea!", and across the Indian Ocean into the corridor of the Red Sea, where on silent nights one can hear the desert stones, scorched in the daytime, freeze and crack one by one as we return to the ancient sea in which all cries are hushed.

Finally, one morning, we drop anchor in a bay filled with a strange silence, beaconed with fixed sails. A few sea birds are quarrelling in the sky over scraps of reeds. We swim ashore to an empty beach; all day plunging into the water and drying off on the sand. When evening comes, under a sky that turns green and fades into the distance, the sea, already calm, grows more peaceful still. Short waves shower vaporous foam on the lukewarm shore. The sea birds have disappeared. All that is left is space, open to a motionless voyage.

Knowing that certain nights whose sweetness lingers will keep returning to the earth and sea after we are gone, yes, this helps us die. Great sea, ever in motion, ever virgin, my religion along with night! It washes and satiates us in its sterile billows, frees us and holds us upright. Each breaker brings its promise, always the same. What does each say? If I were to die surrounded by cold mountains, ignored by the world, an outcast, at the end of my strength, at the final moment the sea would flood my cell, would lift me above myself and help me die without hatred.

At midnight, alone on the shore. A moment more, and I shall set sail. The sky itself has weighed anchor, with all its stars, like the ships covered with lights which at this very hour throughout the world illuminate dark harbors. Space and silence weigh equally upon the heart. A sudden love, a great work, a decisive act, a thought that transfigures, all these at certain moments bring the same unbearable anxiety, quickened with an irresistible charm. Living like this, in the delicious anguish of being, in exquisite proximity to a danger whose name we do not know, is this the same as rushing to our doom? Once again, without respite, let us race to our destruction.

I have always felt I lived on the high seas, threatened, at the heart of a royal happiness.

1953

The Rains of New York

New York rain is a rain of exile. Abundant, viscous and
dense, it pours down tirelessly between the high cubes of
cement into avenues plunged suddenly into the darkness
of a well: seeking shelter in a cab that stops at a red light
and starts again on a green, you suddenly feel caught in a
trap, behind monotonous, fast-moving windshield wipers
sweeping aside water that is constantly renewed. You are
convinced you could drive like this for hours without
escaping these square prisons or the cisterns through
which you wade with no hope of a hill or a real tree. The
whitened skyscrapers loom in the gray mist like gigantic
tombstones for a city of the dead, and seem to sway
slightly on their foundations. At this hour they are deserted. Eight million men, the smell of steel and cement,
the madness of builders, and yet the very height of solitude. "Even if I were to clasp all the people in the world
against me, it would protect me from nothing."

The reason perhaps is that New York is nothing
without its sky. Naked and immense, stretched to the
four corners of the horizon, it gives the city its glorious
mornings and the grandeur of its evenings, when a flam-

ing sunset sweeps down Eighth Avenue over the immense crowds driving past the shop windows, whose lights are turned on well before nightfall. There are also certain twilights along Riverside Drive, when you watch the parkway that leads uptown, with the Hudson below, its waters reddened by the setting sun; off and on, from the uninterrupted flow of gently, smoothly running cars, from time to time there suddenly rises a song that recalls the sound of breaking waves. Finally I think of other evenings, so gentle and so swift they break your heart, that cast a purple glow over the vast lawns of Central Park, seen from Harlem. Clouds of Negro children are striking balls with wooden bats, shouting with joy; while elderly Americans, in checked shirts, sprawl on park benches, sucking molded ice creams on a stick with what energy remains to them; while squirrels burrow into the earth at their feet in search of unknown tidbits. In the park's trees, a jazz band of birds heralds the appearance of the first star above the Empire State Building, while long-legged creatures stride along the paths against a backdrop of tall buildings, offering to the temporarily gentle sky their splendid looks and their loveless glance. But when this sky grows dull, or the daylight fades, then once again New York becomes the big city, prison by day and funeral pyre by night. A prodigious funeral pyre at midnight, as its millions of lighted windows amid immense stretches of blackened walls carry these swarming lights halfway up the sky, as if every evening a gigantic fire were burning over Manhattan, the island with three rivers, raising immense, smoldering carcasses still pierced with dots of flame.

I have my ideas about other cities—but about New York only these powerful and fleeting emotions, a nostalgia that grows impatient, and moments of anguish.

After so many months I still know nothing about New York, whether one moves about among madmen here or among the most reasonable people in the world; whether life is as easy as all America says, or whether it is as empty here as it sometimes seems; whether it is natural for ten people to be employed where one would be enough and where you are served no faster; whether New Yorkers are liberals or conformists, modest souls or dead ones; whether it is admirable or unimportant that the garbage men wear well-fitting gloves to do their work; whether it serves any purpose that the circus in Madison Square Garden puts on ten simultaneous performances in four different rings, so that you are interested in all of them and can watch none of them; whether it is significant that the thousands of young people in the skating rink where I spent one evening, a kind of *vélodrome d'hiver* bathed in reddish and dusty lights, as they turned endlessly on their roller skates in an infernal din of metal wheels and loud organ music, should look as serious and absorbed as if they were solving simultaneous equations; whether, finally, we should believe those who say that it is eccentric to want to be alone, or naïvely those who are surprised that no one ever asks for your identity card.

In short, I am out of my depth when I think of New York. I wrestle with the morning fruit juices, the national Scotch and soda and its relationship to romance, the girls in taxis and their secret, fleeting acts of love, the excessive luxury and bad taste reflected even in the stupefying neckties, the anti-Semitism and the love of animals—this last extending from the gorillas in the Bronx Zoo to the protozoa of the Museum of Natural History—the funeral parlors where death and the dead are made up at top speed ("Die, and leave the rest to us"), the barber shops where you can get a shave at three in the morning, the temperature that swings from hot to cold in two hours, the subway that reminds you of Sing Sing prison, ads filled with clouds of smiles proclaiming from every wall that life is not tragic, cemeteries in flower beneath the gasworks, the beauty of the girls and the ugliness of the old men; the tens of thousands of musical-comedy generals and admirals stationed at the apartment entrances, some to whistle for green, red, and yellow taxis that look like beetles, others to open the door for you, and finally the ones who go up and down all over town like multicolored Cartesian divers in elevators fifty stories high.

Yes, I am out of my depth. I am learning that there are cities, like certain women, who annoy you, overwhelm you, and lay bare your soul, and whose scorching contact, scandalous and delightful at the same time, clings to every pore of your body. This is how, for days on end, I walked around New York, my eyes filled with tears simply because the city air is filled with cinders, and half one's time outdoors is spent rubbing the eyes or removing the minute speck of metal that the thousand New Jersey factories send into them as a joyful greeting gift, from across the Hudson. In the end, this is how New York affects me, like a foreign body in the eye, delicious and unbearable, evoking tears of emotion and all-consuming fury.

Perhaps this is what people call passion. All I can say is that I know what contrasting images mine feeds on. In the middle of the night sometimes, above the skyscrapers, across hundreds of high walls, the cry of a tugboat would meet my insomnia, reminding me that this desert of iron and cement was also an island. I would think of the sea then, and imagine myself on the shore of my own land. On other evenings, riding in the front of

185

the Third Avenue El, as it greedily swallows the little red and blue lights it tears past at third story level, from time to time allowing itself to be slowly absorbed by half-dark stations, I watched the skyscrapers turning in our path. Leaving the abstract avenues of the center of town I would let myself ride on toward the gradually poorer neighborhoods, where there were fewer and fewer cars. I knew what awaited me, those nights on the Bowery. A few paces from the half-mile-long stretch of splendid bridal shops (where not one of the waxen mannequins was smiling) the forgotten men live, those who have let themselves drift into poverty in this city of bankers. It is the gloomiest part of town, where you never see a woman, where one man in every three is drunk, and where in a strange bar, apparently straight out of a Western, fat old actresses sing about ruined lives and a mother's love, stamping their feet to the rhythm and spasmodically shaking, to the bellowing from the bar, the parcels of shapeless flesh that age has covered them with. The drummer is an old woman too, and looks like a screech owl, and some evenings you feel you'd like to know her life—at one of those rare moments when geography disappears and loneliness becomes a slightly confused truth.

At other times . . . but yes, of course, I loved the mornings and the evenings of New York. I loved New York, with that powerful love that sometimes leaves you full of uncertainties and hatred: sometimes one needs exile. And then the very smell of New York rain tracks you down in the heart of the most harmonious and familiar towns, to remind you there is at least one place of deliverance in the world, where you, together with a whole people and for as long as you want, can finally lose yourself forever.

Published in Formes et couleurs, *1947*

II

CRITICAL ESSAYS

The New Mediterranean Culture[1]

❧❧ ❧❧❧ ❧❧

I. THE AIM of the Maison de la Culture, which is celebrating its opening today, is to serve the culture of the Mediterranean. Faithful to the general directions governing institutions of its type, it seeks within a regional framework to encourage the development of a culture whose existence and greatness need no proof. Perhaps there is something surprising in the fact that left-wing intellectuals can put themselves to work for a culture that seems irrelevant to their cause, and that can even, as has happened in the case of Maurras, be monopolized by theoreticians of the Right.

It may indeed seem that serving the cause of Mediterranean regionalism is tantamount to restoring empty traditionalism with no future, celebrating the su-

[1] *This outline of a lecture given at the Maison de la Culture on February 8, 1937, is a very early text. With its insistence on the fundamental difference between political doctrines elaborated in the north of Europe and the more tolerant attitude toward life fed by the Mediterranean, it already contains the essence of Camus's argument in* The Rebel. —P.T.

189

periority of one culture over another, or, again, adopting an inverted form of fascism and inciting the Latin against the Nordic peoples. This is a perpetual source of misunderstandings. The aim of this lecture is to try to dispel them. The whole error lies in the confusion between Mediterranean and Latin, and in attributing to Rome what began in Athens. To us it is obvious that our only claim is to a kind of nationalism of the sun. We could never be slaves to traditions or bind our living future to exploits already dead. A tradition is a past that distorts the present. But the Mediterranean land about us is a lively one, full of games and joy. Moreover, nationalism has condemned itself. Nationalisms always make their appearance in history as signs of decadence. When the vast edifice of the Roman empire collapsed, when its spiritual unity, from which so many different regions drew their justification, fell apart, then and only then, at a time of decadence, did nationalisms appear. The West has never rediscovered unity since. At the present time, internationalism is trying to give the West a real meaning and a vocation. However, this internationalism is no longer inspired by a Christian principle, by the Papal Rome of the Holy Roman Empire. The principle inspiring it is man. Its unity no longer lies in faith but in hope. A civilization can endure only insofar as its unity and greatness, once all nations are abolished, stem from a spiritual principle. India, almost as large as Europe, with no nations, no sovereignty, has kept its own particular character even after two centuries of English rule.

This is why, before any other consideration, we reject the principle of a Mediterranean nationalism. In any case, it would never be possible to speak of the superiority of Mediterranean culture. Men express themselves in harmony with their land. And superiority, as far as culture is concerned, lies in this harmony and in nothing else. There are no higher or lower cultures. There are cultures that are more or less true. All we want to do is help a country to express itself. Locally. Nothing more. The real question is this: is a new Mediterranean civilization within our grasp?

II. Obvious facts. (a) There is a Mediterranean sea, a basin linking about ten different countries. Those men whose voices boom in the singing cafés of Spain, who wander in the port of Genoa, along the docks in Marseilles, the strange, strong race that lives along our coasts, all belong to the same family. When you travel in Europe, and go down toward Italy or Provence, you breathe a sigh of relief as you rediscover these casually dressed men, this violent, colorful life we all know. I spent two months in central Europe, from Austria to Germany, wondering where that strange discomfort weighing me down, the muffled anxiety I felt in my bones, came from. A little while ago, I understood. These people were always buttoned right up to the neck. They did not know how to relax. They did not know what joy was like, joy which is so different from laughter. Yet it is details like this that give a valid meaning to the word "Country." Our Country is not the abstraction that sends men off to be massacred, but a certain way of appreciating life which is shared by certain people, through which we can feel ourselves closer to someone from Genoa or Majorca than to someone from Normandy or Alsace. That is what the Mediterranean is—a certain smell or scent that we do not need to express: we all feel it through our skin.

(b) There are other, historical, facts. Each time a doctrine has reached the Mediterranean basin, in the resulting clash of ideas the Mediterranean has always remained intact, the land has overcome the doctrine. In the beginning Christianity was an inspiring doctrine, but a closed one, essentially Judaic, incapable of concessions, harsh, exclusive, and admirable. From its encounter with the Mediterranean, a new doctrine emerged: Catholicism. A philosophical doctrine was added to the initial store of emotional aspirations. The monument then reached its highest and most beautiful form—adapting itself to man. Thanks to the Mediterranean, Christianity was able to enter the world and embark on the miraculous career it has since enjoyed.

Once again it was someone from the Mediterranean, Francis of Assisi, who transformed Christianity from an inward-looking, tormented religion into a hymn to nature and simple joy. The only effort to separate Christianity from the world was made by a northerner, Luther. Protestantism is, actually, Catholicism wrenched from the Mediterranean, and from the simultaneously pernicious and inspiring influence of this sea.

Let us look even closer. For anyone who has lived both in Germany and in Italy, it is obvious that fascism does not take the same form in both countries. You can feel it everywhere you go in Germany, on people's faces, in the city streets. Dresden, a garrison town, is almost smothered by an invisible enemy. What you feel first of all in Italy is the land itself. What you see first of all in a German is the Hitlerite who greets you with "Heil Hitler!"; in an Italian, the cheerful and gay human being. Here again, the doctrine seems to have yielded to the country—and it is a miracle wrought by the Mediterranean that enables men who think humanly to live unoppressed in a country of inhuman laws.

• • •

III. But this living reality, the Mediterranean, is not something new to us. And its culture seems the very image of the Latin antiquity the Renaissance tried to rediscover across the Middle Ages. This is the Latinity Maurras and his friends try to annex. It was in the name of this Latin order on the occasion of the war against Ethiopia that twenty-four Western intellectuals signed a degrading manifesto celebrating the "civilizing mission of Italy in barbarous Ethiopia."

But no. This is not the Mediterranean our Maison de la Culture lays claim to. For this is not the true Mediterranean. It is the abstract and conventional Mediterranean represented by Rome and the Romans. These imitative and unimaginative people had nevertheless the imagination to substitute for the artistic genius and feeling for life they lacked a genius for war. And this order whose praises we so often hear sung was one imposed by force and not one created by the mind. Even when they copied, the Romans lost the savor of the original. And it was not even the essential genius of Greece they imitated, but rather the fruits of its decadence and its mistakes. Not the strong, vigorous Greece of the great tragic and comic writers, but the prettiness and affected grace of the last centuries. It was not life that Rome took from Greece, but puerile, over-intellectualized abstractions. The Mediterranean lies elsewhere. It is the very denial of Rome and Latin genius. It is alive, and wants no truck with abstractions. And it is easy to acknowledge Mussolini as the worthy descendant of the Caesars and Augustus of Imperial Rome, if we mean by this that he, like them, sacrifices truth and greatness to a violence that has no soul.

What we claim as Mediterranean is not a liking for reasoning and abstractions, but its physical life—the

193

courtyards, the cypresses, the strings of pimientoes. We claim Aeschylus and not Euripides, the Doric Apollos and not the copies in the Vatican; Spain, with its strength and its pessimism, and not the bluster and swagger of Rome, landscapes crushed with sunlight and not the theatrical settings in which a dictator drunk with his own verbosity enslaves the crowds. What we seek is not the lie that triumphed in Ethiopia but the truth that is being murdered in Spain.

IV. The Mediterranean, an international basin traversed by every current, is perhaps the only land linked to the great ideas from the East. For it is not classical and well ordered, but diffuse and turbulent, like the Arab districts in our towns or the Genoan and Tunisian harbors. The triumphant taste for life, the sense of boredom and the weight of the sun, the empty squares at noon in Spain, the siesta, this is the true Mediterranean, and it is to the East that it is closest. Not to the Latin West. North Africa is one of the few countries where East and West live close together. And there is, at this junction, little difference between the way a Spaniard or an Italian lives on the quays of Algiers, and the way Arabs live around them. The most basic aspect of Mediterranean genius springs perhaps from this historically and geographically unique encounter between East and West. (On this question I can only refer you to Audisio.)[2]

This culture, this Mediterranean truth, exists and

[2] *Gabriel Audisio, born in 1900, studied in Marseilles and Algiers, where he was a member of the literary group associated with the publisher Charlot. In 1932 he published a collection of popular folk tales entitled* Les Meilleures Histoires de Cagayous. *These stories, attributed to a popular character named Musette, were originally written by Gabriel Robinet.* —P.T.

shows itself all along the line: (1) In linguistic unity—
the ease with which a Latin language can be learned
when another is already known; (2) Unity of origin—the
prodigious collectivism of the Middle Ages—chivalric
order, religious order, feudal orders, etc., etc. On all these
points the Mediterranean gives us the picture of a living,
highly colored, concrete civilization, which changes doctrines into its own likeness—and receives ideas without
changing its own nature.

But then, you may say, why go any further?

V. Because the very land that transformed so
many doctrines must transform the doctrines of the present day. A Mediterranean collectivism will be different
from a Russian collectivism, properly so-called. The issue
of collectivism is not being fought in Russia: it is being
fought in the Mediterranean basin and in Spain, at this
very moment. Of course, man's fate has been at stake for
a long time now, but it is perhaps here that the struggle
reaches its tragic height, with so many trump cards
placed in our hands. There are, before our eyes, realities
stronger than we ourselves are. Our ideas will bend and
become adapted to them. This is why our opponents are
mistaken in all their objections. No one has the right to
prejudge the fate of a doctrine, and to judge our future in
the name of a past, even if the past is Russia's.

Our task here is to rehabilitate the Mediterranean, to take it back from those who claim it unjustly for
themselves, and to make it ready for the economic organization awaiting it. Our task is to discover what is concrete and alive in it, and, on every occasion, to encourage
the different forms which this culture takes. We are all
the more prepared for the task in that we are in immediate contact with the Orient, which can teach us so much

in this respect. We are, here, on the side of the Mediterranean against Rome. And the essential role that towns like Algiers and Barcelona can play is to serve, in their own small way, that aspect of Mediterranean culture which favors man instead of crushing him.

VI. The intellectual's role is a difficult one in our time. It is not his task to modify history. Whatever people may say, revolutions come first and ideas afterward. Consequently, it takes great courage today to proclaim oneself faithful to the things of the mind. But at least this courage is not useless. The term "intellectual" is pronounced with so much scorn and disapproval because it is associated in people's minds with the idea of someone who talks in abstractions, who is unable to come into contact with life, and who prefers his own personality to the rest of the world. But for those who do not want to avoid their responsibilities, the essential task is to rehabilitate intelligence by regenerating the subject matter that it treats, to give back all its true meaning to the mind by restoring to culture its true visage of health and sunlight. I was saying that this courage was not useless. For if it is not indeed the task of intelligence to modify history, its real task will nevertheless be to act upon man, for it is man who makes history. We have a contribution to make to this task. We want to link culture with life. The Mediterranean, which surrounds us with smiles, sea, and sunlight, teaches us how it is to be done. Xenophon tells us in *The Persian Expedition* that when the Greek soldiers who had ventured into Asia were coming back to their own country, dying of hunger and thirst, cast into despair by so many failures and humiliations, they reached the top of a mountain from which they could see the sea. Then they began to dance, forgetting their weariness and their disgust at the spectacle of their lives. In the same way we do not wish to cut outselves off from the world. There is only one culture. Not the one that feeds off abstractions and capital letters. Not the one that condemns. Not the one that justifies the excesses and the deaths in Ethiopia and defends the thirst for brutal conquests. We know that one very well, and want nothing to do with it. What we seek is the culture that finds life in the trees, the hills, and in mankind.

This is why men of the Left are here with you today, to serve a cause that at first sight had nothing to do with their own opinions. I would be happy if, like us, you were now convinced that this cause is indeed ours. Everything that is alive is ours. Politics are made for men, and not men for politics. We do not want to live on fables. In the world of violence and death around us, there is no place for hope. But perhaps there is room for civilization, for real civilization, which puts truth before fables and life before dreams. And this civilization has nothing to do with hope. In it man lives on his truths.[3]

It is to this whole effort that men of the West must bind themselves. Within the framework of internationalism, the thing can be achieved. If each one of us within his own sphere, his country, his province agrees to work modestly, success is not far away. As far as we are concerned, we know our aim, our limitations, and our possibilities. We only need open our eyes to make men realize that culture cannot be understood unless it is put to the service of life, that the mind need not be man's enemy. Just as the Mediterranean sun is the same for all

---

[3] I have spoken of a new civilization and not of a progress in civilization. To handle that evil toy called Progress would be too dangerous.

men, the effort of men's intelligence should be a common inheritance and not a source of conflict and murder.

Can we achieve a new Mediterranean culture that can be reconciled with our social idea? Yes. But both we and you must help to bring it about.

Published in the first number of the review Jeune Méditerranée, *monthly bulletin of the Algiers Maison de la Culture, April 1937*

On Jean-Paul Sartre's

La Nausée[1]

❦❦ ❦❦❦ ❦❦

A NOVEL is never anything but a philosophy expressed in images. And in a good novel the philosophy has disappeared into the images. But the philosophy need only spill over into the characters and action for it to stick out like a sore thumb, the plot to lose its authenticity, and the novel its life.

Nonetheless, a work that is to endure cannot do without profound ideas. And this secret fusion of experience and thought, of life and reflection on the meaning of life, is what makes the great novelist (as we see him in a work like *Man's Fate,* for example).

The novel in question today is one in which this balance has been broken, where the theories do damage to the life. Something that has happened rather often lately. But what is striking in *La Nausée* is that remarkable fictional gifts and the play of the toughest and most

[1] *When Camus wrote this review of Sartre's first novel and the following one on the volume of short stories published in English under the title of* Intimacy, *the two men had never met.* —P.T.

lucid mind are at the same time both lavished and squandered.

Taken individually, each chapter of this extravagant meditation reaches a kind of perfection in bitterness and truth. The novel that takes shape—a small port in the north of France, a bourgeoisie of shipowners who combine religious observance with the pleasures of the table, a restaurant where the exercise of eating reverts to the repugnant in the narrator's eyes—everything that concerns the mechanical side of existence, in short, is depicted with a sureness of touch whose lucidity leaves no room for hope.

Similarly, the reflections on time, represented in an old woman trotting aimlessly along a narrow street, are, taken in isolation, among the most telling illustrations of the philosophy of anguish as summarized in the thought of Kierkegaard, Chestov, Jaspers, or Heidegger. Both faces of the novel are equally convincing. But taken together, they don't add up to a work of art: the passage from one to the other is too rapid, too unmotivated, to evoke in the reader the deep conviction that makes art of the novel.

Indeed, the book itself seems less a novel than a monologue. A man judges his life, and in so doing judges himself. I mean that he analyzes his presence in the world, the fact that he moves his fingers and eats at regular hours—and what he finds at the bottom of the most elementary act is its fundamental absurdity.

In the best ordered of lives, there always comes a moment when the structures collapse. Why this and that, this woman, that job or appetite for the future? To put it all in a nutshell, why this eagerness to live in limbs that are destined to rot?

The feeling is common to all of us. For most men

the approach of dinner, the arrival of a letter, or a smile from a passing girl are enough to help them get around it. But the man who likes to dig into ideas finds that being face to face with this particular one makes his life impossible. And to live with the feeling that life is pointless gives rise to anguish. From sheer living against the stream, the whole of one's being can be overcome with disgust and revulsion, and this revolt of the body is what is called nausea.

A strange subject, certainly, and yet the most banal. M. Sartre carries it to its conclusions with a vigor and certainty that show how ordinary so seemingly subtle a form of disgust can be. It is here that the similarity between M. Sartre and another author, whom, unless I am mistaken, no one has mentioned in connection with *La Nausée,* is to be found. I mean Franz Kafka.

But the difference is that with M. Sartre's novel some indefinable obstacle prevents the reader from participating and holds him back when he is on the very threshold of consent. I attribute this to the noticeable lack of balance between the ideas in the work and the images that express them. But it may be something else. For it is the failing of a certain literature to believe that life is tragic because it is wretched.

Life can be magnificent and overwhelming—that is its whole tragedy. Without beauty, love, or danger it would be almost easy to live. And M. Sartre's hero does not perhaps give us the real meaning of his anguish when he insists on those aspects of man he finds repugnant, instead of basing his reasons for despair on certain of man's signs of greatness.

The realization that life is absurd cannot be an end, but only a beginning. This is a truth nearly all great minds have taken as their starting point. It is not this discovery that is interesting, but the consequences and rules for action that can be drawn from it. At the end of his voyage to the frontiers of anxiety, M. Sartre does seem to authorize one hope: that of the creator who finds deliverance in writing.

· From the original doubt will come perhaps the cry "I write, therefore I am." And one can't help finding something rather comic in the disproportion between this final hope and the revolt that gave it birth. For, in the last resort, almost all writers know how trivial their work is when compared to certain moments of their life. M. Sartre's object was to describe these moments. Why didn't he go right through to the end?

However that may be, this is the first novel by a writer from whom everything may be expected. So natural a suppleness in staying on the far boundaries of conscious thought, so painful a lucidity, are indications of limitless gifts. These are grounds for welcoming *La Nausée* as the first summons of an original and vigorous mind whose lessons and works to come we are impatient to see.

Review published in Alger républicain
on October 20, 1938

On Sartre's
Le Mur and Other Stories

❧❧ ❧❧❧ ❧❧

JEAN-PAUL SARTRE, whose *La Nausée* was reviewed in this column, has just published a collection of short stories in which the strange and bitter themes of his first novel appear once more, in a different form. Men sentenced to death, a madman, a sexual pervert, a man suffering from impotence, and a homosexual make up the characters in these stories. One might wonder at the bias of these choices. But already, in *La Nausée*, the author's aim was to turn an exceptional case into an everyday story. It is at the far boundaries of the heart and instinct that M. Sartre finds his inspiration.

But this needs further definition. One can prove that the most ordinary person is already a monster of perversity and that, for example, we all more or less wish for the death of those we love. At least, such is the aim of a certain kind of literature. It does not seem to me that this is M. Sartre's aim. And, at the risk of being perhaps a shade oversubtle, I would say that his aim is to show that the most perverse of creatures acts, reacts, and describes himself in exactly the same way as the most ordinary.

And if there were a criticism to be made, it would concern only the use the author makes of obscenity.

Obscenity in literature can attain a certain grandeur. It certainly contains an element of grandeur, if one thinks for instance of Shakespeare's. But at least obscenity must be called for by the work itself. And while this may be the case for "Erostrate" in *Le Mur*, I cannot say the same for *Intimité*, where the sexual descriptions often seem gratuitous.

M. Sartre has a certain taste for impotence, both in the larger meaning of the word and in its physiological sense, which leads him to choose characters who have arrived at the limits of their selves, stumbling over an absurdity they cannot overcome. The obstacle they come up against is their own lives, and I will go so far as to say that they do so through an excess of liberty.

These beings, with no attachments, no principles, no Ariadne's thread, are so free they disintegrate, deaf to the call of action or creation. A single problem preoccupies them, and they have not defined it. From this stems both the immense interest and the absolute mastery of M. Sartre's stories.

Whether one takes young Lucien, who begins with surrealism and ends in the *Action Française;* Eve, whose husband is insane and who wants at all costs to penetrate into the mad domain from which she is excluded; or the hero of "Erostrate"; everything these characters do, say, or feel is unexpected. And from the moment they are introduced to us there is no clue as to what they will do in the next. M. Sartre's art lies in the detail with which he depicts his absurd creatures, the way he observes their monotonous behavior. He describes, suggesting very little but patiently following his characters and attributing importance only to their most futile actions.

It would not be surprising to learn that at the very moment he begins his story, the author himself is not sure where it will lead him. Yet the fascination such a story evokes is undeniable. One cannot put it down, and soon the reader too acquires that higher, absurd freedom which leads the characters to their own ends.

For his characters are, in fact, free. But their liberty is of no use to them. At least, this is what M. Sartre demonstrates. And doubtless this explains the often overwhelming emotional impact of these pages as well as their cruel pathos. For in this universe man is free of the shackles of his prejudices, sometimes from his own nature, and, reduced to self-contemplation, becomes aware of his profound indifference to everything that is not himself. He is alone, enclosed in this liberty. It is a liberty that exists only in time, for death inflicts on it a swift and dizzying denial. His condition is absurd. He will go no further, and the miracles of those mornings when life begins anew have lost all meaning for him.

How does one remain lucid confronted with such truths? It is normal for such beings, deprived of human recreations—the movies, love, or the Legion of Honor—to regress to an inhuman world where they will this time forge their own chains: madness, sexual mania, or crime. Eve wants to go mad. The protagonist of "Erostrate" wants to commit a crime, and Lulu wants to live with her impotent husband.

Those who escape these turnabouts or who do not complete them can always yearn for the self-annihilation they offer. And, in the best of these short stories, *La Chambre,* Eve watches her husband's delirium and tortures herself to discover the secret of this universe in which she would like to be absorbed, of this isolated room in which she would like to sleep with the door forever closed.

This intense and dramatic universe, this brilliant yet colorless depiction, are a good definition of M. Sartre's work and its appeal. And one can already speak of "the work" of an author who, in two books, has known how to get straight to the essential problem and bring it to life through his obsessive characters. A great writer always brings his own world and its message. M. Sartre's brings us to nothingness, but also to lucidity. And the image he perpetuates through his characters, of a man seated amid the ruins of his life, is a good illustration of the greatness and truth of this work.

Review published in Alger républicain *on*
March 12, 1939

On Ignazio Silone's
Bread and Wine

❧❧ ❧❧❧ ❧❧

EDITIONS GRASSET has just given us an excellent translation of Ignazio Silone's novel *Bread and Wine*. Here, once
again, is a work that deals with timely problems. But the
mixture of anguish and detachment with which these
problems are approached enables us to greet *Bread and
Wine* as a great revolutionary work. We can do so for
several reasons.

First of all, the work is without any doubt an anti-
Fascist's. But the message it contains goes beyond anti-
Fascism. For although its protagonist, a revolutionary
who has spent years in exile after having escaped from a
concentration camp, still finds reasons to hate Fascism
when he returns to Italy, he also discovers reasons to
doubt. Not his revolutionary faith, of course, but the way
in which he has expressed it. One of the book's key passages is certainly the moment when the hero, Pietro
Sacca, sharing now the elemental life of Italian peasants,
wonders whether the theories in which he has travestied
his love for them have not simply put a greater distance
between him and them. It is in this sense that the work is

revolutionary. For a revolutionary work is not one that glorifies victories and conquests, but one that brings to light the Revolution's most painful conflicts. The more painful the conflicts, the greater their effect. The militant too quickly convinced is to the true revolutionary what the bigot is to a mystic. For the grandeur of a faith can be measured by the doubts it inspires. And no sincere militant, born among the people and determined to defend their dignity, could miss the doubt that sweeps over Pietro Sacca. The anguish that grips the Italian revolutionary is precisely what gives Silone's book its bitterness and somber brilliance.

On the other hand, there is no revolutionary work without artistic qualities. This may seem paradoxical. But I believe that if our time teaches us anything on this score, it is that a revolutionary art, if it is not to lapse into the basest forms of expression, cannot do without artistic importance. There is no happy medium between vulgar propaganda and creative inspiration, between what Malraux calls "the will to prove" and a work like *Man's Fate.*

Bread and Wine meets this test. Written by a rebel, it flows forward in the most classical of forms. Short sentences, a vision of the world both naïve and sophisticated, terse, natural dialogues give Silone's style a secret resonance that comes through even in translation. If the word poetry has a meaning, one finds it here, in tableaux of a rustic and eternal Italy, in cypress-planted slopes and an unequaled sky, and in the ancient gestures of Italian peasants.

To rediscover the road to these gestures and this truth, and to return from an abstract philosophy of the revolution to the bread and wine of simplicity, this is Ignazio Silone's itinerary and the lesson of his novel. And no small part of its greatness is its ability to inspire us to rediscover, beyond the hatreds of today, the face of a proud and human people who remain our only hope for peace.

Review published in Alger républicain
on May 23, 1939

Intelligence and the Scaffold[1]

❦❦ ❦❦❦ ❦❦

IT IS SAID that when Louis XVI, on his way to the guillo-
tine, tried to give one of his guards a message for the
queen, he drew the following reply: "I am not here to run
your errands but to lead you to the scaffold." This excellent example of propriety in wording and obstinate perseverance to the job at hand is, it seems to me, perfectly
applicable, if not to all the novels in our language at least
to a certain classical tradition in the French novel. Novelists of this genre do indeed refuse to carry messages, and
their only concern seems to be to lead their characters
imperturbably to the rendezvous awaiting them, whether
it be Madame de Clèves to her convent, Juliette to happiness and Justine to her ruin, Julien Sorel to his behead-

[1] *The initial notes for "Intelligence and the Scaffold"
appear in Camus's* Carnets II, *pp. 60–1 (Alfred A. Knopf edition,
pp. 44–5). Since at the time Camus was planning the first version of* The Plague *it is perhaps useful to bear in mind the ideas
he expresses in this essay when discussing the construction of
that novel.* L'Homme révolté (The Rebel) *also contains a long
discussion of the Marquis de Sade and Proust.* —P.T.

ing, Adolphe to his solitude, Madame de Graslin to her deathbed, or Proust to the celebration of old age he discovers in the salon of Madame de Guermantes. What characterizes these authors is their singleness of purpose; one would look in vain through these novels for the equivalent of a Wilhelm Meister's interminable adventures; it is not that pedantry is foreign to us but that we have our own particular kind of pedantry, which is not, fortunately, Goethe's sort. All that can be said is that in art an ideal of simplicity always requires fixity of intention. Hence a certain obstinacy that seems central in the French novel.

This is why the problems of the novel are primarily artistic. If our novelists have proved anything, it is that the novel, contrary to general belief, cannot easily dispense with perfection. Only it is an odd sort of perfection, not always a formal one. People imagine—wrongly —that novels can dispense with style. As a matter of fact, they demand the most difficult style—the kind that does not call attention to itself. But the problems our great novelists set themselves have not concerned form for form's sake. They focused only on the exact relationship they wished to introduce between their tone and their ideas. Somewhere between monotony and chit-chat they had to find a language to express their obstinacy. If their language often lacks outward distinction it is because it is molded in a series of sacrifices. The messages have been omitted; everything is reduced to essentials. This is how minds as different as Stendhal's and Madame de La Fayette's may seem akin: both have worked hard to find the right language. Indeed, the first problem Stendhal set himself is the one that has preoccupied great novelists for centuries. What he called an "absence of style" was a perfect conformity between his art and his passions.[2] For what gives originality to all [French] novels compared to those written in other countries is that they are not only a school of life but an artistic school: the liveliest flame crackles in their rigorous language. Our great successes are born of a particular concept of strength, which might be called elegance, but which needs to be defined.

One must be two persons when one writes. In French literature, the great problem is to translate what one feels into what one wants others to feel. We call a writer bad when he expresses himself in reference to an inner context the reader cannot know. The mediocre writer is thus led to say anything he pleases. The great rule of an artist, on the other hand, is to half forget himself the better to communicate. Inevitably this involves sacrifices. And this quest for an intelligible language whose role is to disguise the immensity of his objective leads him to say not what he likes but only what he must. A great part of the genius of the French novel lies in the conscious effort to give the order of pure language to the cries of passion. In short, what triumphs in the works I am discussing is a certain preconceived idea. I mean intelligence.

But the term needs definition. One always tends to think of intelligence as involving only what is visible —structure, for example. Now it is curious to note that the structure of the typical seventeenth-century novel, *La Princesse de Clèves*, is extremely loose. Several stories are launched and the novel begins in complexity even though it ends in unity. Actually, we have to wait for *Adolphe*, in the nineteenth century, to find the purity of

[2] "If I am not clear, my whole *world* is destroyed." (Stendhal).

line we are so ready to imagine we find in *La Princesse de Clèves*. In the same way, the structure of *Les Liaisons dangereuses* is purely chronological, with no artistic experiments. In Sade's novels the composition is elementary; philosophical dissertations alternate with erotic descriptions right to the end. Stendhal's novels offer curious evidence of carelessness, and one is never surprised enough at the final chapter of *La Chartreuse de Parme*, in which the author, as if anxious to conclude, with the end in sight, bundles in twice as many events as in the rest of the book. It is surely not these examples which justify the claim that French novels possess an Apollonian perfection of form.

The unity, the profound simplicity, the classicism of these novels thus lie elsewhere. It is surely closer to the truth to say merely that the great characteristic of these novelists is in the fact that each, in his own way, always says the same thing and always in the same tone. To be classic is to repeat one's self. And thus at the heart of our great works of fiction one finds a certain conception of man that intelligence strives to illustrate by means of a small number of situations. And, of course, this can be said of any good novel, if it is true that novels create their universe by means of intelligence, just as the theater creates its universe by means of action. But what seems peculiar to the French tradition is that plot and characters are generally limited to this idea and everything is arranged so as to make it echo on indefinitely. Here, intelligence not only contributes the original idea; at the same time it is also a marvelously economical principle that creates a kind of passionate monotony. It is both creative and mechanical at the same time. To be classical is both to repeat oneself and to know how to repeat oneself. And this is the difference I see between French novels and those of other countries, where intelligence inspires the fiction but also allows itself to be carried away by its own reactions.[3]

To take a specific example, it seems to me that Madame de La Fayette's aim, since nothing else in the world appears to interest her, is simply to show us a very special conception of love. Her strange postulate is that this passion places man in peril. And while this is something one might say in conversation, no one ever thinks of pushing the logic quite so far as she did. What one feels at work in *La Princesse de Clèves, La Princesse de Montpensier,* or *La Comtesse de Tende* is a constant mistrust of love. It is apparent in her very language, where certain words really seem to burn in her mouth: "What Madame de Clèves had said about his portrait had restored him to life by making him realize that it was he whom she did not hate." But in their own way, the characters also convince us that this healthy suspicion is valid. They are strange heroes, who die of emotion, who seek mortal illness in thwarted passions. Even the minor characters die through impulses of the soul: "He received his pardon when he was expecting only the death blow, but fear had so possessed him that he went mad and died a few days later." Our most audacious Romantics never dared attribute such powers to passion. Faced with such ravages of feeling, it is easy to understand why Madame de La Fayette makes an extraordinary theory of marriage-as-a-lesser-evil the mainspring of her plot: better to be unhappily married than to suffer from passion. Here is the deep-seated idea whose obstinate repetition gives her work its meaning. It is one idea of order.

Long before Goethe, in fact, Madame de La Fayette balanced the injustice of an unhappy condition

[3] In Russian novels, for example, or in such experiments as James Joyce's.

against the disorder of the passions; and long before him, in an amazing act of pessimism, she chose injustice, which leaves everything untouched. The order she is concerned with is less simply a wordy one than that of a soul and a system of ideas. And far from wishing to make passions of the heart the slave of social prejudice, she uses these prejudices as a remedy for the disorderly impulses that terrify her. She is not interested in defending institutions—they do not concern her; but she does wish to protect the core of her being, whose only enemy she knows. Love is nothing but madness and confusion. It is not hard to guess what burning memories surge beneath such disinterested phrases, and it is this, far more than deceptive questions of structure, that offers us a great lesson in art. For there is no art where there is nothing to be overcome, and we realize then that the monotony of this ceremonious harmony is as much the result of clear-sighted calculation as of heart-rending passion. There is only one feeling present, because it has consumed all others, and it speaks always in the same rather formal tone because it is not allowed to shout. Such objectivity is a victory. Other writers, who can offer lessons but who achieve no such victories, have tried to be objective, because they were capable of nothing else. This is why the novelists who are called naturalists or realists, who have written so many novels and many good ones, have not written a single great one. They could not go beyond description. The grandeur of this lofty art in Madame de La Fayette, on the other hand, is that we are made to feel her limits have been put there *on purpose*. Immediately they disappear, and the whole work vibrates. This is the result of a studied art that owes everything to intelligence and its attempt to dominate. But it is quite obvious that such art is also born of an infinite possibility of suffering, and a firm decision to master suffering by means of language.

Nothing expresses this disciplined distress, this powerful light with which intelligence transfigures pain, better than an admirable sentence from *La Princesse de Clèves:* "I told him that so long as his suffering had had limits, I had approved of it and shared it; but that I would pity him no longer if he gave way to despair and lost his reason." The tone is magnificent. It assumes that a certain strength of soul can impose limits on misery by censuring its expression. It introduces art into life by giving man the power of language in his struggle against his destiny. And thus we see that if this literature is a school for life, it is *precisely* because it is a school of art. To be more accurate, the lesson of these lives and these works of art is no longer simply one of art, but one of style. We learn from them to give our behavior a certain form. And this permanent truth, which Madame de La Fayette never stops repeating, which she expresses in this sentence in unforgettable form, takes on its full significance and illuminates what I mean when we realize that the very man who says it (the Prince of Clèves) will nonetheless die of despair.

It would be easy to find in Sade, in Stendhal, in Proust, and in a few contemporary writers similar lessons in style and life, very different in each case, but always made up of a choice, a calculated independence, and a clarity of aim. The perseverance in sin legitimized in Sade,[4] the litanies of energy in Stendhal,[5] Proust's

[4] "He invented cruelties he never practiced himself, and which he would have no desire to practice, in order to enter into contact with the great problems" (Otto Flake). The great problem for de Sade is man's irresponsibility without God.

Camus noted down this judgment on Sade in Carnets I, *p. 249, in 1942 (Alfred A. Knopf edition, pp. 208–9).*—P.T.

[5] The remark by the Prince of Clèves can be juxtaposed with this notation in Stendhal's *Journal:* "As often happens to

216

heroic effort to portray human suffering within a wholly privileged existence—all say one thing and nothing else. Out of a single feeling that has become a part of them forever, these writers create works that are both various and yet monotonous.

Of course, all I am doing here is making a few suggestions. Perhaps they are enough to demonstrate that the rigor, the purity, and the concentrated force of French classical fiction do not stem purely from its qualities of form (in any case, such a term has no meaning in art), but from the stubborn clinging to a certain tone, a certain constancy of soul, and a human and literary knowledge of sacrifice. Such classicism is a matter of deliberate choices (*partis pris*).[6] The cult of the efficacity of intelligence creates not only an art but also a civilization and a way of life. It's possible, of course, that such an attitude has limitations. But perhaps they are necessary ones. We tend nowadays to undervalue lucid effort. And we are very proud of the universality of our taste. But perhaps this universality diminishes our inner strength. To someone who asked Newton how he had managed to construct his theory, he could reply: "By thinking about it all the time." There is no greatness without a little stubbornness.

men who have concentrated their energy on one or two vital points, he had an indolent and careless look."

[6] This is why Francis Ponge's *Le Parti pris des choses* is one of the few classical works of our day.

Francis Ponge (born 1899) is known for his minute descriptions of individual physical objects. A long letter from Camus to Ponge, in which he described Le parti pris des choses *as "an absurd work in the purest sense of the term" was published in the* Nouvelle Nouvelle Revue Française *in September 1956. It was written in 1943 in reply to a letter from Ponge to Camus, and is reprinted in* Pléiade II, *pp. 1662–6.* —P.T.

In any case, this is how I explain the very strong feeling I have about our great novels. They prove the effectiveness of human creation. They convince one that the work of art is a human thing, never human enough, and that its creator can do without dictates from above. Works of art are not born in flashes of inspiration but in a daily fidelity. And one of the real secrets of the French novel is its ability to show at the same time a harmonious sense of fatality and an art that springs wholly from individual liberty—to present, in short, the perfect domain in which the forces of destiny collide with human decisions. Its art is a revenge, a means of overcoming a difficult fate by imposing a form upon it. From the French novel one learns the mathematics of destiny, which are a means of freeing ourselves from destiny. And if the Prince of Clèves shows that in spite of everything he is superior to the tremors of a susceptibility that will kill him, it is because he is capable of forming that admirable sentence which refuses to depict madness and despair. None of our great novelists has turned his back on human suffering, but we can also say that none has surrendered to it and that they have all mastered it with an inspiring patience, through the discipline of art. A contemporary Frenchman owes his idea of virility perhaps (and naturally his virility needs no beating on the drum) to this series of incisive, scorching works in which the superior exercise of an intelligence that cannot keep from dominating moves unflinchingly forward, to the very scaffold.

> *From a special issue of the magazine* Confluences *on "Problems of the Novel," July 1943*

Portrait of a Chosen Man [1]

❦❦ ❦❦❦ ❦❦

Le Portrait de M. Pouget was published before the war, in installments, in a review of relatively limited influence. At the time, it enjoyed an undoubted but unobtrusive success. It has just appeared in book form,[2] and it still seems to have been relatively little discussed in the unoccupied zone. This is because, in spite of appearances, the world has not changed since the war. It is still very noisy. And if a measured voice undertakes to speak to us of an

---

[1] *Though apparently only of minor interest, this essay throws considerable light upon Camus's attitude toward religion. Like* Diplôme, *which he wrote in 1936 on* Métaphysique chrétienne et Néo-platonisme, *it shows that he had a serious interest in the intellectual history of Christianity, and in the problems which this religion presented. But, unlike* Diplôme, *which retains complete academic objectivity, this essay on Father Pouget shows more of Camus's own opinions. Thus, when he dismisses as "quibbles" (p. 225) the type of problem that drove Ernest Renan from the Church, his own essentially moral objections to Christianity stand out much more clearly by contrast* —P.T.

[2] Published by Gallimard, 1943.

austere and pure example, the probability is that no one will listen. What we mean when we say that a book has "found an audience" is that it has gone beyond the large or small circle of readers it could count upon even before publication. Naturally, I have no doubts that *Le Portrait de M. Pouget* was read enthusiastically in Catholic circles. But it would be a good thing if very different readers had the opportunity to meditate on this fine book, and what I would like to do here is describe its appeal to a mind alien to Catholicism.

It is an extremely difficult enterprise to put intelligence and modesty on stage, or to sketch the portrait and write the novel of a spiritual adventure. *Le Portrait de M. Pouget* belongs to a genre difficult to define, even more tricky to categorize. It is inspired not by friendship, as was Montaigne's essay on La Boétie, but rather by veneration, as Alain was inspired when he tried to revive Jules Lagneau. There is always something moving in the homage one man pays to another. But who can boast that he has defined the intriguing feelings that link certain minds to others with ties of respect and admiration? Such ties are sometimes more solid than those of blood. The man who has not had this experience is indeed poor, while he who has been granted it and has given himself wholly to it is happy indeed. In any case, this is the kind of experience Monsieur Guitton has described for us.

Who was M. Pouget? An old Lazarist priest, three-quarters blind, who meditated on Tradition, and received a few students in the little cell where his life was drawing to its close. His life can be summed up in a few words: peasant, seminarian, teacher, invalid, with forty years of studious retreat in his order's Mother House. So it is lacking in the kind of dramatic events that nourish brilliant biographies. The only earthly happenings are

those contained in an endless reflection on Tradition and
Biblical texts. Writing the biography of M. Pouget thus
involved composing a small manual of exegesis and apol-
ogetics, tracing a spiritual portrait from his works, his
method, and his ideas.

These ideas were not clear-cut. M. Pouget put
them forward with considerable precaution. And M. Guitton has shown all the necessary moderation and respect
in describing them. Consequently, to summarize would
be to distort them. The reader can remedy this difficulty
by making allowances for it. If Pouget had read the rest
of this article, he and M. Guitton would have been justified in exclaiming: "It's much more complicated than
that."

Father Pouget's whole effort seems to have been
devoted to finding a middle way between blind faith and a
faith that knows its reasons. He did not wish to maintain
ideas that are indefensible, to justify ambitions that the
Bible never had. Father Pouget made concessions. He
considered everything in the Bible inspired, but did not
see everything as necessarily sacred. A choice had to be
made. From the point of view of rigid orthodoxy, such an
attitude was dangerous. As a matter of fact, this proved
to be the case, for it appears that Father Pouget suffered
from official disapproval. He made his peace by striving
after serenity and putting forward a postulate: "The
Church is not infallible because of the proofs that she
advances, but because of the divine authority with which
she teaches." This said, his problem was to cut his losses,
to establish an irreproachable minimum in the Biblical
texts, and to show that this minimum was enough to
prove the truths of faith. Father Pouget pointed out, for
example, that we require the Gospels to possess a degree

of historical accuracy that no one would have thought of requiring from the historians of classical antiquity or the Middle Ages. Allowance must nevertheless be made for the mentality peculiar to each historical period, and for the rapid variations in moral climate from one century to another. And we have to make a clear distinction in the Bible between what is attributable to divine inspiration and what results from the mentality peculiar to a historical period. Thus, for a long time, the Bible indiscriminately cast both sinners and the righteous into the same hell. *Ecclesiastes*, for example, clearly states that "the dead know not anything neither have they any more a reward" (Ecc. IX, 5). This is because the idea of moral rewards was foreign to primitive Jewish thought. Consequently, it is impossible to defend these texts, or torture them by allegory until they show evidence of divine inspiration.

To those who might evidence surprise at God's carelessness in thus allowing his ideas to be distorted, Father Pouget would have replied that it was more probably a case of a deliberate plan. God has proportioned his revelations to the ability of men to understand them. The light of God is too bright for human eyes and revelation must be progressive. "God is a teacher," M. Pouget would say.

We had to wait until the twentieth century to believe that it was possible to philosophize without knowing how to spell. Such an idea would have scandalized Father Pouget. Divine pedagogy, like all reasonable pedagogies, proceeds on the contrary by stages. It does not lay down the law, it teaches. It temporizes with the human mind and gives it time to breathe. Thus God has made himself a realist and a politician. Father Pouget also liked to talk of another divine attribute, that of condescension (which we must, I suppose, take in its exact meaning of "coming down to the level of . . ."). God's motto would thus be, according to our author: "Neither too soon, nor too late, nor too much at a time." The result is that God had made his teaching coincide with history. History is the series of manoeuvers organized by God to make the light of truth penetrate the blind hearts of men. We must consequently look upon revelation as something that develops in a stubborn effort to free itself from successive layers of worldly prejudice. There must be no tampering with historical truth. And Monsieur Guitton had considerable justification for replying to critics that: "What is remarkable is not that Judeo-Christianity should be clothed in particular mental attitudes, but that it should transcend them." Let us finally note that the Church supports this effort in her own work of defining the faith, which as Father Pouget points out is almost always negative. The Church gives every liberty to her theologians. She rejects only those theories which threaten the existence of the faith in their time. Revelation teaches what is, the Church rejects what is not. The task of the Church is thus to watch over the march of truth, preventing men from causing it either to hasten or to stray. Heretics, in short, are men who want to go faster than God. There is no salvation for impatience.

These principles of the basic minimum, of respect for the mentality peculiar to a particular period, and of progressive revelation form the basis of M. Pouget's method. This method does not, it is true, go to the root of the problem. That root is the problem of being, and Pouget seems to have been suspicious of metaphysics. In any case, the intellectual esteem inspired by his enterprise makes it the commentator's duty not to go beyond

the author's chosen context. Within this context, however, Pouget's method is exposed to one great objection. It
runs the risk, in fact, of using this respect for the mentality peculiar to a historical period as an easy way out for
problems raised by exegesis. Everything that contradicts
faith is attributed to the mentality of the time, and discussion is thus avoided. On this point M. Guitton offers a
reply that is only half satisfying: "The method is as good
as the mind using it." True. But that involves the risk of
abolishing the very problem of methodology, for there
would no longer be good and bad methods but good and
bad minds. With a few nuances, I would not find this a
completely impossible point of view. But for a person
who accepts Tradition, on the other hand, it is rather
surprising.

One feels much more comfortable in pointing out
what seems invaluable in Pouget's meditations: they
leave the problem of faith intact. Let me make myself
clear. It is scarcely necessary to say that, for Father
Pouget himself, the problem did not arise. But every
exegesis assumes its disbelievers. Like Pascal's *Pensées*,
Pouget's thought has an implicit aim: it is apologetic. But
his method does not try to convince people immediately.
That is the task of grace. Pouget's critique was negative
and preparatory. It aimed at showing that the inspired
texts of the Bible contained nothing really offensive to
common sense. Divine texts cannot be obstacles on the
path to faith. They are just the opposite, sure and certain
guides. "From all this," said Pouget, "we draw not faith,
for this is impossible, but adequate motives for belief."
Thus, from the point of view of intelligence, such a
method, with all its modesty and generosity, leaves the
question intact. Our freedom of choice remains absolute.
It is restored to its true climate.

For a hundred years now, science and religion have been mixed together far too much.[3] More supple examination, indeed, restores complete freedom both to Christians and to unbelievers. The former no longer try to "prove" revelation, while the latter no longer base their arguments on the Bible's doubtful genealogies. The problem of faith does not lie in quibbles of this kind. Pouget uses common sense to restore prestige to grace. On this issue he puts things back into their rightful places, the only way to make the mind progress. These are the real merits of a method like his. And however discreet they may be, these merits are so invaluable as to make us forget the astonishing attitude that kept Copernicus and Galileo on the Index for three hundred years, or that accords divine status to the slightest comma in the Bible.

Is all of Father Pouget contained in this method? We might perhaps expect to find that there is also, in addition, some whiff of existence, some more human resonance. The very method, however, ought to disclose, to those who are looking for it, the secret of a great soul. When M. Guitton writes that the principle Father Pouget followed in his researches was "a courageous indifference to his desires," we seem indeed to stand face to face with the man and, for a second, to possess him completely. Again, we feel completely informed, as to his human side, when Father Pouget confides to us: "There are moments, now that I am drawing near my end, when I have

[3] In fact, contemporary disbelief is no longer based on science in the way that it was at the end of the last century. It denies both science and religion. It is no longer the skepticism of reason when confronted with miracles. It is a passionate disbelief.

questions which might lead toward disbelief." It would be puerile to exaggerate the meaning of these confessions. They are the significant shadows of the portrait, the fold of the lip that Piero della Francesca gave the Duke d'Orbino. It would be nothing without the rest—the hard eyes, the imperious nose, and even the landscape in the background. But, without it, the face would lose its secret and its humanity.

Here, in conclusion, I can repeat the question I asked in the beginning: "But who was M. Pouget?" Today, when India is in fashion, one is certain of an audience if one talks about gurus. Indeed, it is one of those spiritual masters whom this priest calls to mind. Yet this cannot be said of his influence. His teaching is really not aimed at illumination or at the inner god; this strange guru has transformed historical criticism into an instrument of asceticism. He appeals to common sense in order to support the revelation of what goes beyond our senses. I am not competent to judge if he was rewarded in what was dearest to his heart.[4] One can, on the other hand, easily feel that a book like the one that has just been devoted to him is not only a homage but also a proof of the efficacity of such teaching. For I have scarcely discussed the book itself, faithful in this, I suppose, to the intentions of its author. In another book by Guitton we read that "the elect are those who realize their own ideal type." In this respect, we can see that we have today a "portrait of a chosen man" that appears as an exceptional triumph in our literature. To write it required not only talent, but also the powerful motives of admiration and affection. M. Guitton indeed brings clarity to the most

[4] It will nevertheless be noted that Guitton's fine thesis on Time and Eternity in Plotinus and Saint Augustine begins with a methodological distinction between mind and mentality.

delicate ideas, which is a feature of the highest style. He also breathes warmth into abstractions and passion into objectivity. This comes from the soul. A virile piety does the rest and gives this fine book its tone.

It would be ungracious to insist upon the reservations that the ethical *a priori* one feels in certain pages of the book (pp. 130 *passim,* 157) can inspire in a non-Catholic thinker. It is enough to note that such reservations exist. The essential thing is that this book of good faith should be accorded its rightful place: far above the vain remarks that, today, are heard like the sounding brass and tinkling cymbal mentioned by St. Paul.[5]

Review published in the Cahiers du Sud, *April 1943*

[5] *Le Portrait de M. Pouget* was written before the war. Since the armistice, M. Guitton has published books and articles of which I would be less inclined to approve.

On a Philosophy of Expression
by Brice Parain[1]

❧❧ ❧❧❧ ❧❧

IT IS NOT certain that our time has lacked gods. Many
have been proposed, usually stupid or cowardly ones. Our
time does, on the other hand, seem to lack a dictionary.
At least, this is obvious to those—in this world in which
all words are prostituted—who hope for justice that is

[1] *Brice Parain (born 1897) was an author whose political preoccupations coincided with those of Camus at a later
stage in his career. Thus on p. 184 of* Carnets II *(Alfred A.
Knopf edition, p. 144), in November 1946, Camus noted down
Parain's remark that "the essence of modern literature is recanta-
tion," and later used it as one of the main themes of* The Rebel.
Parain had written, in an article published in Combat *on November 11, 1946, and entitled* Le caractère commun des productions
actuelles, *that modern literature was characterized not by despair
but by "palinodes, in other words, a return to commonplaces."
"In the last fifty years," he continued, "we have seen all kinds of
such returns. Once again it was Rimbaud who showed the way.
The others, naturally, have followed. We have had Claudel and
devotion, Gide and duty, Aragon and his voice quivering from
patriotic emotion, Jean Paulhan and rhetoric, surrealism which
has returned from different kinds of magic to different kinds of
rationalism, even to positivism, pacifism which has gone to war*

228

unambiguous and liberty that is unequivocal. The question Brice Parain has just raised is whether such a dictionary is possible, and, above all, whether it is conceivable in the absence of a god to give the words in such a dictionary their meanings. Parain's recent books are concerned with language.[2] But even his early essays took the unreliability of language as their subject matter.[3] Parain's long and scrupulous reflection would be enough to earn him attention and esteem. But his books are timely and important for many other reasons, which I shall mention in my conclusion; and despite the apparent speciality of their subject, they are always pertinent.

What is Parain's originality? He makes language a metaphysical question. For professional philosophers, language poses historical and psychological problems. How did it originate, what are its laws—these are the limits of the inquirer's ambition. But there is a primary question that necessarily concerns the very value of the words we use. We must know whether our language is truth or falsehood: this is the question Parain chooses to discuss.

Yet talking is apparently the easiest thing in the world. We lie when we want to and tell the truth when we must. This is not the problem. What we need to know is whether or not our language is false at the very moment

and even existentialists who have become professors of ethics." *Camus took over this idea himself and made it into one of the central themes of* The Rebel, *arguing in his chapter on the Poet's Rebellion that in Rimbaud, Lautréamont, and surrealism, "complete conformism follows merciless revolt."* —P.T.

[2] *Essai sur le logos platonicien* (1941), *Recherches sur la nature et les fonctions du langage* (Gallimard, 1943).

[3] *Essai sur la misère humaine* (1934), *Retour à la France* (Grasset, 1936).

when we think we are telling the truth, whether words have flesh or are merely empty shells, whether they mask a deeper truth or are merely part of a wild-goose chase. Actually, we already know that words fail us sometimes at the very moment when our heart is going to speak, that they betray us even more often in our moments of greatest sincerity, and that at other times their only use is to trick us by appearing to leave no problems. We know quite well that "to pay one's debt to society," "die on the field of battle," "put an end to one's days," "make total war," "be rather weak in the chest," and "lead a life of toil" are ready-made expressions whose purpose is to camouflage heart-breaking experiences. But the questions Parain asks are even more imperious. For the problem is to know whether our most accurate expressions, our most successful cries are not in fact empty of all meaning, whether language does not, in short, express man's final solitude in a silent universe. What this adds up to is a search for the essence of language, and a quest for words that can give us the same reasons we require of God. For Parain's basic premise is that if language is meaningless then everything is meaningless, and the world becomes absurd. We know only by means of words. If they are proved useless, then we are finally and irredeemably blinded.

But indulging in metaphysics means accepting paradoxes, and the metaphysics of language follows this rule. Either, in fact, our words translate only our impressions, and, partaking of their contingency, are deprived of any precise meaning; or else our words represent some ideal and essential truth, and consequently have no contact with tangible reality, which they can in no way affect. Thus we can name things only with uncertainty, and our words become certain only when they cease to refer to actual things.

In neither of these cases can we count on words to tell us how to behave. And tragedy begins as a consequence. "We cannot," says Parain, "accuse language of being the instrument of falsehood and of error, without at the same time, and for the same reasons, accusing the world of being bad and God of being wicked." [4] And, quoting Socrates in the *Phaedo:* "The misuse of language is not only distasteful in itself, but actually harmful to the soul." [5]

The situation Socrates faced is analogous to our own. There was evil in men's souls because there were contradictions in communication, because the most ordinary words had several different meanings, were distorted and diverted from the plain and simple use that people imagined them to have. Such problems cannot leave us indifferent. We too have our sophists and call for a Socrates, since it was Socrates' task to attempt the cure of souls by the search for a dictionary. If the words justice, goodness, beauty have no meaning, then men can tear one another to pieces. Socrates' effort, and his failure, lay in seeking this impeccable meaning, for the lack of which he chose to die. The value of Parain's *Recherches* lies in a similar concern for these urgent consequences. His first effort is one of honesty. He sets out, with the greatest clarity, the paradox of expression: "If man chooses the sensualist hypothesis, he will obtain the external world but lose knowledge; if he chooses the idealist hypothesis, he will obtain knowledge, but will not

[4] *Recherches*, p. 141.
[5] Hackforth's translation.

know how to deal with tangible reality and his knowledge will be useless. In the first case, his language will become literature; in the second, the logical system, developed from a few simple propositions, will soon appear as the fruit of a dream, or as the appalling amusement with which a prisoner might occupy his solitude." [6] We understand now why language for Parain is not only a metaphysical problem but indeed the root of all metaphysics. And it is not without good reason that he offers his researches both as an inquiry into our condition and as an introduction to the history of philosophy. Any philosophical system is, in the last analysis, a theory of language. Every inquiry about being calls into question the power of words.

The history of philosophy for Parain is basically a history of the failures of the mind, confronted with the problem of language. Man has not managed to find his words. And perhaps it is possible to think of the metaphysical adventure as both an obstinate and sterile quest for the masterword that would illuminate everything, for an adequate "Open Sesame," the equivalent of "Aum," the sacred syllable of the Hindus. In this respect, Parain's researches show that from classical Greek philosophy to modern dialectic, considerations of language have moved toward an attitude of acceptance and resignation. Attempts at justification have been replaced by a study of the rules of expression. This evolution is paralleled by the one which, in our century, has replaced metaphysics with the cult of action, the quest for knowledge with the humble wisdom of pragmatism. "Knowledge and becoming are mutually exclusive," wrote Nietzsche. Thus, if we

[6] *Recherches,* p. 56.

want to live in "the becoming," we must give up all hope of knowledge.

The Greeks, however, those great adventurers of the mind, tackled the problem head on. The pre-Socratics began by defining a motionless and transparent universe, in which every object had its corresponding expression. Nor did they recoil before the consequences of this initial claim. For if each word is guaranteed by an object in this world, nothing can be denied, and Protagoras is right to proclaim that all is true. Knowledge is inseparable from sensation and discussion becomes impossible. This world cannot be objected to, and we need only speak to tell the truth.[7] But Gorgias can just as well say that all is false, since in fact there are more real objects than words to designate them. No word can give a complete account of what it designates, nothing can be proved since nothing can be exhausted.

Greek thought oscillated for a long time between these extreme conclusions. And it is not without significance that it should have found its purest literary form in the dialogue, as if Protagoras and Gorgias had to confront each other tirelessly through centuries of Hellenic thought. Socrates' object, and Plato's, was to find the law that transcended our acts and our expressions. We are not very certain about Socrates' conclusions. We know that he chose to die, perhaps proof he believed more in the virtue of example than in verbal demonstration. But as for Plato, Parain correctly remarks that the *Dialogues*

[7] Similarly, if we conclude that we cannot name what does not exist, everything that has a name therefore exists, and there is not one of man's dreams (Jesus or Pan) that does not possess reality. If, on the contrary, we conclude that we can name what does not exist, we are without any rule.

are nothing but long struggles between language and reality, in which, paradoxically, reality is the loser. For the theory of Ideas marks the victory of words, which are more general than objects and closer to that ideal land of which this world is but a pale copy. For words to have meaning, their meaning must come from somewhere else than the tangible world, so fleeting and so changeable. This "elsewhere," to which so many Greek minds appealed with all their strength, is Being. Plato's solution is no longer psychological but cosmological.[8] He makes language an intermediary stage in the hierarchy that proceeds from matter to the One. The *logos* is a species of being, one of the spheres of universal harmony. Next to it, this world has no importance.

Thus, from the fifth century B.C., the definitive problem is laid out: the world or language, nonsense or eternal light. This is the sharp division that Aristotle, anxious to remain within the familiarity of earthly things, rejects. The Aristotelian theory of proof, whereby words are correct only by convention, but by a convention that rests on an accurate intuition of essences, is an ambiguous compromise. This is the choice Pascal brings back in all its cruelty. Uncertain of language, trembling before the enormity of falsehood, incapable of making paradox reasonable, Pascal merely convinces himself that it exists.[9] But he denounces this paradox better than anyone else: "Two errors," he writes. "1. To take everything literally, 2. to take everything spiritually." Thus Pascal suggests not a solution but a submission: submission to traditional language because it comes to us from

[8] *Essai sur le logos platonicien.*

[9] How words do have meaning! For us, Pascal is a great philosopher. But in Clermond-Ferrand, on the street where he was born, there exists a *Pascal-Bar.*

God, humility in the face of words in order to find their true inspiration. We have to choose between miracles and absurdity; there is no middle way. We know the choice Pascal made.

With a few important nuances that I shall mention further on, it is obvious that for Parain too this dilemma constitutes the basic problem. But he nonetheless studies the considerable effort modern philosophers have made to arrive at a compromise less insulting to reason. Such a compromise already begins in Descartes and Leibnitz, and I should point out that the chapters devoted to these philosophers in Parain's *Recherches* are absolutely original. The compromise, however, finds its best expression in German philosophy, especially in Hegel. We know that, characteristically, German philosophy hit upon the idea of deifying history. Precisely, history, taken as a whole, is considered the common expression of unity and of "becoming." Actually, it is no longer a question of unity or the absolute, in the classical sense. There are no longer any truly atemporal essences. On the contrary, ideas realize themselves in time. One of Hegel's texts quoted by Parain is a striking illustration of this position: "It must therefore be said of the Absolute that it is essentially Result and that it is only when it reaches its conclusion that it succeeds in being what it is in truth, its nature consisting precisely of being at one and the same time its own fact, subject or becoming." [1] This will immediately be recognized as a philosophy of immanence. The absolute no longer stands in opposition to the relative world, but mingles with it. There is no longer any truth, but there is something which is in the process of creating itself, which will become truth. And, similarly,

[1] *Recherches*, p. 149.

language is nothing but the totality of our inner life. The truth of a word is not something it owns, but something which creates itself little by little in sentences, speeches, literature, and the history of literatures. The word "God," for example, is nothing outside its attributes and the phrase that acknowledges Him. Separated from the pile of notions men's hearts and the history of mankind have accumulated and continue to accumulate around it, the word itself is insignificant. All words thus form part of an unending adventure that moves toward a universal meaning. At that point too language is being, because being is everything.

I have not enough space here to discuss the idea. Interested readers may turn to Parain's discussion. What he does, briefly, is to confront Hegel with the objections any philosophy of immanence raises: we cannot conceive of a truth that has neither beginning nor end, that participates at one and the same time in the physical and the universal. Metaphysics is the science of beginnings, and the demands language provokes are more categorical than the replies that one can furnish with it. Is language truth or falsehood? To reply that it is truth "in the process of self-creation" (and with the help of falsehood) is possible only if we carry our abstractions right into the heart of concrete things. In any case, this reply cannot satisfy the trenchant paradox with which the mind is here confronted.

The history of philosophy always brings the thinker back to the Pascalian dilemma. The aim of Parain's *Recherches* is to use new arguments to underline a paradox that is as old and cruel as man himself. It would indeed be a mistake to imagine that what we have here is an argument which simply concludes that the world is

236

meaningless. Because Parain's originality, for the time being at any rate, is to keep the dilemma in suspense. He does of course say that if language has no meaning then nothing can have any meaning, and that anything is possible. But his books show, *at the same time*, that words have just enough meaning to refuse us this final certainty that the ultimate answer is nothingness. Our language is neither true nor false. It is simultaneously useful and dangerous, necessary and pointless. "My words do perhaps distort my ideas, but if I do not reason then my ideas vanish into thin air." Neither yes nor no, language is merely a machine for creating doubt. And as in every problem that involves being, we find as soon as we advance a little further, to the point where our condition is called into question, that we are in the midst of darkness. A brutal "no" would at least be a definite answer. But this is not what we find. However uncertain language may be, Parain does feel, in spite of everything, that it yields the elements of a hierarchy. It does not provide us with being, but it allows us to suspect that being exists. Each word goes beyond the object it claims to designate, and belongs to the species. But if it indicates the species, it is not the species in its entirety. And even if we were to bring together all the words designating all the individuals of this species, this would not make up the species itself. The word contains something further, but this something further is still not enough.

The author refrains from drawing conclusions, and, as he says himself, his book begins and ends with the expression of misgivings. He allows us to guess, though, where his feelings and his experience will lead him. His apparent aim is to maintain choice and paradox: "Any philosophy," he writes, "which does not refute Pascal is vain." This is true, even for minds without a

penchant for the miraculous. In any case, the apparent
objectivity of the writer might give the impression that
his admirable books contain a metaphysics of falsehood
that has already had a very great defender. But while
Nietzsche accepted the falsehood of existence and saw it
as the principle of all life and all progress, Parain rejects
it. Or, at least, if he agrees to acknowledge it, he does not
give it his approval—preferring, at that precise moment,
to resign his judgment into the hands of some higher
power. This philosophy of expression ends indeed as a
theory of silence. Parain's basic idea is one of honesty:
the criticism of language cannot get around the fact that
our words commit us and that we should remain faithful
to them. Naming an object inaccurately means adding to
the unhappiness of this world. And, in fact, the vast
wretchedness of man, which has long pursued Parain
and which has inspired so many moving accents in his
work, is falsehood. Without knowing, or without yet saying, how it is possible, he knows that the great task of
man is not to serve falsehood. When he finishes his analysis, he merely glimpses the fact that language contains a
power that reaches far beyond ourselves: "We ask language to express what is most intimately personal to
man. It is not fitted to such a task. It was made to
formulate what is most strictly impersonal, what, in
man, is closest to other people.[2] It is to this higher banality that we should perhaps limit ourselves, for it is there
that the artist and the peasant, the thinker and the
worker, come together. Because language goes beyond
individuals, and its terrible inadequacy is the sign of its
transcendence. For Parain, this transcendence needs a
hypothesis. We are well aware that here, confronted with

[2] *Recherches,* p. 173.

238

the Pascalian choice, Parain leans toward the miraculous and, through it, to traditional language. He sees as evidence of a god the fact that men resemble one another. The miracle consists of going back to everyday words, bringing to them the honesty needed to lessen the part of falsehood and hatred.[3] This is indeed a path that leads to silence, but toward a silence that is relative, since absolute silence is impossible. Although Parain may tell us that his book stops short of ontology, his final effort is to pursue with the most silent of beings that higher conversation in which words are unnecessary: "Language is only a means of drawing us to its opposite: silence and God." [4]

At this point the critic should call a halt. The essential in any case is not yet to know which to choose: miracles or absurdity. The important thing is to show that they form the only possible choice, and that nothing else matters. But I think I would be justified in pointing out, in my conclusion, that this is where Parain's apparently very highly specialized investigations tie in with our century and its destiny. They have, in fact, never really been removed from them, and it is not irrelevant to learn that in their author's eyes Parain's books constitute one single meditation, extending over a number of years, intimately linked to the history of his life and our times.

[3] "Not to lie means not only refusing to hide our acts or our intentions, but also saying them and meaning them truthfully. This is not easy, and not something painlessly achieved." *Recherches*, p. 183.

[4] *Recherches*, p. 179. But from that point onward, the new problem that arises is how to reconcile the existence of falsehood with the existence of God. This, I assume, is the problem Parain will tackle in his next book.

What characterizes our century is perhaps not so much the need to rebuild the word as to rethink it. This amounts to giving the world its language. This is why some of the great artistic or political movements of our time have called language into question. Surrealism is a good illustration of how a philosophy of expression can be closely related to social criticism. Today, when the questions the world puts to us are so much more urgent, we search for words with even more anguish. The lexicons that are proposed to us don't fit. And it is natural for our best minds to form a kind of passionate academy in quest of a French dictionary. This is why the most significant works of the 1940's are perhaps not the ones people think, but those that call language and expression once more into question. The criticism of Jean Paulhan, the new world created by Francis Ponge, and Parain's historical philosophy seem to me to answer this need, though on very different planes and with very marked contrasts between them. For they do not indulge in Byzantine speculations about grammatical motivation, but ask a number of basic questions that are a part of human suffering. It is in their inquiry that our sacrifices find a form.

Only one thing has changed since the surrealists. Instead of using the uncertainty of language and the world to justify every possible kind of liberty—calculated madness or automatic writing—men are striving for an inner discipline. The tendency is no longer to deny that language is reasonable or to give free rein to the disorders it contains. The trend is to recognize that language has the limited powers to return, through miracles or through absurdity, to its tradition. In other words, and this intellectual move is of the highest importance for our time, we no longer use the falsehood and apparent meaninglessness of the world to justify instinctual behavior, but to defend a prejudice in favor of intelligence. It is a question merely of a reasonable intelligence that has returned to concrete things and has a concern for honesty. It is a new classicism—and one that expresses the two values most frequently attacked today: I mean intelligence and France.

For many reasons, the book Parain promises us on the ontology of language takes on great importance. But in the meantime, over and above any differences of opinion, let us begin by recognizing how deeply he resembles us. A taste for the truth, a lesson in modesty following scrupulous analysis informed by the most extensive documentation, this is the education one receives from Parain's books. We cannot turn our back on such works. We still have much to do, and we are still subjected to the most torturous questions. But it is certain that, whether we turn toward miracles or toward absurdity, we shall do nothing without those virtues in which human honor lies —honesty and poverty. What we can learn from the experience Parain sets forth is to turn our back upon attitudes and oratory in order to bear scrupulously the weight of our own daily life. "Preserve man in his perseverance," we read in *Essai sur la misère humaine,* "it is through this that he becomes immense, and gains the only immensity that he can transmit." Yes, we must rediscover our banality. The question is merely to know whether we shall have both the genius and the simple heart that are needed.

Article published in Poésie 44, *1944*

On Jules Roy's
La Vallée Heureuse[1]

❦❦ ❦❦❦ ❦❦

TODAY's writers talk about what happens to them. Tolstoi centered *War and Peace* around the retreat from Moscow, which he himself had not experienced. In our own day, he would not receive the approval of his contemporaries unless he replaced the first Napoleon with the third, and cast Prince Andrei in the siege of Sebastopol, where Tolstoi himself fought well (though without having been able to overcome his fear of rats).

There are reasons for this, and they are complex. But, in any case, very few of our writers seem blessed with that innocence which enables them to bring imaginary characters to life, detach themselves from these characters enough to love them truly, and, consequently, make other people love them. This is, after all, because

---

[1] *Jules Roy was born in Algeria in 1907. From 1927 to 1953 he was an officer in the French air force, and served with the R.A.F. during World War II. In 1960 he dedicated his book La Guerre d'Algerie to Camus's memory, but disagreed with his friend's refusal to take sides in the Algerian conflict.* —P.T.

we lack both time and a future, and because we have to hasten to create in the interval between war and revolution. Hence we do what is quickest, which is to report what we have done and what we have seen. And it is true that any great work is, in a way, the account of a spiritual adventure. But generally such an account is suggested or transfigured. Today, we go no further than the account, the document, the "slice of life," as the Naturalists ignorantly called it. A minimum of preparation, a few strips of bacon, two or three flowers of fluted paper, and the meat is served raw.

As a result, cooks are becoming scarce; a certain manner is beginning to be lost, or at least forgotten, and finally the best we can do is accept what we are. But this shouldn't keep us from being clear-sighted and from realizing that this new taste for raw meat leads to the loss of what has long been the strength, sometimes the explosive strength, of our literature—I mean a sense of propriety. (To make myself clear, and by straining words a little, I will say, for example, that there is a sense of propriety in Sade.) Candor is becoming obstreperous, and when everyone embraces it, it becomes a new kind of conformism. The attitude is very understandable, of course. The adventures of past writers almost always had to do with love. Through respect for their partners, and consideration for the world, they transposed. Today, the raw material of experience is provided by men whom no one respects, and their frenzied embraces, called war or revolution. What is the point of restraint? Let the meat bleed, since that is its function.

But this does not alter the fact that art cannot do without restraint, whose very impulses it shares. It does not alter the fact that art lies in the distance that time gives to suffering or to joy. And if our time compels us to

turn away from art in order to involve ourselves in new
and fresh suffering, it is still true that the best books are
and will be those which limit the damage, and which,
though rejecting nothing of the cumbersome present, will
nevertheless continue to show a certain restraint.

I have not been able to find a better way than this
long digression to express why I find *La Vallée Heureuse*,
by Jules Roy, a book that meets all the imperatives of the
present and yet is exceptional. It manages to maintain a
certain delicacy in spite of the killing. At the same time it
deals with a personal experience, which the author
scarcely disguises. After ten pages, it is obvious that
Chevrier is Roy himself. Only the conclusion seems to
have been fictionalized. For the rest, it is very clear. Roy
is in command of the crew of a bomber, in the R.A.F.,
and has to carry out the customary tour of duty of thirty
bombing missions over Germany. Statistically, it is rare
for bombers to do more than twenty missions because
they are usually shot down before that. This dangerous
and monotonous struggle against probability forms the
subject matter of the book. Roy climbs into the "B," his
plane, with his crew. He accomplishes his mission. He
returns. He waits for the next mission. He climbs back
into the "B," his plane, with his crew. He accomplishes
his mission. He returns. He waits for the next mission.
He climbs back into the "B," and so on and so forth. All
we have is the description of the various circumstances,
anti-aircraft barrages, delay in reaching the target when
the enemy fighters have already taken off, or collision on
landing, when the bomber, in the normal course of
events, would have crashed with its load of men and
bombs. Finally, we have the death of a friend who has
not had the incredible luck of reaching his thirtieth mis-

sion. The book is therefore the story of a run of luck, but
one enjoyed with suitable humility.

For this is the originality of *La Vallée Heureuse*.
It is possible that, like all of us, Roy has lost his innocence. But he does not make a fuss about it, which is
another way of approaching innocence. He does not gen-
eralize about anything nor does he find a pretext for
lamentation or glorification. In *La Vallée Heureuse*, Roy
has not set out to write a book of morals or heroism. It
contains no theory of destiny. The author talks about
himself and his friends, but does not claim to use his own
experience as a basis for judging other men. If such
judgment is implied, then that is the reader's business. In
other words, Roy has accepted the experience without
trying to place himself above it. He is trapped in it, or,
rather, other people have trapped him like a rat. And he
has found himself caught, as in those formation flights
which he describes so admirably, the airplanes coagu-
lated in the heart of the night, wing to wing, each crew
pursuing its task, isolated in the fantastic noise and the
shadow of the sky, with no feeling except the terrible
perpetual expectation of a possible collision, and the
nervous fear that, when they return, all the bombs will
not have been dropped, and that the instant of landing
will bring new death. Month after month, shoulder to
shoulder, Roy thus pursued his task in the night of a war
for which he had no liking. And, rather than draw from it
some great view on human destiny, he has limited himself to registering the moments when he was afraid and
those when he picked up new courage. This is how he has
been able to speak for all of us, while seeking to speak for
no one, and this is how for the first time, thanks to him,
we can imagine the thoughts of those who, year after

year, traveled across the black sky of our imprisoned towns.

La Vallée Heureuse does not, therefore, take its place among the great books of humanism that we are used to demanding, but among those works of strength and modesty whose taste we had forgotten. When Chevrier tells us that he is afraid (the terrible *Miserere* that mounts in him at the moment when the bomber takes off on a new mission), it is not so that he can beat his breast. It is normal, in certain circumstances, for a man to be afraid. And, similarly, when he gives the order to aim for the target under conditions made ten times more dangerous by the fact that the bomber is late, he does not glamorize his action. It is normal, under all circumstances, for a man to do his duty. On each page of the book, we find the same naïveté (in the sense that Schiller spoke of Greek naïveté). The chapter I like the least, the one where Roy talks about love, reveals indeed that this strange warrior has recognized and accepted his sentimentality for what it was, something defenseless. In other words, he writes naturally about being sentimental, just as he wrote naturally about fear and courage. And that is enough to justify everything.

At this degree of simplicity and honesty, a man should be accepted or rejected as a whole. I would have no difficulty in saying what I feel on this point, as readers will have guessed. But this book is one that makes us think seriously. In other words, it is a book worthy of a man. What other praise can I add? Let me merely say that after we have followed Chevrier in his long struggle against chance, death, and himself, the fraternal esteem that comes irresistibly to us is, I suppose, the truest homage a writer of good faith can hope for from a reader of good faith.

A word finally about the style. It too is a style of struggle. It does not flow easily; it makes an effort. The sentences are generally long, and rather complex. The image is surrounded, approached, released for a moment, then taken up again in the thickness of the words before being finally delivered in its strength and flesh. Such a great tension is, inevitably, accompanied by a few obscurities and excessive complexities of style. But it is this very effort that explains Roy's greatest success as well as his surprising ability to make us see what he is describing. For, after this great pitching of words and sentences, grouped into squadrons, assembled like the airplanes setting out on a raid, traveling wing tip to wing tip, slowly through the night, where at the very end of their journey through clouds and shadows they will make the gigantic flames of war burst forth, so the image bursts forth, in the end, so terrible in its loveliness that it shakes us like an explosion or a cataclysm. This is the passage where the squadron, coming back from a mission, is suddenly surrounded in the darkness by exploding rockets and machine-gunned by enemy fighters, which shoot the heavy bombers down one by one. "New fires were born with the flapping of the heavy gasoline flames as they were flattened by the wind; the bombers rolled over a little, then caught fire from the fuel tanks in the wings, floated on a little longer and exploded like stars."

Published in L'Arche, *February 1947*

Encounters with André Gide

I WAS sixteen when I first met André Gide. An uncle, who had taken part of my education in hand, sometimes gave me books. A butcher by trade, with a fairly wealthy clientele, his only real passion was for reading and ideas. He devoted his mornings to the meat business, and the rest of the day to his library, newspapers, and interminable discussions in the local cafés.

One day, he held out to me a small book with a parchmentlike cover, assuring me that I would find it interesting. I read everything, indiscriminately, in those days; I probably opened *Les Nourritures Terrestres* after having finished *Lettres de Femme* or a volume of the Pardaillan series. I found the invocations rather obscure. I shied away from this hymn to the bounties of nature. In Algiers, at sixteen, I was saturated with these riches; no doubt I longed for others, and then [the evocations of] "Blida, little rose . . ." I knew Blida, unfortunately. I gave the book back to my uncle, telling him that it had indeed been interesting. Then I went back to the beach, to my listless studies and idle reading, and also to the difficult life I led. The encounter had not been a success.

The next year, I met Jean Grenier. He also, among other things, offered me a book. It was a novel by André de Richaud called *La Douleur*. I don't know André de Richaud. But I have never forgotten his admirable book, the first to speak to me of what I knew: a mother, poverty, fine evening skies. It loosened a tangle of obscure bonds within me, freed me from fetters whose hindrance I felt without being able to give them a name. I read it in one night, in the best tradition, and the next morning, armed with a strange new liberty, went hesitatingly forward into unknown territory. I had just learned that books dispensed things other than forgetfulness and entertainment. My obstinate silences, this vague but all-persuasive suffering, the strange world that surrounded me, the nobility of my family, their poverty, my secrets, all this, I realized, could be expressed! There was a deliverance, an order of truth, in which poverty, for example, suddenly took on its true face, the one I had suspected it possessed, that I somehow revered. *La Douleur* gave me a glimpse of the world of creation, into which Gide was to be my guide. This is how my second encounter with him took place.

I began to read properly. A fortunate illness had taken me away from my beaches and my pleasures. My readings were still disorderly, but there was a new appetite in them. I was looking for something, I wanted to rediscover the world I had glimpsed that seemed to me to be my own. From books to daydreams, alone or because of friends, little by little I was discovering new dimensions in life. After so many years, I still remember the amazement of this apprenticeship. One morning, I stumbled on Gide's *Traités*. Two days later, I knew by heart whole passages of *La Tentative amoureuse*. As to the *Retour de l'enfant prodigue,* it had become the book of which I never spoke: perfection seals our lips. I only made a dramatic adaptation of it, which I later put on the stage with a few friends. Meanwhile, I read all Gide's work, responding in my turn to *Les Nourritures Terrestres* with the personal upheaval so often described by others. Mine came the second time round, perhaps because of the first reading I was a young, unenlightened barbarian, but also because for me there was nothing revolutionary in the senses. The shock was decisive in quite a different way. Long before Gide himself had confirmed this interpretation, I learned to read *Les Nourritures Terrestres* as the gospel of a self-deprivation I needed.

From that point on, Gide held sway over my youth, and it is impossible not to be always grateful to those we have at least once admired for having hoisted us to the highest point our soul can reach. In spite of all this, however, I never saw Gide as my master either as a writer or a thinker. I had given myself others. Rather, Gide seemed to me, because of what I have just said, the model of the artist, the guardian, the king's son, who kept watch over the gates of the garden where I wanted to live. There is almost nothing in what he has written about art, for example, that I don't entirely approve of, although our century has moved away from his conception. The reproach made of Gide's work is that it neglects the anguish of our time. We choose to believe that a writer must be revolutionary to be great. If this is so, history proves that it is true only up *to* the revolution, and no further. Moreover, it is by no means certain that Gide did move away from his time. What is more certain is that his time wanted to move away from what he represented. The question is whether it will ever succeed, or will do so only by committing suicide. Gide also suffers from that other prejudice of our day, which insists that we parade our despair to be counted as intelligent. On this point, discussion is easier: the pretext is a poor one.

Yet I had to forget Gide's example, of necessity, and turn away very early from this world of innocent creation, leaving at the same time the land where I was born. History imposed itself on my generation. I had to take my place in the waiting line on the threshold of the black years. We fell into step, and have not yet reached our goal. How could I not have changed since then? At least I have not forgotten the plenitude and light in which my life began, and I have put nothing above them. I have not denied Gide.

In fact, I encountered him again at the end of our darkest years. I was in Paris then, living in part of his flat. It was a studio with a balcony, and its greatest peculiarity consisted of a trapeze that hung in the middle of the room. I had it taken down, I think; I got tired of seeing the intellectuals who came to see me hanging from it. I had been settled in the studio for some months when Gide, in his turn, came back from North Africa. I had never met him before; yet it was as if we had always known each other. Not that Gide ever received me very intimately. He had a horror, as I already knew, of that noisy promiscuity which takes the place of friendship in our world. But the smile with which he greeted me was simple and joyful and, when he was with me, I never saw him on his guard.

Otherwise, forty years difference in age stood between us, together with our mutual horror of embarrassing each other. This is why I spent long weeks next door to Gide, almost without seeing him. Occasionally, he would knock at the double door that separated the studio from his library. At arm's length, he would be carrying Sarah, his cat, who had slipped into his room via the roof. Sometimes, the piano attracted him. On another occasion, he listened by my side to the announcement of the armistice on the radio. I realized that the war, which brings most people an end to their loneliness, was for him, as it was for me, the only true loneliness. Sitting around the radio, for the first time we shared the solidarity of the times. On other days, all I knew of his presence on the other side of the door were footsteps, rustlings, the gentle disturbance of his meditations and musings. What did it matter! I knew that he was there, next door to me, guarding with his unrivaled dignity that secret realm I had dreamed of entering, and toward which I have always turned, in the midst of our struggles and our shouts.

Today, now that he is no longer among us, who can replace my old friend at the gates of this kingdom? Who will look after the garden until we can get back to it? He, at least, kept watch until his death; so it is right for him to continue to receive the quiet gratitude we owe to our true masters. The unpleasant noises made at his departure will in no way alter this. Of course, those who know how to hate are still furious over this death. He, whose privileges have been so bitterly envied, as if justice did not consist of sharing these privileges rather than mingling everything in a general servitude, is argued over even at the end: people are indignant about such serenity. Not a day goes by without his once again receiving the homage of hatred, envy, or that poor insolence which

thinks it descends from Cardinal de Retz, although actually it originates in the scullery.

Yet what unanimity ought to have been performed around this little iron bed. To die is such appalling torture for some men that it seems to me as if a
happy death redeems a small patch of creation. If I were
a believer, Gide's death would be a consolation. But if
those believers I see do believe, what is the object of their
faith? Those deprived of grace simply have to practice
generosity among themselves. As far as the believers are
concerned, they lack nothing, they are provided for; or at
least they act as if that were the case. We, on the other
hand, lack everything but the fraternal hand. Surely this
is why Sartre was able to pay Gide, over and above their
differences, an exemplary act of homage. Certain men
thus find, in their reflections, the secret of a serenity
neither miserly nor facile. Gide's secret is that he never,
in the midst of his doubts, lost the pride of being a man.
Dying was also part of this condition, which he wanted to
assume to the very end. What would have been said of
him, if after having lived surrounded by privilege, he had
gone trembling to his death? This would have shown that
his moments of happiness were stolen ones. But no, he
smiled at the mystery, and turned toward the abyss the
same face he had presented to life. Without even knowing it, we were waiting for that one last moment. And, for
one last time, he kept the rendezvous.

"Homage to André Gide," *from the* Nouvelle nouvelle revue
française, *November 1951*

Roger Martin du Gard[1]

❧❧ ❧❧❧ ❧❧

READ, in *Devenir!*, the portrait of old Mazarelles and his
wife. From his very first book, Roger Martin du Gard
achieves the portrait in depth, whose secret seems to be
lost nowadays. This third dimension, which extends the
range of his work, makes it almost unique in contempo-

[1] *Roger Martin du Gard was born in Paris in 1881 and
died in 1958. He was trained as a historian and archivist, and
his first really important novel,* Jean Barois, *uses some of the
techniques of the professional historian for literary purposes.
Published in 1913, it tells the story of a man who is led by the
discoveries of nineteenth-century science to abandon the Catholic
faith in which he has been educated. He founds a rationalist review called* Le Semeur, *which has similarities to Péguy's* Cahiers
de la Quinzaine, *and plays an active part in the campaign to establish the innocence of Captain Dreyfus. He is highly successful in
his professional career, but nevertheless conscious of how easily he
can relapse into the acceptance of Christian belief. One day, for
example, when he has just delivered a lecture on* The Future of
Disbelief, *his cab is almost involved in an accident, and he finds
himself reciting the* Hail Mary. *This incident makes him realize
the danger that he may, in old age, return to the religion of his
childhood, and he therefore composes a "Last Will and Testa-*

rary literature. Our present literary production could, in fact, when it is valid, claim descent from Dostoevski rather than from Tolstoi. Inspired or impassioned shad-

---

ment" in which he declares his complete lack of belief and states that any future relapse into religion is to be explained solely by old age and the fear of death. As he grows older, he does in fact accept Catholicism again, and dies a believer. On discovering his will, his pious wife, encouraged by a priest, burns this evidence of her husband's intended fidelity to free thought.

Martin du Gard's major work, however, and the one for which he was awarded the Nobel Prize for Literature in 1937, is the long novel Les Thibault. *This began appearing in 1922, and was completed by the publication of the* Epilogue *in 1940. It describes the life of two brothers, Jacques and Antoine Thibault, during the years immediately before the First World War. Jacques, the rebel, is some ten years younger than his more stable brother Antoine, and appears to be the more interesting character. In particular, his love affair with Jenny de Fontanin, sister of his close friend Daniel, occupies a good deal of the first two volumes. However, Antoine takes on more importance in the* La Belle Saison *and* La Mort du Père, *and represents a theme to which Camus himself devotes much attention: the impossibility of explaining, within a religious context, the purely physical suffering that afflicts men, children, and animals alike. Like Dr. Rieux in* The Plague, *Antoine is extremely conscious of the interminable defeat that death inflicts upon a doctor, and he administers to his father, who is dying in agony, the injection that he knows will kill him.*

Originally Martin du Gard had intended to continue the adventures of Jacques and Antoine in a whole series of novels describing their life in the Paris of the 1920's. However, on January 1, 1931, he was involved in a serious car accident, and had to spend a long time in bed. There, meditating on his work, he came to realize that the 1914–18 war had so completely destroyed the world in which Jacques and Antoine had lived that he could not carry on with their story as if nothing had happened. He consequently destroyed the part of the novel that he had already written but not yet published, and composed L'Eté 1914, ows outline the commentary in motion of a reflection on man's fate. Doubtless there is also depth and perspective in Dostoevski's characters; but, unlike Tolstoi, he does not make such qualities the rule for his creation. Dostoevski looks above all for movement, Tolstoi for form. There is the same difference between the young women in *The Possessed* and Natasha Rostov as there is between a character in the movies and one on the stage: more animation and less flesh. In Dostoevski these weaknesses on the part of a genius are compensated for by the introduction of a further, spiritual dimension, rooted in sin or sanctity. But, with a few exceptions, such notions are consid-

---

a two-volume account of the outbreak of the First World War. Jacques, a socialist and fervent pacifist, is killed in an attempt to throw leaflets from an airplane onto the French and German armies as they advance to battle. Antoine is gassed, and eventually kills himself when he realizes that he will never recover. The Epilogue is made up of his diary, and ends with two notations: "Easier than you think" and "Jean-Paul." Dying, he thinks of the son born to Jacques and Jenny, and of the physical survival of humanity and the family that this son represents.

There are a number of analogies between Martin du Gard and Camus that help to explain the long preface Camus wrote to his collected works in 1954. Both were socialists, but were opposed to extremist forms of political thought. Both were agnostics, preoccupied with the problems of death and physical suffering. As artists, both strove to be impersonal, and to write books in which their own personality would not be immediately visible. Yet while Martin du Gard succeeded, so much so that he is more completely identified with his work than any other French writer, Camus failed, and it is perhaps his awareness of this failure which gives such a note of regret. Similarly, Martin du Gard succeeded in organizing his life in such a way that he could devote his life to his work, whereas Camus, as can be seen from his letter to "P. B." (pages 342–4), was constantly distracted from writing by his other preoccupations and duties. —P.T.

ered old-fashioned by our contemporaries, who have as a result retained from Dostoevski only a legacy of shadows. Combined with the influence of Kafka (in whom the visionary triumphs over the artist), or with the technique of the American behaviorist novel, assimilated by artists who have more and more difficulty, emotionally and intellectually, in keeping up with the acceleration of history and who, in order to deal with everything, go deeply into nothing, this imperious example has produced in France an exciting and disappointing literature, whose failures are on a par with its ambitions, and of which it is impossible to say whether it exhausts a fashion or foreshadows a new age.

Roger Martin du Gard, who began writing at the beginning of the century, is, on the other hand, the only literary artist of his time who can be counted among Tolstoi's descendants. But at the same time he is perhaps the only one (and, in a sense, more than Gide or Valéry) to anticipate the literature of today, by bequeathing problems that crush it and also by authorizing some of its hopes. Martin du Gard shares with Tolstoi a liking for human beings, the art of depicting them in the mystery of their flesh, and a knowledge of forgiveness—virtues outdated today. The world Tolstoi described nevertheless formed a whole, a single organism animated by the same faith; his characters meet in the supreme adventure of eternity. One by one, visibly or not, they all, at some point in their stories, end up on their knees. And Tolstoi himself, in his winter flight from family and glory, wanted to recapture their unhappiness, universal wretchedness, and the innocence of which he could not despair. The same faith is lacking in the society Martin du Gard was to depict and also to a certain extent lacking in the author. This is why his work is also one of doubt, of disappointed and persevering reason, of ignorance acknowledged, and of a wager on man with no future other than himself. It is in this, as in its invisible audacities or its contradictions accepted, that his work belongs to our time. Even today it can explain us to ourselves, and soon, perhaps, be useful to those who are to come.

There is a strong possibility, in fact, that the real ambition of our authors, after they have assimilated *The Possessed*, will be one day to write *War and Peace*. After tearing through wars and negations, they keep the hope, even if it's unadmitted, of rediscovering the secrets of a universal art that, through humility and mastery, will once again bring characters back to life in their flesh and their duration. It is doubtful whether such great creation is possible in the present state of society either in the East or in the West. But there is nothing to prevent us from hoping that these two societies, if they do not destroy each other in a general suicide, will fertilize each other and make creation possible once again. Let us also bear in mind the possibility of genius, that a new artist will succeed, through superiority or freshness, in registering all the pressures he undergoes and digesting the essential features of the contemporary adventure. His destiny then will be to fix in his work the prefiguration of what will be, and, quite exceptionally, to combine the gift of prophecy with the power of true creation. These unimaginable tasks cannot, in any case, do without the secrets contained in the art of the past. The work of Martin du Gard, in its solitude and its solidity, contains some of these secrets and offers them in a familiar form. In him, our master and our accomplice at the same time, we can both find what we do not possess and rediscover what we are.

* * *

"Masterpieces," said Flaubert, "are like the larger mammals. They have a peaceful look." Yes, but their blood still runs with strange, young ardor. Such fire and such audacity already bring Martin du Gard's work closer to us. The more so, after all, if it does look peaceful. A kind of geniality masks its relentless lucidity, apparent only upon reflection, although then it takes on added dimension.

It is important to note, first of all, that Martin du Gard never thought provocation could be an artistic method. Both the man and his work were forged by the same patient effort, in withdrawal from the world. Martin du Gard is the example, a rare one indeed, of one of our great writers whose telephone number nobody knows. He exists, very strongly, in our literary society. But he has dissolved himself in it as sugar does in water. Fame and the Nobel Prize have favored him, if I may so express it, with a kind of supplementary darkness. Simple and mysterious, he has something of the divine principle described by the Hindus: the more he is named, the more he disappears. Furthermore, there is no calculation in this quest for obscurity. Those who have the honor of knowing him as a man realize his modesty is real, so real that it appears abnormal. I for one have always denied that there could be such a thing as a modest artist; since meeting Martin du Gard my certainty has begun to waver. But this monster of modesty also has other reasons, apart from the peculiarity of his character, for seeking to live in withdrawal from the world: the legitimate concern every artist worthy of the name has to protect the time needed for his work. This reason becomes imperative the moment the author identifies his work with the construction of his own life. Time then ceases to be merely the place where the work is done, but

259

becomes the work itself, immediately threatened by any diversion.

Such a vocation rejects provocation and its calculated stratagems, instead accepting in everything concerned with literary creation the law of true craftsmanship. When Martin du Gard began his career as a writer, men were entering literature (the history of the *Nouvelle revue française* group is clear proof of this) rather as one enters the religious life. Today, people enter it—or pretend to do so—as if in mockery; it is merely a pathetic derision which can, with a few writers, have its effectiveness. With Martin du Gard, however, there was never any doubt about the seriousness of literature. The first of his published novels, *Devenir!,* is a clear indication of this, being the story of a literary vocation that fails through lack of character. He makes the person in whom he depicts himself say: "Everyone has a little genius; what people don't have anymore these days, because it's something you have to acquire, is a conscience." The same character likes neither too polished an art, which he describes as "castrated," nor "geniuses who are essentially adolescent." I hope readers will forgive the author for the truth and topicality of his second remark. But the "big guy," as Martin du Gard calls him in the novel, continues squarely in the same vein. "In Paris, all writers seem to have talent; actually, they have never had time to acquire any: all they have is a kind of cleverness which they borrow from one another, a communal treasure in which individual values are frittered away."

It is already obvious that if art is a religion, it will not be an attractive one. On this point Martin du Gard quickly cut himself off from the theoreticians of art for art's sake. Symbolism, which caused so much exquisite damage among the writers of his generation, never had any effect on him, except in certain stylistic indulgences [2] which he later outgrew, like adolescent acne. He was only twenty-seven when he wrote *Devenir!*, and the writer who is quoted with enthusiasm in this first work is already Tolstoi. From here on, Martin du Gard was to remain faithful all his life to an ascetic vocation, an artistic Jansenism that would make him shun ostentation and effect, in order to sacrifice everything to uninterrupted labor on a work he wanted to make endure. "What is difficult," says this precocious and perspicacious thinker, "is not to have been someone but to stay that way." Genius runs the risk, in fact, of being no more than a fleeting accident. Only character and work can transform it into fame and a livelihood. Hard work, and the organization and humility that go with it, are thus at the very core of free creation and consequently indispensable in a craft where work, but work humbly pursued, is also the rule of life. It is no exaggeration to say that Martin du Gard's very aesthetic principles made it inevitable that his work, in which individual problems have the starring roles, take on historical dimensions. The man who finds his reasons for living and his delights in free work can, in the end, bear any humiliation except the humiliation justly inflicted on his work, just as he can accept every privilege except those that separate him from his liberty, the work to which he is chained. Works like Roger Martin du Gard's sometimes unknowingly restore artistic toil to its rightful place in the city, and can no longer be divorced then from its victories or defeats.

But even before any other discovery, the result is this work, solid as stone, whose main body is *Les Thi-*

[2] "The milky river of the sky sweeps along its silver spangles" (from *Devenir!*).

bault and whose buttresses are *Devenir!, Jean Barois, Vieille France, Confidence africaine,* and the plays. We can discuss this work, we can try to see its limitations. But we cannot deny that it exists, and does so superbly, with an unbelievable honesty. Commentaries can add to it or detract from it, but the fact remains that we have here one of those works, exceptional in France, around which one can turn, as one walks around a building. The same generation that gave us so many aestheticians, so many subtle, delicate writers, also brought a work rich in people and in passions, constructed according to the plans of a well-tried technique. This nave of men, built solely with the rigor of an art practiced a whole lifetime, testifies that in a time of poets, essayists, and novelists concerned with the soul, a master craftsman, a Pierre de Craon without a religion but not without faith, was born in our land.

Nevertheless, a law exists in art which says that every creator should be buried beneath the weight of his most obvious virtues. The proverbial honesty of his art has sometimes hidden the true Martin du Gard in a time which, for various reasons, put genius and improvisation above everything else, as if genius could do without a work schedule and improvisation without arduous leisure. The critics thought they had done enough by paying homage to virtue, forgetting that in art virtue is only a means placed at the service of risk. There is certainly no lack of audacity in the work that concerns us. It stems nearly always from the obstinate pursuit of psychological truth. It thus serves to emphasize the ambiguity of human beings, without which this truth is meaningless. We are already surprised, reading *Devenir!,* by the cruel modernity of the ending; André, who has just buried his wife in great grief, notices the young servant girl standing at the window. We know that he has desired her, and realize that she will help him digest his sorrow.

Martin du Gard deals frankly with sexuality and with the shadowy zone of darkness it casts over every life. Frankly, but not crudely. He has never given way to the temptation of suggestive licentiousness that makes so many contemporary novels as boring as guides to social etiquette. He has not obligingly described monotonous excesses. He has chosen rather to show the importance of sexual life through its inopportunity. Like a true artist, he has not painted directly what it consists of, but indirectly, what it forces people to become. It is sensuality, throughout her life, for example, that makes Mme de Fontanin vulnerable in the presence of her unfaithful husband. We know this, and yet it is never said, except as Mme de Fontanin watches over her husband on his deathbed. What is also noticeable in *Les Thibault* is a curious intermingling of the themes of desire and death. (Once more, it is the night before the burial of Mother Frubling that Jacques is initiated by Lisbeth.) Certainly we must see this intermingling as one of the obsessions that are an artist's privilege and at the same time as a means of underlining the unusual nature of the sexual life.

But desire is not only mingled with the things of death, it also contaminates morality and makes it ambiguous. The righteous man, the man who observes the outward show of Christianity, the father in *Les Thibault,* writes in his diary: "Do not confuse with the love of our neighbor the emotion we feel at the approach, at the touch, of certain young people, even children." Then he crosses out only the final words, and this omission reconciles him with both modesty and sincerity. Just as Jérôme de Fontanin savors the delight of the repentant libertine when he saves Rinette from the prostitution into which he had cast her. "I am good, I am better than they think," he repeats tenderly to himself. But he cannot resist sleeping with her one last time, adding the pleasures of the flesh to those of virtue. One sentence is all Martin du Gard needs to summarize the mechanical inspiration of the pose: "His fingers were automatically unfastening her skirt, as his lips rested on her forehead in a paternal kiss."

The whole work has this flavor of truth. The admirable *Vieille France* not only offers us Martin du Gard's most sinister character, the postman Joigneau, a sort of Astaroth on bicycle, but it also abounds in pitiless revelations about the provincial heart, and the last page gives an astonishing conclusion. Similarly, in *African Secret,* the very simplicity of an incestuous brother's tone will make his unfortunate adventure seem natural. In 1931, with *Un taciturne,* Martin du Gard dared to put on the stage, without the slightest vulgarity of tone, the drama of a respectable industrialist who discovers he has homosexual leanings. At last, in *Les Thibault,* the brilliant touches multiply. One could quote the scene in which Gise secretly allows the child that the man she loves has had with another woman to suck her virgin breast; or the meal Antoine and Jacques have, after the father's death, that almost in spite of themselves takes on a slight air of celebration. But there are two such touches I rank higher than the others, for they show the great novelist at work.

The first is Jacques' stubborn silence when, for the first time, Antoine comes to see him at the reform school in Crouy. How could there be a better way to convey humiliation than this silence. The rapidly muttered words, the onsets of reticence in which this silence is clothed, and which serve to underline it even further, are so accurately calculated and proportioned that mystery and pity suddenly erupt into what was until then a straightforward story, opening much wider vistas than those of the middle-class Parisian milieu in which it had begun. Humiliation has never been depicted more objectively or more successfully, except by Dostoevski, whose technique is either frenzied or grating (I am not counting Lawrence, who describes a personal humiliation) and by Malraux, in the epic mode (especially in *La Voie royale,* which I persist in liking whatever its author may say). No one, however, has ever tried to paint it in subdued and even colors, and Martin du Gard has perhaps achieved what is most difficult in art. If there are artistic miracles, they must resemble those that come from grace. I have always thought it would be easier to redeem a man steeped in vice and crime than a greedy, narrow-minded, pitiless merchant. Thus, in art, the more prosaic the reality chosen as one's subject matter, the more difficult it is to transfigure. Even here, however, there is a point beyond which we cannot go, that makes any claim to absolute realism quite untenable. But it is here nonetheless, half way between reality and its stylization, that art from time to time achieves the perfect triumph. The portrait of Jacques in his humiliation remains, in my view, one of these triumphs.

To give one last example of Martin du Gard's technique, I shall quote the father's simulated death in *Les Thibault.* A brilliant idea, indeed, on the novelist's part, to make the play-acting that had, in a sense, formed this character's whole life, extend even into death. The man who could not prevent himself from constantly playing the part of a Christian is also incapable, in the idleness and depression of an illness that he does not know is fatal, of resisting the temptation to dramatize the last moments of his life. So he organizes, from his bed, a dress rehearsal, which is half sincere, involving assemblies of servants, exemplary acts of repentance, the praising of virtues, and flights of holiness. The father expects his reward in the form of protests that will dissipate the vague anxiety he sometimes harbors, as does every invalid. But his family's genuine grief, their tacit acceptance of his speeches on his approaching end, suddenly bring him face to face with his true condition. His playacting, instead of producing the good results he had hoped for, brings the cruel reflection of a merciless reality. Having thought himself an actor, he finds himself a victim. From this moment, he begins to die, and fear sterilizes his faith. His great cry "Ah, how can God do this to me!" crowns this dramatic discovery with the emptiness and duplicity of his religious beliefs and also his need of them. He dies reconciled, nonetheless, but in gasps of pain and childish songs that reveal a man broken to the very core, stripped of his pretense and ostentation, delivered naked to death and simple faith.

Such a canvas bears the signature of a master. The novelist able to depict the successive impulses of a soul that transforms being itself into a device for pretense has nothing to learn from anyone. He has only lessons, and durable ones, to offer us.

But even more than his art it is Martin du Gard's themes that coincide with our own preoccupations. The path he has followed with so fortunate and deliberate a pace is one the rest of us have had to race along, with history at our heels. I mean, generally, the personal evolution that leads one to a recognition of the history of all men and to an acceptance of their struggles. Even in this, of course, Martin du Gard has his own particular stamp.

He stands midway between his predecessors and his peers (who talked of nothing but the individual and never let history play more than a circumstantial role) and his successors (who make only embarrassed allusions to the individual). In *Les Thibault*, and in *Jean Barois*, individuals are intact and the pain of history still quite fresh. They have not yet worn each other out. Martin du Gard has not experienced our situation, in which we inherit at the same time shop-worn people and a history tensed and paralyzed by several wars and the fear of final destruction. We can say without paradox that what is alive in our present-day experience lies behind us, in a work like Roger Martin du Gard's.

As early as 1913, in any case, *Jean Barois* outlines the movement that concerns us. The subject of this curious novel is familiar, although its construction is quite unusual. Technically, in fact, there is nothing of the novel about it. It breaks with all the genre's traditions, and there is nothing comparable to it in literature since. Its author seems to have looked, systematically, for the least fictional of mediums. The book is made up of dialogues (accompanied by brief stage directions) and documents, some of them incorporated in their original form. Consequently, the interest of the book never weakens, and it can be read in one sitting. This may be because the subject was perfectly suited to such a technique. Actually, Martin du Gard intended to adopt this form for all his future work. As it turned out, only *Jean Barois* was to profit from it. One might say that in a way this book (more than Zola's novels, which were intended as scientific although their author could not keep them from becoming epic) is the only great novel of the age of scientism, whose hopes and disappointments it expresses so well. This documentary novel is also a monograph, all the more surprising in that it concerns the case history of a religious crisis. It happens that to make a card index of the aspirations and doubts of a soul was, in the long run, an enterprise particularly fitting in a period inspired, with a few exceptions, by the religion of science. In the course of the book, Barois abandons the old faith for the new. If, face to face with death, he betrays this new belief at the very last moment, he still remains the man of that brief new age which was to collapse in 1914. His story is therefore all the more striking, related to us in the style of the new gospels. The case history reads like an adventure tale because its unusual form is deeply wedded to the story it unfolds. The evolution of a man who comes to doubt traditional faith, who thinks he finds a more certain faith in science,[3] could not be reported better than by this technique of quasi-scientific description, which Martin du Gard intended to perfect. In the end, science satisfied neither Barois nor his creator, but its method, or at least its ideal, was fleetingly raised, in this novel, to the dignity of perfectly effective art. The exploit has not been repeated in our literature or even in Martin du Gard's later work. But didn't the faith that inspired it, already threatened in the book itself, also die, prematurely, as a result of the excesses of mechanized savagery? *Jean Barois* remains at least a testamentary work in which we can find moving evidence of a vanished belief and prophecies that affected our lives.

The conflict between faith and science, which so excited the early years of this century, arouses less interest today. We are living out its consequences, nonetheless, which were foreshadowed in *Jean Barois*. To take

[3] "This innate need," says Barois, "to understand and explain, which today finds its wide and complete satisfaction in the scientific development of our age."

only one example: irreligion is portrayed as closely linked to the rise of the socialist movement, and the book consequently lays bare one of the most powerful driving forces in our history. Fleeing from the encounter with God, Jean Barois discovers men. His liberation coincides with the great movement that grew up around Dreyfus. The "Sower's" group links Barois to the rest of mankind; it is there that he reaches full maturity, and that what can be called the cycle of history (struggle and victory) exhausts his manhood. Historical disappointments bring him gradually back to solitude, to anguish, and, faced with death, to the denial of his new faith. Can the community of men, which sometimes helps us to live, also help us die? This is the question underlying all Martin du Gard's work, which creates its tragic quality. For if the reply is negative, the situation of the modern unbeliever is temporarily madness, even if a tranquil madness. This is doubtless why so many men today proclaim with a kind of fury that the human community keeps us from dying. Martin du Gard has never said this, because in truth he does not believe it. But he gives us in his novel, along with Barois, the portrait of a rationalist who does not deny his own beliefs, and who dies without abjuring reason. The Stoic Luce probably represents Martin du Gard's ideal in 1913. A particularly severe and sombre ideal, if Luce himself is to be believed. "I do not acknowledge two moral standards. One must attain happiness, without being the dupe of any mirage, through truth and truth alone." One could hardly give a better definition of the enlightened renunciation of happiness. But let us simply remember that the first portrait of men who reject all forms of hope, determined to confront death in its entirety, who later swarm into our literature, was traced in 1913 by Roger Martin du Gard.

The great theme of the individual caught between history and God will be orchestrated symphonically in *Les Thibault,* where all the characters move toward the catastrophe of the summer of 1914. The religious problem, however, is upstaged. It runs through the first volumes, disappears as history gradually swamps individual destinies, reappearing in negative form in the final volume, with the description of Antoine Thibault's solitary death. The reappearance is nonetheless significant. Like any true artist, Martin du Gard cannot get rid of his obsessions. It is significant, therefore, that his great work ends with the constant theme of all his books, the death agony, in which man is, if I may put it this way, finally faced with the ultimate question. But in the *Epilogue* that ends *Les Thibault,* Martin du Gard's two main characters —the priest and the doctor—have disappeared, or come very near to doing so. *Les Thibault* ends with the death of a doctor, alone among other doctors. It seems that for Martin du Gard, as for Antoine, the problem has now ceased to present itself solely on the individual human level. And it is indeed the experience of history, and his enforced involvement in it, which explains this evolution on Antoine's part. Historical passion (in the two senses of the word) is atheistic today, or seems to be. In simple terms, this means that the historical misfortunes of the twentieth century have marked the collapse of bourgeois Christianity. A symbolic illustration of this idea can be seen in the fact that the father, who represents religion to Antoine,[4] dies just after Antoine has proclaimed his atheism. War breaks out at the same time, and a world that thought it could live by trade and still be religious collapses in bloodshed. If it is legitimate to see *Les Thi-*

---

[4] "I have never, alas, seen God except through my father."

bault as one of the first committed novels, the point should simply be made that it has better claims to this description than those published today. For Martin du Gard's characters, unlike ours, have something to commit and something to lose in historical conflicts. The pressure of immediate events struggles in their very being against traditional structures, whether religious or cultural. When these structures are destroyed, in a certain way man himself is destroyed. He is simply ready to exist, some day. Thus Antoine Thibault first becomes aware that other people exist, but this first step leads him only to confront death in an attempt to discover, beyond any consolation or illusion, the final secret of his reasons for living. With *Les Thibault,* the man of our half-century is born, the human being we are concerned with, and whom we can choose to commit or to liberate. He is ready for everything, so long as we have not decided what he is.

It is Antoine who most strikingly embodies the theme. Of the two brothers, Jacques is the one most often praised and admired. He has been seen as exemplary. I, on the other hand, see Antoine as the true hero of *Les Thibault.* And, since I cannot undertake to comment on the whole of so vast a work, I feel that its essential features can be underlined in a comparison between the two brothers.

Let me begin by giving my reasons for choosing Antoine as the central character. *Les Thibault* opens and closes with Antoine, who constantly grows in importance throughout the work. Besides, Antoine seems closer to his creator than Jacques. A novelist certainly expresses and betrays himself through all his characters at the same time: each of them represents one of his tendencies or his temptations. Martin du Gard is or has been Jacques, just as he is or has been Antoine; the words he gives them are sometimes his own, sometimes not. An author will, by the same token and for the same reasons, be nearest the character who combines the largest number of contradictions. From this point of view, Antoine, because of his complexity, the different roles he plays in the novel, is a richer character than Jacques. Finally, and this is my principal reason, the basic theme of *Les Thibault* is more convincing in Antoine than in Jacques. Both of them, it is true, leave their private universe to rejoin the world of men. Jacques even does so before Antoine. But his evolution is less significant since it is more logical and could have been foreseen. What is easier than to pass from individual revolt to the idea of revolution? But what is more profound, and more persuasive, on the other hand, than the inner metamorphosis of a happy, well-balanced man, full of strength and sincere self-esteem (a mark of nobility, according to Ortega y Gasset), that brings him to the recognition of a common misery in which he will find both his limits and his fulfillment?

The interest *Les Thibault*'s first readers took in Jacques is understandable, of course. Adolescents were in fashion at the time. Martin du Gard's generation popularized the cult of youth in France, a cult at first merry and then fearful, which has contaminated our literature. (Nowadays, every writer seems riddled with anxiety to find out what young people think of him, when the only interesting thing would be to know what he really thinks about them.) However, I am not sure that the reader of 1955 will be tempted for very long to prefer Jacques to Antoine. Let us admit at least that Martin du Gard succeeded, with Jacques, in giving us one of the finest portraits of adolescence our literature offers. Thin-skinned, courageous, self-willed, determined to say everything he thinks (as if everything one thinks were worth saying),

272

passionate in friendship but clumsy in love, stiff and stilted like certain virginities, uncomfortable with himself and with other people, doomed by his purity and intransigence to lead a difficult life, he is superbly depicted by his creator.

But here again we have an exceptional destiny, a character who tears through life like a blind meteor. In a sense, Jacques is not made for life. His two great experiences, love and the revolution, are proof of this. It is worth noting, first of all, that Jacques experiences the revolution before he experiences love. When he sleeps with Jenny, he tries to live them both at the same time, a hopeless idea. When the revolution betrays both him and itself, he leaves Jenny suddenly and goes off to face a solitary death that he hopes will be exemplary. His disappearance is the only guarantee that their love will endure. The wild, intractable Jenny, who begins by hating Jacques, without, moreover, being very fond of anyone, cannot bear to be touched, which has curious implications. Yet, separated from Jacques, she discovers she has a kind of hard passion for him, in which there is little tenderness. She can find lasting fulfillment, if this word has any meaning for her, only as a widow. It would seem that Jenny is the stuff of which suffragettes are made; faithfulness to the ideas of her dead husband, and the care given to the child of this curious love will be enough to keep her going. And in truth, what other ending is conceivable for the adventure of these two trapped souls? Their love—in the Paris of August 1914, with Jenny in mourning following Jacques into all the public places where the socialist betrayal, and the beginnings of disaster, will unfold, with both of them running through the scorching afternoon as bells boom out the order to mobilize—is filled more with pain than delight. It is not without surprise that we learn these two lovers have occupied one bed; we would prefer, in fact, not to think about this formality. Artistically, the two characters are more than convincing; they are true. In a human way, Jacques alone touches our hearts, because he is a figure of torment and failure. Setting out from his solitary revolt, he discovers history and its struggles, joins the socialist movement on the eve of one of its greatest defeats, lives through this defeat in anguish, discovers Jenny for the briefest of moments, abandons her in the same dreamlike state in which he had made her his mistress, and, despairing of everything, retreats into solitude, but this time to the loneliness of sacrifice. "To give oneself, to achieve deliverance by giving one's all." One definitive act removes him from this life, which he has never really known, but which at least he thinks he is serving this way. "To be right against everyone else and escape into death!" The formula is significant. In reality, Jacques does not participate, even after having discovered participation. A solitary figure, he can rejoin other people only through a solitary form of sacrifice. His deepest desire (ours, too, after all) is to be right, along with everybody else. But if this is only a dream, which it is, in order to be consistent he would prefer to be right against everybody else. In his case, dying, deliberately, is the only way of being right once and for all. In reality, Jacques has not only never been able to feel at one with other people, except through a great idea; but he has always felt hemmed in by them. "I always think of myself as the prey of other people; that if I escaped them, if I managed somewhere else, far from them, to begin an entirely new life, I would finally achieve serenity." Here Jacques expresses something all of us think, at one time or another. But there is no "somewhere else," no new life either, or at least not one without other people. Someone who insists on always being right will always feel alone against everyone else; it is impossible to live with others and be right at the same time. Jacques does not know that the only real progress lies in learning to be wrong all alone. But this presupposes a capacity for patience, the patience to make and to build, the only capacity that has ever produced great works, in history or in art. Such patience is beyond the capacity of a certain type of man, however, who can be satisfied only by action alone. At the summit of this sort of men is the terrorist, of whom Jacques is one of the first representatives in our literature. He dies alone; even his example is useless, and the last man who sees him, a policeman, insults him as he finishes him off, because he hates having to kill him. Those like Jacques, who want to change life in order to change themselves, leave life untouched and, in the end, remain what they are: sterile and disturbing witnesses for everything in man that refuses and always will refuse to live.

The portrait of Antoine offers different problems and teaches different lessons. Unlike Jacques, Antoine loves life, carnally, with passion; he has a physical and wholly practical knowledge of it. As a doctor, he reigns in the kingdom of the body. But his nature explains his vocation. In him, knowledge always passes through the medium of the senses. His friendships, his loves, are physical. The shoulder of his friend or brother, a woman's radiance, are the paths by which feelings set fire to his heart or kindle his intelligence. Sometimes he even prefers what he feels to what he believes. He defends Protestantism, in front of Mme de Fontanin,[5] solely out

[5] One can almost speak of love between Mme de Fontanin and Antoine, although they never exchange a guilty word or gesture.

of physical attraction, for he never has any traffic with it otherwise.

A liking for the physical sometimes leads to flabbiness or the cynicism of the sensualist. But it is balanced in Antoine by two complementary things, work and character. His life is ordered, occupied, and has, above all, a single purpose: his profession. Immediately, his sensuality is an advantage. It helps him in his job and gives him a sense, an orientation no doctor can do without that guides his probings of the human body. It also softens his excessive determination. The result, his unshakable balance, his informed tolerance, and also his excessive self-assurance. For Antoine is far from perfect: he has the defects of his virtues. In the man who enjoys being what he is, a certain form of solitary happiness does not exist without selfishness and blindness. Jacques and Antoine help us understand that there are two kinds of men; some will still be adolescents when they die, the others are born adult. But the adults run the risk of imagining that their balance is the general rule, and consequently that unhappiness is a sin. Antoine seems to believe that the world he lives in is the best possible and that anyone, indeed, can choose to live in a large town house on the rue de l'Université, to pursue the honorable calling of doctor of medicine, and welcome life in all its goodness. This is his limitation, in the first volumes at least, and it leads him to adopt a number of unattractive attitudes. Born a bourgeois, he lives with the idea that everything around him is eternal, since everything surrounding him suits his convenience. This conviction even influences his true nature, which he drapes in the doublet of being a "Thibault son and heir." He behaves as a man of wealth, even in his sexual adventures: he pays cash for his pleasures, striking an air of importance and authority.

Antoine will therefore not have to accept life. He will merely have to discover that he is not the only person living. In keeping with his nature, he will simply follow an opposite path to his brother's. Here the profound truth of the novel is revealed. Martin du Gard knows that men learn not from circumstances themselves, but from the contact of their own natures with circumstances. They become what they are. And, quite naturally, it is a woman who breaks the shell with which Antoine protects himself. Truth can reach a carnal man only through the flesh. This is why its path cannot be foreseen. Here the path is called Rachel, and the episode of her affair with Antoine remains one of the most beautiful in *Les Thibault*. The love affair between Rachel and Antoine, unlike so many affairs in literature, does not hover in the blissful heavens of verbal effusions. But it fills the reader with a secret joy, and gratitude for a world in which such truths are possible. Rachel's physical beauty radiates the whole of *Les Thibault*, and until the very eve of his death Antoine continues to draw warmth from it. He finds in Rachel not the tired or humiliated prey to which he had been accustomed, but his generous equal. She admires Antoine, of course, but she is not his subordinate. She has lived, seen the world, she remains slightly mysterious for him, and cannot free herself from what she has been. Without ceasing to love Antoine, she says, "I am like this," and he has to admit that people can exist independently of him, that this is nevertheless something good, which gives an added taste to life. From their first meeting, they are equals. On the stormy summer night when Antoine operates on a little girl with the emergency resources at his disposal, Rachel holds the lamp steadily and Antoine discovers that the doctor in him is helped simply by the fact that she is there. Later on, exhausted, sitting side by side, they fall asleep. Antoine wakes, feeling a gentle warmth along one side of his body: Rachel has dozed off against him. They will become lovers a little later on, but they are already intimate, linked to each other so that each pours into the other a richer life. From this moment on, Antoine abdicates, joyfully and gratefully. When Jacques meets his brother again in Lausanne, after long years of separation, he finds him "changed." What a hundred sermons could not have accomplished a woman has achieved. But this woman does not belong to the world Antoine had thought unique and unchangeable. She is one of those who never stay, who are always nomads; what one inhales in her presence is liberty. A sensual freedom, of course, in which Antoine discovers for the first time that equality within difference which is the highest dream of minds and bodies. But this liberty is also a freedom from prejudices Rachel does not fight against; she does not even know that they are there, and her very existence quietly denies them. This is why Antoine becomes less complicated with her and discovers the only valid aspects of his own nature: his personal generosity, his vitality, and his power to admire.[6] He does not become better, but he fulfills himself a little more, outside himself and yet nearer to what he really is, in joyfully responding to a person who in turn acknowledges and welcomes him. Perhaps a certain royal truth is defined in this—a man who feels entitled to be just what he is, at the same time freeing another being by loving her very nature.

Long after their separation, this realization con-

[6] Admiration is also Martin du Gard's subject matter in the beautiful scenes between Antoine and his teacher, Philip. This is not surprising. Where admiration is lacking, both heart and work are weakened.

278

tinues to inspire Antoine. "He was laughing the deep, youthful laugh he had so long repressed, that Rachel had permanently freed." They do in fact separate, without seeing each other, on a foggy, rainy night; their story is apparently a short one. Rachel follows the darker slope of her character, returning to Africa to rejoin the mysterious man who dominates her (here, the motivation seems a bit romantic). Actually, she is moving toward death, with which this living creature has a natural complicity. But she has helped Antoine to grow up, and she will even have helped him to die better since it is toward her that he turns once more when he is close to death. "Do not despise your uncle Antoine," he writes in the notebook that he is keeping for Jacques' son . . . "this poor adventure is, after all, the best thing that happened in my poor life." The word "poor" is excessive here, but it is written in self-pity by a dying man. Antoine's love life has doubtless not been a very rich one, but, in this life, Rachel has been a royal gift that enriched him without obligation. When Jacques, to whom Antoine risks confiding something of this love, proclaims from the height of his ignorant purity: "Ah, no, Antoine, love is something different from that," he does not know what he is talking about. There is a lesson he has missed, a knowledge worth having, which would make him humbler about love according to the flesh and freer for the joyous gifts that life and people can bestow.

Liberty and humility, these are the virtues Rachel awakens in Antoine. Life is bad, Antoine sometimes tries to tell himself, "as if he were talking to some stubbornly optimistic interlocutor; and this stubborn, stupidly satisfied person was himself, the everyday Antoine." It is this Antoine, better informed, who survives the liaison with Rachel. He knows that life is good, he moves easily

279

through it, can lie when he has to, and patiently waits for life to justify this confidence. Most of the time it does. But, somewhere within him, a concern awakened by Rachel has at the same time humanized his assurance. Antoine now knows that other people exist, and that, in love, for example, we do not take our pleasure alone. This is one way, but a sure and certain one, of learning that during the historical events to come he will not be the only one to suffer. France goes to war. Jacques refuses the war and dies from this refusal. Antoine agrees to fight, with no love for war,[7] and eventually dies from this acceptance. He leaves behind his life as a wealthy and famous doctor, the newly-decorated town house whose paint is chipped off by his army equipment. He knows that he will never return to the world he is leaving behind. But he keeps the essential thing, his profession, which he can pursue even during the war and even, as he sincerely remarks, into the revolution. Carried along in the crazy course of history, Antoine is now free; he has given up what he owns, not what he is. He will know how to judge the war: a doctor reads communiqués as lists of wounds and death agonies. Gassed, crippled, certain that he is going to die, he regrets nothing of the old world. In the *Epilogue* his only two concerns are the future of mankind (he hopes for a "peace with neither victory or humiliation," so that wars will not arise again) and Jean-Paul, Jacques' son. As for himself, he no longer has anything but memories, among them the memory of Rachel, which make up his knowledge of life and which help him to die.

Les Thibault ends with the diary of a sick doctor

[7] "It would really be too easy to be a citizen only until the outbreak of war and then no longer."

and the death of the hero. A world is dying along with him, but the problem is to discover what one generous individual can pass on from the old world to the new. History overflows and floods whole continents and peoples, then the waters recede and the survivors count up what is missing and what remains. Antoine, a survivor of the war of 1914, transmits what he has been able to save from the disaster to Jean-Paul—that is to say, to us. And here is his greatness, which is to have come back, lucidly, to everyone's level. From the moment Antoine sees his death warrant in the eyes of his teacher, Philip, until his final solitude, he never ceases to grow in stature, but he does so precisely as he comes to recognize one by one his weaknesses and doubts. The petty, self-satisfied doctor now discovers his ignorance. "I am condemned to die without having understood very much about myself or about the world." He knows that pure individualism is not possible, that life does not consist solely of the selfish glow of youthful strength. With three thousand new babies every hour, and as many deaths, an infinite force sweeps the individual along in the uninterrupted flow of generation, drowning him in the vast, unfillable ocean of collective death. What else can he do but accept himself with his limitations, and try to reconcile the duties he has toward himself with those he has toward others? As to the rest, he has to wager once again. Gassed and fallen from his throne, Ulysses seeks a definition of his wisdom, and realizes it must have an element of folly and of risk. To avoid being a burden on anyone, first of all he will kill himself, all alone, in a way both so humble and deliberate that one hesitates to say whether he is like a successful Barois or a bourgeois Kirilov. And in spite of this sensible suicide, or because it is so reasonable, his wager will be irrational and optimistic: he bets on the continuity of the human adventure, writing his last words for Jacques' son. This double obliteration, by death and by fidelity to what will live on, makes Antoine vanish into the very stuff of history, of which men's hopes are made, and whose roots are human misfortune. In this respect, the remark of Antoine's that touches me most deeply is the one he jots down shortly before his death: "I've only been an average man." This is true, in a way, whereas Jacques, by the same standards, is someone exceptional. But it is the average man who gives the whole work its strength, illuminates its underlying movement, and crowns it with this admirable *Epilogue*. After all, the truth Ulysses represents includes Antigone's as well, although it does not hold the other way round.

What are we to think of the creator who can build, silently and without commentaries, two characters who are so different and so commanding?

Since I have concentrated on the relevance of Martin du Gard's work to the present day, I still must show that his very doubts are our own. The birth of an awareness of history in the Thibault brothers is paired with the posing of a problem we can well understand. *Summer 1914*, which reveals along with the impending war the failure of socialism in circumstances decisive to the future of the world, offers a summary of all Martin du Gard's doubts. He was not lacking in lucidity. We know that *Summer 1914*, appearing in 1936, was published long after *The Death of the Father* (1929). During this long interval, Martin du Gard carried out a veritable revolution in the structure of his work. He abandoned his original plan, and decided to give *Les Thibault* an ending different from the one he had originally intended. The first plan involved thirty or so volumes; the

second reduces *Les Thibault* to eleven. Martin du Gard
had no hesitation next about destroying the manuscript
of *L'Appareillage* (*Setting Sail*), a volume which was to
follow *The Death of the Father* and which had cost him
two years' work. Between 1931, the date of this sacrifice,
and 1933, the year when armed with a new plan he
began to write *Summer 1914*, there were two years of
quite natural confusion. This is perceptible in the book's
very structure. After a long pause the machine at first
had some difficulty getting started again, and really gets
going only in the second volume. But it seems to me that
we also feel this change in a number of new perspectives.
Begun at the moment of Hitler's ascendance to power,
when the Second World War could already be sensed on
the horizon, this great historical fresco of a conflict men
tried to hope would be the last is almost compelled to call
itself into question. In *Vieille France*, written during the
years when Martin du Gard had given up *Les Thibault*,
the schoolmistress was already asking herself a formidable question: "Why is the world like this? Is it really
society's fault? . . . Is it not rather man's own fault?"
The same question worries Jacques at the height of his
revolutionary fervor, just as it explains most of Antoine's
attitudes toward historical events. One can therefore suppose it must have haunted the novelist himself.

    None of the contradictions of social action are, in
any case, eluded in the long, perhaps overlong, ideologi-
cal conversations that fill *Summer 1914*. The main
problem, the use of violence in the cause of justice, is discussed at great length in the conversations between
Jacques and Mithoerg. The famous distinction between
the yogi and the commissar has already been made by
Martin du Gard: within the revolution, in fact, it brings
about the confrontation between the apostle and the tech-

nician. Better still, the nihilistic aspect of the revolution is isolated, in order to be treated in depth, in the character of Meynestrel. The latter believes that after having put man in the place of God, atheism ought to go even further and abolish man himself. Meynestrel's reply, when asked what will replace man, is "Nothing." Elsewhere, the Englishman Patterson defines Meynestrel as "the despair of believing in nothing." Finally, like all those who join the revolution from nihilism, Meynestrel believes that the best results are achieved by the worst means. He has no hesitation about burning the secret papers Jacques has brought back from Berlin, which prove the collusion between the Prussian and Austrian general staffs. The publication of these documents would risk altering the attitude of the German social democrats, thus making the war, which Meynestrel considers as the "trump card" for social upheaval, far less likely.

These examples are enough to show that there was nothing naïve in Martin du Gard's socialism. He cannot manage to believe that perfection will one day be embodied in history. If he does not believe this, it is because his doubt is the same as the schoolteacher's in *Vieille France*. This doubt concerns human nature. "His pity for men was infinite; he gave them all the love his heart contained; but whatever he did, however hard he tried, he remained skeptical about man's moral potentialities." To be certain only of men, and to know that men have little worth, is the cry of pain that runs through the whole of this work, for all its strength and richness, and that brings it so close to us. For, after all, this fundamental doubt is the same doubt that is hidden in every love and that gives it its tenderest vibration. This ignorance, acknowledged in such simple terms, moves us because it is the other side of a certainty we also share. The service of man cannot be separated from an ambiguity that must be maintained in order to preserve the movement of history. From this come the two pieces of advice that Antoine bequeaths to Jean-Paul. The first is one of prudent liberty, assumed as a duty. "Don't let yourself be tied down to a party. Feeling your way in the dark is no joke. But it is a lesser evil." The other is to trust oneself in taking risks: to keep going forward, in the midst of others, along the same path that crowds of men have followed for centuries, in the nighttime of the species, marching and stumbling toward a future that they cannot conceive.

Clearly, there are no certainties offered here. And yet this work communicates courage and a strange faith. To wager, as Antoine does, over and above doubts and disasters, on the human adventure, amounts in the end to praising life, which is terrible and irreplaceable. The Thibault family's fierce attachment to life is the very force that inspires the whole work. Father Thibault dying takes on an exemplary quality; he refuses to disappear, comes unexpectedly to life again, lunges at the enemy, struggles physically against death, bringing nurses and relatives into the fray. Inevitably, we are reminded of the Karamazovs' love of life and pleasure, of Dimitri's despairing remark, "I love life too much. It's even disgusting." But life is not polite, as Dimitri is well aware. In this great struggle to escape by any and every means from annihilation lies the truth of history and its progress, of the mind and all its works. Here indeed is one of those works conceived in the refusal to despair. This refusal, this inconsolable attachment to men and the world, explains the roughness and the tenderness of Martin du Gard's books. Squat, heavy with the weight of flesh in ecstasy and humiliation, they are still sticky with the life that has given them birth. But, at the same time, a vast indulgence runs through all their cruelties, transfiguring and alleviating them. "A human life," writes Antoine, "is always broader than we realize." However low and evil it may be, a life always holds in some hidden corner enough qualities for us to understand and forgive. There is not one of the characters in this great fresco, not even the hypocritical Christian bourgeois who is painted for us in the darkest colors, who goes without his moment of grace. Perhaps, in Martin du Gard's eyes, the only guilty person is the one who refuses life or condemns people. The key words, the final secrets, are not in man's possession. But man nevertheless keeps the power to judge and to absolve. Here lies the profound secret of art, which always makes it useless as propaganda or hatred, and which, for example, prevents Martin du Gard from depicting a young follower of Maurras except with sympathy and generosity. Like any authentic creator, Martin du Gard forgives all his characters. The true artist, although his life may consist mostly of struggles, has no enemy.

The final word that can be said about this work thus remains the one that it has been difficult to use about a writer since the death of Tolstoi: goodness. Even then I must make it clear that I am not talking about the screen of goodness that hides false artists from the eyes of the world while at the same time hiding the world from them. Martin du Gard himself has defined a certain type of bourgeois virtue as the absence of the energy necessary to do evil. What we are concerned with here is a particularly lucid virtue, which absolves the good man because of his weaknesses, the evil man because of his generous impulses, and both of them together because of their passionate membership in a human race that hopes and suffers. Thus Jacques, returning home after long years of absence, and having to help lift up his dying father, finds himself overwhelmed by the contact with this enormous body, which in his eyes had formerly symbolized oppression: "And suddenly the contact with this moistness so overwhelmed him that he felt something totally unexpected—a physical emotion, a raw sentiment which went far beyond pity or affection: the selfish tenderness of man for man." Such a passage marks the true measure of an art that seeks no separation from anything, that overcomes the contradictions of a man or a historical period through the obscure acceptance of anonymity. The community of suffering, struggle, and death exists; it alone lays the foundation of the hope for a community of joy and reconciliation. He who accepts membership in the first community finds in it a nobility, a faithfulness, a reason for accepting his doubts; and if he is an artist he finds the deep wellsprings of his art. Here man learns, in one confused and unhappy moment, that it is not true he must die alone. All men die when he dies, and with the same violence. How, then, can he cut himself off from a single one of them, how can he ever refuse him that higher life, which the artist can restore through forgiveness and man can restore through justice. This is the secret of the relevance to our times I spoke of earlier. It is the only worthwhile relevance, a timeless one, and it makes Martin du Gard, a just and forgiving man, our perpetual contemporary.

Preface to the Pléiade edition of the complete works of Martin du Gard, published in 1955.

Herman Melville

❦❦ ❦❦❦ ❦❦

BACK IN the days when Nantucket whalers stayed at sea for several years at a stretch, Melville, at twenty-two, signed on one, and later on a man-of-war, to sail the seven seas. Home again in America, his travel tales enjoyed a certain success while the great books he published later were received with indifference and incomprehension.[1] Discouraged after the publication and failure of *The Confidence Man* (1857), Melville "accepted annihilation." Having become a custom's officer and the father of a family, he began an almost complete silence (except for a few infrequent poems) which was to last some thirty years. Then one day he hurriedly wrote a masterpiece, *Billy Budd* (completed in April 1891), and died, a few months later, forgotten (with a three-line obituary in *The New York Times*). He had to wait until our own time for America and Europe to finally give him his place among the greatest geniuses of the West.

It is scarcely easier to describe in a few pages a

---

[1] For a long time, *Moby Dick* was thought of as an adventure story suitable for school prizes.

288

work that has the tumultuous dimensions of the oceans where it was born than to summarize the Bible or condense Shakespeare. But in judging Melville's genius, if nothing else, it must be recognized that his works trace a spiritual experience of unequaled intensity, and that they are to some extent symbolic. Certain critics [2] have discussed this obvious fact, which now hardly seems open anymore to question. His admirable books are among those exceptional works that can be read in different ways, which are at the same time both obvious and obscure, as dark as the noonday sun and as clear as deep water. The wise man and the child can both draw sustenance from them. The story of captain Ahab, for example, flying from the southern to the northern seas in pursuit of Moby Dick, the white whale who has taken off his leg, can doubtless be read as the fatal passion of a character gone mad with grief and loneliness. But it can also be seen as one of the most overwhelming myths ever invented on the subject of the struggle of man against evil, depicting the irresistible logic that finally leads the just man to take up arms first against creation and the creator, then against his fellows and against himself.[3] Let

[2] In passing, let me advise critics to read page 449 of *Mardi* in the French translation.

[3] As an indication, here are some of the obviously symbolic pages of *Moby Dick*. (French translation, Gallimard): pp. 120, 121, 123, 129, 173–7, 191–3, 203, 209, 241, 310, 313, 339, 373, 415, 421, 452, 457, 460, 472, 485, 499, 503, 517, 520, 522.

Camus probably read Moby Dick in the French translation by Lucien Jacques, Joan Smith, and Jean Giono, which was published by Gallimard in 1941. If this is the case, then the page numbers correspond to these page numbers in the Everyman edition and refer more or less to the following episodes:

120—p. 114: of chapter XXX. Ahab's leg.

121—p. 115: beginning of chapter XXXI.

us have no doubt about it: if it is true that talent recreates life, while genius has the additional gift of crowning it with myths, Melville is first and foremost a creator of myths.

I will add that these myths, contrary to what

123—p. 117. Whether a whale be a fish.
129—pp. 122–3. Black Fish—Narwhal.
173–7—pp. 163–7: chapter XLI. The Whiteness of the Whale.
203—p. 192. "Now the advent of these outlandish strangers . . ."
209—p. 197. Queequeg as the standard bearer "hopelessly holding up hope in the midst of despair."
241—p. 227: chapter LIII. The Town-Ho's story of how the mate Radney was eaten by Moby Dick.
310—p. 290. The Right Whale's Head.
313—end of chapter LXXIV. Resolution in facing death.
339—pp. 317–18: end of chapter LXXXII, beginning of chapter LXXXIII.
373—p. 350: chapter XC. The smell of the Rosebud.
415—pp. 393–4: chapter CIII.
452—p. 420: chapter CXXII. The tempering of the harpoon.
457—p. 425. The meeting with the Bachelor.
460—p. 248: beginning of chapter CXVI.
472—pp. 438–9: chapter CXX.
485—p. 451: end of chapter CXXV.
499—p. 463: beginning of chapter CXXX, "The Symphony." Ahab weeps into the sea.
503—p. 480. Moby Dick breaks Ahab's ivory leg.
520—end of chapter CXXXIII.
522—p. 482. "I meet thee, this third time, Moby Dick."
It should be noted that there is a difference in the chapter numberings between the French translation and the Everyman edition referred to here. Thus, the French edition is consistently one chapter number ahead, so that chapter CXXXIV in the Everyman edition is chapter CXXXV in the French edition. The chapter headings here refer to the Everyman edition. —P.T.

people say of them, are clear. They are obscure only insofar as the root of all suffering and all greatness lies buried in the darkness of the earth. They are no more obscure than Phèdre's cries, Hamlet's silences, or the triumphant songs of Don Giovanni. But it seems to me (and this would deserve detailed development) that Melville never wrote anything but the same book, which he began again and again. This single book is the story of a voyage, inspired first of all solely by the joyful curiosity of youth (*Typee, Omoo,* etc.), then later inhabited by an increasingly wild and burning anguish. *Mardi* is the first magnificent story in which Melville begins the quest that nothing can appease, and in which, finally, "pursuers and pursued fly across a boundless ocean." It is in this work that Melville becomes aware of the fascinating call that forever echoes in him: "I have undertaken a journey without maps." And again: "I am the restless hunter, the one who has no home." *Moby Dick* simply carries the great themes of *Mardi* to perfection. But since artistic perfection is also inadequate to quench the kind of thirst with which we are confronted here, Melville will start once again, in *Pierre: or the Ambiguities,* that unsuccessful masterpiece, to depict the quest of genius and misfortune whose sneering failure he will consecrate in the course of a long journey on the Mississippi that forms the theme of *The Confidence Man.*

This constantly rewritten book, this unwearying peregrination in the archipelago of dreams and bodies, on an ocean "whose every wave is a soul," this Odyssey beneath an empty sky, makes Melville the Homer of the Pacific. But we must add immediately that his Ulysses never returns to Ithaca. The country in which Melville approaches death, that he immortalizes in *Billy Budd,* is a desert island. In allowing the young sailor, a figure of beauty and innocence whom he dearly loves, to be condemned to death, Captain Vere submits his heart to the law. And at the same time, with this flawless story that can be ranked with certain Greek tragedies, the aging Melville tells us of his acceptance for the first time of the sacrifice of beauty and innocence so that order may be maintained and the ship of men may continue to move forward toward an unknown horizon. Has he truly found the peace and final resting place that earlier he had said could not be found in the Mardi archipelago? Or are we, on the contrary, faced with a final shipwreck that Melville in his despair asked of the gods? "One cannot blaspheme and live," he had cried out. At the height of consent, isn't *Billy Budd* the worst blasphemy? This we can never know, any more than we can know whether Melville did finally accept a terrible order, or whether, in quest of the spirit, he allowed himself to be led, as he had asked, "beyond the reefs, in sunless seas, into night and death." But no one, in any case, measuring the long anguish that runs through his life and work, will fail to acknowledge the greatness, all the more anguished in being the fruit of self-conquest, of his reply.

But this, although it had to be said, should not mislead anyone as to Melville's real genius and the sovereignty of his art. It bursts with health, strength, explosions of humor, and human laughter. It is not he who opened the storehouse of sombre allegories that today hold sad Europe spellbound. As a creator, Melville is, for example, at the furthest possible remove from Kafka, and he makes us aware of this writer's artistic limitations. However irreplaceable it may be, the spiritual experience in Kafka's work exceeds the modes of expression and invention, which remain monotonous. In Melville, spiritual experience is balanced by expression and invention, and constantly finds flesh and blood in them. Like the greatest artists, Melville constructed his symbols out of concrete things, not from the material of dreams. The creator of myths partakes of genius only insofar as he inscribes these myths in the denseness of reality and not in the fleeting clouds of the imagination. In Kafka, the reality that he describes is created by the symbol, the fact stems from the image, whereas in Melville the symbol emerges from reality, the image is born of what is seen.[4] This is why Melville never cut himself off from flesh or nature, which are barely perceptible in Kafka's work. On the contrary, Melville's lyricism, which reminds us of Shakespeare's, makes use of the four elements. He mingles the Bible with the sea, the music of the waves with that of the spheres, the poetry of the days with the grandeur of the Atlantic. He is inexhaustible, like the winds that blow for thousands of miles across empty oceans and that, when they reach the coast, still have strength enough to flatten whole villages. He rages, like Lear's madness, over the wild seas where Moby Dick and the spirit of evil crouch among the waves. When the storm and total destruction have passed, a strange calm rises from the primitive waters, the silent pity that transfigures tragedies. Above the speechless crew, the perfect body of Billy Budd turns gently at the end of its rope in the pink and grey light of the approaching day.

T. E. Lawrence ranked *Moby Dick* alongside *The Possessed* or *War and Peace*. Without hesitation, one can add to these *Billy Budd, Mardi, Benito Cereno,* and a few others. These anguished books in which man is over-

---

[4] In Melville, the metaphor suggests the dream, but from a concrete, physical starting point. In *Mardi*, for example, the hero comes across "huts of flame." They are built, simply, of red tropical creepers, whose leaves are momentarily lifted by the wind.

293

whelmed, but in which life is exalted on each page, are inexhaustible sources of strength and pity. We find in them revolt and acceptance, unconquerable and endless love, the passion for beauty, language of the highest order—in short, genius. "To perpetuate one's name," Melville said, "one must carve it on a heavy stone and sink it to the bottom of the sea; depths last longer than heights." Depths do indeed have their painful virtue, as did the unjust silence in which Melville lived and died, and the ancient ocean he unceasingly ploughed. From their endless darkness he brought forth his works, those visages of foam and night, carved by the waters, whose mysterious royalty has scarcely begun to shine upon us, though already they help us to emerge effortlessly from our continent of shadows to go down at last toward the sea, the light, and its secret.

Article published in Les Ecrivains célèbres, *Editions Mazenod, Volume III, 1952*

On the Future of Tragedy[1]

❦❦ ❦❦❦ ❦❦

AN ORIENTAL wise man always used to ask in his prayers that God spare him from living in an interesting age.
Our age is extremely interesting, that is to say, it is
tragic. To purge us of our miseries, do we at least have a
theater suited to our time or can we hope to have one? In
other words, is modern tragedy possible? This is the
question I would like to consider today. But is it a reasonable question? Isn't it the same type of question as: "Will
we have good government?" or "Will our authors grow
modest?" or again, "Will the rich soon share their for-
tunes with the poor?"—interesting questions, no doubt,
but ones that lead to reverie rather than to thought.

[1] *Like his early association with the Théâtre de l'Equipe
when he lived in Algiers, and his later adaptations of Faulkner's*
Requiem for a Nun *and Dostoevski's* The Possessed, *this lecture
demonstrates the continuity of Camus's interest in the theater
and his concern for its wider implications. As he points out in a
program note to the adaptation of* Requiem for a Nun *(pages 311–
15), his own ambition in the theater was to write a modern
tragedy.*

295

I don't think so. I believe, and for two reasons, that one can legitimately raise the question of modern tragedy. First, great periods of tragic art occur, in history, during centuries of crucial change, at moments when the lives of whole peoples are heavy both with glory and with menace, when the future is uncertain and the present dramatic. Aeschylus, after all, fought in two wars, and Shakespeare was alive during quite a remarkable succession of horrors. Both, moreover, stand at a kind of dangerous turning point in the history of their civilizations.

It is worth noting that in thirty centuries of Western history, from the Dorians to the atomic bomb, there have been only two periods of tragic art, both of them narrowly confined in both time and space. The first was Greek and presents remarkable unity, lasting a century, from Aeschylus to Euripides. The second lasted scarcely longer, flourishing in the countries bordering the edge of western Europe. Too little has been made of the fact that the magnificent explosions of the Elizabethan theater, the Spanish theater of the Golden Age, and French seventeenth-century tragedy are practically contemporary with one another. When Shakespeare died, Lope de Vega was fifty-four and had already had a large number of his plays performed; Calderón and Corneille were alive. Finally, there is no more distance in time between Shakespeare and Racine than between Aeschylus and Euripides. Historically, at least, we can consider them a single magnificent flowering, though with differing aesthetics, of the Renaissance, born in the inspired disorder of the Elizabethan stage and ending with formal perfection in French tragedy.

Almost twenty centuries separate these two tragic moments. During these twenty centuries, there was nothing, nothing, except Christian mystery plays, which may be called dramatic but which, for reasons I shall explain, cannot be considered tragic. We can therefore say that these were very exceptional times, which should by their very peculiarity tell us something about the conditions for tragic expression. I think this is a fascinating subject for study, one that should be thoroughly and patiently pursued by real historians. But this is not within my competence and I would simply like to enlarge on what I think about it as a man of the theater. Looking at the movement of ideas in these two periods, as well as at the tragic works that were written at the time, I find one constantly recurring factor. Both periods mark a transition from forms of cosmic thought impregnated with the notion of divinity and holiness to forms inspired by individualistic and rationalist concepts. The movement from Aeschylus to Euripides is, roughly speaking, the development from the great pre-Socratic thinkers to Socrates himself (Socrates, who was scornful of tragedy, made an exception for Euripides). Similarly, from Shakespeare to Corneille we go from a world of dark and mysterious forces, which is still the Middle Ages, to the universe of individual values affirmed and maintained by the human will and by reason (almost all the sacrifices in Racine are motivated by reason). It is the same transition, in short, that links the passionate theologians of the Middle Ages to Descartes. Although the evolution is more clearly visible in Greece, because it is simpler and limited to one place, it is the same in both cases. Each time, historically, the individual frees himself little by little from a body of sacred concepts and stands face to face with the ancient world of terror and devotion. Each time, literarily, the works move from ritual tragedy and from almost religious celebration to psychological tragedy. And each time the final triumph of individual reason, in the fourth cen-

297

tury in Greece and in the eighteenth century in Europe, causes the literature of tragedy to dry up for centuries.

What can we draw from these observations on the subject that concerns us? First of all, the very general remark that the tragic age always seems to coincide with an evolution in which man, consciously or not, frees himself from an older form of civilization and finds that he has broken away from it without yet having found a new form that satisfies him. It seems to me that we, in 1955, have reached this stage, and can therefore ask whether this inner anguish will find tragic expression in our world. However, the twenty centuries separating Euripides from Shakespeare should encourage us to be prudent. After all, tragedy is one of the rarest of flowers, and there is only the slimmest chance that we shall see it bloom in our own day. But there is another reason that encourages us to wonder about this chance, a very particular phenomenon that we have been able to observe in France for some thirty years now, which began with the reform carried out by Jacques Copeau.[2] This phenomenon is the advent of writers to the theater, which up to then had been the exclusive domain of theatrical brokers and business interests. The interference of writers has led to the resurrection of the tragic forms that tend to put

[2] *Jacques Copeau (1878–1949) was one of the outstanding theatrical directors of the twentieth century. After an initial association with Antoine and the realism of the* Théâtre libre, *he founded his own theater, the Vieux-Colombier, in 1913. There he was able to put into practice his idea that the staging of a play should be subordinated to the meaning of the text and not to the ambition of the famous actor performing the main part. His concept of drama as involving the active participation of the audience as well as the combined efforts of the actors, the director, and the designer is already visible in Camus's work in 1936, in the play* Révolte dans les Asturies. *—*P.T.

dramatic art back in its rightful place, at the summit of the literary arts. Before Copeau (except for Claudel, whom nobody performed) the privileged place for theatrical sacrifices in France was the double bed. When the play was particularly successful, the sacrifices multiplied, and the beds as well. In short, it was a business, like so many others, in which the price of everything was marked—with, if I may say so, the mark of the beast. This, moreover, is what Copeau used to say about it:

> . . . If we are asked what feeling inspires us, what passion urges, compels, forces, and finally overwhelms us, it is this: *indignation.*
>
> The frantic industrialization that, more cynically every day, degrades the French stage and makes the educated public turn away from it; the monopolization of most of our theaters by a handful of entertainers hired by shameless merchants; everywhere, and even in places where great traditions ought to preserve some modesty, the same spirit of ham acting and commercial speculation, the same vulgarity; everywhere bluff and every conceivable kind of exaggeration and exhibitionism feed like parasites on a dying art, itself now no longer even mentioned; everywhere the same flabbiness, disorder, indiscipline, ignorance and stupidity, the same contempt for the creator, the same hatred of beauty; an ever more vain and stupid output of plays, ever more indulgent critics, and ever more misguided public taste: these are what inspire our indignation and revolt.

Since this magnificent protest, followed by the creation of the Vieux-Colombier, the theater in France, for which we are indebted to Copeau, has gradually recovered its claim to nobility, that is to say, it has found a style. Gide, Martin du Gard, Giraudoux, Montherlant, Claudel, and so many others have restored a glory and ambitions that had disappeared a century ago. At the same time a movement of ideas and reflections on the theater, whose most significant product is Antonin Artaud's fine book *Le Théâtre et son double*,[3] and the influence of such foreign theoreticians as Gordon Craig [4] and Appia, have once more brought the tragic dimension to center stage in our thoughts.

By bringing all these observations together, perhaps I can clearly define the problem I would like to discuss for you. Our time coincides with a drama in civilization which might today, as it did in the past, favor tragic modes of expression. At the same time many writers, in France and elsewhere, are engrossed in creating a

---

[3] *Antonin Artaud's* Le Théâtre et son double *was published in 1938. Artaud puts forward the view that the Western theater is wrong to attempt an imitation of life. The true aim of the theater, he argues, should be to shock the spectator into an awareness of the violence that lies beneath civilization and the importance of man's more primitive instincts. Artaud began his career as a member of the surrealist movement, and his views have recently found a possibly accidental echo in the plays of Jean Genet—see Robert Brustein:* The Theatre of Revolt (*Boston and Toronto: Little, Brown and Co.; 1962*). In her study of Camus's work, Professor Germaine Brée also discusses a possible influence of Artaud's ideas on* La Peste (*see* Camus [*Rutgers University Press; 1959*], p. 116*). —*P.T.

[4] *Arthur Gordon Craig (1872–1966). Son of Ellen Terry, and a famous theatrical designer and director. In 1908 he founded* The Mask, *in Florence, and ran a school of acting. Like Copeau, he tended to increase the importance of the director at the expense of the "star" actor, and, like Artaud, he was extremely interested in Oriental forms of drama.* —P.T.

tragedy for our epoch. Is this a reasonable dream, is this enterprise possible, and under what conditions? This is the timely question, I believe, for all those who find in the theater the excitement of a second life. Of course, no one today is in a position to give so definite a reply to this question as: "Conditions favorable. Tragedy to follow." I shall therefore limit myself to a few suggestions about this great hope that inspires men of culture in the West.

First of all, what is a tragedy? The problem of defining "the tragic" has greatly occupied both literary historians and writers themselves, although no formula has ever received universal agreement. Without claiming to solve a problem that so many thinkers hesitate over, at least we can proceed by comparison and try to see, for example, how tragedy differs from drama or melodrama. This is what seems to me the difference: the forces confronting each other in tragedy are equally legitimate, equally justified. In melodramas or dramas, on the other hand, only one force is legitimate. In other words, tragedy is ambiguous and drama simple-minded. In the former, each force is at the same time both good and bad. In the latter, one is good and the other evil (which is why, in our day and age, propaganda plays are nothing but the resurrection of melodrama). Antigone is right, but Creon is not wrong. Similarly, Prometheus is both just and unjust, and Zeus who pitilessly oppresses him also has right on his side. Melodrama could thus be summed up by saying: "Only one is just and justifiable," while the perfect tragic formula would be: "All can be justified, no one is just." This is why the chorus in classical tragedies generally advises prudence. For the chorus knows that up to a certain limit everyone is right and that the person who, from blindness or passion, oversteps this limit is heading for catastrophe if he persists in his desire to assert a right he thinks he alone possesses. The constant theme of classical tragedy, therefore, is the limit that must not be transgressed. On either side of this limit equally legitimate forces meet in quivering and endless confrontation. To make a mistake about this limit, to try to destroy the balance, is to perish. The idea of a limit no one should overstep, beyond which lies death or disaster, also recurs in *Macbeth* and *Phèdre*, though in a less pure form than in Greek tragedy. This explains, finally, why the ideal drama, like Romantic drama, is first and foremost movement and action, since what it represents is the struggle between good and evil and the different incidents in this struggle. The ideal tragedy, on the other hand, and especially Greek tragedy, is first and foremost tension, since it is the conflict, in a frenzied immobility, between two powers, each of which wears the double mask of good and evil. It is of course true that between these two extreme types of tragedy and melodrama, dramatic literature offers all the intermediary stages.

But if we restrict ourselves to the pure forms, what are the two forces, in Greek classical tragedy for example, that enter into conflict? If we take *Prometheus Bound* as typical of this kind of tragedy, we can say that there is, on the one hand, man and his desire for power, and on the other, the divine principle reflected by the world. Tragedy occurs when man, through pride (or even through stupidity as in the case of Ajax) enters into conflict with the divine order, personified by a god or incarnated in society. And the more justified his revolt and the more necessary this order, the greater the tragedy that stems from the conflict.

Consequently, everything within a tragedy that tries to destroy this balance destroys the tragedy itself. If the divine order cannot be called into question and admits only sin and repentance, there is no tragedy. There can only be mysteries or parables, or again what the Spaniards call acts of faith or sacramental acts, that is to say, spectacles in which the one truth that exists is solemnly proclaimed. It is thus possible to have religious drama but not religious tragedy. This explains the silence of tragedy up to the Renaissance. Christianity plunges the whole of the universe, man and the world, into the divine order. Hence there is no tension between the world and the religious principle, but, at the most, ignorance, together with the difficulty of freeing man from the flesh, of renouncing his passions in order to embrace spiritual truth. Perhaps there has been only one Christian tragedy in history. It was celebrated on Golgotha during one imperceptible instant, at the moment of: "My God, my God, why hast thou forsaken me?" This fleeting doubt, and this doubt alone, consecrated the ambiguity of a tragic situation. The divinity of Christ has never been doubted since. The mass, which daily consecrates this divinity, is the real form religious theater takes in the West. It is not invention, but repetition.

On the other hand, everything that frees the individual and makes the universe submit to his wholly human law, especially by the denial of the mystery of existence, once again destroys tragedy. Atheistic or rationalist tragedy is thus equally impossible. If all is mystery, there is no tragedy. If all is reason, the same thing happens. Tragedy is born between light and darkness and rises from the struggle between them. And this is understandable. In both religious and atheistic drama, the problem has in fact already been solved. In the ideal tragedy, just the opposite, it has not been solved. The hero rebels and rejects the order that oppresses him, while the divine power, by its oppression, affirms itself exactly to the same extent as it is denied. In other words, revolt alone is not enough to make a tragedy. Neither is the affirmation of the divine order. Both a revolt and an order are necessary, the one supporting the other, and each reinforcing the other with its own strength. There is no Oedipus without the destiny summed up by the oracle. But the destiny would not have all its fatality if Oedipus did not refuse it.

And if tragedy ends in death or punishment, it is important to note that what is punished is not the crime itself but the blindness of the hero who has denied balance and tension. I am talking, of course, of the ideal tragic situation. Aeschylus, for example, who remains close to the religious and Dionysiac origins of tragedy, granted Prometheus forgiveness in the last section of the trilogy; the Furies are replaced by the Kindly Ones. But in Sophocles the balance is most of the time scrupulously maintained, and it is in this respect that he is the greatest tragedian of all time. Euripides, on the other hand, will upset the tragic balance by concentrating on the individual and on psychology. He is thus a forerunner of individualistic drama, that is to say, of the decadence of tragedy. Similarly, the great Shakespearean tragedies are still rooted in a kind of vast cosmic mystery that puts up an obscure resistance to the undertakings of its passionate individuals, while Corneille ensures the triumph of the individual ethic and by his very perfection announces the end of the genre.

People have thus been able to write that tragedy swings between the two poles of extreme nihilism and unlimited hope. For me, nothing is more true. The hero denies the order that strikes him down, and the divine order strikes because it is denied. Both thus assert their existence at the very moment when this existence is called into question. The chorus draws the lesson, which is that there is an order, that this order can be painful, but that it is still worse not to recognize that it exists. The only purification comes from denying and excluding nothing, and thus accepting the mystery of existence, the limitations of man—in short, the order where men know without knowing. Oedipus says "All is well," when his eyes have been torn out. Henceforth he knows, although he never sees again. His darkness is filled with light, and this face with its dead eyes shines with the highest lesson of the tragic universe.

What can be drawn from these observations? A suggestion and a working hypothesis, nothing more. It seems in fact that tragedy is born in the West each time the pendulum of civilization is half way between a sacred society and a society built around man. On two occasions, twenty centuries apart, we find a struggle between a world that is still interpreted in a sacred context and men who are already committed to their individuality, that is to say, armed with the power to question. In both cases, the individual increasingly asserts himself, the balance is gradually destroyed, and the tragic spirit finally falls silent. When Nietzsche accuses Socrates of having dug the grave of ancient tragedy, he is right up to a certain point —to exactly the same extent that it is true to say of Descartes that he marks the end of the tragic movement born in the Renaissance. At the time of the Renaissance, the traditional Christian universe is called into question by the Reformation, the discovery of the world, and the flowering of the scientific spirit. Gradually, the individual rises against the sacred order of things and against destiny. Then Shakespeare throws his passionate creatures against the simultaneously evil and just order of the world. Death and pity sweep across the stage and once again the final words of tragedy ring out: "A higher life is born of my despair." Then the pendulum moves increasingly in the opposite direction. Racine and French tragedy carry the tragic movement to its conclusion with the perfection of chamber music. Armed with Cartesianism and the scientific spirit, triumphant reason then proclaims the rights of the individual and empties the stage: tragedy descends into the street with the bloody scaffolds of the Revolution. No tragedies, therefore, will spring from romanticism, but only dramas, and among them, only Kleist's or Schiller's reach true greatness. Man is alone, and thus confronted with nothing but himself. He ceases to be a tragic figure and becomes an adventurer; dramas and the novel will depict him better than any other art. The spirit of tragedy consequently disappears until our own day, when the most monstrous wars have inspired not a single tragic poet.

What then leads one to hope for a renaissance of tragedy among us? If my hypothesis is valid, our only reason for hope is that individualism is visibly changing today and that beneath the pressures of history, little by little the individual is recognizing his limits. The world that the eighteenth-century individual thought he could conquer and transform by reason and science has in fact taken shape, but it's a monstrous one. Rational and excessive at one and the same time, it is the world of history. But at this degree of *hubris,* history has put on the mask of destiny. Man doubts whether he can conquer history; all he can do is struggle within it. In a curious paradox, humanity has refashioned a hostile destiny with the very weapons it used to reject fatality. After having defied human reign, man turns once more against this new god. He is struggling, as warrior and refugee at the same time, torn between absolute hope and final doubt. He lives in a tragic climate. Perhaps this explains why tragedy may seek a renaissance. Today, man proclaims his revolt, knowing this revolt has limits, demands liberty though he is subject to necessity; this contradictory man, torn, conscious henceforth of human and historical ambiguity, is the tragic man. Perhaps he is striding toward the formulation of his own tragedy, which will be reached on the day when *All is well.*

And what can in fact be observed in the French dramatic renaissance are the first tentative movements in this direction. Our dramatists are looking for a tragic language because no tragedy can exist without a language, and because this language is all the more difficult to formulate when it must reflect the contradictions of the tragic situation. It must be both hieratic and familiar, barbarous and learned, mysterious and clear, haughty and pitiful. In quest of this language, our writers have thus gone back instinctively to its sources, that is to say, to the tragic epochs I have mentioned. So we have seen Greek tragedy reborn in our country, but in the only forms possible to highly individualistic minds—either derision or highly mannered literary transposition. That is to say, humor and fantasy, since comedy alone is in the individual realm. Two good examples of this attitude are provided in Gide's *Oedipe* or Giraudoux's *La Guerre de Troie.*

[reads] [5]

[5] *Unfortunately, the French text does not show what passages Camus read during the lecture.* —P.T.

What is also visible in France is an effort to reintroduce the language of religion to the stage. A logical thing to do. But this had to be done by classical religious images, while the problem of modern tragedy lies precisely in the need to create new sacred images. So we have seen either a kind of pastiche, in both style and sentiment, as in Montherlant's *Port-Royal*, which is at the moment triumphing in Paris.

[reads]

or the resurrection of authentic Christian sentiments, as in the admirable *Partage de midi*.

[reads]

But here we can see just how the religious theater is not tragic: it is not a theater in which the creature and creation are pitted one against the other, but a theater in which men abandon their love for what is human. In a way, Claudel's works before his conversion, such as *Tête d'Or* or *La Ville* are more significant for our purposes. But however that may be, religious theater always precedes tragedy. In a way, it anticipates it. So it is not surprising that the dramatic work in which the style, if not the situation, is already perceptibly tragic should be Henry de Montherlant's *Le Maître de Santiago*, from which I should now like to read the two principal scenes:

[reads]

I find authentic tension in a work like this, although it is slightly rhetorical and, above all, highly individualistic. But I feel that a tragic language is taking shape in it and that this language gives us more than does the play itself. In any case, if the attempts and researches that I have tried to present to you through some of their most outstanding examples do not give you the certainty that a dramatic renaissance is possible, they do at least leave us with this hope. The path still to be traveled must first of all be made by our Society itself, in search of a synthesis between liberty and necessity, and by each of us. We must keep alive our power of revolt without yielding to our power of negation. If we can pay this price, the tragic sensibility that is taking shape in our time will flourish and find its expression. This amounts to saying that the real modern tragedy is the one that I cannot read to you, because it does not yet exist. To be born, it needs our patience and a genius.

My only aim has been to make you sense that there does exist in modern French dramatic art a kind of tragic nebula within which various nuclei are beginning to coagulate. A cosmic storm may, of course, sweep the nebula away, along with its future planets. But if this movement continues despite the storms of time, these promises will bear their fruit and the West will perhaps experience a renaissance of the tragic theater. It is certainly in preparation everywhere. Nevertheless, and I say this without nationalism (I love my country too much to be a nationalist), it is in France that the first signs of such a renaissance are visible. In France, of course, but I have surely said enough to make you share my conviction that the model, and the inexhaustible inspiration, remains for us the genius of Greece. To express to you both this hope and a double gratitude, first of all the one French writers feel for Greece, their common fatherland, and secondly my own gratitude for the welcome you have given us, I can find no better way of ending this lecture than reading you an extract from the magnificent and learnedly barbarous transposition that Paul Claudel has made of Aeschylus's *Agamemnon,* in which our two languages are mutually transfigured into one wondrous and inimitable tongue.

[reads]

Lecture delivered in Athens, 1955

William Faulkner

§ Foreword to *Requiem for a Nun*, 1957

THE GOAL of this foreword is not to present Faulkner to the French public. Malraux undertook that task brilliantly twenty years ago, and thanks to him, Faulkner gained a reputation with us that his own country had not yet accorded him. Nor is it a question of praising Maurice Coindreau's translation. French readers know that contemporary American literature has no better nor more effective ambassador among us. One need only imagine Faulkner betrayed as Dostoevski was by his first adapters to measure the role Monsieur Coindreau has played. A writer knows what he owes to his translators, when they are of this quality. I wish only, since I brought *Requiem for a Nun* to the stage, to make a few remarks for the benefit of those who are interested in the problems that making a stage adaptation poses. The publication of the two texts [the novel and Camus's adaptation] now makes possible a comparison I would like to encourage.

It will be seen first of all that the original novel, although it is divided into acts, includes, along with the scenes in dialogue form, chapters that are lyrical and historical describing the origin of the buildings in which the action proper takes place. These structures are the court house, the capitol, seat of the governor of the state, and the prison. Each of them serves to introduce an act and the place where the scenes occur. The dialogues of the first act take place in the living room of the young Stevens family, but they occur just after the trial and concern the death sentence that has just been pronounced. The great scene of Temple's confession, the main point of the second act, takes place in the governor's office, in the capitol at Jackson. Finally, the meeting between Temple and the condemned woman, in the third act, takes place in the prison. Faulkner's intention is plain. He wanted the Stevens drama to be knotted and unknotted in the temples built by man to a painful justice that Faulkner does not believe is of human origin. From this point of view, the courthouse can be seen as a temple, the governor's office as a confessional, and the prison as a convent in which the condemned Negro woman atones for her crime, and Temple's. To breathe life into these sacred buildings, Faulkner has had recourse to poetic evocations that lay the human and historical foundation for the events that take place in them.

It goes without saying that these chapters could not be used on the stage, except for a few details. I cut them, therefore, aware of what I was losing, but resigned to confide to the scene designer and the director the task of discreetly making evident the religious nature of the places where the play would unfold. Only the scenes in dialogue, then, could furnish the raw material of a dramatic action.

The reader of this book will quickly see that they

could not be lifted as is; in many respects, they remain scenes in a novel. Here one senses how different dramatic and fictional time can be. Terseness, condensation, the alternation of tension and explosion are the laws of the former, free development and a certain musing quality are inseparable from the latter. It was necessary, therefore, to redistribute the dialogue in an appropriately dramatic continuity that would permit the action to move forward without ever ceasing to leave it in suspense, that would underline the evolution of each character and lead it to its conclusion, that would clarify motives without throwing too crude a light on them and, finally, that would bring together in the last elevation all the themes touched upon or orchestrated during the action. From a practical point of view, this meant eliminating the prologue to the trial, rearranging the scenes in the first act, developing the character of Gowan Stevens—to whom I gave one whole scene with the governor and whom I had reappear in the final scene to bring to a conclusion the matter of the blackmail letters. In addition, for reasons of dramatic effectiveness, it was necessary to rework the scene with the jailkeepers.

With this new framework established, the most difficult problem, the problem of language, remained. Despite appearances, Faulkner's style is far from resistant to dramatic transcription. After reading the *Requiem*, I was even sure that Faulkner had resolved in his manner, and without even being aware of it, a very difficult problem—the problem of a language for modern tragedy. How can characters in business suits be made to speak a language ordinary enough to be spoken in an apartment and unusual enough to sustain the high level of tragic destinies? Faulkner's style, with its staccato breathing, its interrupted sentences, its repeats and prolongations in

repetitions, its incidences, its parentheses and its cas-
cades of subordinate clauses, gives us a modern, and in
no way artificial, equivalent of the tragic soliloquy. It is a
style that gasps with the very breathlessness of suffering.
An interminably unwinding spiral of words and sentences
that conducts the speaker to the abyss of sufferings
buried in the past. Temple Stevens to the delicious
hell of the Memphis bordello she wanted to forget, and
Nancy Mannigoe to the blind, stunning, ignorant pain
that will make her a murderer and a saint at the same
time.

It was necessary to retain these effects of style at
any cost. But if this breathless, agglutinated, insistent
language can bring something new to the theater, it can
do so only when used sparingly. Without this language
the play would certainly be less tragic. But by itself it
could destroy any play by a monotonous effect that would
tire the most well-disposed spectator, and it would also
run the risk of reducing the tragedy to the melodrama it
always threatens to become. What I had to do was make
use of this language and at the same time deliberately
neutralize it. I am not sure that I succeeded. In any case,
this is what I decided: during all the scenes in which the
characters refuse to surrender, when the action hangs on
a kind of apparent mystery, during all the transitions,
also, that serve to bring forward a development, to expose
new facts, or to change the rhythm of the scene—briefly,
in anything that is not suffered directly by the character,
and therefore by the actor, but simply experienced and
enacted on the exterior—I chose to simplify Faulkner's
language, and to make it as direct as I could, adding only,
for unity of composition, a few echoes, a few touches, of
his "breathless" style. To compensate, in everything that
concerned naked irrepressible suffering, and particularly

in Temple's confession and her husband's reactions, I
have imitated Faulkner's style in French.

One further word that will doubtless interest
those who, after having listened to the last scene in
which Nancy proclaims her faith, asked me if I had been
converted (please note that if I translated and staged a
Greek tragedy, no one would ask me if I believe in Zeus).
I did considerably rework the last scene. One will be
able to see in this book that it consists above all of
long speeches by Nancy Mannigoe and Gavin Stevens
on faith and Christ. Faulkner reveals herein his strange
religion, developed still further in *A Fable,* a religion less
strange in its substance than in the symbols he proposes
for it. Nancy decides to love her suffering and her
own death, like many great souls before her; but,
according to Faulkner, she thus becomes a saint, the
strange nun who suddenly invests the bordellos and
prisons in which she has lived with the dignity of a
cloister. This basic paradox had to be preserved. The rest
—that is, the long enlightening speeches—are liberties a
novelist may take, if he really wishes to, but prohibited to
the dramatist. I therefore cut and tightened these
speeches and made use of Temple instead in order to
challenge the paradox that Nancy illustrates and throw it
into stronger relief. I can therefore accuse myself of
abbreviating Faulkner's message. But in so doing I only
responded to dramatic necessities, and I believe that I
respected the essentials.

§   On Faulkner

In his preface to *Sanctuary,* André Malraux wrote that Faulkner had introduced the detective story into classical tragedy. This is true. There is, moreover, something of the detective story in every tragedy. Faulkner, who knows this, didn't hesitate to choose his criminals and heroes from daily newspaper stories. In my opinion this is what makes his *Requiem* one of the very few modern tragedies we have.

In its original form, *Requiem for a Nun* is not a play. It is a novel in dialogue form. But it has a dramatic intensity. First of all because it gradually discloses a secret and sustains throughout an expectation of tragedy. Secondly, because the conflict that brings the characters face to face with their destiny, centering around the murder of a child, is a conflict that cannot be solved except through the acceptance of this destiny.

Faulkner has contributed then to hastening the time when the tragedy at work in our history can also take its place in our theater. His characters are our contemporaries and yet they are confronted with the same destiny that crushed Electra or Orestes. Only a great artist could attempt to introduce the noble language of pain and humiliation into our public rooms this way. Nor is it accidental that Faulkner's strange religion is experienced in this play by a Negro woman who has been a prostitute and is a murderer. On the contrary, this extreme contrast summarizes the human grandeur of the *Requiem* and all Faulkner's work.

William Faulkner

Let me add in conclusion that the great problem of modern tragedy is language. Characters in business suits cannot talk like Oedipus or Titus. Their language must at the same time be simple enough to be our own and lofty enough to reach the tragic. In my view, Faulkner has found such a language. I have tried to recreate it in French, and to betray neither a work nor an author I admire.

1956

Program note to the Camus adaptation of Requiem for a Nun.

§ Excerpts from Three Interviews

I

"I had to put the form back in, to prune the text; it is not a play, it's a world into which I introduced logic. For the French public, the theater is inconceivable without unity. . . .

I like and I admire Faulkner; I believe I understand him rather well. Even though he did not write for the stage, he is in my opinion the only truly tragic dramatist of our time. . . . He gives us an ancient but always contemporary theme that is perhaps the only tragedy in the world: the blind man stumbling along between his destiny and his responsibilities. A simple dialogue must be found, acceptable for people who are simple too, [but] who have access to grandeur despite their coats and ties. Only Faulkner has known how to find an intensity of tone, of situation, intolerable to the point of making the

317

heroes deliver themselves by means of a violent, superhuman act."

Combat, *1956*

II

"The *Requiem* was not a play, but a novel in great dialogued scenes filled with a historical-poetic accent and a psychological climate that I have taken pains to preserve. . . .

I wanted to clear the way for a more theatrical than fictional progression. . . .

I developed only the role of the husband which I find admirable. . . .

The play poses no racial problem. Faulkner is too great a creator not to be universal. In the *Requiem,* the religion of suffering, notably in the seventh scene, becomes one with the catharsis, that ancient purification."

Nouvelles littéraires, *1956*

III

Is the meeting of Albert Camus and William Faulkner equivalent to a first modern tragedy?

The stage setting will already have told you that the detective element in this tragedy plays a strong role. It does in all tragedies for that matter. Take *Electra* or *Hamlet.* Faulkner, who has never been reluctant to look for his characters in news items reported in the newspapers, knows this well.

A secret, then. And a conflict. Something which sets the protagonists against their destiny and is resolved with their acceptance of this destiny. These are the keys to ancient tragedies. Faulkner used them to open the way to modern tragedy. Even though it was not written for the stage, his work, whose intensity is wholly dramatic, seems to me one that most nearly approaches a certain tragic ideal.

This problem of modern tragedy, I believe, has always interested you. Is this the reason you agreed to produce the Requiem?

It is precisely the reason. Together with the admiration that I plainly hold for someone I consider the greatest American novelist. You see, we are living through a highly dramatic time that does not yet have a drama. Faulkner permits us to catch a glimpse of the time when what is tragic in our own history can at last reach the footlights.

Doesn't the whole difficulty consist of making contemporary people speak a tragic language?

Without a doubt, but I hope to have surmounted it. Faulkner's "breathless" style, that I did my utmost to imitate, is the style of suffering itself.

The basis of his whole religion . . .

Just so. A strange religion, more clearly expressed in his latest work, *A Fable,* whose symbols give a glimpse of the hope for redemption through pain and humiliation. Here, Nancy Mannigoe, murderer and prostitute, is his message bearer. This is not accidental.

And the meaning of his title: Requiem for a Nun, *did he explain it to you?*

He? Not at all. I saw him for only ten minutes and he didn't say three words to me. No, the title takes on its meaning when one knows the role that bordellos and prisons play in Faulkner's universe. Nancy and Temple are two nuns who have entered the monastery of abjection and expiation.

As diffuse as it is, doesn't Faulkner's faith run counter to your own agnosticism?

I don't believe in God, that's true. But I am not an atheist nonetheless. I would even agree with Benjamin Constant that there is something vulgar . . . yes . . . worn out about being against religion.

Should one see in this the sign of a certain evolution in your thinking, and doesn't this interest in Faulkner foresee an eventual rallying to the spirit if not the dogma of the Church? Certain readers of The Fall *seemed to hope for this.*

Nothing really justifies them in this. Doesn't my judge-penitent clearly say that he is Sicilian and Japanese? Not Christian for a minute. Like him, I have a good deal of affection for the first Christian. I admire the way he lived, the way he died. My lack of imagination keeps me from following him any further. There, in parentheses, is my only similarity to the Jean-Baptiste Clamence with whom people stubbornly insist on identifying me. I would like to have called that book "A Hero of Our Time." Originally it was only a short novel, meant to appear next January in a collection that will be called *Exile and the Kingdom.* But I let myself get carried away with the idea: to paint a portrait of a small prophet like so many today. They proclaim nothing at all and find nothing better to do than accuse others in accusing themselves.

Le Monde, *August 31, 1956*

René Char[1]

❧❧ ❧❧❧ ❧❧

ONE CANNOT do justice in a few pages to a poet like René Char, but one can at least place him in the right context. Certain works justify our seizing any pretext to testify, even without shades of meaning, to what we owe them. And I am happy that this German edition of my favorite poems gives me the opportunity to say that I consider René Char our greatest living poet, and *Fureur et Mystère* to be the most astonishing book French poetry has given us since Rimbaud's *Les Illuminations* and Apollinaire's *Alcools* . . .

The originality of René Char's poetry, actually, is startling. He came to it by way of surrealism, no doubt, but by lending rather than giving himself to that move-

[1] *René Char, a close personal friend of Camus, was born in Provence in 1907. He was initially associated with the surrealist movement, but broke with it in 1937. During World War II he fought as a member of the Resistance. References to his experiences, which also inspired his book* Feuillets d'Hypnos *in 1946, can be found in* Carnets II, *pp. 216–17; Alfred A. Knopf edition, p. 170.* —P.T.

321

ment, staying just long enough to realize that his step was firmer when he walked alone. Since the publication of *Seuls demeurent,* a handful of poems have been enough to set a free and virgin wind blowing through our poetry. After so many years devoted to the manufacture of "inane trifles," our poets relinquished the lute only to put the bugle to their lips, transforming poetry into a salubrious funeral pyre. It blazed, like those great bonfires of grass which in the poet's own country give scent to the wind and richness to the earth. At last we could breathe. Natural mysteries, with living waters and sunlight, burst into a room where poetry still lay spellbound in echoes and shadows. I am describing a poetic revolution.

But I would have less admiration for the originality of this poetry if its inspiration were not, at the same time, so ancient. Char rightly lays claim to the tragic optimism of pre-Socratic Greece. From Empedocles to Nietzsche a secret has been passed from summit to summit, and after a long eclipse, Char once more takes up this hard and rare tradition. The fires of Etna smoulder beneath some of his unendurable phrases, the royal wind of Sils Maria irrigates his poems and makes them echo with the sound of clear and tumultuous waters. What Char calls "wisdom with tear-filled eyes" is revived here, at the very height of our disasters.

His poetry, at once both old and new, combines refinement with simplicity. It carries day and night in the same impulse. In the intense light beneath which Char was born we know the sun sometimes grows dark. At two in the afternoon, when the countryside is replete with warmth, a dark wind blows over it. In the same way, whenever Char's poetry seems obscure, it is because of his furious concentration of images, a thickening of the light that sets it apart from the abstract transparence we usually look for only because it makes no demands on us. But at the same time, just as on the sun-filled plains, this black point solidifies vast beaches of light around itself, light in which faces are stripped bare. At the center of the *Poème pulvérisé*, for example, there is a mysterious hearth around which torrents of warm images inexhaustibly whirl.

This is also why Char's poetry is so completely satisfying. At the heart of the obscurity through which we advance, the fixed, round light of Paul Valéry's skies would be of no use. It would bring nostalgia, not relief. In the strange and rigorous poetry René Char offers us, on the other hand, our very night shines forth in clarity and we learn to walk once more. This poet for all times speaks accurately for our own. He is at the heart of the battle, he formulates our misfortunes as well as our renaissance: "If we live in a lightning flash, it is the heart of the eternal."

Char's poetry does indeed exist in a flash of lightning—and not only in a figurative sense. The man and the artist, who go hand in hand, were tempered yesterday in the struggle against Hitlerian totalitarianism, and today in the denunciation of the rival but allied nihilisms that are tearing our world apart. Char has accepted sacrifice but not delight in the common struggle. "To leap not in the festival, but in its epilogue." A poet of revolt and liberty, he has never succumbed to complacency, and never, to use his own words, confused revolt with ill temper. It can never be said enough, and all men confirm it every day, that there are two kinds of revolt— one that conceals a wish for servitude, and another that seeks desperately for a free order, in which, as Char magnificently puts it, bread will be cured. Char knows well that to cure bread means to restore it to its rightful place, to place it above all doctrines, and give it the taste of friendship. This rebel thus escapes from the fate of so many noble insurgents who end up as cops or accomplices. Char will always protest against those who sharpen guillotines. He will have no truck with prison bread, and bread will always taste better to him in a hobo's mouth than in the prosecuting attorney's.

It is easy to understand, then, why this poet of revolutionaries has no trouble being also a poet of love, into which his poems sink fresh and tender roots. A whole aspect of Char's ethic and his art is summed up in the proud phrase of the *Poème pulvérisé:* "Bow down only in order to love." For him, love is a question of bowing down, and the love that runs through his work, however virile, has the stamp of tenderness.

This is again why Char, caught up as we all are in the most confusing history, has not been afraid to maintain and celebrate within this history the beauty for which it has given us so desperate a thirst. Beauty surges from his admirable *Feuillets d'Hypnos*, burning like the rebel's blade, red, streaming from a strange baptism, crowned with flames. We recognize her then for what she is, not some anaemic, academic goddess, but the sweetheart, the mistress, the companion of our days. In the middle of the struggle, here is a poet who dared to shout at us: "In our darkness, there is no one place for beauty. There is space for beauty everywhere." From that moment on, confronting the nihilism of his time and opposing all forms of betrayal, each of René Char's poems has been a milestone on the path to hope.

What more can one ask of a poet in our time? In the midst of our dismantled citadels, by virtue of a generous and secret art, are woman, peace, and liberty hard to maintain. And far from diverting us from the fray, we learn that these rediscovered riches are the only ones worth fighting for. Without having meant to, and simply because he has rejected nothing of his time, Char does more than express what we are: he is also the poet of our tomorrows. Although he remains alone, he brings us together, and the admiration he arouses mingles with that great fraternal warmth within which men bear their best fruit. We can be sure of it; it is in works like his from now on that we will seek recourse and vision. Char's poems are messengers of truth, of that lost truth each day now brings us closer to, although for a long time we were able only to say that it was our country and that far away from it we suffered, as if in exile. But words finally take shape, light dawns, one day the country will receive its name. Today a poet describes it for us, magnificently, reminding us, already, to justify the present, that this country is "earth and murmurs, amid the impersonal stars."

Preface to the German edition of René Char's Poésies,
written in 1958 and published in 1959

On Jean Grenier's Les Iles

❧❧ ❧❧❧ ❧❧

I WAS TWENTY in Algiers when I read this book for the first time. I can do no better than compare its overwhelming effect, its influence on me and many of my friends, to the shock a whole generation in France received from *Les Nourritures Terrestres*. But the revelation offered by *Les Iles* was of a different order. It suited us, whereas Gide's glorification of the senses left us at once full of admiration and puzzled. We really had no need to be freed from the winding sheet of morality, or to sing of the fruits of the earth. They hung on our doorstep in the sunlight. All we had to do was sink our teeth into them.

Some of us knew, of course, that poverty and suffering existed. We simply rejected them with all the strength of our youthful blood. The truth of the world lay only in its beauty, and the delights it offered. Thus we lived on sensations, on the surface of the world, among colors, waves, and the good smell of the soil. This is why *Les Nourritures*, with its invitation to happiness, came too late. Happiness was a faith that we proclaimed, insolently. We needed, quite the opposite, to be diverted a bit

from our greed, to be torn, in fact, from our happy barbarity. Of course, if gloomy preachers had stalked across
our beaches hurling anathema at the world and at the
creatures who enchanted us, our reaction would have
been violent, or sarcastic. We needed more subtle teachers, and a man born on other shores, though like us
enamoured of light and bodily splendors, came to tell us
in peerless language that these outward appearances
were beautiful, but that they were doomed to perish and
should therefore be loved in despair. Immediately, this
great, eternal theme began to echo in us like an over-
whelmingly new discovery. The sea, the light, people's
faces, from which a kind of invisible barrier suddenly
separated us, receded, but still exercised their fascination. *Les Iles*, in short, had just initiated our disenchant-
ment; we had discovered culture.

Without denying the physical reality that composed our realm, this book coupled it with another reality
that explained our youthful uneasiness. What Grenier
did was to remind us that the moments of bliss, the
instants when we said "Yes," which we had experienced
only obscurely and which inspire some of the finest pages
in *Les Iles,* were essentially fleeting and would perish.
Immediately, we understood our sudden melancholies.
The man who labors painfully between a harsh earth and
a somber sky can dream of another world where bread
and the sky will both be light. He hopes. But men whose
longings are fully satisfied every hour of the day by the
sunshine and the hills have ceased to hope. They can
only dream of an imaginary elsewhere. Thus men from
the North flee to the shores of the Mediterranean, or into
deserts of light. But where can men of sun-drenched
countries flee, except into the invisible? The journey
Grenier describes is a voyage into imaginary and invisible

lands, a quest from isle to isle, such as the one Melville, using other means, illustrates in *Mardi*. Animals take their pleasure and die, man marvels and he dies—where is his harbor? This is the question that echoes through the book. It is answered only indirectly. Grenier, like Melville, ends his voyage with a meditation on the absolute and on God. Speaking of the Hindus, he writes of a port that can be neither named nor situated in any particular place, of another island, but one forever distant, and in its own way deserted.

Once again, for a young man brought up outside traditional religions, this prudent, allusive approach was perhaps the only way to direct him toward a deeper meditation on life. Personally, I had no lack of gods: the sun, the night, the sea . . . But these are gods of enjoyment; they fill one, then they leave one empty. With them alone for company I should have forgotten the gods in favor of enjoyment itself. I had to be reminded of mystery and holy things, of the finite nature of man, of a love that is impossible in order to return to my natural gods one day, less arrogantly. So I do not owe to Grenier certainties he neither could nor wished to give me. But I owe him, instead, a doubt which will never end and which, for example, has prevented me from being a humanist in the sense that it is understood today—I mean a man blinded by narrow certainties. From the very day I read *Les Iles*, I admired its pervasive tremor, and wanted to imitate it.

"I have long dreamed of arriving alone in a foreign town, alone and stripped of everything. I would have lived humbly, in poverty even. Above all else, I would have kept the secret." This is the kind of music that almost intoxicated me as I repeated it softly to myself, walking in the Algerian evenings. I felt that I was entering a new land, that one of those high-walled gardens which stood on the heights of my city, past which I often walked, catching only a whiff of invisible honeysuckle, and of which, in my poverty, I had dreamed, was finally left open to me. I was not mistaken. A garden of incomparable wealth was opening up to me; I had just discovered art. Something, someone was stirring dimly within me, longing to speak. Reading one book, hearing one conversation, can provoke this rebirth in a young person. One sentence stands out from the open book, one word still vibrates in the room, and suddenly, around the right word, the exact note, contradictions resolve themselves and disorder ceases. Already, at the same moment, in response to this perfect language, a timid, clumsier song rises from the darkness of our being.

I believe I already wanted to write at the time I discovered *Les Iles*. But I really decided to do so only after reading this book. Other books contributed to this decision. Their role accomplished, I forgot them. But this book has not stopped living within me, and I have been reading it for twenty years. Even today, I find myself repeating, as if they were my own, phrases from *Les Iles* or other books by the same author. I don't regret it at all. I simply admire my good fortune, in that I, who more than anyone else needed to bow down before someone, should have found a teacher, at just the right moment, and that I should have been able to continue to love and admire him from year to year and from work to work.

For it is indeed lucky to be able to experience, at least once in one's lifetime, this enthusiastic submission to another person. Among the half-truths that delight our intellectual society this stimulating thought can be found —that each conscience seeks the death of the other. At once we all become masters and slaves, dedicated to mutual annihilation. But the word master has another

329

meaning, linked to the word disciple in respect and gratitude. It is no longer a question of one mind seeking to kill the other, but of a dialogue, which never ceases once it has begun, and which brings absolute satisfaction to certain lives. This long confrontation involves neither servitude nor obedience, only imitation, in the spiritual sense of the word. In the end, the master rejoices when the disciple leaves him and achieves his difference, while the latter will always remain nostalgic for the time when he received everything and knew he could never repay it. Mind thus engenders mind, from one generation to another, and human history, fortunately, is built as much on admiration as on hatred.

But this is not a tone in which Grenier would speak. He prefers to tell us about a cat's death, a butcher's illness, the scent of flowers, the passage of time. Nothing is really said in this book. Everything is suggested, with incomparable strength and sensitivity. The delicate language, at once so accurate and dreamlike, has the fluidity of music. It flows, swiftly, but its echoes linger. If a comparison has to be made, one should speak of Chateaubriand or Barrès, who drew new accents from French. But why bother? Grenier's originality goes beyond these comparisons. He merely speaks to us of simple and familiar experiences in an apparently unadorned language. Then he lets us translate, each in his own way. It is only on these conditions that art is a gift which carries no obligations. I, who have received so much from this book, recognize the extent of this gift and acknowledge my debt. The great revelations a man receives in his life are few, rarely more than one or two. But, like good fortune, they transfigure us. To anyone eager to live and to know, this book offers in each one of its pages a similar revelation. It took *Les Nourritures Terrestres* twenty years to find a public to overwhelm. It is time for new readers to come to this book. I would still like to be one of them, just as I would like to go back to that evening when, after opening this little volume in the street, I closed it again as soon as I had read the first lines, hugged it tight against me, and ran up to my room to devour it without witnesses. And I envy, without bitterness, but rather, if I may say so, with warmth, the unknown young man today who picks up *Les Iles* for the first time . . .

Essay published in Preuves, *1959, and reprinted as a preface in the same year*

III

CAMUS ON HIMSELF

Preface to The Stranger [1]

I SUMMARIZED *The Stranger* a long time ago, with a remark that I admit was highly paradoxical: "In our society any man who does not weep at his mother's funeral runs the risk of being sentenced to death." I only meant that the hero of my book is condemned because he does

[1] *When* L'Etranger (The Stranger) *was published in 1942, Camus noted down his reactions to some of the criticisms and interpretations that appeared in the French press. In 1942, for example, he wrote in his* Carnets II *(pp. 32–4; Alfred A. Knopf edition, pp. 20–2) the draft of a long letter pointing out how completely his book had been misunderstood by a critic who had "not taken into account" the scene in which Meursault explains his attitude to the priest. In all probability, this letter was inspired by a review the Catholic critic André Rousseaux had published in* Le Figaro littéraire *on July 17, 1942. At that time, however, Camus insisted mainly on the way in which his character "defined himself negatively," and did not really present him as potentially heroic. He took a further step toward doing this in an interview published in* Le Littéraire *on August 10, 1946, when he told Gaëton Picon that the critics had failed to see the importance of the Algerian atmosphere in* The Stranger. *The men in Algeria, he explained, "live like my hero, in complete*

not play the game. In this respect, he is foreign to the society in which he lives; he wanders, on the fringe, in the suburbs of private, solitary, sensual life. And this is why some readers have been tempted to look upon him as a piece of social wreckage. A much more accurate idea of the character, or, at least, one much closer to the author's intentions, will emerge if one asks just *how* Meursault doesn't play the game. The reply is a simple one: he refuses to lie. To lie is not only to say what isn't true. It is also and above all, to say *more* than is true, and, as far as the human heart is concerned, to express more than one feels. This is what we all do, every day, to simplify life. He says what he is, he refuses to hide his feelings, and immediately society feels threatened. He is asked, for example, to say that he regrets his crime, in the approved manner. He replies that what he feels is annoyance rather than real regret. And this shade of meaning condemns him.

For me, therefore, Meursault is not a piece of social wreckage, but a poor and naked man enamored of a sun that leaves no shadows. Far from being bereft of all feeling, he is animated by a passion that is deep because it is stubborn, a passion for the absolute and for truth. This truth is still a negative one, the truth of what we are and what we feel, but without it no conquest of ourselves or of the world will ever be possible.

One would therefore not be much mistaken to

---

simplicity. Naturally, you can understand Meursault, but an Algerian will do so much more freely and more fully."

The 1955 preface is directed first and foremost against critics like Father Troisfontaines, Wyndham Lewis, Pierre Lafue, and Aimé Patri, who have argued that Meursault was "a schizophrenic," or "a moron," or have seen him as an example of the mechanization and depersonalization of modern life. —P.T.

read *The Stranger* as the story of a man who, without any heroics, agrees to die for the truth. I also happened to say, again paradoxically, that I had tried to draw in my character the only Christ we deserve. It will be understood, after my explanations, that I said this with no blasphemous intent, and only with the slightly ironic affection an artist has the right to feel for the characters he has created.

January 8, 1955

Published as a preface to the American University edition, 1956

Letter to Roland Barthes

on The Plague[1]

❦❦ ❦❦❦ ❦❦

Paris, January 11, 1955

My dear Barthes,

    However attractive it may appear, I find it difficult to share your point of view on *The Plague*. Of course, all comments are justifiable, within an honest critical appraisal, and it is both possible and significant to venture as far as you do. But it seems to me that every work contains a number of obvious factors to which the author is justified in calling attention if only to indicate the

---

[1] *In an article in the review* Club, *Roland Barthes had argued that* The Plague *was an inadequate transposition of the problems of the Resistance movement because Camus had replaced a struggle against men by a struggle against the impersonal microbes of plague. This is a fairly common criticism of* The Plague, *and it could be argued that Camus also neglected an important aspect of the Resistance movement when he made no reference to the moral problem created by the German habit of executing innocent hostages. The Resistance fighter risked having on his conscience the death of fifteen or twenty people executed as a direct result of his act of sabotage.* —P.T.

338

limits within which the commentary ought to go. To say, for example, that *The Plague* lays the foundation for an antihistorical ethic and an attitude of political solitude, involves, in my view, exposing oneself to a number of contradictions, and, above all, involves going beyond a certain number of obvious facts which I shall briefly summarize here:

1. *The Plague,* which I wanted to be read on a number of levels, nevertheless has as its obvious content the struggle of the European resistance movements against Nazism. The proof of this is that although the specific enemy is nowhere named, everyone in every European country recognized it. Let me add that a long extract from *The Plague* appeared during the Occupation, in a collection of underground texts, and that this fact alone would justify the transposition I made. In a sense, *The Plague* is more than a chronicle of the Resistance. But certainly it is nothing less.

2. Compared to *The Stranger, The Plague* does, beyond any possible discussion, represent the transition from an attitude of solitary revolt to the recognition of a community whose struggles must be shared. If there is an evolution from *The Stranger* to *The Plague,* it is in the direction of solidarity and participation.

3. The theme of separation, whose importance in the book you bring out very well, throws a good deal of light on this point. Rambert, who embodies this theme, does in fact give up private life in order to take his place in the common struggle. Parenthetically, this character alone shows how misleading it is to contrast the friend and the militant. For the one virtue common to them both is active fraternity, which no history, in the last resort, has ever done without.

4. *The Plague* ends, moreover, with the promise

and acceptance of struggles yet to come. It is a testimony of "all that had had to be done, and that [men] would doubtless have to do again against terror and its tireless weapons, whatever their personal anguish . . ."

I could develop my point of view further. But even if I already find it possible to consider the ethic at work in *The Plague* inadequate (and it must then be stated what more complete morality it is being compared with), and legitimate to criticize its aesthetic (many of your remarks are clarified by the very simple fact that I do not believe in realism in art), I find it, on the contrary, very difficult to agree with you when you say in your conclusion that its author rejects the solidarity of our history-in-the-making. Difficult and, permit me to say in all friendship, a little disappointing.

In any case, the question you ask: "What would the fighters against the plague do confronted with the all-too-human face of the scourge," is unjust in this respect: it ought to have been asked in the past tense, and then it would have received the answer, a positive one. What these fighters, whose experience I have to some extent translated, did do, they did in fact against men, and you know at what cost. They will do it again, no doubt, when any terror confronts them, whatever face it may assume, for terror has several faces. Still another justification for my not having named any particular one, in order better to strike at them all. Doubtless this is what I'm reproached with, the fact that *The Plague* can apply to any resistance against any tyranny. But it is not legitimate to reproach me or, above all, to accuse me of rejecting history—unless it is proclaimed that the only way of taking part in history is to make tyranny legitimate. This is not what you do, I know; as far as I am concerned, I am perverse enough to believe that if we resigned ourselves to such an idea we should be accepting human solitude. Far from feeling installed in a career of solitude, I have, on the contrary, the feeling that I am living by and for a community that nothing in history has so far been able to touch.

Here, too briefly expressed, is what I wanted to tell you. I would merely like to assure you in conclusion that this friendly discussion in no way alters the high opinion I have of your talent or of you as a person.

Albert Camus

Letter published in Club, *the review of the* Club *du meilleur livre,*
February 1955

Letter to P. B.

❦❦ ❦❦❦ ❦❦

February 15, 1953

My dear friend,

I will begin with the apology I owe you for last Friday. It was not because of a lecture on Holland, but that I was summoned at the last moment to sign books on behalf of the flood victims there. This exercise, which I was doing for the first time, seemed something I couldn't refuse, and I thought you would forgive my inconveniencing you. But this is not the question, the question is what you describe as the difficulties of our relationship. On this point, what I have to say can be expressed simply: if you knew one quarter of my life and its obligations, you wouldn't have written a single line of your letter. But you cannot know them, and I neither can nor should explain them to you. The "haughty solitude" that you, along with many others who lack your quality, complain of, would be a blessing for me, if it existed. But people are quite wrong to assume I enjoy such paradise. The truth is that I fight time and other people for each hour of my work, usually without winning. I'm not complaining. My life is what I

342

have made it, and I am the first person responsible for the way and the pace at which I spend it. But when I receive a letter like yours, then I do feel I want to complain, or at least ask people not to heap abuse on me so easily. To be equal to everything today, I would need three lives and several hearts. Of the latter, I have only one, which can be judged, as I often judge it myself, to be of only average quality. Physically I do not have the time, and above all the inner leisure, to see my friends as I would like to (ask Char, whom I love like a brother, how many times we see each other in a month). I haven't the time to write for reviews, neither on Jaspers nor on Tunisia, even in order to clear up one of Sartre's arguments. You will believe me if you want to, but I have not the time, nor the inner leisure, to be ill. When I am sick, my life is all upside down and I spend weeks trying to catch up with myself. But what is most serious is that I no longer have the time, or the inner leisure, to write my books, and it takes me four years to write something which, if I were free, would have taken one or two. Besides, for several years now, rather than freeing me, my work has enslaved me. And if I keep on, it's because I cannot do otherwise and because I prefer it to anything else, even liberty, wisdom, or true creativity, even, yes even, to friendship. It is true that I try to organize myself, to double my strength and my "presence" by a timetable, by organizing my day, by an increased efficiency. I hope to be equal to it someday. For the moment, I am not. Each letter brings three others, each person ten, each book a hundred letters and twenty correspondents, while life continues, there is work to do, people I love and people who need me. Life continues, and some mornings, weary of the noise, discouraged by the prospect of the interminable work to keep after, sickened also by the madness of the world that leaps at you from the newspaper, finally convinced that I will not be equal to it and that I will disappoint everyone—all I want to do is sit down and wait for evening. This is what I feel like, and sometimes I yield to it.

Can you understand this? Of course, you deserve to be respected and talked to. Of course your friends are as good as mine (who are not so grammatically inclined as you think). Even though I find it hard to imagine (and this is not a pose) that my esteem can matter to anyone, I do admire you. But for this esteem to transform itself into active friendship, we should indeed require real leisure, and many opportunities to meet. I have met a number of fine people, this has been the blessing of my life. But it is not possible to have that many friends, and unfortunately this condemns me to disappoint people, I know. I can understand that other people find it unbearable. I find it unbearable. But this is how things are, and if people cannot like me under these circumstances I expect them to leave me to a solitude that, as you see, is less haughty than you think.

In any case, I am replying to your bitterness without any of my own. Letters like yours, coming from someone like you, only make me sad, and compound the reasons I have to flee this town and the life I lead here. For the moment, although this is what I long for most in the world, it is not possible. I am thus compelled to continue this alien existence, and must count what you tell me as the price—rather a high one, I think—that I must pay for having let myself be driven to it.

Forgive me, in any case, for having disappointed you, and believe me to be,

Faithfully,

Albert Camus

344

Three Interviews

❦❦ ❦❦❦ ❦❦

§ I No, I am not an existentialist . . .

"No, I am not an existentialist. Sartre and I are always surprised to see our names linked. We have even thought of publishing a short statement in which the undersigned declare that they have nothing in common with each other and refuse to be held responsible for the debts they might respectively incur. It's a joke, actually. Sartre and I published all our books, without exception, before we had ever met. When we did get to know each other, it was to realize how much we differed. Sartre is an existentialist, and the only book of ideas that I have published, *The Myth of Sisyphus*, was directed against the so-called existentialist philosophers.

· · · · · ·

Sartre and I do not believe in God, it is true. And we don't believe in absolute rationalism either. But neither do Jules Romains, Malraux, Stendhal, Paul de Kock, the Marquis de Sade, André Gide, Alexandre Dumas, Mont-

345

aigne, Eugène Sue, Molière, Saint-Evremond, the Cardinal de Retz, or André Breton. Must we put all these people in the same school? But we had better leave this aside. After all, I don't see why I should apologize for being interested in those who live outside Grace. It is high time we began concerning ourselves with them, since they are the most numerous.

Doesn't a philosophy that insists upon the absurdity of the world run the risk of driving people to despair?

All I can do is reply on my own behalf, realizing that what I say is relative. Accepting the absurdity of everything around us is one step, a necessary experience: it should not become a dead end. It arouses a revolt that can become fruitful. An analysis of the idea of revolt could help us to discover ideas capable of restoring a relative meaning to existence, although a meaning that would always be in danger.

Revolt takes a different form in every individual. Would it be possible to pacify it with notions valid for everyone?

. . . Yes, because if there is one fact that these last five years have brought out, it is the extreme solidarity of men with one another. Solidarity in crime for some, solidarity in the upsurge of resistance in others. Solidarity even between victims and executioners. When a Czech was shot, the life of a grocer in the *rue de Beaune* was in jeopardy.

The individualism of the French makes it difficult for them to have a real experience of this solidarity.

That remains to be proved. And besides, in a world whose absurdity appears to be so impenetrable, we simply must reach a greater degree of understanding among men, a greater sincerity. We must achieve this or perish. To do so, certain conditions must be fulfilled: men must be frank (falsehood confuses things), free (communication is impossible with slaves). Finally, they must feel a certain justice around them.

You wrote in "The Myth of Sisyphus": "A man without hope, and conscious of this condition, no longer belongs to the future." Since you do not believe that men can escape into religion, are you not afraid that young people today will be led into a dangerous neglect of action?

If it were not possible nowadays to live or act without reference to God, then perhaps a very great number of people in the West would be condemned to sterility. Young people know this very well. And if I feel so great a solidarity with so many students, for example, it is because we are all confronted with the same problem, and because I am confident that, like me, they want to solve it by trying to act more effectively and to serve man.

Since you know young people so well, does this mean that you have been a teacher?

Never. But to continue my studies, I had to work at a number of jobs. I sold spare parts for automobiles, worked in a meteorological office, in a shipping firm, and in a *préfecture*. I was an actor (I belonged to a company that performed for a fortnight each month, and during the rest of the time I prepared my *licence*), and, finally, I worked as a journalist, which gave me the chance to travel.

To write after having had a number of jobs is more usual in America than in France. Your first novel,

347

The Stranger, *recalls certain works by Faulkner and Steinbeck. Is this simply coincidence?*

No. But the technique of the American novel seems to me to lead to a dead end. I used it in *The Stranger,* it is true. But this was because it suited my purpose, which was to describe a man with no apparent awareness of his existence. By generalizing this particular technique, we would end up with a universe of automatons and instincts. It would be a considerable impoverishment. That is why, although I appreciate the real value of the American novel, I would give a hundred Hemingways for one Stendhal or one Benjamin Constant. And I regret the influence of this literature on many young writers.

You are nevertheless considered a revolutionary writer.

I don't know what that means. If it is revolutionary to ask oneself questions about one's art, then perhaps . . . but I cannot imagine literature without style. I know of only one revolution in art; it belongs to all ages, and consists of the exact adjustment of form to subject matter, of language to theme. From this point of view, I love, deeply, only the great classical French literature. It is true that I include here Saint-Evremond and the works of the Marquis de Sade. It is also true that I exclude certain academicians, both present and past.

What are your projects?

A novel about the plague, an essay on man in revolt. And perhaps I ought to make my mind up to study existentialism . . .

An interview with Jeanine Delpech, in Les Nouvelles littéraires,
November 15, 1945

§ II   Encounter with Albert Camus

Albert Camus, who is still a young writer, is con-
sidered one of the intellectual leaders of the younger
generation.

However, I will say at once that not for a moment
when I was with him did he seem to have the strained
look of a Master or a director of consciences. I will even
go so far as to say that he seemed very little interested in
such matters. "I am often depicted as an austere charac-
ter," he told me, not without the kind of irony that
breaks almost imperceptibly through the gravity of his
writings.

There is also a discreet smile on his tormented
face, a high, wrinkled forehead beneath very dark, crisp
hair, a manly, North African face that has grown paler in
our climate. A discreet but frequent smile, and his rather
deep voice is not afraid of humorous inflexions.

The world was not hostile to me at first. I had a
happy childhood . . .

Happy in its poverty, in spite of its poverty. Born
in a village in the province of Constantine, Mondovici,
the birthplace of General Juin, he was only a year old
when his mother, widowed in the First World War, took
him to Algiers where she had to work hard to bring up
her two sons. Nevertheless, he will never hear an envious
or a bitter word. So that he doesn't know what envy or
bitterness are like. He feels himself rich in natural
bounty. In Africa, of course, this is easier. He enjoys the
sun and the sea, lives happily in the street or on the

beach, until the day when he allows himself to be convinced of the usefulness of acquiring knowledge. He studies at the Lycée d'Alger, has to take a number of jobs in order to carry on up to the licence. *He even works as an actor . . .*

I have had my share of difficult experiences. However, I did not begin my life with a feeling of anguish. Similarly, I did not go in for literature scorning or sneering of it, as many people do, but with admiration.

How did you first get the urge to write? Can you remember the first feeling?

It is rather difficult to say. But I can remember how overwhelmed I was by a book written by a young man and lent to me by Jean Grenier. It was called *La Douleur*, by André de Richaud. You must understand that this shock took place in the life of a very young man. At the time, I read everything, even Marcel Prévost. But Richaud, in *La Douleur*, talked about things I knew: he depicted poor areas; he described the nostalgias I had felt. I saw, while reading his book, that I too might perhaps have something personal to express.

You spoke of Jean Grenier. I believe he was your teacher in the Lycée d'Alger.

Yes, Grenier gave me the taste for philosophical meditation; he guided my reading. Both in style and by sensibility, he is one of our leading writers. Perhaps we should be sorry that his modesty, and a certain detachment, prevent him from showing himself more frequently. But the fact remains that *Les Iles* is an admirable book. And what a marvelous friend, always bringing you back to the essential, in spite of yourself. Grenier was my teacher, and still is.

350

The highly classical purity of your art has often made me think that Gide was your master as well.

He reigned over my youth—while Grenier nonetheless remained the keeper of the garden—Gide, or to be more accurate, the Malraux-Gide conjunction . . . Montherlant also affected me very deeply at that time. Not only by the ascendancy of his style: *Service inutile* is a book that moved me. . . . As for the earlier writers, the ones you go back to when you are tired of reading your contemporaries, it is Tolstoi I most like to reread nowadays. There is an anguish in Tolstoi and a tragic sense doubtless less spectacular than Dostoevski's, but which I persist in finding overwhelming since it remained his own fate until the very end: of the two, it was Dostoevski after all who died in his own bed. . . .

You yourself are often thought of as riddled with anguish. You are seen as a pessimistic writer. What do you think of this weighty reputation?

First of all that I very obviously do not adopt the opposite attitude. Comfortable optimism surely seems like a bad joke in today's world. Having said this, I am not one of those who proclaim that the world is hurtling toward its doom. I do not believe in the final collapse of our civilization. I believe—without, of course, nursing anything but . . . reasonable illusions on this subject—that a renaissance is possible. If the world were hurtling toward its doom, we would have to blame apocalyptic modes of thought. Not every pose horrifies me. But I have no sympathy at all for that of *poète maudit.*

When I do happen to look for what is most fundamental in me, what I find is a taste for happiness. I have a very keen liking for people. I have no contempt for the human race. I think that one can feel proud of being the contemporary of a certain number of men of our day whom I respect and admire. . . . At the center of my work there is an invincible sun. It seems to me that all this does not make up a very sad philosophy?

Not sad. Grave and concerned. How could this fail to be the case, when one is as sensitive as you are to the drama of our century?

I am, in fact, very sensitive to it, and perhaps it is this sensitivity which has led me to write books which are, up to now, "blacker" than I would have liked.

But it is also this sensitivity which has given you the attention and trust of a large section of young people. In turn, the new generation looks on you today as one of its masters . . .

(This time, the author of *The Plague* laughs out loud.)

A master, already! But I don't claim to teach anybody! Whoever thinks this is mistaken. The problems confronting young people today are the same ones confronting me, that is all. And I am far from having solved them. I therefore do not think that I have any right to play the role you mention. . . .

What are young people looking for? Certainties. I haven't many to offer them. All I can say definitely is that there is a certain order of degradation I shall always refuse. I think this is something they feel. Those who trust me know that I will never lie to them. As to the young people who ask others to think for them, we must say "No" to them in the clearest possible terms.

That is all I have to say.

Let us go back to your own formation. You acknowledge having learned from André Gide. But which André Gide? For there are several, are there not? And in any case there are no traces in your work, which never gives away secrets about your own life, of the Gide of "Si le grain ne meurt" *or the* Journals.

Well, my cult was directed above all to the artist, the master of modern classicism, let us say to the Gide of the *Prétextes*. Being fully aware of the anarchy of my nature, I need to give myself limits in art. Gide taught me how to do this. His conception of classicism as a romanticism brought under control is something I share. As for his deep respect for artistic matters, I agree with him completely. For I have the highest possible idea of art. I place it too high ever to agree to subject it to anything.

Then I shall not have to ask Albert Camus what is by now the ritual question on "committed" literature. You have just heard his reply. But immediately, with that care for accuracy which characterizes him, both a scruple and a taste for nuance:

Nevertheless, I do not want to defend aesthetic ideas and artistic forms that are out of date. The writer who allows himself to be fascinated by the political Gorgon is doubtless making a mistake. But it is also a mistake to pass over the social problems of our time in silence. . . . And besides, it would be quite useless to run away from them: turn your back on the Gorgon, and it starts to move. . . . What, in fact, is the aim of every creative artist? To depict the passions of his day. In the seventeenth century, the passions of love were at the forefront of people's minds. But today, the passions of our century are collective passions, because society is in disorder.

Artistic creation, instead of removing us from the drama of our time, is one of the means we are given of bringing it closer. Totalitarian regimes are well aware of

353

this, since they consider us their first enemies. Isn't it obvious that everything which destroys art aims to strengthen ideologies that make men unhappy? Artists are the only people who have never harmed the world.

Would you say the same of philosophers?

The evil geniuses of contemporary Europe bore the label of philosopher: they are Hegel, Marx, and Nietzsche.

Nietzsche? I thought he was one of your spiritual ancestors?

He is, undoubtedly. What is admirable, in Nietzsche, is that you always find in him something to correct what is dangerous elsewhere in his ideas. I place him infinitely higher than the two others.

We are living in their Europe, the Europe they have made. When we have reached the final stage in their logic, we will remember that another tradition exists; one that has never denied what makes man's grandeur. Fortunately, there is a light that we Mediterraneans have known how to keep lit. If Europe were to reject certain values of the Mediterranean world—moderation, for example, true moderation, which has nothing to do with the more comfortable variety—can you imagine what the results would be? They are in fact visible already.

Yes, of course, the Mediterranean has its word to say at this tragic juncture. But isn't it too detached to assume such a role, too skeptical?

It was, until it was afflicted with its own truths. It is far less detached and skeptical today, now that it is stifling in a barbarous Europe. I am judging, it is true, as

354

a Mediterranean from North Africa, which is a harder
and a harsher earth than your Provence.

But equally fecund in new talents, it seems to me.

Indeed. It's a regular nest of singing birds: The
generation before ours did not know even how to read.
And now we have an Audisio, a Roblès, a Jules Roy, a de
Fréminville, a Rosfelder, a Pierre Millecan, etc., and a
young author who is going to make his debut with Gallimard, with a very curious novel. Fruits grow quickly
there. Of course, it was the country of Jugurtha and Saint
Augustine. A singularly explosive mixture, don't you
think?

*Let us come back to sad Europe. I am thinking
of certain European novelists many people will be surprised not to have heard you name among your intellectual mentors. The Czech writer, Franz Kafka, for example, the great painter of the absurd.*

I look upon Kafka as a very great storyteller. But
it would be wrong to say that he has influenced me. If a
painter of the Absurd has played a role in my idea of
literary art, it is the author of the admirable *Moby Dick,*
the American, Melville. . . . I think that what repels me
a little in Kafka is the fantastic element. I am not at
home in fantasy. The artist's universe should exclude
nothing. But Kafka's universe excludes practically the
whole world. And then . . . then, I really cannot entertain an affection for a literature of total despair.[1]

---

[1] One shouldn't put too much stock in these cutting remarks. Camus expressed himself very thoughtfully on Kafka in
The Myth of Sisyphus. According to René Char, Camus remained
deeply troubled, even obsessed, by Kafka, and near the end of his
life rendered him unlimited homage. —Roger Quilliot, note from
p. 1342, *Pléiade II.*

To what extent should we look upon your books, whether they are novels or plays, as symbolic translations of the philosophy of the Absurd? People have often done this.

This word "Absurd" has had an unhappy history, and I confess that now it rather annoys me.

When I analyzed the feeling of the Absurd in *The Myth of Sisyphus*, I was looking for a method and not a doctrine. I was practicing methodical doubt. I was trying to make a *"tabula rasa,"* on the basis of which it would then be possible to construct something.

If we assume that nothing has any meaning, then we must conclude that the world is absurd. But does nothing have a meaning? I have never believed that we could remain at this point. Even as I was writing *The Myth of Sisyphus* I was thinking about the essay on revolt that I would write later on, in which I would attempt, after having described the different aspects of the feeling of the Absurd, to describe the different attitudes of man in revolt. (That is the title of the book I am completing.) And then there are new events that enrich or correct what has come to one through observation, the continual lessons life offers, which you have to reconcile with those of your earlier experiences. This is what I have tried to do . . . though, naturally, I still do not claim to be in possession of any truth.

Robert de Luppé seems to have brought out this constant development of your ideas very well in the little book on your work he has just published.

At any rate, it's a book written in a spirit of sympathetic objectivity, and for this I am grateful to its author. I appreciate the way he has not presented me as a doctrinal writer enslaved to one particular system.

356

What is more complex than the birth of thought? The right explanation is always double, at least. Greece teaches us this, Greece to which we must always return. Greece is both shadow and light. We are well aware, aren't we, if we come from the South, that the sun has its black side?

The sun that a painter like Jean Marchand likes to bring bursting into his skies?

Exactly. René Char has also given very fine expression to this duality. I consider him one of the few French poets who are great today and will still be great tomorrow. . . . I mean that he is ahead of his time, although he is at one with it. The truth is that it is a hard fate to be born in a pagan land in Christian times. This is my case. I feel closer to the values of the classical world than to those of Christianity. Unfortunately, I cannot go to Delphi to be initiated!

Interview with Gabriel d'Aubarède *in* Les Nouvelles littéraires,
May 10, 1951

§   III   Replies to Jean-Claude Brisville [2]

At what time in your life did you become clearly aware of your vocation as a writer?

Vocation is perhaps not the right word. I wanted

[2] J.-C. Brisville, a writer of whom Camus had a high opinion, is a critic and novelist, and reader for the publishing house of Julliard. His study of Camus in the collection entitled "La Bibliothèque idéale" was published by Gallimard in 1959.

to be a writer when I was about seventeen, and at the
same time I was vaguely aware that I would become one.

Were you thinking then of another profession?
Teaching. By necessity. But I have always wanted
to have a second profession to ensure my freedom to
work as a writer.

At the time of The Wrong Side and the Right
Side *did you have any idea of what your literary future
would be?*
After *The Wrong Side and the Right Side* I had
doubts. I wanted to give up. And then an overwhelming
sense of life burst to express itself in me: I wrote *Noces.*

*Do you find it difficult to reconcile your role as a
creator with the social role you see yourself obliged to
play? Is this an important problem for you?*
Of course. But our century has reached the point
where it gives so derisory or odious a face to "social
preoccupations" that it helps us to feel freer in this respect. The fact remains that writing while others are
gagged or imprisoned is a delicate undertaking. So as not
to fall short, either in one direction or in the other, we
have to remember that the writer lives for his work and
fights for liberties.

Do you feel at ease in your personality as a writer?
Very much at ease in my private relationships.
But the public aspect of my calling, which I have never
liked, is becoming unbearable.

*If for any reason you had to give up writing, do
you think that you could nevertheless be happy? Would
the simple "agreement between the earth and the foot" of*

which you speak in Caligula *be enough to compensate for the happiness of expressing yourself?*

When I was younger, I could have been happy without writing. Even today I have great gifts for silent happiness. However, I have to acknowledge now that I probably could not live without my art.

Do you think that your early success—the fact of having been considered, whether you wanted it or not, as an "intellectual master" after the publication of The Myth of Sisyphus—*has given any particular direction to your work? Do you, in short, think that you would have written the same books if you had composed them in relative obscurity?*

Of course, having a reputation changed many things. But, on this point, I have few complexes. My rule has always been a simple one: refuse all that could be refused quietly; in any case, make no effort to gain either reputation or obscurity. Accept either in silence, if it is to be one or the other, and perhaps accept them both. As to being an "intellectual leader," it simply makes me laugh. To teach, you need to know. To guide other people, you must know how to guide yourself.

Even so, it is true that I have known the servitudes of having a reputation before having written all my books. The most obvious consequence of this is that I have been obliged, and still am obliged, to struggle against society to find time for my work. I manage, but at a high price.

Do you consider the main part of your work as completed?

I am forty-five, and have a rather disturbing vitality.

Does the development of your work follow a general plan established long in advance, or do you discover this plan while you are actually writing?

Both. There is a plan that circumstances, on the one hand, and the actual writing of my books, on the other, tend to modify.

What is your method of working?

Notes, scraps of paper, vague musing, and this for years on end. One day, the idea, the conception that causes these scattered fragments to coagulate, comes along. Then the long and painful task of setting everything to order begins. And this task is all the longer because of the immensity of my profound anarchy.

Do you feel the need to talk about the work while you are writing it?

No. When, once in a while, I happen to talk about it, I am not pleased with myself.

When it is completed, do you ask the views of a friend—or do you content yourself with your own opinion?

I have two or three friends who read my manuscripts and note down what they don't like. Nine times out of ten, they are right, and I make the correction.

What, in your work as a writer, is the moment you prefer (the conception, the first draft, the working over of what you have written)?

The moment of conception.

Do you see any kind of relationship in the artist between the life of the body and his inspiration (or the nature of his work)? *If so, what do you think this relationship is?*

Physical life in the open air, in the sun, sport, and a proper balance in my body are, for me, the conditions under which I do my best intellectual work. Together (and the two things are connected) with a good timetable. To tell the truth, I rarely find myself in these conditions. But in any case I know that creation is an intellectual and bodily discipline, a school of energy. I have never achieved anything in anarchy or physical slackness.

Do you work regularly?

I try to. When everything is going well: four or five hours at the start of every day. When everything is going badly! . . .

Do you find fault with yourself when you put your work off to the next day?

Yes. I feel guilty. How shall I put it? I don't like myself.

Is there a character in your work of whom you are particularly fond?

Marie, Dora, Céleste.[3]

There seem to be two families of people in your work: the first, illustrated by Caligula, seem to correspond to a taste for powerful individuality; the second,

---

[3] *Marie is Meursault's mistress in* The Stranger. *Dora is Kaliayev's mistress in* The Just. *Céleste is the owner of the little restaurant where Meursault takes his meals. When Meursault is on trial for shooting the Arab, Céleste tries to defend him by showing how good a person he is, but can say nothing but:* "He is a man." (*See* "Summer in Algiers," *p. 87.*) —P.T.

which might be represented by Meursault, correspond to the temptation of self-effacement. Can you recognize this double direction in yourself?

Yes, I have a liking for energy and conquests. But I soon tire of what I have obtained. This is my great weakness. I also have a liking for obscurity, for self-effacement. But the passion for life urges me forward again. In short, I never solve the dilemma.

Which technique—fiction, the theater, or the essay—gives you the most satisfaction as a creator?

The alliance of all these techniques in the service of a single work.

It seems from some of your writings that you see an art of living in the theater. Do you agree with this?

That would be saying a great deal. But I sometimes feel that I could have been an actor and been satisfied with this profession.

To what values in a work of art—and especially in a literary work of art—are you most sensitive?

Truth. And the artistic values that reflect it.

Is there a theme in your work that you think is important and that you consider has been neglected by your commentators?

Humor.

How do you look on the part of your work which is already completed?

I don't reread it. It is dead for me. I would like, I want, to do something else.

What, in your view, distinguishes the creator?
The ability to renew himself. He always says the
same thing, no doubt, but he tirelessly renews the forms
in which he says it. He has a horror of rhymes.

*Which writers have formed you—or, at least,
have helped you to become aware of what you wanted to
say?*
Among the moderns: Grenier, Malraux, Montherlant. Among classical writers: Pascal, Molière. Nineteenth-century Russian literature. The Spanish writers.

*What importance do you attribute to the plastic
arts?*
I would have liked to be a sculptor. Sculpture for
me is the greatest of arts.

And music?
When I was young, I used to get drunk on it.
Nowadays, very few musicians move me. But Mozart still
does.

What do you think of the cinema?
And you?

*There are often misunderstandings in the way
artists are admired. What is the compliment that annoys
you the most?*
Honesty, conscience, humanity—you know, all
the modern mouthwashes.

*What, in your view, is the most marked feature of
your character?*
That depends on the day. But, often, a kind of
blind, heavy obstinacy.

Which human characteristic do you value highest?

There is a mixture of intelligence and courage, which is fairly rare, that I like very much.

Your last hero, the narrator in The Fall, *seems discouraged. Does he express what you feel at the present moment?*

My hero is indeed discouraged, and this is why, as a good modern nihilist, he exalts servitude. Have I chosen to exalt servitude?

You once wrote: "Secret of my universe: imagine God without the immortality of the soul." Can you define more exactly what you meant?

Yes. I have a sense of the sacred and I don't believe in a future life, that's all.

Is the simple pleasure of being alive, and the dispersion which it implies, threatened, in your view, by a vocation—an artistic one, for example—and by the discipline it demands?

Yes, unfortunately. I like burning, active days, a free life. . . . And this is why discipline is hard, and necessary. And this is why it is good to escape from it sometimes.

Have you a rule for living—or do you improvise, according to the circumstances and your reactions at the time?

I make strict rules for myself, in order to correct my nature. It is my nature in the end that I obey. The result is by no means brilliant.

364

What, for example, was your first reaction to the personal attacks directed against you in the press after the award of the Nobel Prize?

Oh, first of all, I felt hurt. When a man has never asked for anything in his life, and is then suddenly subjected to excessive praise and excessive blame, both praise and blame are equally painful. And then I soon rediscovered the notion I normally rely on whenever things go against me: that this was in the order of things. Do you know the remark of a man who was a great solitary being in spite of himself? "They have no love for me. Is this a reason for not blessing them?" No, everything that happens to me is good, in a sense. Besides, these noisy events are essentially secondary.

What wish would you make, at this stage in your life?

"Within a superabundance of life-giving and restoring forces, even misfortunes have a sunlike glow and engender their own consolation." This remark of Nietzsche's is true, and I have experienced it myself. And all I ask is that this strength and this superabundance should be given to me again, even if infrequently. . . .

La Bibliothèque Idéale, *Gallimard, 1959*

A NOTE ABOUT THE AUTHOR

ALBERT CAMUS was born in Mondovi, Algeria, in 1913. In occupied France in 1942 he published *The Myth of Sisyphus* and *The Stranger*, a philosophical essay and a novel that first brought him to the attention of intellectual circles. Among his other major writings are the essay *The Rebel* and three widely praised works of fiction, *The Plague, The Fall,* and *The Exile and the Kingdom.* He also published a volume of plays, *Caligula and Three Other Plays,* as well as various dramatic adaptations. In 1957 Camus was awarded the Nobel Prize for Literature. On January 4, 1960, he was killed in an automobile accident.

A NOTE ON THE TYPE

THE TEXT of this book was set on the Linotype in a new face called PRIMER, designed by RUDOLPH RUZICKA, earlier responsible for the design of Fairfield and Fairfield Medium, Linotype faces whose virtues have for some time now been accorded wide recognition.

The complete range of sizes of Primer was first made available in 1954, although the pilot size of 12 point was ready as early as 1951. The design of the face makes general reference to Linotype Century (long a serviceable type, totally lacking in manner or frills of any kind) but brilliantly corrects the characterless quality of that face.

This book was composed, printed and bound by Kingsport Press, Inc., Kingsport, Tennessee. Binding based on designs by George Salter.